Crossroads in the Sandhills

by T.B. Kitsmiller

I've waited a long time to tell this story. Partly because life is busy and time races. Another reason I waited is my parents were still alive. Mom battled a long time with cancer. Dad took good care of her. When she passed his heart broke; he followed her eight months later. I've spent time settling their estate, an odd and emotional exercise, ripe with misplaced memories. I've come to appreciate their sacrifices, while gaining some measure of the debt I owe and can never repay them.

While I was digging through my parent's belongings, putting away old papers, photos, and documents, I came across an envelope addressed to me at the "St. Paul Phonograph", my first job in Nebraska. The postmark was from Fridley, Minnesota, dated December 1983, and forwarded from the paper to my parent's home in Des Moines, Iowa. The letter was addressed to me, Mr. Willy Beam, from Kelly Patterson-Allen. I opened it with a mixture of caution and curiosity...

Dear Mr. Beam.

I apologize that I have taken so long to respond to your letter and I am sorry for being so rude when you called. I knew Mary Steward and remember the day at the chapel but my memories from that awful time after my mother passed are almost too painful to recall. Still you can be assured the journal entry is true. Mary saved me that day; saved my whole family. The change in my father after she went to see him at the house was profound. He never drank again, that I know of. He never struck me again and he became kind and gentle, more patient with my brother and I. He was a wonderful father and grandfather until his passing a few years ago.

It was strange to read, in the letter you sent, but I believe her recollection is more accurate than mine. To tell you the truth, I had almost come to believe it was a dream. I had all but forgotten or tried to; maybe even convinced myself that I had imagined it all, but the story from Mary's journal allowed me remember. She was a remarkable woman, kind and full of mercy, loving and healing. She was the miracle that saved us from a cycle of abuse and neglect that I see so much of in the world today.

I wish more people knew what wonderful people she and Joe were. They gave so much of themselves to everyone and anyone who came to their little chapel. I hope this helps you in some way. I

know your letter has helped me.
        All the best,
        Kelly Patterson-Allen.

        The misplaced letter unleashed a flood of memories for me.
Like Kelly Patterson, I had almost convinced myself that my
recollections were no more than a dream. I had set them aside, as if
they didn't matter much at all. Kelly Allen's lost misplaced letter
convinced me of what I always knew to be true but have never told
anyone. Gabe was right; it's taken me a long time to work it out;
some days I'm still trying. Now I'm ready, I think, to remind myself
and others of all the struggles and heartbreaks in the American
heartland during the nineteen eighties. John Mellencamp and Bruce
Springsteen sang about it, but their lyrics sometimes get lost in all
the big hair and Fast Times at Ridgemont High. This is a story,
misplaced, forgotten and neglected, of Mary Steward, her cross and
chapel that offered shelter to so many sojourners, like me who found
themselves at crossroads the Sandhills.

Chapter 1

He was an old man sitting in an antique rocker with an oxygen hose looped around his ears and tubes under his nose. The rhythmic sound of air being forced into his lungs filled the small, stale smelling room. His eyes were closed, his chest rose and fell in time with the machine. His skin was frail wrinkled leather with dark purple splotches of age on the backs of his hands and forearms. His hair was slicked over, receding and gray. He'd done his best to maintain a style popular to when he was a young man, in the early twenties or maybe early thirties. I hated to disturb him, a little afraid of what might happen if I startled him but I needed to speak with him. I was on the trail of a story. A mystery had caught hold of me. I was compelled to uncover the meaning behind the cross and chapel.

"Excuse me," I said. "Sir, could I speak with you?"

He stirred, a loud growling snort escaped when he inhaled through his mouth. His eyes fluttered and came open, "What the, what in the world," he stammered.

"Sorry to bother you sir. My name is Willy; Willy Beam. Can I ask you some questions?"

He rocked forward, fumbled in his shirt pocket for his glasses, squinting at me with watery blue eyes until he got the pair of horned rimmed glasses in place. "What, what do you want?" he asked in a gruff filmy voice.

"I want to ask you about the cross and chapel on the hill up by the old Steward's place," I said. "I was told you might be able to tell me about them, who made the cross and why."

His mouth opened and closed, his hands flexed over the arms of the rocker. His hands were big workingman's hands, hands of a laborer with bulging knuckles, scared fingers, memories of a life spent working with tools. He rocked slowly, gazing down at the floor between his feet. I thought maybe he suffered from some kind of memory loss and had already forgotten my question.

"Sir, can you tell me about the cross?" I asked.

He grinned, a simple ironic grin, "Yes son, I can tell you about Mary's cross. I carved it, from a single piece of white oak taken from the Loup River valley, nearly thirty-five years ago."

I first read about the cross and the chapel in the newspaper. The Daily Independent ran a story about a couple who purchased a ranch along Highway 92 just east of Broken Bow in Custer County,

Nebraska. The land included an unusual landmark, a twenty-foot-tall cross and a small one room chapel. The cross was illuminated by a single spotlight pointing up from a cement slab at its base. The couple didn't know the history of the cross or who had put it up, when or why; but when the light went out, they wanted to fix it. They soon discovered there was a bit of mystery surrounding the cross sitting on their land. The electricity costs for the light were not charged to their utility bills. The clerk at North Loup Electric Coop didn't know how exactly the bill got paid, but every month for the past few years the bill had been paid. The wife, intrigued by the mystery, began to dig a little deeper. She discovered neither the cross nor the chapel at its base, belonged to them at all. They had purchased the land but the cross and the small patch of land where the chapel sat was the property of a trust managed by a law firm out of Lincoln, Nebraska. The story went on to say; a repair crew came out within a few days to repair the light. A representative of the trust sent a letter thanking the couple for their inquiry and assured them the light would be serviced more regularly in the future. It apologized for any further inconvenience. The reporter for the newspaper had done a little digging to discover the land had once belonged to the Steward family dating back to the turn of the century. The eldest son, Joe Steward, had moved off the land in the late seventies. The ranch had been sold to Glenn and Dorothy Adams, the couple who now owned it. According to locals, the cross had been put up first, and a short time later the small chapel was built on the low bluff sometime in the spring of 1947. The story concluded with some speculation on the significance of the cross as a beacon and the chapel a way station for travelers. I thought the reporter got a little preachy toward the end of the report, implying the growing social and economic distress of America could somehow be traced to the neglect of the cross and its small chapel. I'm not from Nebraska, had never been to Broken Bow but after trying to forget the newspaper story that lay on my coffee table for a few weeks I felt strangely compelled to make a road trip to see the cross and chapel for myself.

I left out of St. Paul, Nebraska, my new home, before sunrise on a Thursday morning with a cup of coffee and donut for breakfast. I drove north of town on Hwy 281, turned west on US92 until I was beyond the town of Farwell. I passed over the Middle Loup River as I skirted the edge of Loup City; all the while the scenic road rising and falling over the ancient grass covered dunes of the Sandhills. Occasionally, standing far off the road in the expanse of green hills, a windmill and barn disturbed the landscape. Hints of domestic inhabitance and ownership marked the landscape with rows of plowed ground or herds of cattle grazing on a hillside.

The little town of Ansley forced me to slow down at the awkward convergence of roadways: US Hwy 92 from the east, Historic Hwy 2 running alongside the Burlington Northern railroad climbing out of Grand Island from the southeast and Hwy 183 cutting straight through from north to south. There was a road sign just past Ansley telling me it was twenty more miles to Broken Bow. At CR-441, on a low hill stands a magnificent wooden cross and twenty yards or so further north, a small wooden chapel.

I turned onto the county road and pulled off the side of the road. I climbed out of my little Honda Civic, over a rusty barbed-wire fence, stepping around the scrub trees, wading through buffalo grass until I discovered a fading footpath leading up the incline. I squinted up into the sun at the cross towering above. Maybe I was looking for something important, miraculous even. So when the sun hit the old wooden cross, weathered, wind-hardened and true, my emotions caught in my throat. I tried to swallow them down; to control the powerful ache forcing my eyes to water. I felt something inviting, no, drawing me up to see the cross and chapel.

It was big, every bit of twenty feet tall. It's arms fifteen feet from tip to tip and a base like a tree trunk. It stood back above the road, the small chapel sitting like an afterthought beneath its outstretched arms. I imagined it could be seen for miles along the collection of roads. On a clear night and with the spotlight illuminating it from below, it must indeed shine like a beacon with the chapel a welcoming shelter in the wide-open grasslands and rolling hills. I asked out loud, "Who put you here and why?"

The trail continued around the chapel and along a natural ridge leading to a single-story ranch style home. The house faced to the east with a wide circular gravel driveway. There were outbuildings in back of the house. Barbed wire supported by gray weathered fence-posts staggered down the rise and into a wide green pasture. In the distance stood the expected windmill and water tank surrounded by a small herd of red and cream-colored cattle.

I walked back to stand at the foot of the cross. Its base was as wide as a tree trunk. I ran my hand across its surface; it was smooth like finished furniture. Up close, the color wasn't white but a weathered silver gray. The sunlight and shadow made it appear whitish from a distance. I looked up to the cross beam and noticed it was not a beam at all; more like branches, carved at right angles from the base. There were images carved into the trunk; nothing vulgar or ugly. There was no heart framing 'Billy + Sally'. There were a few religious symbols, beautifully carved, almost folk art; a star, the fish symbol, a peace dove and anchor. Each engraving appeared to have been applied with great significance.

The grass rustled with the wind, drawing my attention to the chapel. It was silver gray like the cross, except for the door that was fading rose red. A fine, wood-framed stained-glass window decorated the side of the clapboard structure. The colored glass, placed with artistic care, produced a kaleidoscope of reds, purples, yellows, greens and blues. The steps and foundation were stacked limestone blocks, just like the pioneers used for cabins in the 1800's. A small facade' with an inspired steeple protruded out from the main building. The single room building looked sound, did not sag or lean in any way. It looked well built to withstand the elements, winter and summer.

I considered going up to the house to talk with the family but decided there was nothing I needed to know that I hadn't already read in the paper. I stood there between the cross and the chapel looking down at the roadways below. The wind blew, the sun bore down, and the highways hummed with traffic from both directions. I inhaled deeply and held my breath for a heartbeat or three before exhaling; the tension in my shoulders released and floated away. There was a sense of peace followed by a burning desire to know more about this place.

I began my query at the public library in Broken Bow. Like a lot of Nebraska towns, the downtown business district was a square with a courthouse at its center. The shops, offices and diners filled the business fronts facing inward toward the two-story red brick courthouse. The library was just off the square. The plaque on the walkway said it was built by the Andrew Carnegie Foundation. The classic arch structure with an art deco style looked out of place in the small town, but it was inviting none-the-less.

I asked the large gray-haired woman at the desk for directions to the public records. She eagerly showed me the way to the archives in the back corner of the building. I found a desk and began my search.

I read the short history of the town. A man named Hewitt and a few neighbors wanted a post office and so they began applying for the post office to the government. He submitted several names, all rejected for being too similar to other towns and post offices in the region. Finally, Mr. Hewitt remembered that an old Indian burial ground had recently been unearthed a few miles from his farm and among the artifacts was a broken bow. He thought the discovery a grand name and quickly submitted it to the United States Post Office. It was approved, and Broken Bow was soon a growing, industrious town.

The archival photographs looked like the work of Solomon Butcher who recorded most of the earliest images of the homestead life in the Nebraska Sandhills. Like the sod house of the homesteader; the treeless prairie offered free land, possibilities, isolation, wind, drought, floods and endless struggles for the families who chose to settle here. Those settlers planted trees for future generations to use as windbreaks and decoration. They took root along the shallow Loup River and reached deep down into the Ogallala aquifer, the largest underground reservoir of water in North America. The dry sandy soil was poor farmland but excellent pasture for beef cattle. The Kinkaid Act of 1904 amended the Homestead Act to allow a farmer in the lands west of the 100th Meridian in the Sandhills to claim 640 acres. The Kinkaiders who benefited from the expanded land act gave birth to a huge cattle industry, which explained the large number of feedlots around Broken Bow. The stench from those feedlots hung over the town like a cloud on this clear spring day.

I skimmed newspaper articles from the turn of the century when Broken Bow was growing and prospering. The Great Depression brought unbearable plagues, natural, political, economic and personal; The population of the county dropped by thirty percent. A quarter of a million souls gave up and moved away.

On the drive up Hwy 2 from Grand Island I had noticed how quickly the landscape changed from flat open cornfields to wide low hills with cattle in the valleys, stretching towards the rivers. The sandy hills act like a filter for the Ogallala Aquifer lying beneath a thin green carpet of coarse, stubborn prairie grasses and a wide array of wild flowers. In spring the hills can be breath-taking beautiful against a backdrop of endless blue sky, but by July the landscapes become brittle and brown, awaiting a prairie fire. I found all the historical stuff interesting, but it was nothing I couldn't have found in the library in St. Paul or Grand Island.

I went back to the desk and asked the librarian, "Do you know anything about the cross out on the edge of town?"

She smiled. "The old Steward's place?"

"Joe Steward's, yes. Do you know his wife's name?" I asked.

"Yes, Mary," she said. "Everyone called her Mary Ann."

"Do you know if the Stewards put the cross up?" I asked.

"Well now, I know it was made by a local craftsman," she paused. "Why are you so interested in that old cross, may I ask?"

"Well, see," I stammered, not really sure why I was so interested. "I'm working on a story for a magazine." I lied. I'm a terrible liar. I knew the old librarian was looking at me with questions I was sure to fail answering so I blurted out, "I'm a freelancer, hoping to sell an idea to the Saturday Evening Post."

She smiled at my fib and said, "Well, wouldn't that be something. A story about our little town in a national magazine. You should see Amos Tensley."

I fumbled for my notebook, "Amos, who?"

"Amos Tensley. You'll find him at Valley Acres, the retirement home over on Twelfth Street."

"Who?" I asked again.

"A carpenter, a handyman of sorts and a sculptor at times. He can tell you all about it."

"And he will know about the cross?" I asked.

"Amos will be able to fill your notebook with stories. Yes, he knows all about the cross and chapel."

Chapter 2

Amos adjusted his weight in the rocker and the tube in his nose; straightened his glasses and looked me over. "What do you want to know about it?"

"Well," I said as I got out my notebook and clicked my pen. "When did you make it?"

"It was the fall of nineteen hundred and forty-seven. Mary Ann came down to the shop I had over on Elm earlier that summer. I learned my craft of wood working from Edgar Bargeman, a true artist from the old country. He spoke very poor English yet he could realize the potential in a raw piece of wood. He could peel away the layers and shape it to his desire with chisel and hammer." He looked to be drifting from the subject.

I nudged him back, "Mary Ann came to ask you to make a cross?"

"Oh, yes, yes she came down, like I said. She was a nice woman, polite, always said "sir" and "thank you." People don't say that anymore. Anyway, she said to me, 'Amos, I need you to make me a cross.' I asked her what kind of cross she wanted. She said, 'I would like it big as an oak tree and it must be carved from a single piece of wood.' That took me back. It seems she'd had a dream of a huge cross carved from a single tree. I told her I didn't know where I would find a tree that would allow me to carve a cross as big as she wanted from a single tree. Well, she said, and this is the part that really got me, she said, 'You will find a tree to fit our needs along the South Loup River.'"

He adjusted his breathing tube and took a couple of shallow breaths.

"Sir, are you okay?" I asked.

"Please call me Amos," he said. "And yes, I'm fine young man. What is your name again?"

"I'm Willy Beam."

"Like the whiskey," he said.

I smiled and nodded. It was not the first or the last time the association had been made.

"Well, it'd be nice if you had a nip with you," he said.

"Maybe next time," I said. "So, Amos, did you find the tree?"

He looked at me for an awkward moment. I almost said something but remembered my professor at Iowa State had warned against breaking the silence after a question, so I waited.

"She was a healer. Some might say a prophet. Shoot, she may have been the voice of God." he said.

"Excuse me?" I asked. "Do you mean she had some magic powers or something?"

"No, no, not magic!" He leaned forward, rubbed his hand over his mouth and chin. "I'm not talking about tricks or spells like you think, nothing like that. She had the gift that 'passes all understanding'. She was pure and holy as the Truth."

I lowered my pen waiting out an uncomfortable pause. I didn't feel the impulse to break it this time. The old man looked up at the ceiling; at first, I thought I had lost him again, but his stare was more concentrated. He said, "She was touched by the power of the Lord." His attention was not focused on me. "That's the only way I can explain it. She had the power of Elisha or Elijah, them prophets in the Old Testaments."

I didn't know what to say or how to respond. I could tell he was serious. He went on, "She knew things, could tell you things that later on proved to be exactly as she had said they would be. Like the cross. She told me exactly where it would be. I'd never made a cross of that size before and most certainly not from one piece of wood."

He settled in to tell me a story. "She said I would find a tree of white oak growing along the South Loup River. Boy, do you know anything about the trees that grow around here?"

I shook my head no, so he began to tell me. "When the Homesteaders came out here in the late 1850's this was still a great prairie. The Sioux and Pawnee roamed this land following the buffalo from time immemorial. The Indians burned the prairie. They'd start these huge fires that burned for days. The fire gave way to new grass in the spring, which in turn brought the buffalo to feed. The Indians hunted the buffalo and used every bit of bone, meat, entrails and sinew for their way of life. But the fires destroyed the tree saplings you see. So when the pioneers came out here there were no trees. The grass waved and rolled in the wind like the ocean. The Mormons, who with their two wheeled carts passed over this land, said the grass moved like ocean tides."

He took a few slower breaths of oxygen before returning to the story. "Anyway, like I was saying, the folks that came out here, the Homesteaders, found no wood to build with. There were a few cottonwoods growing along the rivers; not the forest of trees like back East or even over in Colorado. That's where the Indians got poles for their tepees, from the Black Hills, and aspens from over in Wyoming. The early Settlers made sod houses. This whole area used to be called the sod house region. Anyway, the trees around here got planted by those pioneers. They planted evergreens as wind rows along with maple, and oak and they let the cottonwoods grow; all of this after the Civil War. Son, do you know how long it takes a white oak tree to grow?"

I shook my head again.

"A long damn time, decades; season after season trees mature and the rings form around the heart of a tree, each season leaving its mark on the character of the tree. Besides, trees don't grow like that, they're forked. They split off from the trunk at angles. You look next time you walk along a grove of trees and see if you can spot a tree that has limbs at right angles. By damn, I'll bet you dollars to donuts you won't find too many."

This was a carpenter, a craftsman who knew wood and trees. I made a note to look more closely at the trees on my way home.

"You know what? I found that tree, just as she said I would, growing along the Loup river. I went down by Scotia over in Valley County. I knew an old farmer over that way. I asked him if I could look on his land for some wood, told him I was working on a job and needed a particular tree. He was an old German, spoke very little English but understood more than he let on. He says to me 'Ja, ja go find de vood, come tell me before ja take any.'"

Amos chuckled at his imitation of the old German. "Anyway, I'm walking along the river looking up and down for a tree that I might be able to carve into a cross. Like I said, there were plenty of trees but nothing to fit the bill. Then just as I came around a bend in the river, right along the bank stood this huge white oak." He raised his hands to show me the height of the tree. "Its branches reached forty feet in the air. The trunk was four foot across, straight as a beam and about halfway up, growing out at perfect right angles were two limbs." He stretched out his arms looking wide-eyed from hand to hand as if he were looking at the tree as he first saw it. "It was just as Mary Ann said it would be."

I was scribbling fast in my notebook trying to get every word. Old Amos was sitting forward in his chair. "I could see the cross in the tree. It was there, in my mind's eye, I could see the cross just beneath the bark and leaves. It was amazing. I've never told anyone this." He was beaming at me, "I saw the cross in that tree just as you see it today."

"You saw how you were going to make it?" I asked.

"No," he said lowering his arms. "I saw a cross, glowing and bright, shining from the tree. I could have walked up and touched it. It was that real; that clear."

He sat back in his chair to catch his breath. He was getting tired but I felt like the story wasn't finished and maybe I would be the only one to hear it. If not today, then the story might fade away with old Amos. I tried to draw a picture of what he was telling me. I'm no artist; still I did my best to sketch a tree with a cross. I hoped it would remind me of the look on the old man's face as he told me of his discovery, but I could never capture the expression of wonder that had been there just a moment ago.

He was breathing more normal now. With his eyes closed, he began to speak again. "The strangest thing happened when I went back to talk to the old German. He was out in the field on an antique walk behind tractor. Have you ever seen one of them things?"

"No," I said.

"They're huge, with steel wheels, belts and pulleys to move them; truly amazing things. Anyway, Fritz, the old German stopped when he saw me coming. I told him I'd found a tree I wanted. He nodded and said, 'You find the big oak on the bend, ja?' I said yes. I would give him what I didn't need for firewood. That was always our agreement, for most carpenters in those days. Wood was far too valuable to give away, but you could barter for what you needed." He opened his eyes and grinned. "Do you know what that old man said?" He didn't wait for my reply. "He said, 'You want the cross hidden in the tree.'"

I stopped my scribbling and looked up. "What?"

Amos opened his eyes and his face broke into a toothy wide smile. "That's precisely what I said." He chuckled. "I asked him what he meant? Fritz said, 'I, too, have seen da cross in dat tree. I dreamt it a few nights ago. I knew you vood come to ask me for dis tree.' He told me to take the tree and keep the wood, a huge gesture; enough wood for a season of work."

I stopped writing. Amos was smiling a wide gray smile. "I've never told a soul that story, not to anyone but I swear to you it's true."

"You think the old German farmer knew you were coming for the tree?" I asked, just for clarification.

"You're damn right. I don't think it, I know it, for a fact." Amos stopped smiling, his eyes challenging and angry.

"I believe you," I said. "I just wanted to be sure I understood you, to clarify the story."

"It's not a story young fella, it's the gospel truth and I don't give a damn if you believe a word of it."

I needed to get him back to the story, the truth, whatever he wanted to call it. "How did you carve the cross from the tree?"

He looked away toward the windows. The light streaming in through the wide commercial blinds indicated it was late afternoon. I wondered if maybe I should come back another day. Just as the idea crossed my mind, the question on the tip of my tongue, Amos said, "Hardest work I've ever done."

"Why?" I asked.

He was still looking out the window, his eyes were focused. "Just to fell the damn thing without breaking one of the arms was a miracle. I came back in the fall after the leaves had fallen and harvest was in. The corn would've prevented me from getting in there before October. It was cold that morning. I thought about putting it off but awoke before dawn with an urgent feeling. I had to go and get it that day. I can't say exactly why, it was a nagging urgency, a sense of foreboding. I packed a lunch, filled a thermos with coffee, hooked up the trailer to my old International truck and headed for the South Loup. I pulled through the gate and called up to the house, just to let the old German know I was there for the tree. He smiled and waved but made no offer to help. The tree was swaying a little in the wind. A strong north wind was against me. The tree stood along the northwest side of the river. The problem was I needed it to fall into the wind. Now before you lay ax to trunk, you've got to decide exactly which way you want your tree to fall. If you just go at it half-cocked you can end up in trouble in a great big hurry."

He looked up to the ceiling. "It was beautiful, straight and true as a beam. I can't imagine when it would have been planted. It must've been seventy or eighty years old; one of the first trees." He was no longer aware of my presence. He was standing beneath the giant tree on a late October morning in the nineteen-forties.

"The trunk was five foot across with roots that went down and drank deep from the river. You could smell the rich wet earth providing life to the branches reaching like a prayer toward the sky.

God, she was one of those natural beauties most people take for granted. When you stop to consider the energy, the strength and endurance it takes to survive out here, well it's nothing short of miraculous." He shook his head slowly, "I almost hated to take her down, but Mary Ann had said this was the tree. The old German had seen it in a dream and I'll admit, I could see the cross, its form and stance, captured within. There was no real choice; still it was not easy."

"What made it so hard?" I asked.

He looked up at me with a mixture of surprise and excitement. I got the impression he usually told this story to himself and was not used to interruptions. "Boy, have you ever taken down a forty-foot tree?" Again, not waiting for my reply. "There are too many things that can go wrong. I needed this monster to fall flat; couldn't risk it might twist this way or that and snap off one of the branches. Remember, she said, 'One piece', I had to keep both of those huge arms."

He rubbed his chin, "I took a notch out of the south side, lined it up with the horizon, that's the way I needed it to fall. I wedged in a shim to keep the damn thing up right. I went around to the north and began to saw. Fritz's boy Henry, he came down to help. Fine boy, strong and steady on the other end of a two man saw. We made our straight cut into the heart of the tree. Then we came above that cut at a thirty-degree angle. It was a chore, but we worked the saw and it didn't bind. Still it was fifteen minutes of hard sawing before it creaked. For a moment I was sure it was going the other way. I hurried around to the other side and took a swing at the wedge with the flat side of my ax, but my shim was too shallow, and the tree was top heavy. Just then the wind came up. A mighty wind from the south, straight out of the Bible, I swear to you. It was as if God himself pushed it over. I just knew that damn tree was going straight into the water and the wind pushed it; pushed it right where I planned for it to fall."

"Don't you think it could have been just a coincidence," I said. "The wind blows where it will."

The old man looked at me, a glint of frustration. "Some people say the wind moves the trees and others say the tree is swaying in the wind. I believe the Spirit moves things and that morning it caused a tree to fall against the angle of the earth, away from the geometry of the land. It fell perfectly where I needed it to." He was adamant in his statement, his posture forward and defiant. I didn't challenge his assertion or his faith.

He went on "I let the wood age all winter. Come spring I had carved out the base and the top. See, it's fairly simple to make a cross with two timbers, you just notch out the post and attach the crossbar into the notch. But Mary Ann insisted, she wanted the cross made from a single tree."

"Any idea why?" I asked.

He looked away, off into space, "I don't know for sure. I got the feeling it was inspired."

"Inspired?" I asked. "Like from a dream or..."

"Or God," he said. "I think Mary Ann was given a calling to make the cross, build a chapel and a mission to help folks."

"I don't understand," I said, "There are lots of churches here in Broken Bow. Why would Mary be called?"

He smiled a pitiful smile, reserved for children or fools. "Son, there's more to this than you can see and less grace in them churches than you want to know."

I wrote the statement down and put a question mark by it. This was indeed the mystery I had hoped for and plenty to consider about the cross, chapel and Mary Ann Steward.

"I finished the cross in the spring of 1947. We put it up as soon as the ground thawed enough to dig the hole." He continued the story. "Joe poured concrete in and with some help from the ranch hands we got her up. It was a magnificent sight. That big son of a gun gleaming in the sunlight, up on that hill. God what a sight to behold." His eyes were far away again, seeing the cross as it was on that spring day years ago.

"What was the reaction from the town?" I asked.

His expression darkened, he said, "I'm tired, need my rest. You'll have to come again another time to hear about that."

The sunlight from the windows was stretching across the room. Evening was approaching, it was time for me to go. "Thank you for the information, Mr. Tensley, I mean Amos. It was very helpful. I'd like to come back, if you don't mind."

He waved his hand, a dismissive tired gesture. I reached out my hand to shake his. He took my hand in both of his and looked me in the eyes. "It's not just a story; it's the Gods honest truth."

I was a little shaken by the spiritual references in the old man's story. Maybe the guy was a Holy Roller or soft in the head. I wasn't sure of anything. I knew it was important to him and maybe in some strange way to me as well. I drove to the edge of town, slowed and pulled over to look at the cross. It towered over the landscape, inviting and powerful, its arms stretching out wide to the east and west. Something Amos said, 'Less grace than you would think in them churches', whatever that meant. It didn't matter, I was hooked. I had to find out more, about Mary Ann Steward, the cross and chapel.

Chapter 3

I told the librarian I was a freelance writer. That was my ambition. Currently I worked for a small-town paper, the St. Paul Phonograph. It paid just enough so I could eat and pay rent. My parents helped a lot, with things like paying the phone bill. My mother insisted I have a phone, so she could call her son on Sunday nights.

My parents were older, ten years older, than my friends' parents. My dad, William Randell Beam, an accountant with McAllister and Maloney CPA in Des Moines, loved Husker Football. Bill was your typical bean counter; a good guy, a loving father and husband. Mom; Linda Sue, was the proper housewife; a stay at home mom. She worried, volunteered and baked. A caring, devout woman, always ready to serve wherever needed. She was always concerned about the future of young people of this country, with good reason. I was fortunate to be loved and raised by them. However, recently I learned something about them, about myself that made me willing to take a job in Nebraska, four hours from home. I needed space. I had graduated from Iowa State's School of Journalism in the spring and that's when I found out I was not my father's son, nor my mother's for that matter. When the job offer came from a small paper in St. Paul Nebraska I decided it was a good place to go.

The story about the cross and chapel captured my imagination. I dreamed of publishing it as an article, maybe a short story or novelette. In the meantime, I had a job to do and there was plenty local news to write about.

Since the waning days of the Carter Administration, the American farmer has been facing a looming crisis. I grew up in the city but the economies in Iowa, South Dakota, Nebraska, Minnesota and Kansas are intertwined with agriculture. Everyone and everything is impacted. There were stories of farming families who had worked the land for three or four generations, who suddenly, overnight, and with no warning to anyone, found a foreclosure sign in their yard with the bank scheduling an auction.

"Beam, get in here!" My editor yelled from across the news room.

I grabbed my notebook and ran. John P. Hendrick had been a sergeant in the Korean War, a field reporter, decorated for wounds sustained during combat. I know this because of the award hanging prominently on the wall in his office. Almost every week John P. aka

Sarge made some reference to his military service and the price he paid for my freedom. His war stories were used to convey a message or make a point I was clearly missing. My long hair, open collar and elbow covered corduroy jacket was clearly the uniform of a commie sympathizer.

"Beam," he would say in a deep bark of a voice. "I once had to slog through snow up to my ass, in temperatures so cold, hot water froze the minute it was removed from the fire to get a story my editor wanted about the weather conditions. Now, I could have told him to stick his damn head out the window and he'd get all the news he needed about the weather for the soldier at the front, but I didn't." He paused for dramatic effect. "Now, I expect you to go out and find a story, without complaining, or asking me where you can find it. I pay you to find the stories for me to edit."

The other reporters said the P. in John P. stood for Prick. When they first referred to the big powerful man in that way, I was a little offended. I thought it was disrespectful and petty. However, since I'd been under his management for a few months, I fully concurred. Sarge could be a prick. He ran a tight ship and a little discipline could be good for my commie soul.

"Beam, you need to go see Mr. William Oldfather at the bank. He's expecting you. I told him I would send a reporter over to see him this afternoon. Understand, I'm using the term reporter loosely in sending you over, I think this might be a good story for you."

"What's the story boss?" I liked to act as if I didn't hear his jokes about my reporting.

"I want you to dig into these farm foreclosures. See how it's affecting local banks." He paused and leaned forward in his chair. "There's been a few banks in trouble the past few months. I want you to listen for any hint that our local bank might be in trouble."

"Do you think there is?" I asked.

"Damned if I know. That's why I'm sending a reporter over there to see what he can find out." Sarge looked at the ceiling and shook his head. "Now, he's not going to tell you straight out, so don't ask him. You've got to be more subtle. Ask good questions and wait for the answers."

"I will, sir." He liked it when his reporters called him sir, so he could reply. "I'm not a sir, I was a sergeant in the Army, a working man. Now get your ass out of here and do some research before you go see Oldfather."

Mr. William Oldfather, Bill to friends, Billy to family was not as old as his name implied. The Oldfather family was old, old money, big on tradition and powerful in the family business of banking. Three Oldfather brothers started the First Bank of Creston Iowa in 1869. They each had three sons, who each had three sons. Billy was the youngest son and grandson, a bit of a rebel. If rumors are true he had wanted to pursue a career in music. His grand-father squashed the idea with demands he follow the plan laid out for him, by the family.

Still, Billy was often the lead actor in local theater productions. From all reports he was the hit of last fall's musical production of South Pacific. The First National Bank of St. Paul sponsored every production of the area thespian group, The Sandhill Theater. Bill could be counted on to support the high school's theater department as well.

I arrived at the bank a few minutes before one o'clock. I did my banking here, that is to say, I cashed my paycheck here and I opened a small savings account at the First National Bank of St. Paul. The exterior was red brick, steel commercial windows and doors. The interior was illuminated by fluorescent lights hung along with rectangle ceiling tiles supported by a metal grid. The desks were dark wood, the carpet an odd geometric pattern that made my head hurt.

Ms. Tilly, the receptionist, greeted me with a wide smile on her chubby face. "Hello William, how are you today?"

"Fine Mrs. Tilly," I said.

"You're here to see Mr. Oldfather." It wasn't a question. "He's with someone. Have a seat and he'll be with you in a minute."

"Thank you," I said.

She went back to her typing. I meandered over to the group of chairs lined up along the dark paneled wall just outside of Mr. Oldfather's office. I took out my notebook to review the questions I had prepared for the interview. I could hear muffled but clearly agitated voices coming from the office. I couldn't make out the words, but the tone was clearly not friendly or business like. I wasn't eavesdropping but couldn't help being curious; as a good reporter, it's important to pay attention to everything. Suddenly the door banged opened. A man in blue jeans and a checkered shirt stepped out of the office. He turned back to the door and shouted, "I'll tell you one thing, you send them sons-a-bitches out to my place and I'll run'em off with buckshot."

Mr. Oldfather came to the door. "Jim, this is no way to act."

"Act; don't tell me how to act," the old farmer said. "I've been doing business with the bank since I come back from the war in nineteen forty-three, my family before that. I never thought I'd see the day when it would turn its back on us."

The farmer turned his back to the banker and walked toward the door. He stopped in front of Ms. Tilly's desk. "Don't think I'll take this laying down. I'll not lose my land to you money grubbin' bastards." He shoved the ball cap in his hand onto his head, pulled the bill down sharply and stormed out the door.

The pause in activity all across the bank stretched out to a count of ten which I counted in my head. The reaction of the customers, employees and Mr. Oldfather was a mixture of shock and embarrassment. Bill Oldfather still stood in the doorway of his office. He pulled his attention from the doors the farmer had exited and slowly looked around the bank. His eyes passed over each employee causing them to return to their activities, as if his gaze released them from a trance. The customers tried to ignore the gaze and smile, pretending nothing out of the ordinary had happened. His gaze eventually fell on me. I smiled and nodded in my own awkward way.

Mr. Oldfather was a tall man, over six feet with broad shoulders and sandy blond hair, starting to retreat from his dark eyebrows. His dark suit and white shirt was exactly the uniform you expect a banker to wear. He turned and walked back into his office. Ms. Tilly hurried into his office.

"The reporter from the newspaper is here. Do you want me to send him away?" I heard her ask.

"No, no send him in," he said.

Ms. Tilly walked slowly out of the office, forced a smile across her face and said, "He'll see you now."

I should have been excited to get a scoop, to confront the bank president just after a heated argument with a patron. This was an ideal time to bring up the subject of farming and banking. This was a great opening to discuss the issues and impact of the problem on our small community. All I felt was embarrassment, for everyone. I stepped into the wood paneled room expecting to face a man who had just had an uncomfortable confrontation.

"Welcome, young man." He said with an engaging smile, "J.P.

told me you were coming."

If I had not witnessed the preceding altercation, I would have believed he was having a great day with nothing amiss. Old Billy was an actor, he knew how to smile and put on a show.

"Thank you, sir," I said. "I appreciate you taking time out to meet me."

He pointed to the chair for me to sit in, across from his desk. "Glad to, glad to."

I took out my pen and small cassette recorder from my jacket pocket. I held it up for the banker to see. "Do you mind if I record our conversation? I'll take notes of course, still the recorder helps me remember voice inflection and tone when I review the conversation later."

"Not at all, I guess this means everything is on the record." He chuckled at his joke.

I placed the recorder on the desk between us and pressed the record buttons. "Mr. Oldfather, again thank you for speaking with me today," I began. "Forgive me for being forthright but it appears the farming industry across the Midwest is suddenly in trouble. What is your assessment of the current situation?"

"I'm not sure if my assessment is of any value. I'm just the local banker," he said with a shrug as he sat forward in his chair. "I would say the farm economy is facing some powerful outside forces, both politically and economically. I'm sure it's short term, as you might imagine farming has always been difficult."

"I understand," I said. "The banks in some of the small towns are dealing with some of the same forces, the one up in Taylor being the most recent. How would you assess the overall banking industry here in Nebraska?"

The small town of Taylor, Nebraska, about hundred miles north, just a few miles from the South Dakota border had one bank. The Bank of Taylor had unexpectedly closed overnight, leaving the community without a lender. Many of the good people of the area lost their life savings. It had scared more than a few business people in the region and maybe old J.P. as well.

"I believe the banks here in rural Nebraska are sound. The issues in Taylor were unique to that community and not, I believe, an indication of the majority of banks serving the farming communities across the state." His reply was well rehearsed, as polished as if delivered from the community theater stage.

"There have been several foreclosures and auctions over by Palmer and Boelus. The Randall place seems to have taken a lot of folks by surprise. Do you expect more farms to fail in the coming year?"

The banker paused before answering; I could see him considering the options. "I would like to tell you all the farms in the area are sound. I cannot speak to the Randall situation; it's highly probable that some farms will be affected by this ongoing crisis."

"So you do consider it a crisis?"

He paused again, "Forgive me, I misspoke, I wouldn't characterize anything as a crisis. There may be some foreclosures; there are always losses in any industry. I assure you we'll do everything possible as responsible bankers to avoid the loss of any of our farm clients."

"Mr. Oldfather," I had decided to go another route in hopes of getting him off his pat answers, "can you tell me why this happened? I mean I've heard people say it's just a few bad operations, which is clearly the position of the current administration in Washington. Do you think this is a bigger problem? Maybe not here but in other states?"

He leaned back in his chair, pressed his hands together like he was going to pray, then spread them out fingertip to fingertip. He sat like that for a few seconds, working his fingers in and out before answering.

"The current farming situation is the result of a number of factors, not all of them easily understood but causally related." He ticked off the reasons. "Over inflated land values, this has led to some over extended loans against the properties. The value of land skyrocketed about ten years ago, when exports were at an all-time high. No one ever expects the market to drop; then again no one would have expected the President of the United States to boycott the Olympic Games to make a political statement."

"How could President Carter's decision to boycott the Olympics lead to the current situation?"

"That's another good question," he said with a smile. "I see why J.P hired you."

When I didn't smile back or respond to his compliment he cleared his throat and shifted upright in his chair. He looked over my head in a vague distracted way. "I'm not sure I have time to give you an economics lesson today."

"I appreciate that your time is valuable," I said. "I know you're very busy but could you give me some idea of how the two are connected?"

He leaned his forearms on the desk "The Soviet Union was one of the largest importers of American wheat and corn in the world. We exported thousands of tons of grains to the USSR. When the president announced the Olympic team would not compete in the Olympics hosted by Russia in 1980, the Russian Premier took his business elsewhere."

"Couldn't we just sell the grain to someone else?" I asked.

"To whom? What other country could pay the high price we were asking to transport the grain?"

"I don't understand? Why couldn't they just pick it up at the dock?"

"Well now you may be asking the right questions," he said. "See, we pay our politicians to protect interests and whoever pays the most gets the most protection. Some people have more interests to protect so they are willing to pay more."

I was taking notes, glad the recorder was still running so I could double check my notes later.

"Some congressmen from the port cities passed a law in the mid-sixties that said American commodities shipped to foreign markets had to be transported on our merchant ships. Furthermore, these merchant ships could charge whatever the market would bear."

"So the shipping companies don't have to compete with foreign shippers," I said with surprise.

"Excellent," he said with the satisfaction of a teacher. "Not only don't they have to compete, when they don't have the ships to move the necessary grains, they don't have to allow a foreign shipping agent to move the grain. It just sits there until the ships come back."

"So, why would Russia pay more for grain?" I asked.

"I think that's the question old Boris must have asked himself and guess what, he found plenty of South American countries willing to sell wheat, corn and barley for less money and with less hassles."

I was starting to see the complexity of the problem. "So, are you saying, the problems we are facing here, in Nebraska and other states are global problems?"

"The problems the local farmer is facing is a symptom, the results of a larger problem. Still the local issues are real and very personal," he said.

"What's causing farmers to suddenly default on their loans? I would think most of the farmers would be willing to pay back what they owe if they are able, right?"

"I think that's a fair statement. Let me ask you, do you know the current interest rates?"

I had to admit I didn't. I was not in the habit of borrowing money. My father being an accountant you would've thought I would have some knowledge of interest rates, but I did not. "No sir."

"In February of 1976, about the time Jimmy Carter took office, a thirty-year fixed mortgage rate was eight and three quarter's percent. Today as we sit here, that same mortgage rate is sixteen and a half percent and that's down from a high earlier this year of over seventeen percent."

I tried to do some math in my head, math not being my strong suit. "So the cost of borrowing money has doubled in the past six years?"

"That's correct. Now do you know the current land value for a farm in Howard County?"

"Not exactly," I replied.

"Land values can be highly speculative from region to region. Dry land values, like we have here, are down almost seventeen percent. The value of a farmer's property is what we use as collateral, so you can see the problem, correct?"

I did indeed see the problem. "Why the sudden shift in interest rates and land values?"

"This is where monetary policy, political ideology and market conditions converge to cause unintended consequences," he said with a bit of exasperation. "The Federal Banks want to slow inflation or stag-flation as some call it, so they've raised interest rates. The higher yield of corn in the past few seasons has created a surplus. As I'm sure you know supply and demand influences price." He raised his fingers to count off the issues. "So, lower corn prices, lower land value, raising interest rates, a surplus of corn with no export market to ship to, these problems alone have put us all in a very difficult situation. Now add to that the rising cost of fuel and you have all the elements needed to cause problems for everyone"

He paused to let me catch up with my notes. I looked up when he hadn't continued. "What about President Reagan's ideology don't you like?" I asked.

"It's not that I don't like it or disagree in principle. The government should allow for business to succeed or fail without interference in a capitalistic economy. The problem is that the government has been providing assistance to the farmer since before the Great Depression. This administration's attitude toward farming, in my opinion, is naive at best. Ideology is all well and good. You have to stand for something but like I said, all of this led us to a load of unintended consequences."

"So, you think the presidents farm agreement is..?"

"There is not farm policy to speak of. The Secretary of Ag has said some farmers need to fail and that's just what is going to happen."

"Where does that leave the farmer?" I asked.

"The farmer wants a fair price for his crops and right now doesn't feel that's what he's getting. The American people have a true advantage as compared to other countries in that the cost of their groceries is relatively low. The real cost of the cereal on your breakfast table doesn't equate with the true cost of production: again, political deals come home to roost."

The banker had clarified some of the facts I had dug up in my research. His answer had been honest and forthright. I was generally pleased to have some good quotes for an article. "Mr. Oldfather, I want to thank you once again for taking the time to speak with me. I'll get out of your hair. Before I go, can I ask one more question?"

He raised his hands, palms up and said, "Go ahead."

"Is the farmer who was just here going to lose his farm because of a shipping company in New Jersey, banking policies, political ideology and Russia invading Afghanistan?"

Suddenly Mr. Oldfather was the Bank President of the First National Bank of St. Paul. Not the patient instructor he had been just seconds ago. "That is a banking matter." He rose to his feet, "Thank you for coming in. I hope I was helpful. I'll tell J.P you did a fine job."

He extended his hand. I rose to shake it, realizing I was being dismissed. I gathered up my notes. He escorted me to the door. Before I knew it, I was out on the sidewalk walking toward my car. I was very worried. I didn't have the story Sarge sent me to get. I knew a great deal more about the overall farm situation and almost nothing about the affairs of the First National Bank of St. Paul.

I had a thought. Maybe there was another angle. I had a gut

reaction to the scene I had witnessed before and decided to go see the old farmer, Jim Taylor, whose farm was in trouble. I didn't know the Taylors except for a few passing introductions at community events or maybe at church. I remembered they were mannerly and polite whenever I'd met them, which made his outburst at the bank seem out of character. I felt a strong desire to talk with him and at the same time I had butterflies fluttering in my gut. You never know how folks will act when you go poking round in their business.

Chapter 4

The Taylor's place was east of town along the Middle Loup River, a sub branch of the Loup River, flowing into the Platte at Columbus. Today, from what I could tell, it was a river in name only. Most of the year it was no more than waist deep; a few weeks of each season it swelled to a current large enough to be called a river. Right now, it was either too early or too late to earn the designation, river.

The farm started on the north bank and rolled back toward the Sandhills, the western edge of the great American desert, part of the grand span of land that mountain-men explored, and Indians inhabited a hundred odd years ago. To the west of the ninety-eighty meridian, roughly US Hwy 81, the land changes dramatically, with each mile traveled toward the sunset. The trees, rivers and terraces of Iowa give way to wide open skies and low rolling hills. Further on, before you reach the Rocky Mountains, the land becomes sparse and so flat you can see from horizon to horizon with nothing but the steel gray mountains in the distance, as far away as the moon, in the windshield.

Just down the road in Grand Island the soil is richly abundant with corn and bean fields. Here, where the Middle Loup slithers like a wide shallow snake, the land starts to change. In the sandy hills north of the Loup the land is different. The unique topography of low grassy dunes changes from farmland to ranch land, from corn and beans to cows and hogs. The Taylor place sat gingerly along the borders of the changing landscape.

I thought of what Amos had said about trees as I drove. I noticed the maples and cottonwoods growing among the cedar and evergreens, all of them forked out and up. None looked like a cross at all.

The Taylor's homestead sat back off the road, up on a low rise, surrounded by wide based evergreen trees. Most of the farms out here had long ago planted rows of trees as windbreaks. The trees stood like the walls of a fortress or Santa's Christmas soldiers, adding shade from the summer heat and protection from the howling winter winds sweeping down from Canada, racing across the wide open Northern Plains. The house was white clapboard with a high peaked roof and wide flat wings on each side, and an open porch across the front with lower awnings on each side. A swing hung on one side of the porch and two rocking chairs sat on the other. A large

German Shepherd raced towards my car as I pulled up the gravel drive. I parked back away from the house in the yard. I gathered my note book and waited for someone to come and call the dog away from my car. I didn't expect the dog would bite; most farm dogs would just as easily lick you to death as bite, but when their master isn't home they can be very protective.

I saw Jim Taylor come out of the Quonset building across the driveway from the house. He was wiping his hands and looking to see who had pulled up in his yard and excited the dog. I opened the door and got out, waving a friendly hand. I remembered Jim had left the bank angry and didn't want him to mistake me for an auctioneer.

"Hello," I called. "It's Willy from the paper." I walked towards him, the dog walking along beside me, sniffing my legs. I got a few yards away and stopped, "I met you at the church social a few times," I said hoping to jog his memory.

"I recall who you are. I saw you this noon at the bank, too," he said in a less friendly tone.

"Yes," I said. "Yes, sir you did, I wanted to ask a couple of questions about that?"

He didn't respond but called the dog over by him. He didn't bend over and pet the dog, yet it dutifully sat down at his side and waited.

"If you're busy, I can come back another time," I said.

"What kind of questions?" he asked.

"Well, sir I hoped you could help me understand the problems some of the farmers seem to be having," I said.

"That banker tell you I was having problems?" he asked.

"No, no sir. I did see how upset you were and thought you might have a story to tell." I was melting under the weight of his stare. "See, my editor told me to go see the banker, but he didn't tell me nothing, nothing of interest anyway, and I thought maybe I should talk to some of the farmers instead of bankers and politicians."

He was about to tell me to get the hell off his place when a small grandmotherly woman called to him from the porch. "Jim." He turned and looked toward her, "Jim, invite the young man up, he must be burning alive out there."

She didn't wait for him to do as he was told but turned and sat a tray of drinks down on a low bench by the rocking chairs. Jim Taylor removed his hat and waved me up to the house.

"Now, you're the news reporter for the paper, right?" she asked handing me a tall glass of iced tea. Jim took a glass from the tray and sat down in one of the rockers.

"Yes ma'am," I said. "I'm Willy Beam."

"Well, what brings you all the way out here?" she asked.

I took a long drink from the glass and considered my response. "Mrs. Taylor," I began.

"Call me Eunice," she said with a smile. "Now, sit down right here."

I took the rocker opposite Jim and Eunice sat on a low bench next to the house. She was a small woman, not more than five one. She wore a light sun-dress, faded and comfortable. Her hair was almost completely white, cut short almost boyish; her face was lined with the wisdom of a grandmother and the patience of a saint.

"Well, Eunice, my boss asked me to report on how the farming problems were affecting the local community. So, I went to see Mr. Oldfather at the bank, but"

"But you saw me yell at that prissy son of a bitch and thought you'd follow me out here," Jim said with plenty of resentment.

"Now Jim," she said. "Be nice. Go on Willy."

"Well, yes I did see you at the bank. Like I said, Mr. Oldfather didn't tell me anything. Still I thought maybe I should hear your side of the story."

Jim was brooding, and Eunice was looking at me with a worried smile.

"I don't want to pry and would not use your names. I just wanted to see if you might tell me some of the stories of your neighbors and how all this is affecting them."

"We don't hold with gossip," Jim said. "If you want to know my neighbors' business, you go ask them. Don't come snooping around here."

"Yes sir," I said. "I don't want to offend. I just hoped you could help me to understand all this."

Jim squinted his eyes at Eunice, scratched his chin with his thumb and forefinger. I took another drink of my tea to break away from his hard eyes.

"We are not doing too badly," said Eunice. "We've got a good crop in the field and if we get a little rain between now and October we'll be able to settle up with the bank."

"I don't want to know your business," I said. "I wanted to know if you knew how all this got started."

"Who knows, I'll tell you this. That banker was out here five times in three months back in seventy-six, begging for my business. He could lend me enough money back then and he wasn't the only one. Hell, bankers were knocking on farmer's doors like they was brush salesmen."

"We don't borrow much, not like some," said Eunice.

"No, your granddad taught us that," Jim was warming to the conversation. I wanted to take out my notebook but was afraid to interrupt. "Her granddad Martin was working this land back in the thirties. He survived the worst of the Depression because he didn't borrow money and saved ten percent of everything."

"The man never got rid of anything," said Eunice with a smile. "He would pull nails from boards, straighten and save them. I bet Jim's still got mason jars full of bolts and nuts my grandfather salvaged."

"We toss too damn much away these days," Jim said. He took another drink of his tea before going on. "Folks just throw things away, things that could be used. More than that, nobody makes anything to last. We got a bed and dresser in the house there that belonged to my grandparents and it's as solid as the day they bought it."

"It's in the guest room and it's starting to show some age," Eunice said with a smile.

Jim went on. "People don't give a damn about quality or craftsmanship, just throw it away and get a new one."

Eunice added from behind her hand, "He keeps everything; the man can't even get into the shed."

"Tell me," I asked, "do you think the worst of this is over?"

Jim looked past me to the fields beyond the row of trees and the river out past that. The wind blew, and the moment stretched out. He ran a callused hand over his face. "Son, I wish I could tell you the worst of this is over. I just can't believe it."

Eunice ran the palm of her hand over his back. She knew this man and the load of worries he carried to the fields and back. "The folks around here have worked too hard to see it all just go. I'm afraid that's what will happen to some but not to us."

Jim smiled at his wife, his bride of thirty some odd years, "We'll be fine. Mark my words though, there will be families that have been working together for generations whose farms will be lost, and it'll be a sad, bad day when it happens."

I thanked them for the cool drink and got up to leave, when a question stopped me at the edge of the porch, "Jim, do you know the cause of it all?"

He stood, looked me square in the eyes. "Kid, in my opinion, folks stopped listening and stopped believing."

I must have had a question on my face because he shook his head, "Stopped listening to the Word of God, stopped believing in the Proverbs"

The simplicity and complexity of his statement struck me as profound. Mr. Oldfather gave me an explanation of the economics and political, unintended consequences and miscalculations but in the end those reasons were subject to perspective and agenda. The truth always seems to lay somewhere between those two poles, agenda and perspective. The facts are less appealing, less satisfying and less revealing than either. Truly there is nothing new under the sun.

Chapter 5

I told Sarge I had some good information and was working on the story. He gave me a stern warning, "Have a draft on my desk by Friday." He neglected to provide the consequences if I failed to produce the assigned document for his editorial review, so I felt I could put him off a little. I really wanted to go back to Broken Bow. There was something there, pulling on me, demanding I dig a little more into the life of Mary Ann Steward.

So I headed back up Hwy 281, into the Sandhills and toward the setting sun. The FM radio station out of Broken Bow was playing top 40 hits for my afternoon drive. Big Jim Tuner was playing the Dr. Hook hit from seventy-nine, "In Love with a Beautiful Woman" followed by "Bad Case of Loving You" by Robert Palmer and "The Rose". I hate to admit it but Bette Midler and I sang to the outskirts of town, where the smell from the feedlots and a couple hundred head of cattle, all shitting themselves, is enough to squelch the imagery of a rose in bloom. The methane stench mixed with the heat are signature facts of life in Broken Bow. The town's people seem to be completely oblivious to it. A waitress at the local café told me once, "That's the smell of money, and God knows we need all of that we can get." I wanted to tell her money don't smell like cow shit, but who was I to say what money smells like.

The library stayed open until seven during the summer. I wanted to dig into the newspaper archives. I had a feeling there might be something to Mr. Tensley's statement that not everyone thought of Mary's cross as good for the community. I hoped there might be something in the public records to send me off in the right direction.

I spent almost two hours reading old newspapers, some on microfiche. The last hour I flipped through full page stories, bound in giant book volumes, with pages yellowed and beginning to fade. I felt like Jack and the Bean Stalk, reading stories in the Giant's library. The gray-haired librarian who helped me the first time was not on duty. A thin dark-haired biddy working this evening was no help at all. She got me what I asked for, but I could not entice her to engage in any type of conversation. She looked sternly over the old fifties style reading glasses, which she wore with a gold chain attached at the temples. It was so cliché I thought she was playing a role, "The part of the old biddy, prune faced librarian, will be played by Miss Wiggins." I could hear the announcer's voice in my head saying. The fact I was hearing announcers in my head told me it was time to leave just before Miss Wiggins told me the library was closing in ten minutes. I looked at my Swatch. It did indeed say six fifty. I gathered my giant books and returned them to the information desk, took my notes and headed for the door, with nothing to show for my two hours of work. I had run across some vague references, still nothing to go on. The whole trip was a waste of time. Outside, the sun was an hour from setting, so the heat and smell had not waned, both assaulted me as I walked toward my car.

"Hey, you," I heard behind me call. I kept walking, not realizing anyone was talking at me.

"Don't just walk away from me," a girl said. I stopped and turned to see her striding toward me in an aggressive manner. She stopped less than a yard in front of me, placed fists on her hips, leaned a little to one side, leaned forward and stuck her chin out. "Who are you? What do you want?" Not waiting for me to answer either question she went on. "I know you've been asking around about my Great Aunt Mary and I want to know why!"

I was not used to verbal confrontations or rapid-fire questions from anyone, especially on the streets from a pretty teenage girl. When I didn't answer within the millisecond she asked, "Well, are you going to answer or just stand there with that stupid look on your face?"

I decided to introduce myself, in hope of easing the strain. "I'm Willy, Willy Beam like the bourbon, and you are?"

"Nun'ya," she replied.

"Nun, what?" I asked.

"Nun'ya darn business. Now answer my questions," she said.

I almost laughed but decided that would be a mistake. "Which question would you like me to answer?"

"What? What question?" She looked away, flabbergasted. When she turned her head, so I could see, she had a full mass of dark brown curls pulled up into a ponytail. It was lighter in places, almost tan. The color looked natural not dyed but streaked by the sun. Her face was tanned, with very little makeup.

"I'm sorry," I said. "Did you say you're Mary Steward's niece?"

She looked back at me. Her stance still aggressive with a piercing stare from the brightest green eyes I'd ever seen.

"Are you stupid or deaf," she said.

Now I was getting a little irritated. "Look, that's the second time you've called me stupid and I've had about enough of your attitude."

I turned to walk away.

"I didn't call you stupid," she said. I turned back to her. She had dropped her arms to her side but was still not giving an inch. "I asked if you were stupid and said you had a stupid look on your face, but I didn't call you stupid."

This time I did laugh. "Well now, those are facts."

She looked away. I could see she was trying not to smile. "What are you doing here?"

"I'm a reporter for the St. Paul Phonograph," I offered. "I'm interested in doing a story about the cross and chapel your aunt put up outside of town."

"That cross has been there damn near forty years and Aunt Mary's been passed for six, so why all of the sudden is it so interesting?"

"Well, I just got here," I said.

She finally let loose a smile. It was a great smile with dimples as highlights. She wasn't as young as I had first thought. She could be in college, but I doubted it. I looked at the sun, raised my hand to shield my eyes and wiped a hand across my face. "Can I buy you a pop and we can talk about it?" I asked.

She looked toward the sun, "We could walk over to the Pizzeria, I guess."

I nodded. She turned to walk up the street. I hurried up beside her, "So, Nun'ya, do you have a last name?"

She grinned, "I'm Amanda Steward."

The Pizzeria was dim and cool, an oasis from the heat, with arcade games in each corner and booths along each wall. There were six smaller tables with four high-backed heavy wood chairs around them. In the middle of the room sat a Pac-man machine with a small stool at each end. The walls were dark paneling and the floor was ceramic paver, laid out in a herringbone pattern. The shades were drawn on the windows. Shards of yellow white sunlight made odd lines across the tops of the tables.

Amanda took a booth and I went to get drinks. I ordered two sodas and waited at the counter for the schoolgirl to fill the glasses with ice and pop. I sat down opposite of Amanda and placed the drink in front of her. She had taken her hair down out of the ponytail and shook it out. It was almost shoulder length, brown curly and wild. She took a long drink of the Cola with her eyes closed and set it aside.

"Okay, now who are you?" she asked.

"I'm Willy Beam," I said. "I'm a reporter with the St. Paul Phonograph."

"Are you doing a story for the paper on Aunt Mary?"

"Well, not exactly,"

"What exactly is your interest in my family and that dumb old cross?"

"See," I looked down into my glass.

"Don't you lie to me," she said.

"I'm not going to lie to you," I said looking up into those emerald green eyes.

"You were going to. My daddy's a darn good card player. He plays down at the firehouse every Tuesday evening and he taught me to look for a person's tell. You were about to tell me a lie." She flipped her hair back. "Most people can't look you in the eyes when their lying."

"I was not going to lie," I said defiantly to her accusation.

"If not a lie, then damn sure not the whole truth." Challenging me with her eyes, "You told Mrs. Jenkins you were a writer for a magazine, Harpers Weekly or some such bullshit and now you're a reporter. So, Mr. Willy Beam, like the whiskey, which is it?"

I took a drink of my pop and leaned back. "You appear to know a great deal. Why are you so concerned with who I talk to and what I do?"

She took a drink but only offered a shrug in responding to my question.

"I'm a reporter. I am hoping to write a story because I think it might sell to a magazine. I don't know if it would be anything as big as Harper's."

"Where are you from?" she asked.

"Grew up in Iowa, outside of Des Moines. I graduated from Iowa State in the spring." We seemed to get on more even footing so I asked, "You going to school in the fall?"

She blushed just a little, her dimples showing. "How old you think I am?"

"I don't know," I said. "Maybe seventeen?"

"I'm eighteen. Well, I will be next month."

"So you're a senior?" I asked.

Her eyes flashed a bit of suspicion, "Don't change the subject. Why are you so interested in that old cross?"

This was the question I had been asking myself and still had not settled on a satisfactory answer. "You keep saying cross but there's a small chapel up there as well. Have you ever been up there?"

She shrugged like a child "I have been up there plenty of times, just not since they sold it."

I decided to come clean, "I don't know exactly. It's just that they hold some kind of mystery, all kinds of intrigue and controversy." I leaned forward with my arms on the tabletop. "Do you know what Mr. Tensley told me? He said your aunt had the spirit of God on her. He talked like she was an Old Testament prophet, like miracles and stuff. He's old I know but not delusional. I think he's sincere, you know. The story of how he found the tree to make the cross and all. I can't get it out of my head."

Amanda had a sad sympathetic look on her face. She leaned forward as if to share a secret. "My mom says she was a crazy old fool, but she knew things, understood things, felt things."

"You knew her, Mary Steward, I mean?"

"She was my aunt."

"I know, but you would have been young when she passed," I said.

"I was about twelve," she said. "I spent time with her, before she got sick and Uncle Jimmy tells me things."

"Who's Uncle Jimmy?" I asked, realizing how foolish it sounded. "I know, you have an uncle, Is he Mary's brother or Joe's?"

"Neither."

I cocked my head in confusion. She gave me a playful dimpled grin before saying, "He's a distant cousin on my father's side; everybody just calls him Uncle Jimmy. Some people think he's a little crazy, but I find him eccentric."

"But he knew Mary?" I asked.

"Maybe," she answered coyly.

I had lost control of the interview, as if I ever did have control. "Hey, look, I don't want to cause any trouble for your family. I certainly don't want to be disrespectful to Mary's memory, I just need to know more about the cross and why she put it there."

"Mr. Tensley died," she said with an even sadness.

I stared at her, half expected her to smile, hoping she was just making fun. She didn't change expression.

"He passed on Tuesday. The funeral is tomorrow."

"How?"

"He was old, you know," she said with a shrug. "One of the nurses told me you went to see him."

I was struck dumb. I had gotten the story from him before it passed with him. That had to mean something. It wasn't just a coincidence. Suddenly I felt the need to get out of there. I needed to think.

"Amanda, I need to go. I would really like to talk to your Uncle Jimmy sometime. Do you think I could do that?"

She thought about it for a moment, "Yeah, I think he would talk to you, Willy Beam."

"I have to get back to St. Paul. You can reach me at the paper." I handed her a card from my wallet. "Will you see if your uncle can meet with me? I'll come back over whenever it's good for him."

"What about me?" she asked. "Don't you want to talk to me, too?"

"Sure," I said. "I would like to talk to you again, about your Aunt."

She smiled with her eyes and dimples. "I'll see what I can do."

"And you'll let me know?"

"I'll be in touch, as they say in the movies," she said

I hopped out of the booth and hurried for the door. I can't say what was more disturbing, the death of Amos or my encounter with the beautiful Amanda Steward.

Chapter 6

When I drive sometimes, I'll turn down the radio and talk to myself. Most of the time the conversation takes place between my ears, in my head, sometimes it spills out of my mouth. To this day if you pass me on the road or sitting in traffic, you might notice me speaking to the steering wheel or pointing my finger at an invisible adversary on the other side of the windshield. I'm sure I look like a complete idiot but that's how I work my way through things; out loud and between my ears.

On the way back to Saint Paul I took up one such conversation. I remember it started with Mr. Tensley, "His story was important. His passing so soon after I interviewed him couldn't be a coincidence, could it? The old man experienced something profound and I was the last person, maybe the only person, he told it to. I hope I took good notes or recalled most of it. I needed to remember to rewrite my notes, to be sure I recalled everything about the conversation."

"The encounter or whatever you want to call it with Amanda was strange, wasn't it? I mean she came out of nowhere, fired-up and startling. Shit, she was pretty, those eyes, her hair. Seventeen will get you twenty. In a small town like Broken Bow; it might get me killed. I better keep it professional, keep my distance."

Then I asked myself, "What have I got myself into? What kind of story is this anyway?"

"It's my reporter's instincts coming to life," I assured myself. "I know a good story when I run across it; maybe a prize winning one." In my head I thought, "Amos sure believed he had experienced something miraculous. Everyone has something they believe in, most people believe in a God or a higher power involved in the affairs of mankind to some degree or another. How involved and on what level is a matter of faith and theology? I believe in God. I believe in evolution. I don't believe it's one or the other. Both are consistent with the world as I know it. However, religion is another thing. I don't put as much stock in religion. Religion holds too strong a place in the world because people want to know what to believe. They want to know if they are in or out; saved or damned, redeemed or lost; I don't necessarily believe that's what it's all about. Maybe that's why the cross is such a draw for me. Church can be a lot about judgment and condemnation and very little about love and forgiveness."

The conversation in my head ended there. I drove on for a while until the vibration of the tires on the road made me sleepy. I turned on the radio, spun the dial in time to catch the opening cords to John Cougar's "Jack and Diane". I had to sing along. I admit to thinking of Amanda with some high school jock. The song felt true to the times.

That night I had a dream. I was inside a small clapboard building, only about twelve by twelve feet square. The oak floor boards creaked and moaned. The wind whistled through the window frames. The building was sturdy and clean. I knew it was a chapel. No, I knew it was Mary's chapel. There were only four small pews, two on each side of the room. There was a small platform, only six or eight inches higher than the floor. Up on the riser was a small lectern, set to one side, with an open Bible on it. It was night, a bright glowing full moon beamed through a skylight in the roof. The celestial light illuminated the whole room but focused on the Bible.

I stepped up on to the small stage to look at the open book. It was old, like Gutenberg old, its pages frail as parchment. The lettering was almost calligraphy, with large flowing letters at the start of each verse. It was hard to read at first because the style was so ornate. The page was open to the book of Ezekiel, "The word of the LORD also came unto me, saying, Son of man, thou dwellest in the midst of a rebellious house, which have eyes to see, and see not; they have ears to hear, and hear not: for they are a rebellious house."

I was raised in the Methodist church, attending most services whenever the doors were open. The Bible classes I attended focused primarily on the New Testament, Jesus and the disciples. The Book of Ezekiel was not one I knew, still the words sounded like Jesus in the parables. The verse was clearly illuminated, almost glowing, not from the light of the moon, still it was glowing.

I looked up to the moonlight then around the small chapel. It was peaceful here. I felt safe in the space. I turned my attention again to the Bible; the page had turned. "And it shall come to pass afterwards, that I will pour out my spirit upon all flesh; and your sons and your daughters will prophesy; your old men will dream dreams and your young men will see visions." Joel chapter two, verse twenty-eight.

When I looked up, the pews were full of people. There were old and young, men and boys, women and young girls but they were not a group. Each was dressed in clothes from different years: there was a long-haired hippie with an army jacket and elephant ear flared corduroy pants; a girl of fifteen or younger with braided pigtails, freckles and pale blue eyes; and a grandmother with a bib apron over a blue gingham dress, her hair pulled up in a tight gray bun.

There were others sitting and standing around the edges of the room. They all looked so comfortable and pleasant, at peace. I felt each one had a story to tell, stories full of sadness and hurt but I perceived they had found comfort here, in this place. I didn't see them as ghosts, more the essence of the people who had passed through here. This was something important to the people. But why did it feel so familiar to me?

I heard a ringing, a distant but persistent beckoning for me from outside the chapel. I started toward the door. As soon as I stepped off the platform I was falling. I landed with a thud on the floor of my apartment. I could still hear the phone ringing. The pain in my side made me lay there for a moment hoping the sound was part of the dream.

Within a half hour I was speeding down a gravel road toward the Jenkins place. I didn't know the Jenkins, had never been to their place before this morning. Right now, they were potentially the biggest story in the state and Sarge wanted me there. I could see the sheriff's cruiser with the lights flashing from a quarter mile away. The two-story farmhouse sat back under the shade of trees along a white gravel drive. The house was yellow with white trim. The yard was well kept, the equipment parked systematically and in good order near the out buildings. If it wasn't for the three police cars out front this would've been a picture-perfect scene of rural America. This morning it was a hostage situation.

I parked in the drive, twenty yards or so back from the squad cars. I saw a cluster of people standing in the yard, well back from the house. I grabbed my notebook and took off to get the story.

On the phone Sarge had told me all he knew as I had gotten dressed. It seems Harold Jenkins was holed-up in the family farmhouse with his wife Anna and was threatening to take her life as well as his own. The Thomas and Mason auction company had sent Terry Mills out to do an evaluation on the property. The Jenkins home, equipment, livestock and land were in foreclosure and an auction had been requested by the Archer County Bank. When Terry Mills approached the house, Mr. Jenkins had fired a shot in his direction. Terry ran like a scalded dog from the property and drove back to town to get the sheriff. When Sheriff Griffith arrived, all hell broke loose. Harold had fired at the sheriff, or at least in his direction, threatening him with bodily harm if he came any closer. The Sheriff had called for his deputies, hence the current standoff.

That's where I came in. The deputies stationed behind their patrol cars, each parked sideways to form a protective barrier, their guns at the ready and the sheriff pacing back and forth behind them. I approached the group of people standing back from the scene and said, "Good morning, I'm Willy Beam with the paper, does anyone know what's going on?"

"Daddy's not well," said a woman with wispy red hair, the wind blowing it in her face so that she kept turning her head and brushing it back. The wind can be persistent in the plains. She finally turned her face to the wind and away from the house, forcing me to move to see her face.

"And you are?" I asked.

"I'm the daughter, well one of them, Marie, Marie Childers,"

"Nice to meet you," I said. "Your father isn't well. Is he physically sick?"

"Well, yes and no. I mean, he has been under a lot of stress with the farm and all." She looked over her shoulder toward the house. Marie looked worn out; I noticed wrinkles, tired crow's feet around her mouth and eyes. She had on no mascara, so her brown eyes looked small and faded. She was wearing jeans and a tee shirt, no bra. I imagined she had been awakened in a manner as I had and rushed out the door without any thought of appearance.

"I don't understand," I said.

"He just can't take losing this farm," she said. She wiped at the corner of her eyes "It's all he's ever known. He was born here. My great grandfather homesteaded this land." Her voice broke a little. "He's worked so hard all his life and for them to just come take it like this, it's not right." She bent over to pick up a little girl. I had hardly noticed the toddler until Marie sat her on her hip.

I looked up toward the house wondering about her father inside. I regarded the group, a few other children huddled together, two younger ones, both boys, maybe seven or eight and an older girl around ten or eleven. They were dressed in jeans and tee shirts, with work boots and ball caps, the girl's hair in pig tails. They all had red hair like their mother.

I heard a truck door slam and turned toward the sound. A large barrel-chested man was walking over, while looking over his shoulder at the house. He was big, six four or more, dark beard and small eyes with a mass of black hair bristling out from under his ball cap. Marie, tentatively waved and took a few steps toward the man. His expression softened as he approached. He picked up the smallest boy and held him to the side. The girl reached out and took his hand and stood at his side.

"What's going on?" he asked Marie.

"It's Daddy, he's threatened the man from the auction and took a shot at the sheriff." She stood looking up at her husband, fighting off the tears.

I decided to move away to see if I could find out anything from the Sheriff.

Sheriff Griffith, despite the name, looked nothing like Andy Griffith from Mayberry. He was short, stout and always looked like he needed a shave. He had squinty eyes and fat fingers. I normally don't notice a man's hands, but the sheriff licked his thumb a lot. He would bring his hand up to his small pink mouth and lick the tip of his thumb, as if he was about to count money or deal cards. It was odd. I walked up next to him, he turned, looked at me and licked the tip of his thumb. "What're you doing up here?" the chubby Sheriff Griffith asked.

"Sarge sent me out to see what's going on," I said.

"Son, you need to get back and stay out of the way," he said.

"Did Harold really shoot at you?" I asked.

He squinted at me, breathing through his nose, exhaling hard and slow. "Crazy old bastard; thinks the government is out to get him." He looked toward the house, still talking but more to himself than to me. "These damn militia groups, nothing more than angry fools stirring up trouble. The leaders spouting bullshit about Ben Franklin and George Washington, how they didn't want to allow Jews into the country because they would take it over. Going on about Jews and Bankers are in some conspiracy to destroy the American way of life; preaching from the pulpit of patriotism."

"That sounds a little nuts," I said.

He nodded in the direction of the house. "Well, desperate people will accept crazy if it gives' em someone to blame or someplace to focus their fear."

The sheriff looked over at the family. "The real problem for me is they have this notion that the Sheriff is the only real legal authority, and if I don't do the job as they see it, well I'm to be strung up at the crossroads and replaced by the Posse's Citizens Grand Jury."

"Is that why Harold shot at you?"

"Look, Willy," that was the first time Sheriff Griffith had called me by my name. To tell the truth I wasn't sure he knew my name. I was so shocked it took me a second to hear what he was saying.

"You need to move back and stay low. And don't report anything I just said in the paper, OK?"

"Sure, no problem," I said. "I may go do some research on it though."

"Fine, just don't say I said anything. I got enough shit on my plate."

I moved back to my car and jotted some notes to remind myself to look into the government conspiracy groups when I got back to the office. Just then Harold called out from the house, "Sheriff."

"Yep," the sheriff called back.

"I know you don't work for them evil bastards down at the bank. I know you're a good man but I'm not givin' up my place."

"Harold, can I come up and talk?"

There was a long pause. All I could hear was the wind blowing in the trees. The family looked nervous, the daughter biting her nails and holding her little girl close. Harold called out again, "Come on. I'm warning you though, don't try anything squirrelly."

The sheriff stepped out from behind the squad car and started toward the house. He turned, said something to the deputy behind the car, and walked on as if he was going to his own funeral. I walked up a little closer before realizing I was standing in the middle of the driveway, halfway in between, with no cover if something bad went down. I moved closer to the car and knelt down by the deputy. He looked at me but didn't say anything. We both looked toward the house.

The sheriff held his hands up in the air and gently climbed the wooden steps to the porch. He stopped with one foot on the last step and the other on the porch, looking like he could turn and run like a scalded dog at any second. The farmer was just inside the screen door. We could see the outline of his face, but his body was back out of sight. The two talked cautiously through the screen door; the sheriff nodding his head sympathetically.

"Hey, George," I said to the deputy next to me, "do you know anything about this anti-government group, Possi Calamitous?"

"Posse Comitatus," he corrected with a smile. "There have been some reports over the wire. The North Platte departments have been having trouble; crazy sons of bitches been telling the farmers to file lawsuits against the IRS and stuff like that. It's a real problem, especially since they've uncovered some guns and ammo."

"Guns and ammo, everyone's got guns and ammo," I said.

"I don't mean hunting rifles and thirty-thirty shells, you dumb-ass. I'm talking M16's with stockpiles of military type ammo, real bad shit. Anyway, these groups are springing up all over the place and it appears we got us a true believer right here in Howard County."

Just then the sheriff turned and started walking back toward the car. He looked frustrated. He reached the end of the sidewalk and then the farmer called out. "I'm not going to give up. Go back and tell them kyke bankers to kiss my ass. I'll not be run off my land by them scheming devils."

The sheriff turned and looked back toward the house and then thought better of it. He hurried over to the car, then kept walking to the family. I left my cover to slip closer hoping to hear what was said.

The sheriff took off his hat and wiped his forehead. The family gathered around, daughter, son-in-law and grand kids. "Now listen," said the sheriff with a lick of his thumb. "Someone needs to talk some sense into him. If he doesn't give up and come out soon I'm going to call in for help."

He looked at the son-in-law and then down to the daughter before licking his thumb again. "If I call in help that means federal authority, FBI and maybe a S.W.A.T. team. This could get ugly in a hurry, understand?"

"Let me see what I can do," said the son-in-law. He sat the little boy in his arms down and started toward the house. He walked with long deliberate strides, like he was going in to wash up for supper. He hopped up on the porch and opened the door. Harold must have stepped back because they both disappeared in the shadows of the house.

We stood there, silent and awkward. The sun and wind made my face warm and I could feel sweat running down my spine. The Sheriff scuffed the dirt and tried to offer a reassuring smile to Marie. Suddenly the screen door banged open and the two men walked out on to the porch.

"We're coming out," called the son-in-law. They walked toward the cars with Harold taking cover behind the big man. Sheriff Griffith hurried over to meet them. The three men stood at the end of the sidewalk and talked for a second and then Harold held out his hands for the sheriff to handcuff him. I heard the daughter sob a few feet away.   I tried to talk to the son-in-law when he returned to his family. He looked at me with the coiled anger of a whip and said nothing.

I hurried back to the office to work on the story and do research on the Posse Comitatus. The library had little or no information on the group. I made a note to stop at the Grand Island library for more research. I did find out the name was Latin for "of the country" and its roots seem to go back to a pro-Nazi, pro-Hitler group from the thirties and forties. The very idea of pro-Hitler groups in America was surprising to me. I made some notes but had no idea about how this was tied to the Harold Jenkins story.

Chapter 7

While there may have been anti-government posses in the heartland and the family farm struggling; hell, even the sky might be falling and the end near, but for Nebraska there was always one saving institution; Cornhuskers football. Coach Bob Devaney built the program from the ground up, winning back to back national titles in '70 and '71, then passing the mantle to his young offensive coordinator and Hasting Nebraska native, Tom Osborne; a dynasty was born. On any given Saturday, from Labor Day to the Friday after Thanksgiving, 72,000 fans flocked to Memorial Stadium in Lincoln for every home game. Those who didn't have or couldn't get home game tickets followed the team on the road to Manhattan or Lawrence Kansas, over to Columbia Missouri and down to Stillwater and Norman Oklahoma. The game that always mattered the most was the Cornhuskers and the Sooners: Tom vs. Barry for the Big Eight Championship, a trip to the Orange Bowl and a shot at the National Title.

Dr. Tom Osborne's teams were developed from an aggressive walk-on program which allowed every aspiring young man in the state with a lick of ability, a desire to work and the aspiration to be a part of a championship, to come play for the Huskers. They would come from all over the state: Alliance, Bertrand, Cozad, McCook, Grand Island, Columbus and Norfolk. They might work for four years to play one meaningful season. They would tell you it was all worth it when the crowd rose as one and cheered "GO BIG RED, GO BIG RED."

I was raised in Iowa with the Hawkeyes and Cyclones. My father was a Huskers fan and I was one as well. When I was eleven he took me to my first Nebraska football game. It was bigger and better than I had seen on TV. The year after Johnny the Jet Rodgers 'put them in the aisles' for the win over Oklahoma in the game of the century. I can still see the run, the spin, the cutback and the clear path to the end zone for the game winning touchdown. It's a moment every Husker fan knows and revels in. I wasn't at that game. I had been to others, and to be in the stadium; to see the balloons released after the first score; to join the roar of the crowd. There's nothing to describe it. I loved to see the Big Red roll, even over an early season patsy, who had no chance of competing with the greatest team of the decade. It was a thrill to be awash in the sea of red inside Memorial Stadium on any Saturday in the fall.

In the spring St. Paul was abuzz with the idea one of their own might play for the Huskers, not just another walk-on hoping to go from practice dummies to player, but a real scholarship player. The Walker kid was being recruited by the Cornhuskers, not that they needed to really recruit. If Coach Tom wanted a kid anywhere in the state, all he needed to do was ask. It would've been a sin, a true damn sin for a kid to go somewhere else. The fact that one of Nebraska's coaches had come to the Walker home in February was news. When another coach came back a few weeks later, the town was a whirl of rumors and speculation.

Now, being a member of the press made it seem like I might know more than the next guy. Truly, I knew nothing more than what I read in the paper or heard Sarge speculate about. Truth be told, J.P didn't know anything either. The facts never stop folks from asking and I was proud to play the role of insider.

I stopped by the greasy spoon on the square for a bite. Even before I could slip into a booth, Mindy the waitress was there with a menu. "Hey Willy, did you hear Jimmie Walker was offered a full ride?"

"No, what position?"

"Well, I've heard linebacker, maybe fullback," she said.

"He's big enough for a linebacker. I don't think he's got the speed for it though," Bill Adams said from the next table over.

"Jimmy's fast," said Mindy.

"He's St. Paul fast, not Big Eight fast and he'll have to get a lot stronger if he's got a chance," said Bill's lunch companion.

"They'll get him in that weight room and to the training table and he'll get bigger and stronger in hurry," said Mindy.

"What do you know about it?" asked Bill.

"I know plenty. When Coach McBride was here last fall he talked about the weight program, the meal plans and all about how they develop athletes. He told us how they can turn a boy to a man in just a few months."

"I bet you've turned a few boys to men, Mindy," said Bill.

"Oh, you," she said with a half-hearted swat of her dishrag in Bill's direction. Mindy had been pretty thirty years ago but too many hours on her feet, too many cigarettes and too much fried food had robbed her beauty. Her blond hair came from a bottle, her blue eyes were weepy, and the corners of her mouth turned down until her smile was upside down.

"What can I get you doll?" she asked me.

"I'll have a burger with a side of fries," I said.

Mindy took my order to the counter. I looked over at Bill, gave him a nod of the head and picked up the Omaha World Herald left by the window.

"Willy," said Bill. "What you hear over at the paper about Harold?"

I knew he had been arrested and booked into the local jail before they moved him to county. Harold was there now, waiting on a hearing. He was a good man, a fine farmer but shooting at a sheriff is a serious matter. Actions have consequences, is what my father always told me. I thought Bill Johnson probably knew all this or more. Most of it was in the weekly edition of the St. Paul Phonograph. No, I figured Bill wanted to know what wasn't in the paper. I guess there's some or at least one in every community who wants to be the one who knows the latest news, gossip and rumor. Mr. Johnson likes to know everything about everyone. His small group of regular coffee drinkers at the café expected him or Mindy to know. That's why they came, to hear what was going on.

Something my journalism prof said struck me, 'Don't trade a story for status. The rumor mill will go along fine without you, but a story is yours. Don't trade it away too cheaply.' This was my first real story and if they wanted to know the details, they were going to pay their quarter to Sarge at the paper.

"All I know is what I read in the funny paper," I said, stealing a line from another newspaper man, Will Rogers.

"Oh, come on," said Bill. "I heard he was going on about conspiracies between Yankee lawyers and Jew bankers. Everyone in cahoots to take his land and enslave the white race or some such shit. I hear they have him on suicide watch, in the psycho ward. He's headed for Hastings, I'll bet."

I drank my coffee and didn't say a word. There was some murmured astonishment from the group. Bill went on. "I tell you what I think, its them corporations we need to fear. The boys dressed up in their high-priced suits sitting around their boardrooms, buying up land like it's a damn game. Don't give two shits about the people or the land." Bill paused to get the approval from his congregation. When I asked Mindy for a refill he continued. "Folks around here need to wake up and realize the value of the land. It's got to be valued and protected."

I was curious now, "Protected from what?"

"The corporate assholes who want to swallow up the small farmer with their investments. Hell, they don't care about anything but profits and shares." He was on his soap box now and the lesson was about to begin. "Take Iowa for example."

"I'd rather not take anything from those Idiots Out Wandering Around," one of his cohorts chirped.

Everyone chucked at the old joke "No offense," Mr. Johnson said with a wink as back up.

"Over in Iowa half the land is owned by corporations, swine outfits and feedlots everywhere. The smell and the filth is bad. The real sad thing is the operations are run by managers." He spoke the word as if he could smell the aroma from those managed feedlots.

"Managers run grocery stores and banks, not farms. Farms are owned by families who stay on the land, care for it, nurture it, and protect it. They preserve the wildlife and fishing. Family farms are important. Managers are overseers. They're not vested in the land, the legacy of the crops or the animals. Managers move on when the seasons change, or the work runs out. Families stick it out, work through it and keep going."

"Corporate farming is dangerous," he declared. "Dangerous to the land, to the communities and to the people of Nebraska. Corporations are all about squeezing a dollar out of every nickel invested. Now, don't get me wrong, everyone wants to make money. Some years the winter's too hard or the rains don't come or come too late and everything goes to hell. Nothing to be done, just start over and pray for better next year. Folks get by on what they raise and grow. You let a corporation get hold of the land and there'll be hell to pay."

Everyone agreed with nods and murmurs of approval. I didn't have an opinion but decided I better get one soon. This was something I needed to look into, check Bill's facts and consider how it fit with my interview with Mr. Oldfather at the bank. Most people put out the idea the farmers who were going bankrupt were poor farmers or bad managers. Somehow, I was getting the feeling there was more to this. I didn't understand the economics or the politics of all this. Clearly this farm problem was not simply about poor management, supply and demand or weather conditions. Someone among Bill's clan said, "I heard Taylors are in trouble with their place."

I put my coffee down to listen. "Old Man Taylor was down at the bank seeing Oldfather and he came out the banker's office spitting fire. I never heard such a ruckus; Taylor called the banker a son of a bitch and stormed out. I don't know but sure sounded like the bank was calling the note."

"The Taylors are not getting foreclosed on." I felt the need to protect the old couple; their situation didn't have anything to do with my story. Besides a rumor can do a world of damage in a small town. "I was at the bank the same time and spoke to Mr. Oldfather and Jim Taylor afterwards. I can tell you the Taylor place is fine, and the bank is not foreclosing."

"Well that's good to know," said Mindy as she poured refills around the tables. Bill Johnson looked at me without comment. The questions were in his eyes, but he kept them to himself.

Chapter 8

I learned how to fit into small town life. The pace is different. I admit it requires a level of fortitude and patience. Driving forty or fifty miles one way to get a part or to fix equipment is arduous, the weekly trip into town for groceries and basic supplies and the oddity that the same trip doubles as family entertainment. I discovered the pleasure of gathering at the ball field for little league baseball or softball. The experience of the fireworks on the 4th of July was like nothing I'd ever known. In Iowa fireworks are outlawed from the general public. In Nebraska the unrestricted access to every form of explosive device imaginable was liberating. I admit to spending too much on fireworks: bottle-rockets, black-cats and M80's. I joined the patriotic bombardment of kids and teenagers in the neighborhood along with the semi-professionals hired by the Kiwanis Club to light up the sky on Independence Day; it was alarming, thrilling and just plain fun.

I can tell you from experience, there is no better opportunity to enjoy homemade ice cream and a slice of chocolate cake than at the church potluck. I love comfort food served on folding tables on the lawn next to the parish. It's the best chance for a starving young man to get a home cooked meal, for an unbelievable low price of a little mild flirting with the doting ladies of the church.

The pace of life mirrored the growth of the crops, corn as high as an elephant's eye by the fourth of July, followed by de-tasseling in early August. Labor Day marks the start of football practice and harvest would be just around the corner. The corn harvest and football season overlap in a splendid way. Football was and is the biggest and best distraction for everyone. The high school games on Friday nights and the Cornhuskers on Saturday afternoons.

Small towns are loyal to old and sometimes bitter high school rivalries, passed down from fathers and uncles to sons and cousins. Everyone is involved in the Friday night production. The coaches and players may be the center of attention, but cheerleaders have spent hours practicing routines, their sponsors choreographing every move and jump. The band, along with twirlers and the flag corps at the direction of the drum major performing a well-rehearsed marching routine for the halftime while not neglecting the crescendo of the Star-Spangled Banner nor the fight song played with tempo and passion. The student council members, with parental supervision, man the concession to sell popcorn, candy and hot-dog.

The public-address announcer, clock operator, statistician, video-man and the local radio announcers crammed into the press box, all ready to do their part. Everyone goes to the games except the farmer in the field who listens to the live broadcast from any number of radio stations. If their town's game isn't on the dial, you can bet they'll check the recap with box scores in their local newspaper. From eight-man, class D2 to the class A school, sports would fill three pages in the Saturday morning edition of the St. Paul Phonograph.

High school sports is my favorite past time: football, basketball, baseball, volleyball, wrestling, even track and field are all great ways to spend your time, and getting paid to write about sports was the best. I love the vocabulary of each sport, each with its established adverbs and adjectives. Besides there were a few perks that come with a press pass: a good spot in the press box late in November, the ground level view of the games, as well as a view of the comely backsides of the cheerleaders jumping and screaming to rally the crowd. There is no better way to spend a Friday night in a small town than at a High School football game in the heartland of America.

I switched games so I could cover Broken Bow Indians vs the Chanticleers of Ord High School. It was a good game with Broken Bow leading at halftime by a touchdown. Amanda was in the band. I saw her leaving the field after halftime, but she passed by without the slightest sign of recognition. Her lack of response as she passed by distracted me somewhat, but I forced myself to focus and do my job. I recorded observations on my hand-held tape recorder, took a couple of excellent action shots and later checked my stats against the official numbers.

Adam Purcell, the tailback from Broken Bow, had an impressive night, with over one hundred and fifty yards rushing and two second half touchdowns. Broken Bow had a good team and Ord was over matched. Still, the effort on both sides was first rate. I enjoyed the game and planned to write a well-structured story which Sarge expected me to file before going to bed.

I took my time leaving the field, hoping to see Amanda. She had rushed off with the band. For some reason it surprised me she played the saxophone. I briefly pondered if she was a good musician or if she played to fill a spot in the night's activities. It didn't matter but I wondered about it anyway.

Following the Friday night games, in any small town, the social activity is cruising the drag. Cruising is the art of seeing and being seen. The drag in Broken Bow started down around the square and required at least one loop around the courthouse, then out along Second Street all the way to the highway, where a U turn is required in the parking lot of the Hop and Sack convenience store. One then cruises back toward the square in the opposite direction, repeating the drag until someone calls you over. The parking spots are neither arbitrary nor casual. They are held by tradition, the turf by different classes and cliques: jocks, preps, druggies and shit kickers. There is always an arcade where groups can co-mingle with the less cool pedestrian class, in most cases freshmen or younger.

I found myself cruising the drag in Broken Bow on the first Friday after Labor Day. While I cruised the strip in hopes of finding Amanda, I pondered the cross and chapel. "Why did Mary want the cross made in just such a way? Why build a chapel too? Wasn't the cross enough of a statement? Was Mary Ann Steward really some kind of prophet, as old Amos said, 'speaking with the voice of God'?" I had a million questions. I just knew there was more to this story and the only lead I had was Amanda and her Uncle Jimmy.

After a few trips around the drag, I pulled into the convenience store and bought a six pack of beer and a fried burrito. I was twenty-two and a fried burrito was not the regretful belly buster that it is today. I figured beer would attract high school kids like a flower attracts bees. I wasn't wrong. Soon enough a skinny, pimple faced boy walked over from across the parking lot. He looked like he was in junior high.

"Hey man," he said with a nod of his head. "Buy us some beer?"

I was not opposed to contributing to the delinquency of a minor as long as it got me information. "I can, if you tell me where I can find Amanda."

"Amanda who?"

I suddenly forgot her last name. I knew she was a relative of Mary's, but did that make her a Steward? All I could think of was nun'ya. So I punted. "She plays a tenor sax in the band, dark brown hair, a senior."

"Why are you looking for her?"

A good question. I clearly had not thought this all the way through. "Hey, you want beer or not?"

He nodded.

"Okay, tell her Willy Beam needs to talk to her."

"Alright," he said. I reached into the car and handed over the six- pack of Coors. He tucked the brown paper bag of beer under his arm and held out five dollars.

I shook my head and said, "Tell her I need to talk to her, tonight."

He put the five back in his pocket and ambled back across the parking lot toward a red Z28 Camaro. To my surprise, when he opened the door, Amanda got out. She walked toward me with a strut of confidence that could've made a runway model blush.

"Looking for me?" Her smile was as coy as her eyes were flirtatious. "I saw you down on the field. You looked like you were working."

"And you were busy being a woodwind," I said.

She tiptoed to look over my shoulder. "Got any more beer or did you give it all to my nephew?"

"Nephew?" I said with surprise.

"My oldest sister is twenty years older than me," she said. "Her boy's close to my age." She turned and leaned against my car. Amanda didn't look like anyone's aunt and didn't act like a school girl. She seemed more confident than I had been in high school. Maybe girls do mature faster than boys.

"So, beer?" she asked.

"Oh, ah no," I said. "But if you'll help me answer some questions I'll go get another six-pack."

Her eyes twinkled, she pursed her lips, "This could get interesting." She looked toward the group of boys across the parking lot. "You better make it a case; the team gets real thirsty after a win."

I followed a trio of pickup trucks down a country road. We turned off into a pasture. My little rice burner bumped and hopped over the rough terrain until the convoy came to a stop near a grove of trees along Mud Creek. There was an old barn with a rusting tin roof, leaning to one side. A collection of trucks were already parked in a hapless arch around a roaring bonfire with tailgates down. There were members of the football team, a few couples snuggled close near the fire. It was right out of John Cougar's 'Jack and Diane'.

I kept my distance from the party. I may have provided the beer, but I was an outsider who wanted to stay an outsider. I worked for a local paper. Rumors spread quickly, and stories usually got better on down the line. Amanda walked over and leaned against my car with her arms crossed looking up at the night sky. For a moment we stood staring at the constellations, the Big Dipper, the Bear and Orion's Belt. Those were about the only ones I remembered from my astrology class, sophomore year.

"So here you are again. Still worrying about that old cross," she said looking a little annoyed.

"I don't know exactly. The mystery is still here, and the story Amos Tensley told me is bugging me."

She walked away a few steps and looked toward the fire. The high school boys were loud; someone cranked up the music, 'Running with the Devil'. Suddenly Eddie Van Halen was being accompanied by a host of jubilant boys all playing air guitar.

She spoke to the stars, "My mom says that cross is nothing but trouble, best forgotten."

"What do you mean, best forgotten?" I asked.

"I don't know. She wishes everyone would forget about Mary, Joe and everything to do with their place."

"Why?" I asked with intrigue. "Did something bad happen?"

"No, nothing specific, that I know of. She just believes anything out of the ordinary is by its nature bad. She once told me Aunt Mary was a crazy old lady and I shouldn't listen to anything she said."

"Really, does everyone feel that way?" I asked wishing I had a notepad to write on.

"I don't know. Dad never talked much about Mary or Joe, but Jimmy's still upset the family didn't keep the ranch."

"Do you ever hear anyone in town talk about it?" I asked.

"People talk, just not where I can hear."

"Why is that?"

She turned back to me. "Family may bitch about each other and we may fight amongst ourselves but let someone else criticize one of them, well there's going to be a fight."

I smiled but the set of her chin told me she was dead serious.

"I'd like to know what the deal is with all this," I said. "Will you still help me? Can I meet Uncle Jimmy?"

She gave me a dimpled, mischievous smile. "Sure. Why not? Nothing else to do. Besides, I'd like to know too"

"So, when can I meet Uncle Jimmy?" I asked.

"You know if you really want to know about Aunt Mary you probably should talk to my Uncle Joe."

"Joe Steward's alive?" I asked in surprise.

She nodded her head, "He's in a home over in Ravenna. You didn't know? Man, you're not a very good investigative reporter"

She was right. I should have checked the records and known Joe was alive.

"Will you go with me, to introduce me?" I asked.

She shook her head, "No, I hate to see him like that. You're a big boy, go by yourself. Ask your questions and if it gets you something, maybe I'll introduce you to Jimmy."

The sound of a beer bottle smashing against the old barn drew our attention. There was a howl of laughter. The beer was starting to have its effects and I suddenly felt very uncomfortable. "Okay," I said. "I should go."

She looked over at me, "You are always rushing off, just as things are starting to get interesting."

Suddenly there were shouts and two silhouettes against the firelight, squaring off in fighting positions.

"I need to go, now," I said.

I got in my car, thanked Amanda with a wave of my hand and drove off. I felt like a fool for not checking to see if Joe Steward was still around. "You're such a great reporter" I said to myself. "What a rookie mistake." I chastised myself all the way back to St. Paul to file my sports story. I was proud of the sports report I filed and as always thrilled to see it in print the next morning, even though it was a small-town paper with a total readership of a few hundred.

Chapter 9

Joe Steward was alive. How could I have missed that? I assumed and as my college roommate loved to say, 'when you assume, you make an ass of you and me'. I certainly felt like an ass, a rookie with a lot to learn about digging up a story. I needed to ask more questions, better questions of myself and if I got a chance, Joe. The important thing to remember was I had a source. I had no idea if the source was willing to talk to me. Still it was the lead which could shed light on this growing mystery and I was jacked up.

Sarge had other ideas for how I should spend my week. When he passed out assignments in our Monday morning planning meeting the big guy told me I would be continuing my investigation into the farming and potential banking issue. He strongly suggested Melvin and I go up to O'Neill to a farm auction. I wasn't altogether sure if I was the right reporter for this story. I wondered to myself why Sarge assigned me the story. The answer didn't really matter, the boss was firm. It was my story and Melvin would be a good resource and guide up to the auction.

Sarge said, "That way you don't stick out like a sore thumb in that commie Iowa rice burner."

The auction was on Tuesday about ninety miles north of St. Paul. Melvin insisted we get an early start, so by 7:00 AM we were on Highway 11 headed north to O'Neill. Melvin was old, older than me anyway, at the time I would guess late-thirties. He did freelance work for the paper as well as writing a semi-syndicated column picked up by several farm publications across the region: Nebraska, Iowa, Kansas, Minnesota, South Dakota and Colorado. His column ran just after the advertisements for cattle auctions and farm equipment but before the Cowboy poet and cartoon. Melvin's stories addressed farm policy with a touch of humor and sarcasm. Mel said he tried to make it funny to keep folks from crying.

Melvin was originally from Chadron, way out northwest almost to the South Dakota border. His wife's family had a place west of town. Sarge said Melvin's writing was just a hobby. His real job was ranching. His herd boasted about five thousand head of Black Angus, prime Nebraska beef. I couldn't imagine a stranger team. Sarge assured me it would be good for both of us, besides what else was I going to do?

We took his Ford pickup, a work truck with a toolbox and cow shit in the bed, work gloves on the dash and a cracked windshield.

"We'll want to blend in, look like one of the crowd," Melvin said. "We want to look and listen." He said "try to get a feel for the mood of the crowd."

He wore a straw hat with a cowboy brim. His face was flush, rosacea I think. It made his nose and cheeks look raw and blotchy. I noticed his hand on the wheel; they were working man's hands, rough, scarred and calloused. This man worked for a living and I was just a kid along for the ride.

I cannot stand to ride without talking, even to myself. We rode for ten miles or so listening to the news from the Nebraska Rural Radio Network on KRVN AM 880 out of Lexington. "The price of corn is down a quarter; hog futures are flat and beans down a half. The weather is going to be foggy to start the day but will burn off with high expected in the mid-seventies," the Farm Director said. The rattle of the passenger's window, the drone of the announcer and the hum of the engine was making me crazy.

"What do you think is going on?" I asked.

He looked over at me and back to the road. He adjusted his hands on the wheel and his butt in the seat but didn't reply for a mile or more. I was about to rephrase the question when he asked, "What'd the banker tell you?"

I considered my conversation with Bill Oldfather and said, "He blames a combination of loosely connected events and market factors, over production, bad foreign and monetary policies. I get the feeling he believes it's more bad luck and poor timing than anything."

Melvin nodded, "He may be right. I got a similar story from a professor of economics at Kearney State. He's of a mind that it's a correction, an adjustment in the market."

"You think it's just a few bad farmers, who needed to get out?" I asked, a line often repeated by national and AP publications.

He looked at me like a bull with a bastard calf, "Do you know how many farm auctions there were in 1979?" Before I could offer a guess, he went on. "Twenty-six for the five-state region. Those were mostly estate sales, farmers with no family to take over the homestead or no death insurance coverage. Maybe there were a few bad apples in that lot. In 1980 there were 68 in Iowa, Minnesota and Nebraska alone. We are on our way to the hundredth farm auction this year in that same basic area. I've heard speculation there will be another twenty-five before Christmas."

Melvin paused to let those numbers sink in. His response had caught me off guard. I hadn't heard him mutter more than a couple of questions and nod in response in my short time at the paper.

"So, no." he said. "This is not a few bad farmers. This is a big damn problem, and it's spreading. I know a family over at Fremont, good people, hardworking and productive. One day he's square, in good standing with the bank, so he goes in after the first of the year to secure his production loan. The bank tells him the value of his land dropped by half. He's now over extended and the bank wants to minimize its exposure. Well, they denied the loan. He turns to the Farmer's Union and they offer him a loan but with corn prices falling the likelihood of him covering the note is somewhere between slim and none. That scenario is happening all over the middle west. Lots of families are caught between a rock and a hard place. Damned if you do, damned if you don't. They'll lose the farm by the end of the year and there's nothing can be done."

I looked out the window for a while after Melvin finished until I realized he hadn't answered my question. "So, what do you think is the cause?"

"Kid, there isn't just one thing. It's a whole host of factors and failures. If you're asking my opinion, I would tell you yes: over production, bad advice and corruption by government bureaucrats; corporate intervention for sure, maybe an act of God and the devil to pay."

I was content to ride in silence for a while to consider what Melvin, Oldfather and Jim Taylor had told me. My thoughts were dark and sad. I was sure the auction was not going to improve my mood.

O'Neill is the Irish capital of Nebraska. The huge shamrock painted in the main intersection downtown was illustration of the town's commitment to St. Patrick, beer and the luck of the Irish. We found a café along the downtown strip serving simple country fare with breakfast as a specialty. I had eggs, sausage, buttermilk biscuits with gravy, hash browns and coffee. Melvin had juice, pancakes and bacon, "Break it, don't bend it," he told the waitress who took our order. The place was busy with plenty of out-of-towners there for the sale. Melvin talked with a couple of guys from up around the Valentine area. They knew a friend or relative of his, either way they knew his column. Turns out I was traveling with a bit of a celebrity. Melvin suggested I lay back and gauge the mood. I think he said, 'get the vibe' of the place. My feeling was the vibe was down if not morose. I'd never been to a farm auction, but my father loved to take me to auctions around Des Moines. As I recall, there was always excitement, not just for me but for everyone. The anticipation of finding some forgotten treasure and getting it for a song always accompanied the sale. The vibe of this auction resembled a wake, and not the Irish kind.

The auction was set up out in the open on the edge of the Fairgrounds. There was a good crowd with a variety of trucks and trailers; two dozen half ton trucks with flatbed trailers, six semis with box trailers and a fleet of pickups. Sarge was right; my Honda would have stood out like a sore thumb and might have gotten squashed by any number of these rigs.

Farm equipment was lined up in three directions from the small stage set up by the auction house. The stage had a squat picket fence around it and a portable speaker's stand with speakers at each corner connected to a simple mixing box at the back of the stage.

We split up to walk around the grounds, again, to get the vibe of the buyers. I stopped to listen near two old farmers discussing the price of the tractors. They were looking at a like-new Ford next to an antique Massey Ferguson. "This is a damn shame" one man said to the other.

"Yeah, I know this rig isn't three years old," replied the other

"Really thought they ran a solid operation but I guess not," said the first one.

"Bankers could've found a way to keep them going. It's a crying shame," the other replied.

I walked away not paying much attention to the equipment and trailers. I couldn't have told you the difference between a White's planter and a Caterpillar combine. I came upon rows of tables with plates and bowls on it, wedding china and tarnished silverware, dishes, pots and pie pans stacked all together. There were quilts and bed frames, dressers and nightstands. I got uncomfortable walking by these tables as it occurred to me, "this is not a business being dissolved but a family's life being sold."

I heard a commotion nearby and went to see what it was about. A man dressed in coveralls, a seed corn hat and boots was standing on the running board of the huge machine, waving a piece of paper in one hand and calling the crowd. "This is not just a farm sale, no sir, this is part of a larger scheme to take away our way of life," he announced in a strained high-pitched voice. "Every one of you knows in your heart, this could be your property or your neighbor's for sale today. This is not just a farm being sold off here today but a legacy, the heritage of this great country. Your heritage is on the block. Don't be fooled. These corrupt agents, working within and outside of our government want to destroy the enterprise of the independent, freedom loving, family farms." The crowd grew, and the speaker picked up on the vibe. "I'm not talking about these fools conducting this nasty business here today. No, they're nothing but pawns in a sinister plot, put in motion by Jew bankers and corrupt judges out to take over our country. Our forefathers, the founders of this great country didn't want to allow those killers of Christ into the country. They knew what could happen..." He waved the paper in his hand and raised his voice a little higher. "There's a new world order being introduced in the halls of our government and it starts with controlling the food supply. Whoever produces the food and who holds it, has the power, the power to rule us. These evil bastards realize the independent farmers are the biggest threat to their plans. Take a flier, read it through and come join us in the fight for liberty and independence from illegal government bureaucracy, like the IRS"

I walked away. While I could sympathize with the tragedy of a lifestyle being lost, I don't believe the government could organize a circle jerk much less a conspiracy. Besides it angered me. He was playing on the fears of desperate people to advance his message of anti-Semitism. It's not that I doubted the sincerity of the speaker. In fact he sounded like a true believer, and misguided true believers make for vigilantes, extremist and radicals.

Many of the farmers and ranchers walked away too but not all. There was a group who stayed to listen, some nodding and reaching for a copy of the flier a young boy was passing out at the instruction of the radical on the tractor. I thought later, I should have taken one of the fliers to see what the plot was, but the sale was starting so I wanted to find Melvin.

Chapter 10

Melvin was standing on one side of the crowd, out of the way of the buyers, close enough to see and hear the auctioneer and the crowd. The auctioneer was a chubby faced fellow of about fifty. He wore a dark western style suit with pearl buttons, a felt gray Stetson and black dress cowboy boots polished to a high shine. Around his neck was a funny looking wire harness holding a small square microphone. The harness positioned the mike so it appeared to stick out from his chin. The contraption did the trick of projecting his rich baritone voice clearly out over the gathering crowd. "Welcome folks," the auctioneer began.

"We're about ready to start the sale. Before we do; a few reminders. This is a cash sale, you must settle up with the lady." He pointed to a thirty something platinum blond seated at a desk to his right. "She will take your money and give you a bill of sale. Okay, folks, the first item for sale is a nineteen eighty Ford tractor, model 150 with a rocker set and bush hog attachment. This tractor has only two hundred hours of use and comes with the original dealer's warranty. What will you give me for an opening bid." While he spoke, he waved and pointed with his hands. I could see why he wore the harness. If you took away his hands, even one, it would severely restrict his ability to communicate.

He launched into the rapid fire, staccato cadence of the auctioneer. "Give five, can I have a five-thousand-dollar bid, five, I need five thousand to start. Now I'll take forty-five, four five to open, can I get forty-five hundred from ya?"

Melvin whispered in my ear, "New tractor like that is ten thousand dollars." I knew it was more like twelve from overhearing the earlier conversation between the two farmers. Still the crowd didn't move. The auctioneer went down, "Alright then, I'll take four to open, give me four thousand for a starting bid."

A voice from the back called, "I'll give you a nickel."

The auctioneer stopped and looked out over the crowd; he raised his hand above his eyes, to shield the sunlight or to peer out into the crowd. He took his hand down and smiled a big winning smile. "Now folks, this is a serious matter. The proceeds from this sale will go to settle a debt owed and allow this family to move on."

The voice from the crowd yelled, "This is stealing, and you're a thief for taking part in..."

"We're not going to have any of this." The auctioneer was still smiling. His eyes flashed a caution to the crowd. "Folks we all understand this auction is not a joking matter and I won't accept any of this nonsense. Now, can I take an opening bid of five thousand for this fine piece of equipment?"

One of the fellows I overheard discussing the tractors earlier raised his hand and called, "Yep!"

The auctioneer took up the cadence and the bidding increased as several bidders drove the price up to a respectable eight thousand dollars. We stayed an hour or so until most of the larger items had been sold. Melvin tapped me on the arm and walked off toward the truck. I had plenty of questions. The look in Melvin's sad brown eyes caused me to hold my thoughts until we were gone from the place.

I held off until we were ten miles south of town. I was scribbling in my notebook, trying to remember the ideas and images from the morning. I was beginning to recall the story and was writing fast while trying to keep it legible for later reference.

"That could've gone bad if Ted hadn't handled it the way he did," Melvin said out of the blue.

"What, who's Ted?" I asked.

"Ted Anderson, the auctioneer," Melvin said. "He's a pro. He smiled right through the whole thing. You could tell he don't take no shit. I heard of a sale up by Mankato, Minnesota where nobody bid on anything. They refused to allow anyone to bid, the whole community was in on it, maybe the sheriff too."

"What's the point?" I asked.

"Defiance, a protest of sorts, solidarity for the family," Melvin said. "The folks up in Minnesota wanted to return all the belongings to the family. The bank just shut down the auction and moved it to another area where the emotions were not running so hot."

"Did you hear the guy over at the combine?" I asked.

"No, what was it about?"

"He was talking judges, Jewish bankers and government conspiracies," I smirked.

"Posse Comitatus or John Birch maybe a little of both," Melvin said. "They're no laughing matter."

"He sounded like a radical, a lunatic," I said.

"Radicals will always attract a crowd. Small groups of radicals have changed the world," he said.

I looked at him with questioning surprise. "Really?"

"Radicals speak to the emotions of the marginalized. Ever hear of the Boston Tea Party?" He paused for effect then went on. "When a group of people begin to feel those in authority are no longer dealing fairly with them and they don't trust their motives, the natural response is to rebel."

"How do you know this?" I asked.

"I was sociology major with a minor in history," he said with a grin. He let the statement hang in the truck to let me know I wasn't as bright or as educated as I thought I was.

"Those small radical groups may be shifting the political landscape as we speak. The Moral Majority and its following elected Reagan, an act that may very well have flipped the identity of the two major parties in this country, like a shift at the poles."

"What?" I asked.

"You watch. A decade from now the democrats will be the liberal party and the republicans will be the conservatives. Reagan may have been the first major candidate to switch parties and win a national election. He won't be the last."

"Reagan was a democrat?" I asked.

"You kids today don't know anything," he said with a smirk.

"What about the Posse Comitatus? When the sheriff was out to Harold's place one of the deputies was talking on about this group. Do you know anything about it?"

Melvin adjusted himself in the seat and looked at me out of the corner of his eye. His lack of response made me uneasy, but I was learning to wait for him to answer. After a few miles Melvin said. "If you want to know about the Posse because you're a reporter working on an angle, I'll tell you to be careful with what you write. I did a piece on them for the Fence Post a while back and got some very interesting mail."

Now I was interested, "What kind of mail?"

"Let's just say it wasn't fan mail. Then a few days later I came out to my truck to find my tires cut. A week later one of my new calves went missing. I found it a mile from its mother, gutted and skinned. That was a thousand-dollar calf."

"And you think," I began.

"No, I know," Melvin said turning to look me in the eye. "I know Sarge has you working on a farm story, but you need to think long and hard before you drag any of these radical groups out into the light."

I rode in silence; my mind was working on the story, on the

farm crisis and more. Politics was not my thing and radical government hate groups were way out of my league. I should start to pay more attention; I just might be in the middle of something historical. When we got to the edge of town I gathered my courage to ask Melvin about the Posse. "Could you tell me where I would find information on these radical groups?"

He cut me a look.

I went on, "I've looked in the library but couldn't find much. Do you think they'd have anything in Grand Island or over at Kearney?"

"Okay, if you're going to dig into this start at the courthouse."

"Courthouse?"

"One of the elements of this group is they will file papers with the court, challenging income taxes and property taxes. They seem to be spreading the idea that a farmer can sue the IRS in court, because as they see it, income taxes are unconstitutional. You'll find out a good bit from those documents, who is filing and for what. Sometimes they will file a formal certificate of formation for a charter with the clerk. They want to appear as legitimate as possible. They don't always get upset at news stories. They like to have their names in the paper to show their cause and their claims are real but I'm warning you kid, be careful. This could be big and it could also be bad."

Chapter 11

It was two weeks before I could make my trip over to Ravenna to introduce myself to Joseph Steward. I left my small two-bedroom apartment on a misty fall morning. I could've stayed in bed after eating a bowl of Captain Crunch cereal. I could have just spent the afternoon listening to the Cornhuskers football game on the radio. But something made me get up and move.

Still, my attitude, as I drove out of town, was decidedly gray; as gray as the clouds negating the sun's desire to peek through. When I first moved out here I imagined myself like one of the early pioneers, leaving Iowa behind, crossing over the Missouri River at Council Bluffs and on to the great western road. While I wasn't traveling by horse or prairie schooner at the rate of eight miles a day; I was off on an adventure, starting a new chapter, a career with the opportunity to re-invent myself. Today I was home-sad, not sick, but just low.

I headed out here for all those reasons and one more. I had a great childhood. Parents were good, not perfect but supporting, loving and nurturing. There were a few awkward seasons in junior high I had to outgrow. High school was busy and fun. I got my heart broken a few times, drank a few too many beers, played basketball, and my AC/DC albums were too loud. Nothing out of the ordinary, no deep dark hidden secrets, or at least I thought. Then I found out I was adopted. I should have noticed some of the genetic differences but who really wants to consider such things. The crazy thing is, my parents, when I confronted them, and they finally told me, had this incredible, unbelievable story. I mean truly, I didn't believe it. It was so odd. I'd never known my parents to lie, other than their big lie of omission, which has made me question everything, including myself.

I said some things I want to take back but hadn't, not yet anyway. I talked to them every week on Sunday night when the rates are lower. They always want me to call collect, but I don't. I use the excuse of a high phone bill to get off the phone. I'm not mad at them anymore. I just need some room to think. Maybe that's why the story of the cross keeps coming back to me. I literally dreamed about them, the cross and chapel. It worries me a little; more than anything it excites my curiosity, my journalistic spirit for solving a mystery. These random thoughts cycled through my head as I drove to meet Joe Steward.

The nursing home was a single story yellow building with white trim. Its two wings stretched out from the center rectangle with a church like steeple of a roof. The lobby was divided by a wide carpeted walkway. On one side was a group of chairs loosely arranged to face the TV. A small upright piano stood against the outside wall in front of a large picture window. The other side was set up as a dining area, with cards and dominoes sitting on the table, clearly now being used as recreation space. The home was not as drab or institutional as the one Amos passed away in, but I could still sense the angels of death hovering in the corridors. Sitting at the nurses' station was a smiling middle-aged woman, wearing a bright yellow apron over a white uniform.

"Good morning," she said. "How may I help you?"

"I'd like to see Joe Steward," I answered.

"Family or friend?" she asked. She looked down at a chart in front of her and when I didn't reply she looked up. "Are you a family member or a friend of Joe's?"

"Neither," I answered. Her mouth was still smiling, her eyes were not. "See, I'm a reporter for the St. Paul paper and we're developing a story, a story about the Steward homestead. They were Kinkaiders who received more than forty acres and a mule, because of the difficulties of farming in the Sandhills." When her expression didn't change I knew my ability to lie was not improving. "Anyway, I want to ask Mr. Steward a few questions."

She looked down the hall. "Well isn't that nice." She smiled without really meaning it. "I'm not sure you'll get much in the way of answers from Joe. Some days he's better than others."

I hadn't thought too much about Joe's health or his memory. I said, "Well, isn't that the way for everyone,"

She nodded and said "Ain't that the truth."

"Can I see him?"

"Sure, he could use the company. Since you're not family, let me have you speak with Dr. Waddell first," and she asked me to take a seat in the lobby.

I wasn't sure if a doctor was going to be sympathetic to my cause. I needed to think what I was going to do, how I was going to explain this. I decided, based on the fact that I was still a novice liar and would surely get tripped up on my own back-story, I would tell the truth, as I see it. The truth is always subjective.

Dr. Tom Waddell introduced himself as Dr. Tom, a clear homage to Coach Tom Osborne. I'm sure most people around here made the same association, especially on a football Saturday. Dr. Tom led me to a small office and offered me a seat, coffee and water. I declined all. "What is it you want to ask Mr. Steward?" the doctor asked with his arms crossed and head cocked to one side.

"About the cross and the chapel he built on his place outside of Broken Bow." I said.

Dr. Tom uncrossed his arms but kept his head cocked to one side. "What?"

"I know it was a long time ago but we, I mean the paper, is interested in doing a story on it and I..." the doctor was looking at me like I had two heads or something.

"What did you say your name was, again?" he asked.

"Willy Beam with the St. Paul Phonograph," I answered.

Doctor Tom walked a few steps and took the seat he had offered me just a few seconds ago. He looked amused or confused it was hard for me to say which. "If you want to ask Joe questions go slow. He sometimes needs to hear questions more than once to respond. He gets tired quickly so don't be upset if he falls asleep in the middle of your interview. If you wait he may just be thinking, so don't give up too quickly." The doctor stood up and pointed me toward the door. "Joe is down in room thirty-eight, at the end of the hall on the right."

I was now the one confused, "Doc, what's going on?"

He said, "I'm not sure Mr. Beam. I believe Joe has been waiting for you."

"Huh?"

"For the past week every time the nurses gave Joe his medicine or fed him a meal, he'd talk about the Wily Beans coming to see the cross and talk about his Mary."

I headed down the hall to see Joe Steward with an odd sensation in the pit of my stomach. I peeked around the door frame into room thirty-eight. The door stood open, filtered sunlight came into the room from a large east window. There was a silhouette of a man sitting in a high-backed chair looking toward the window, waiting for my arrival. I stepped into the room to stand just inside the doorway. The old man turned his head my way.

"Good morning," I said.

He nodded.

"My name is Willy Beam. I'd like to sit with you for a while, maybe ask a few questions, if you don't mind."

He adjusted a blanket laying across his lap but didn't reply. I was about to speak again when he said, "Come on in." His speech was gravely but clears enough to understand. I took a cautious step into the room. He was grinning with his eyes and his lips; his teeth didn't show. His hair was white, full, parted and combed to one side; the tracks of the comb distinctive as furrows across a corn field. He was clean shaved with bright eyes that I liked right away.

"Mr. Steward," I began.

"I'm Joe," he said. "Just a plain old Joe."

"Oh, okay, Joe. Do you feel like talking?"

He nodded, again. I took out my notebook and pulled up a yellow plastic chair with a simple but sturdy metal frame.

"Joe, there's a cross and chapel up on the hill next to your homestead outside of Broken Bow. Do you remember?"

He nodded then looked toward the window but didn't reply. I looked around the room. The floor was covered by nine-inch commercial tiles. A large oval braided rug was under Joe's chair. Next to the chair stood a small wooden stand with a glass of water and tissues on it. The walls were a light blue to complement the darker flecks in the floor tile. A full-size sleigh bed dominated the room. It was homey and a little out of place in the institutional setting.

"It was the stranger came to see Mary in the spring of '46 who asked her to put it up," he said.

I was caught off guard by his sudden reply, "A stranger?" I asked.

"I saw him coming from a long way off." Joe was still looking toward the windows. "He was walking along the road coming from the west, along the highway, right out of the sun. I was away from the house, checking the cattle and mending a fence. It was hot and I wanted to make sure the livestock had plenty of water so they didn't knock down the fence to get over to the creek. I'd driven out with a load of hay, pulling the trailer with my horse in it. I needed the truck for the supplies, but I always liked to ride a horse when working cattle. A good cow horse is a joy and a blessing to an old cattleman like me." Joe looked toward me. "Do you ride?"

"A little; summer camps."

"Then you know. I had a sweet bay mare with a black mane. She was dependable and gentle. She didn't take no crud from the cows though," he smiled at the memory.

"There was a stranger walking along the road," I said to encourage the story line.

"Huh, oh yes, Gabe," he said, reluctant to leave the memory of riding a bay mare. "I was out away from the house. I could see the road from atop the rise and the house back up to the north. Like I said, he was a long way off but I knew he was coming. You ever have that feeling?"

"What feeling?" I asked.

He raised a shaky hand with his index finger extended, like he was checking the wind "A feeling like the winds are changing. A feeling that a storm is coming, bringing big changes."

I thought about what Dr. Tom had said and was surprised how lucid and clear Joe seemed.

"I worked the herd up the valley a little toward the stock tank. It wasn't no time, maybe a half hour or so, before I looked back over to the road, and Gabe, though I didn't know his name at the time, was on the road up to the house. I remember being surprised he could travel so far in so short a time."

"How far do you think it was?" I asked.

Joe rubbed his chin with a big knuckled hand, "Well, now I would have to say twenty miles or more."

"Twenty miles?" I asked. "You could see that far along the road?"

He bobbed his head and smiled with his eyes. He pointed his finger at me and winked. He took the glass from the table and drank. His hands shook so; I thought he would spill it. The water sloshed around but he returned it to the table, carefully with both hands, pulling back his hands from the glass as if he had solved a puzzle. I tried to stay calm and wait.

"You know," he said at last, "I've thought about it and I can't tell you for sure that I saw him as much as I could perceive him coming, like the wind. Either way he came to the house where Mary was so I headed up to the house. It was my habit to take a break around three in the afternoon anyway. The day was hot, like I said, and I liked to nap in the heat of the day. Sometimes a nap can refresh you like nothing else before the evening chores. Do you nap?"

"What, no" I said. "Not since kindergarten."

"You should, a nap is a wonderful thing." He returned to the story. "Anyway, I came in through the back porch and took off my boots. Mary didn't allow work boots in the house. It might've been a farmhouse, but it was her house to keep clean. So I sat down on the back steps and took off my boots. While I was sitting there I heard voices coming from the kitchen or better a voice. I called to Mary and she came out to the porch and told me we had a guest."

He paused in the narrative and looked toward the hall. I turned to see a nurse with a tray pass by. I looked back to Joe and smiled. "Sometimes they bring me a snack about this time."

"Do you need me to get you something?" I asked

"No, no, just didn't want those nosy nurses listening in." We waited while the nurse delivered medication to the resident next door. Joe's eyes darted back and forth between the noise in the next room and the hall. When the nurse wheeled her cart back up the hall he picked up the story again. "Now understand it's not unusual to have a guest stop by. We didn't live too far from town and family and friends often came out to visit. Mary attracted people to her like moths to a flame. She loved to have folks drop by to catch up on what was happening, but this was no neighbor stopping out for a visit."

Joe dropped his gaze to look at his hands, bobbing his head a few times before answering. "He had a presence about him, a powerful stature. I can't say it any plainer than that. He was dusty from the road, his face tanned, his hair windblown. The wind and the sun left impressions on his face. He had on work jeans and boots; nothing remarkable about his dress, just a traveler from off the road. All the same he wasn't a wanderer but a messenger. My first response was to be unsettled."

"Why?" I asked.

"Instinct maybe, a gut feeling left over from the service, like the fear I got in my belly when a battle was brewing or when we got the order to move out." He looked back toward the window. "Gabe sure brought change to our lives. Not all of it bad, mind you. Still change just the same."

"What changed?" I asked.

"I've thought about it quite a bit, more so lately. I knew then, I know it now, the stranger sitting at my kitchen table radiated a profound presence..."

"A vibe," I interjected. This was a terrible thing to do in the middle of an interview. My college professor would be ashamed. You never, ever put words into your subject's mouth. Don't feed him lines or ideas; it taints the process, although I hear it all the time now, especially in TV news stories, and it's a cardinal sin in the news gathering business. The word caught Joe off guard, he looked at me odd for a moment. "I suppose that's a good description."

"You called him Gabe?" I asked. I half expected Joe to be reluctant to talk, maybe having trouble remembering but he was lucid and eager to share.

"Gabe, yes that's his name. He was a good looking fellow, a nice smile, brown hair a little long for my tastes but all the kids like to wear it that way." I self-consciously brushed hair from my face. "I remember he looked like he'd just got off a motorcycle. You know how a person's hair will be blown back and up by the wind?" Joe smiled at the thought. "He was tall, well over six foot, closer to six four or five with strong hands. He shook my hand and I felt an energy."

Joe held up his hand as if to shake my hand. "I don't have the words to describe it, electric, a charge. Almost like when you touch the ends of jumper cables together and you get a spark. The spark's in the wires but you feel a little jolt in your hands." He looked to me for assurance and I gave him a nod of understanding.

I was scribbling, trying to sketch the story in my notebook.

"Son," Joe started again. "I've known that I'd be required to tell someone this story, someday. I've tried to work it out in my mind, to find the words, an explanation. Now I'm old. Hell, I'm just a busted-up rancher from the Sandhills and this was something biblical. Bigger than Mary and I."

"What do you mean, biblical?"

Joe's eyes sparked and his jaw set. "The stranger sitting at my kitchen table was sent by God. He gave us a mission. He gave her a calling and I was caught up in it like a whirlwind but only a part of it."

"You believe Gabe, the stranger, was an angel?" I asked.

"I know it. I know it as well as I know my own name."

Skepticism must have registered on my face because Joe bristled. "I don't give a care what anyone else believes. Call me crazy if you want. These damn doctors think I'm soft in the head, but yes. Yes, Gabe was a messenger from God; an angel as you said, and for some reason, I don't, I can't understand why, he chose my Mary to do his work. You can write that down. I got nothing to hide and no reason to lie." He was leaning forward in the chair with his jaw set and his eyes ablaze.

I recalled Amos's defiant challenge when he told me his story. I was learning not to doubt the memories of old men. "I believe you, Joe."

He eased back a little in his seat and we spent the rest of the morning and most of the afternoon talking, recalling. We had lunch together. He told me some remarkable stories. I will admit the idea of a messenger with a divine calling trekking across the Sandhills, along a Nebraska state highway to deliver a message, a "calling" as Joe described it, to a rancher's wife in the summer of 1946 was more than strange. It's unbelievable but I tried to maintain an open mind.

Gabe told Mary to build a small chapel, close to the road and mark it with a cross carved from a single piece of wood. The building materials and dimensions of every window, wall and door was spelled out, even who was to build the cross. It seemed Amos was known to the messenger as well. Every detail and time line for completion was given. As is often the case it seems the reasons were not fully revealed at the time.

He told me about the ranch and his cattle. He spoke of his favorite horse, Buckshot and how they built the chapel. He said they got the pews from a church over in Thedford, just like Gabe had said. The church had burned earlier in the year. The congregation was building a bigger building and didn't need the old pews, so they just gave them away. Joe said the skylight came from two pieces of round glass a scrapper had in his junk pile.

"When we showed up and asked for them, the old guy didn't seem too surprised," Joe said with a laugh. "He told us to 'take em. God only knows what you'll do with em'. Mary laughed about that all the way home."

He said the small steeple and stained glass came from a reservation church up near the Pine Ridge Agency. "That's where the massacre of Wounded Knee happened," Joe said with a shake of his head. "You know they awarded more medals of honor for the killing of women and children in the snow than in any American battle since?"

"No," I said. "I didn't know."

"We hauled the steeple down and built the entrance to connect with the foundation. We sat the steeple on top and the rest is just a simple rectangle, for some reason a steeple makes it a chapel."

Joe talked about how they put the cross up and Amos was amazed it could be made out of one piece of wood. The whole project took about three months from foundation to completion. "We built it on faith. Like Noah there were plenty of people calling us crazy. Lots of good Christians whispered behind our backs but Gabe said, 'build it,' and that's just what we did."

"What happened after it was done?" I asked. "Did people start showing up right away?"

"No, the place stood empty without a soul coming to visit for most of that year. I remember thinking maybe we were crazy. Mary believed though. One day I got up to take care of the animals and noticed someone in the chapel. I called to Mary and we went to see who was there."

Joe cleared his throat and coughed so hard I was about to go get the nurse. He waved me off and continued. "It was a tramp, a hobo from the railroad. He looked sheepish when we opened the door. I thought he would run like a jackrabbit. Mary just smiled and offered him some breakfast." Joe shook his head and smiled. "She could put people at ease with just her smile and cornbread pancakes."

"Did more people start to come after that?"

"It was hit and miss, but eventually people of all ages and for all reasons came. Some stayed for a night or two. Some came and worked for a good little bit. Mary would let them stay for a few nights. If they stayed more than a week, she'd put them to work."

"Doing what?" I asked.

"Cleaning stalls, feeding chickens, hanging laundry, cleaning the chapel, whatever there was to do. She would just ask them, and most were glad to be of use. I had a few turned out to be good hands. One old boy, Peter, stayed most of the year with us and came back every spring to work. I was glad to have him and to call him a friend."

"Did you pay him?"

"Room and board till the branding time and then wages for his work. Most wouldn't take charity. They'd work for a meal. You know, Mary's Sunday dinners were worth a week's wages." Joe laughed.

"Why?" I asked, after Joe had paused to take a drink of water.

"Why, indeed," he replied. "Why Mary, why here, why put all that burden on us? I've asked that question a thousand times and searched the Bible for answers. All I can tell you is God chooses whom He will for His own purposes. 'My ways are not your ways, neither are my thoughts your thoughts'; Isaiah 55." I wrote the verse in my notes.

"Do you wish God had chosen someone else?"

"Some days, yes. Sometimes I wish He had left us alone. I've been angry with it, wanted to curse Gabe for coming to my kitchen that day. Not Mary." He shook his head. "She was an angel herself. Not just my angel but a lot of people's angel of mercy. She never faltered to my knowledge. Then again, I've never read her journals."

"What?" I asked. "Mary kept a journal?"

Joe chuckled, "Yes son. Isn't that what you came here for?"

My heart was racing; a foolish grin swept my face. "What I came for?"

Joe just smiled as if I should know what he knew.

"Do you have them? Can I read them?"

"I don't have them here, but I suppose, yes you can, if you want."

Why wouldn't I want to read them? I thought. "How can I get them?" I was suddenly desperate to read Mary's journals. I wanted to know what she knew, to hear the details from her point of view, to understand this story, the messenger and whatever else was preserved in her own handwriting. I was ready to set off in search of them. Wherever Joe sent me I was prepared to go.

"I suspect you'll find them at James place," Joe said.

"James?" I asked.

"James McCray, my great nephew, I think the kids call him Jimmy."

"Uncle Jimmy," I thought.

Chapter 12

The very idea that Mary Ann Steward kept a record over the years was awesome. I could hardly contain myself. The urge to run to my car was barely containable as I left the nursing home. I raced my little rice burner out of Ravenna and straight for Broken Bow. I needed to find Amanda, to meet Uncle Jimmy and get a look at the journals of Mary Steward. Halfway there it occurred to me that I didn't know where Amanda lived, what her parent's first names were or how to get in touch with her. We had left it very vague when she told me where to find Joe weeks ago. I hadn't met her parents and it might be weird to just show up looking for their daughter. Folks get very protective of teenage girls.

I could drive around the drag all night and not find her. I could ask around, maybe at the library but my first encounter with Amanda told me the librarian could be a bit of a gossip. Never-the-less, my spirits were soaring, my imagination aflame with ideas of what might be. I rolled past the cross and the chapel, standing as a beacon of hope while housing a story alive with mystery. I waved as I passed. What a foolish thing. How full of naiveté; how blind I was to the stories it held.

I decided to call from the pay phone. I parked along the outside of the square and almost sprinted to the booth. I opened the creaky bi-fold door, pulled up the phone book attached by a chain to the underside of the shelf below the pay phone. The phone book was sun faded with some water damage. The S section was not marred. I didn't know her father's name. Fortunately, the list of Stewards included sub-listings of other residents and beneath William Steward were Amy, Todd, Andy, Sam and Amanda.

I dialed the rotary phone without thinking of what I would say. The phone rang once, twice, three times. Common courtesy and social protocol dictated five rings to be maximum, after which one hung up. I let it ring four, then five times; it rang a sixth, seventh and eighth time and still I didn't hang up. I decided to let it ring ten times, double the norm. I needed to speak to someone. I was about to hang up when a female answered.

"Hello!" she said with a great deal of annoyance in her tone.

"Hello," I said. "Is Amanda home?"

"No, she's gone," she said. "Who's calling?"

"My name is Willy Beam," I said. "I'm a reporter for the Phonograph. I need to speak with Amanda."

There was a pause, then she sounded concerned. "What's this about? Is there some kind of trouble?"

"No, no. No trouble," I said. Realizing only then my excitement and place of employment might imply something was wrong. "I've been working on, that is Amanda has been helping me with, a project for the paper and I just needed; that is. I wanted to talk with her about some ideas, for a piece of an article."

"What kind of story?" she asked. "This is Amanda's mother, she better not be ignoring her schoolwork."

"Mrs. Steward," I said. "I'm sure Amanda is taking care of her schoolwork. This is a little history; an ancestry story Amanda was helping me with. She may get extra credit at school for the work." I was deep into a lie I couldn't support, and one Amanda might not confirm. "Do you know when Amanda will be home?"

"She's gone to Kearney. She should be back before dark," Mrs. Steward said. "What was your name again?"

"Willy Beam, ma'am " I said. "Just let Amanda know I called."

I hung up before I said anything else. I did remember to write down the number, and Amanda's father's name, William Steward. I looked up James McCall's number and thought about calling it. Then I thought better of it. I remembered Amanda said Jimmy was a little squirrelly and decided to wait for her.

I left the phone booth and stood at the corner of the square deciding what to do. It had been an exciting day with lots of information to digest. I spotted the diner and decided I needed pie. A warm slice of pie and a cup of coffee was just the ticket. I took a booth seat facing away from the door. The game was on the radio. Several patrons were seated at the counter drinking coffee and listening to the Huskers and Auburn. Nebraska had lost two of its first three games and needed a win over the Tigers or War Eagles (Auburn can't make up its mind about mascots) before the Big 8 Conference schedule started next week with Colorado.

I ordered peach pie and coffee adding both cream and sugar to my drink before consulting my notes. The story Joe told me was amazing and unbelievable. I believed every word; the angel, a calling, and prophecy. Still to my way of thinking biblical missions happened in Palestine and Babylon or maybe fourteenth century Spain or Rome, not twentieth century America. I had been taught God stopped talking directly with humans after Jesus and the Apostles. Why would an angel travel on foot to visit a farm wife in the Sandhills of Nebraska in the nineteen-forties?

I could think of a half dozen places where angels would be needed in the late forties: Russia, Germany, Japan, China all came to mind. However, the fifties in the good old U.S. of A. was "Leave it to Beaver", "My Three Sons", Yankees Baseball and the Boston Celtics. Why would God need to commission a cross and chapel along this lonely stretch of highway in the Sandhills? I supposed Jack Kerouac might need a place to crash.

Maybe Joe was delusional. Still he appeared reflective, introspective and thoughtful. He talked like the story had been with him a long time. I got the same feeling I had with Amos, that he was unburdening himself by telling it to me. The doctor even said something about Joe expecting me or someone like me. How was that possible?

I was caught up in these many questions, trying to sort through my thoughts when a cheer went up. Some of the fans at the counter were yelling. I could hear the faint roar of the crowd from the speakers on the radio. The Sea of Red in Memorial Stadium was in full voice and Lylle Bremser announced another Cornhusker touchdown. The Big Red was rolling this afternoon, victory sounded all but guaranteed. When Nebraska won all was right with the world. If they lost every exchange, every transaction slowed and the whole economy of the state was affected. When Nebraska won, even the lessons from the pulpits were more hopeful on Sunday morning.

I started to return to my notes when I overheard a conversation in the booth behind me. "Did you hear about Will Steward," an older man asked the younger man sitting across from him. I could see the man talking because of a large round mirror mounted in the corner above me. He looked to be about fifty with gray hair. His face was long and weathered, a stubble of beard on his cheeks. I could see the back of the younger man's head and it boasted a wild mop of brown hair.

"Yeah," the younger said. "I can't believe it. Will runs a good operation."

"Nobody is safe from this plague," said the older. "it will be a generation before land values come back."

"You really think so?" asked the younger.

"Afraid so, there are banks failing all over the place. Thing is, a few years back, they were beating down the farmer's door to loan money. Now can't squeeze a nickel out of any of them."

"I just don't understand, how this is happening," said the younger. "Hell, interest rates are up so damn high and prices dropping like a stone. No way to catch up or make a dime."

Another cheer went up and I lost the conversation. When the noise died down the two had moved on to discussing Cornhusker football and how they might fare against Oklahoma at the end of the season.

Their comments reminded me of Melvin's predictions, Mr. Oldfather the banker, Sarge's story and the growing fear that lurked in the back of everyone's mind. The name Steward buzzed in my ear and for the first time I was worried about Amanda.

The conversation also reminded me. I had a deadline to meet and a story to file. Sarge had been on me about getting something local to go with the national stories. I wanted to talk with a professor at Kearney State College whom Melvin had recommended. I already had lots of material, too much material and that was my problem. I didn't know where to start or stop. It was hard to decide what was important and what was just fear and wild speculation. I needed to get a handle on the story, pay my bills and worry less about some wild story about angels from an old man in a nursing home. Still, the practical side of my brain couldn't quite convince my heart not to follow this lead. The sun was setting, and I realized Amanda might have trouble explaining why I called or what we were working on. She had said her mother was not a supporter of Mary. My rash and excited call may have caused more trouble then I intended. I paid my bill and headed back to St. Paul.

Chapter 13

I spent the week doing research and working on the final draft of the farm story. It may have been just a small-town newspaper but Sarge took great pride in putting out a quality paper. One thing I felt I needed was an expert's viewpoint. The banker had been helpful and important from a local perspective. Still I needed an expert. Melvin's recommendation of Dr. Talbert at Kearney State was a perfect choice.

Dr. Matthew Talbert, PhD of Economics was a large man with big square rimmed glasses and a full head of hair. His office was as disheveled as his suit. The closet size room was dominated by three metal cabinets and a desk, overrun by piles of papers. I squeezed into a chair behind the door with my notebook and questions. I could've done the interview over the phone but with the college within easy driving distance the face to face interview was a good excuse for me to visit a city. Kearney had twenty-thousand people and there were restaurants, stores; a little civilization.

"Agriculture is a cyclical industry," Talbert began after my first question about the state of the farm economy. "At its most simple form, it follows a predictable course. When crops are plentiful, prices drop which leads to less acres planted the following year. A reduced supply should cause prices to rise, increased plantings and excessive production; prices decline, and the cycle repeats itself."

He leaned back in his chair with his hands folded across his ample belly. The springs on the antique wooden chair gave a sad creak. "Obviously, outside factors can affect the pattern."

"What kind of factors?" I asked.

"In my opinion global weather patterns are the most important driver of the economic cycle in agriculture. Of course, political or monetary events can alter the economic outlook along with outside investors looking for new opportunities for profits."

"Why would outside investors buy into crops? Do you mean commodities?"

"Commodities can play a factor and sometimes speculation disrupts the usual cycle. When that happens a cycle of speculative excess occurs followed by a reaction of crisis and panic. Such speculative cycles are not uncommon."

"What happens in a speculative cycle?" I asked.

"Characteristically, speculative cycles, in the manic phase, cause individuals with wealth or credit to purchase land and equipment to meet the expected demand. The odd thing about these cycles is that no one ever believes they are going to end. The rising prices may persist for years but eventually they always fail. Then everyone is surprised. Nobody caught up in these speculative bubbles is able to anticipate a reversal of fortunes and therefore cannot avoid the losses when the bubble bursts."

"Do you believe the farming industry is in such a cycle?" I asked.

"I'm afraid so," Talbert said with a nod of his over-sized head. "We're coming to the end of a very attractive period of speculative excess. It began in the 1970s. The boom was essentially driven by a substantial rise in crop prices during the first half of the decade, but supply and demand are only two factors." He counted off the others on his hands: "raising land values, inflation, a weak dollar and strong farm income, a lucrative export market, plus readily available credit. All these factors have made agriculture very attractive for investors both in and out of the industry.

He leaned forward causing another loud screech from the chair. "High inflation rates have meant huge capital gains on farm real estate. I mean real return on investments that dwarfed those of preceding decades. A farm income in the seventies was twice that of the sixties. This new wealth allowed farmers to purchase additional acreage. The bigger operations meant farmers needed to buy more efficient machinery, combines, tractors, planters and bigger barns to house all the new assets. All this land and equipment is justified in an effort to meet the increased demand from foreign markets."

He frowned as he searched something in the pile on the desk, "The export commodities market looked so promising only a short time ago. Here it is." Pulling a sheet of paper from among the litter, "The Secretary of Agriculture declares, 'The era of chronic overproduction is over.'"

"So the farmers are just doing what is expected of them," I said. "They need to grow more crops to meet a demand, what's wrong with that?"

"Everyone always expects a boom to last and are thoroughly surprised when it doesn't," he said again. "The problem is all this new technology requires capital investments."

"So, banks are willing to make loans." I said

"More than willing. The favorable speculative conditions and the boom mentality made credit almost limitless. All these conditions made farming look like a good bet only two years ago."

"What's changed to cause the crisis?" I asked.

"I'm not sure crisis is the correct word, just yet. The situation is changing. As I said, this is a natural cycle."

"So is the current cycle leading us to a...." I searched for the proper phrase... "bust?"

"It's highly probable, not a certainty, but regionally likely." The doctor like everyone else wanted to maintain some glimmer of optimism. "Obviously not all the machinery acquired is justified and such excesses might contribute to financial problems for some. Still, if producers used their gains to pay down debt and maintain their cash flow they will survive."

"What if they don't?"

He raised his hands palms up to give a big shrug. "Obviously debt can be crippling. If the income from the additional acreage is insufficient to meet the higher debt-service payments, financial difficulties will most certainly follow. You cannot borrow your way out of debt. And if the farmer signed a variable rate loan then the rising interest rates will accelerate the failure."

"Do you think there are a lot of variable rate loans out there?"

"I don't know" he said with real concern on his face.

"The real problem is the decline in export commodities. The worldwide supply and demand for agricultural commodities is tanking at the same time as domestic production is at an all-time high."

He shuffled through some papers again. "Look here," he pointed to charts on a graph. "U.S. exports of agricultural products increased at an annual rate of 5.9 percent between 1973 and 1980. This may be the peak." He put the paper down and lifted the newspaper lying next to his coffee cup. He turned a few pages to the financial section, then turned it so I could see the headline. "Fed Hikes Interest Rate."

"The Feds new interest rate has strengthened the dollar, which is good overall but at the same time..."

I jumped in with, "Which makes our exports less affordable to foreign markets." Dr. Talbert nodded his big head with approval.

"This is a complex global issue," I said finally starting to understand how it was all connected. Like three blind men all trying to identify an elephant. Only what we feel are we able to express.

"The boom in farmland values had led to explosive growth in farm debt." Talbert interrupted my thoughts "An interesting fact is farmland values per acre increased every year since 1970, while gross income per acre has decreased several times over the decade."

Searching again through the papers he said. "Right here, the gross income per acre for corn and soybeans declined year to year in 1973 to 75, 1976 to 77, and again 1980 to 81, which leads me to believe that farmland values and investment returns have become decoupled."

"What does that mean?" I asked.

"It means the decision-making process, for both lenders and producers, is very subjective." He laid the papers down and put his hands together as if to pray. "On one hand land as collateral has been very attractive," he turned over his right hand and looked at it for a moment. "On the other hand," he turned over his left hand, "the increased cost of production has badly hampered cash flow." He clasped his hands back together. "The farmer needed more operating capital to maintain his increased costs of production. So he asked for more money but with the grain markets contracting and harvest value..." dropping both hands. "And now there may not be any way to repay the loan," he said with a frown.

"And that's the question everyone is trying to answer," I said with confidence.

"Very good," the doctor said. "In the end, it's a mathematical equation. The current farmland values in America are at an all-time high but falling. The return on investment for corn and soybeans is almost half of what it was in 1973. If overproduction continues to create a surplus, the value of farm commodities will further decline. The raising interest rate will make farm investments less attractive and cash flow will replace land values as the collateral currency. Those farmers unable to pay cash for their operation costs will find borrowing almost impossible."

"In the black one day; foreclosed on the next?"

"I'm afraid so," he said with a shake of his head.

As I got up to leave the teacher said, "The consequence of a failed farm economy will be realized by the next generation."

"How do you mean?"

"The loss of jobs will mean a forced migration by whole families toward more viable job markets. The fewer job opportunities will divest the small town of it population. The consolidation of operations will accelerate the depopulation of these small communities and that loss of ingenuity and innovation that has always been a part of the American west will be irreplaceable."

I left the good doctor's office with an expert's opinion for my article. More than anything I had a growing fear for all the farmers and their families.

Chapter 14

When I got back to working on the article Sarge pushed me
hard, editing and demanding I verify statistical references. I revised
whole sections because he felt I had interjected too much opinion.
"This is a news story," he said. "If I want your opinion I'll beat it out
of you."

The story would go to press only after it "passed muster" and in
the end I was very proud of it. I sent a copy to my mom. I knew she
would like to keep a copy and I kept a copy for myself.

The Farm Crisis on Display in O'Neill

October 1982 – The cost of another family farm lost to the
growing farm crisis was on full display at yet another farm auction in
O'Neill, NE on Tuesday morning. The estate of Mr. Arthur J.
Williams and his family was put up for sale to settle debts owed to
local creditors. On the block were the usual implements and
equipment needed to produce crops and maintain the land: tractors,
trucks, combines, disks and plows. These valuable items and more,
attracted a crowd of interested bidders from across the area.

Those who came to bid on the farm equipment also found on
display the heritage of a farming family. The Williams family has
been working the land west of O'Neill since the late 1800's. Four
generations of farming the land came to an end with the call of the
auctioneer and his gavel.

This has become all too familiar to some here in the Midwest.
The number of farms lost this year in Nebraska, Iowa and Kansas
has reached the hundreds, numbers not seen since the Great
Depression. With interest rates on the rise and crop prices "dropping
like a stone" to quote one local producer, the family farm is facing a
crisis. However, the farming communities which depend on the
economics of agriculture are also feeling the pinch.

Terry Atkins owner of John Deere Equipment says, "Every farm
we lose costs the town not just a good citizen but real dollars and
cents. The grocer, the bank, the church, the feed store; everyone
loses when one of these auctions takes place."

The loss of another farm also means default on another loan at
the local bank. "The farmer is facing pressures from outside forces,"
said Bill Oldfather, the President of St. Paul's First National Bank.
"A whole host of issues, not just local or national but international,
have conspired to make turning a profit in farming very difficult."

"Farming has always been difficult" said one local producer at the O'Neill action. "Farming today is a nonprofit operation."

The current administration has called this a natural free market process. The loss of a few bad managers is to be expected from a free market economy.

"Farming by its very nature is based on cycles," says Dr. Matthew Talbert, professor of economics at Kearney State College. "The current cycles which began in the 1970's appear to be ending and the factors contributing to this change are complex and global." Talbert doesn't feel these changes are as yet a crisis, but farm and ranch operations are feeling the pain of the administration's hands-off approach.

Many in the region believe the new administration has failed to understand the depth of the farm issues. They campaigned and were elected on the ideals of less government interference, but farming has been dependent on federal assistance to maintain lower food costs for the American consumer since the 1930's.

"Their philosophy is costing us good farmers as well as bad and it will get worse if they continue with their approach," states Oldfather.

The most telling items on display at Tuesday's auction were the personal possessions: an antique bedroom set, a steamer trunk, family photo albums, wedding dresses and china, the dishes and flatware, a cast iron skillet and pots and pans. The life of the Williams family was there for the highest bidder.

A growing issue for these families forced off the farm is not simply the loss of vocation but the failure to hold on to their inheritance and the inability to pass it on.

The farm sale in O'Neill felt more like a funeral. The overwhelming vibe around the fairgrounds was sadness. However, there was anger as well. One group tried to call upon that anger by suggesting the current crisis is a well-planned conspiracy by our government to control the food supply. A group called the Posse Comitatus seemed to suggest open rebellion against the Internal Revenue Service. The voices of suspicion and rebellion may appeal to some, but the cost of such propaganda could be tragic. We've seen as much from the recent arrest of a local farmer here in St. Paul.

All these problems and issues facing the farmers seemed to be on display at the O'Neill auction and no one has a simple solution, nor do answers appear close at hand. Most agree the farm situation will get worse before it gets better.

Dr. Talbert suggests, "If farm producers can pay down their debt and maintain cash flow, without incurring additional debt, their chances of surviving this downward cycle are very good. However, if commodities prices stay low and product cost high, then some farm operations will fail."

The timing of my newspaper article was interesting. The state legislature, the lone unicameral in the country, was debating the prohibition of corporate farming. I didn't understand at the time how divided the state was over the proposed I-300 bill. Suddenly my article had made me a sounding board for every Ag related story in the state. I got a call from a local farmer, Mr. Floyd, a proponent of the bill to restrict corporate ownership of farms and for the protection of the rural communities. "Son," he called me, "farming is not just raising crops it's a calling, a way of life that must be protected."

I wasn't sure what his call had to do with my article but once he had my ear he intended to fill it. "We knew without a doubt if we let these companies start buying up the family farm it will be the end of small towns all over the state. These kids are already heading off to Omaha, Lincoln, Kansas City, Denver and Lord knows where. If the family farm is sold to a company, the town dies."

"Isn't that already happening?" I asked.

"It is but you let some dog-gone company manager with a time clock get a hold of the farms, the land, well hell, them corporate investors don't give a damn for the land. All those bastards care about are profits. These investors have no sense of history or tradition. They will abuse the land and its resources for the almighty dollar." Mr. Floyd went on for some time, educating me on the evils of corporate farmers. He was most passionate about supporting bill I-300.

I found the other side of the story had a personal and passionate group of people too. I was downtown at the diner, enjoying a donut and coffee when a cattle rancher named Ed Gill sat down across from me. "You're Willy Beam," he said more than asked. A mouth full of donut kept me from doing anything other than nod.

"I liked your story. This thing is going to cost the state a lot of good people," he said. "Now the thing is, this bill they're pushing to keep corporate farming out isn't going to save anyone."

I swallowed my donut with a sip of coffee and waited for the rancher to pontificate.

"See, we're all between a rock and a hard place. No profits in anything; crops, cows or hogs. The land in these Sandhills is most generally used to graze cattle. It's taken a couple of generations to acquire the land and now the land has lost its value. Now some say irrigation could help both crops and cattle but when commodities are in decline like they are now there's no money for that kind of investment."

He looked to the waitress for a refill of his coffee and so I said, "Some people feel companies will misuse the land for profits."

He took a sip and winced at either the temperature or the taste. "Well now, a bad manager is a bad manager. Ain't no guarantee the farmer will be a better steward of the land. That's not the problem," he said with a wave of his hand. "The problem is interest rates and credit."

"How's that?"

"Well let's say I need to get out to sell my cattle and the land. Who's going to buy; who can I sell to?" He raised his hand and raised the index finger. "The bank or a corporation?" He raised his middle finger and turned two fingers around, so they made a peace sign. "There's nobody else got the capital, even at these land values. Ain't no family farm got that kind of money and no banker will lend a penny. Too damn scared to write a note for a stick of gum much less a thousand acres of land.

He went on, "With these interest rates at seventeen, eighteen, twenty percent, hell, there's not enough money in anything to pay the interest much less the principal. No sir."

"So, you think corporate farming is a good thing?" I asked.

"I believe this is a capitalist society and the government should let it be. Damn politicians picking winners and losers are a recipe for disaster. Hell, this ain't Russia, we're not communist. Let the market work itself out"

Mr. Gill went on for some time about the evils of government interference, the consequences and the slippery slope of meddling in people's affairs. In the end he said, "It all depends on whose ox is being gored."

The reason my little story seemed to spark commentary locally and across the state was that both sides strongly disagreed on the reasons for the crisis and therefore the possible solutions to it. The farmer in the café might be right. It would take a generation for the value of land to return, and what were the people to do in the meantime?

I asked Sarge what he thought, "Some of the family farmers will survive," he said. "The ones with little or no debt. You know what they say, 'you can't borrow your way out of debt'. This debate over corporate farming is going to get heated and I believe the voters will decide it"

"Isn't that the way to decide?" I asked.

Sarge leaned back in his chair and crossed his arms. This was a sure sign he was about to lecture me. "When the public gets involved there is always a percentage that has no interest or understanding of the questions. Most of them will vote according to how the media tells them to. The news is a powerful thing. Most people want to believe the news is neutral on political subjects. We are not."

"I am," I said.

"You're a kid," Sarge said. "You still believe what your professor told you. There is no neutral voice in the news. I try to keep it even, staying even as possible but, have you read any of the op-ed stuff in the Herald?"

"I've read some," I said.

"The editor over in Omaha has an agenda and it's very different from the Lincoln Journal's agenda. The Omaha market is a corporate market. The rest of the state is a rural market. The two have different views. Money buys the news. Those who have money influence what goes in the paper."

I didn't like the sound of that. I wanted to be a reporter to report the news, not make it. I was as foolish then as now. Let the folks decide for themselves. But, then again, what do the people know?

Chapter 15

I don't normally dream; not like I did in the Sandhills. I've heard dreams are supposed to mean something; to reveal suppressed anxiety. The week after I met with Joe I had the most vivid dream. I was with Joe and we were working the cattle down in a valley. We were on horseback and dressed in western outfits, boots and chaps, hat and jeans, even a western shirt with pearl buttons. I thought we looked like characters from a spaghetti western.

I looked to the northwest and could feel someone coming along the road, a traveler a long way off. The sun was bright overhead. It grew in intensity until the light fell over me, enveloping me, transporting me. Suddenly I was standing in a clean, bright yellow kitchen, a Formica counter-top with chrome trim. The kitchen tabletop was a yellow pattern of geometric shapes with chrome edges. The floor was linoleum with flecks of primary colors: yellow, blue and green. An old-fashioned Frigidaire refrigerator with chrome handles and rounded edges stood next to an oven and cook-top built into the counter.

Two people were sitting at the table having coffee. The woman was small, with short sun streaked brown hair and sympathetic green eyes. Her skin was tanned with freckles across the bridge of her nose. She was dressed in jeans and a plaid work shirt. She was listening to a giant of a man sitting across from her. He was tall, but even more than the physical stature, his presence dominated the space. He had a dark complexion with light colored eyes and flowing brown hair. His clothes were threadbare and worn; his boots scuffed and dusty. I understood him to be the traveler. She was leaning forward intently listening to him.

There was a noise at the back porch and a voice called out a hello. The woman rose and went to the back door. A much younger Joe Steward came into the kitchen. I was there, in the room, yet no one saw me. I was the fly on the wall, an observer from another time, as if I were viewing the whole thing from the protection of a two-sided window. The image was so vivid, so detailed, a snapshot fraught with implications.

The light from a kitchen window began to brighten and then shimmer. It reached out for me, pulling me in and transported me instantly to the space where the cross stood. I looked out from atop the hill, across the rolling dunes of the Sandhills. There was the sound of people talking, calling, crying, yelling, laughing and moaning. Their voices were distant yet somehow clear, projected as a collective voice. The sound rose toward me like a force. I had the impression of their mutual energy passing through me. When it passed I could taste sorrow in my mouth, the wet tears of a fleeting sob or an angry cry.

I turned and felt myself falling; the wind in my hair, the rush of air in my ears. I fell for a time; then I was running toward something. I was racing along a path, my breath was labored, my lungs burned. I was excited and frightened. Suddenly the door to the chapel was ahead. I ran inside, and I was safe. The woman from the kitchen was there. She came to me and held me like a mother holding a frightened child. She comforted me until I woke up to the sound of rain.

A storm was blowing against the windows and battering the roof. Rain can be a joy, a celebration in the heartland. Just as often rain brings destruction. It's a hard fact here in tornado alley. You cannot have the rain without a storm, wind and tragedy. Crops need rain, not the hail and wind often accompanying it. Rain blesses the soil and knocks down the dust along rural county roads and just that quickly makes the roads impassable. You take the good with the bad, giving praise for all of God's blessings. I knew a storm was coming and I would have to look for the good amongst the bad.

I shook off the dream. Then a few days later, when I allowed myself to think about it, the images were still very real and vivid, a movie playing over in my mind, the sounds in my ear and the tastes in my mouth. I knew the woman was Mary Ann Steward. Joe hadn't described her to me, not her appearance, but I knew it was she. He had spoken of her spirit; her nature and I could feel it in the residue of the dream. I thought about how I could know someone I had never met; a woman long since dead. Amanda hadn't said anything about what Aunt Mary looked like, the same for Amos. Why was I so sure?

The man, the messenger, traveler whom Joe called Gabe, was not a man. I knew that as well. I understood he was a being, maybe a celestial being that came to see Mary. I knew something else. I knew Joe's story was true. I had seen it for myself. Years removed from the actual event, I had witnessed it. I witnessed the scene in the kitchen, clearly reliving the story Joe had told me. Surely there was some psychological explanation for it; maybe suggestions or empathy for the subject or simply a piece of the larger mystery.

I ate mushrooms at a party when I was in college. The warping of time, the over-awareness of colors and light was a trip. I laughed at the most ordinary things, got lost in my likeness in a mirror. The experience was amusing at first, but eventually my inability to make it stop made me seek out a corner and curl up in a ball. My dreams in that state evolved from sounds. I was forced to talk myself out of freaking the hell out.

Part of me wanted the dream to be a flashback. I heard John Lennon had said that dropping acid was like opening a trap door in your mind to what you previously didn't know existed, and once you stepped through that door, you could never completely go back, like Alice down the rabbit hole. I didn't think mushrooms were exactly the same as acid; still maybe the trap door in my mind had been left open a little.

That idea was somehow more appealing than the alternative, which I was in the midst of a religious experience. I was being compelled by forces beyond my control to follow a path, not entirely of my own choosing. I had pursued the story, of course, but somehow, I was now a part of the story, part of the past not removed from it. The whole thing was freaky. I thought about letting it go but knew I wouldn't, couldn't. Not before reading Mary's journals.

I called Amanda's house on Wednesday afternoon and got no answer. I tried again on Thursday and briefly spoke to her mother to leave a message for Amanda to call. On Friday afternoon I tried again but got no answer. I was as foolish and exasperated as I had been in high school, calling a girl for a date. The fact she wasn't returning my call made me feel jilted. By Saturday morning I had all but decided to call Uncle Jimmy myself. I went to the paper to think and read my story from the game I covered on Friday night. A blowout win between two eight men squads, Greeley 72 and Wahoo 32. I was drinking coffee and reading the area papers when the high-pitched ring of the phone startled me. I answered it half expecting whoever it was to be looking for the editor. "Phonograph, this is Willy," I said.

"Hey, Willy Beam from the Phonograph."

"Amanda!" I didn't keep the excitement out of my reply. "thanks for calling me back."

"Sorry about that, I've been really busy. What did you want?"

"Well, I uh, see I got to visit with your Uncle Joe and well,"

"How was he? How did he look?"

"He was good, he looked good."

"Good, I worry about him, I should go see him but like I said, I've been so busy."

"He would enjoy seeing you, I think. Anyway, see the thing is he told me something incredible, a story about, well it's hard to explain."

"What kind of story?"

I paused, not sure how to answer without sounding like a lunatic. I decided I couldn't do it over the phone without making Joe or myself sound crazy.

"Listen, Amanda, I need to meet your Uncle Jimmy."

"Okay," she said cautiously. "Is something wrong?"

"No, it's just, well Joe said Mary kept journals and that Jimmy has them. I'd really like to get a look at them."

There was a long pause and then she asked, "What's in the journals that you need to see?"

"I don't know," I answered honestly. "I really don't know what's in them. The story Joe told me makes me believe they're important."

"Important how?" she asked.

This was far too complicated for me to explain over the phone. I bet up in Broken Bow there could still be party lines, some nosy neighbor listening in right now. "Look," I began, then changed my mind. "Amanda, can I buy you lunch?"

She brightened with her answer. "Okay, yeah, sure."

"Super, I'll meet you at the Pizzeria." In fifteen minutes I was on my way to see Amanda.

Chapter 16

The radio stations were all playing country ballads that fall. While I can appreciate the sadness of Willie Nelson's 'Blue Eyes Crying in the Rain' and the enthusiasm of Dolly and Kenny's 'Islands in the Stream' as much as the next guy, I needed a little rock and roll. I opened the glove box and rifled through my cassettes. Some people meticulously protect and categorize their tapes. Me, I just throw them in the glove box or the passenger seat. It took me a few miles to find the right tape then to rewind it to find the right song. I sang along with Eddie Money on his "No Control" album. I sang over him on "Running Away" and "My Friends My Friends". I played the steering wheel on "Think I'm in Love" and "It Could Happen to You". Eddie and I crankin' out the hits from the front seat of my little rice burner

I met Amanda at the Pizzeria. The place was as dark as a cave. We ordered a pizza and sodas then found a seat in the corner. It was good to see her.

"So, what's this about Aunt Mary having journals?" she asked.

"Joe told me that Mary kept journals," I said. "I was talking to him about the cross, and he told me this unbelievable story about how a stranger came to see them one day and told them to..." I looked around and lowered my voice. "An Angel told Mary and Joe to have the cross made by Amos and to build the chapel."

"What?" she asked.

"I know, believe me I know, but that's what Joe said and that Mary kept journals telling all about it.

"About the cross?" she asked.

"Maybe, maybe more," I said. "I have to believe, from what Joe said, these journals would have amazing stories."

"What all did my Uncle Joe tell you?" she asked.

I took a deep breath and told her the whole story: the stranger, the calling to build the chapel and the cross. I told her most of what Amos told me. It came out as mysterious and strange as I thought it might. She listened without interruption until I was finished.

Just about that time they called our number to come pick up the pizza. I returned to the table with the pizza, plates and napkins. She was staring into space. She hardly stirred when I placed the pizza on the table in front of her. I felt better now that I had told someone. I wasn't sure if Amanda felt the same. I hadn't put it all out there for anyone to consider besides me. I was unburdened for the moment and suddenly had an appetite.

She sipped her drink. I ate two slices before she said a word. "And you think an angel came to see my Aunt Mary, told her to do all kinds of stuff and Uncle Joe knew all about it?"

I started to answer but she went on. "That's crazy. Why here, why then, why..."

"I agree," I said. "The why is the thing that keeps gnawing at me too. I hope if we have the journals we can figure it out."

"We? As in me and you, from the journals that Uncle Jimmy is supposed to have?" she asked.

"It's you and I, but yes," I said. "You said you'd help me?"

She took a piece of pizza and began to pick the cheese off the top to eat it. The cheese slipped between her fingers and onto her chin. She dropped her head down and scooped the cheese into her hand, then lifted the gooey mess up again as she leaned her head back and let the whole thing fall into her mouth. I chuckled, and she smiled between bites. When she had taken a drink to wash it down she asked, "You really believe all this?"

I took a deep breath and let it out slowly, "Yes, I do. Don't ask me to explain, because I can't, but I truly believe Joe and Amos were telling me the truth. So, I have to move forward with the idea that all of it really happened until I find out differently. And the only way I, we, can find that out, is to get a hold of Mary's journals which Joe says Jimmy has."

She took another bite of pizza. I did the same. We ate without talking until she said, "Okay, I'll help."

"Great, can we go see Uncle Jimmy?"

She scrunched her eyebrows together and picked at a pepperoni with her fingers, then said. "We need to approach him," she looked up searching for a word, "carefully."

"Why?" I asked.

"Jimmy can be strange, maybe a little paranoid."

I took another piece of pizza. "He's crazy?"

"No," she said defensively. "He's not crazy but he can get moody sometimes."

We ate in silence as I tried to decide if she was fooling around or if I really need to be worried. Finally, she said, "Tell you what. Let me see how he is this afternoon. You meet me later, on the drag. If he's cool, we'll go see him tonight."

"What time?" I asked. "How will I find you?

She laughed. "Willy, in that rice burner, you stick out like a sore thumb."

Since I had a few hours to kill I decided to go back to the library. I dug around in the archives and spun some reels of microfiche, looking at old newspaper stories. The town of Broken Bow, like most towns in America in those golden years after the Second World War, was prosperous and industrious. The GIs who came back were full of innovations and business minded. They built churches, businesses and families, went to school and brought home an energy born of optimism and courage born of the mindset that they could conquer anything. I don't think anyone will really fully explain or understand the dynamic energy unleashed by these heroes of war. Everything was possible and most things probable, resources were available, and money was readily available. Every page of the newspapers seemed full of illustrated black and white advertisements, events, and opportunities. The humorous part for me was social pages; they read like local gossip columns.

"The Simpson's had a visitor from Fremont over the weekend. Melba Thompson the mother of Earl Simpson traveled from the northeastern part of the state to celebrate the birth of a granddaughter born in April. The family attended the baby shower of Beverly Anderson hosted by Betty Jane Smith."

"The Bakers are the proud owners of a new Packard. Fred Baker traveled to Omaha to pick up the latest model, a 1952 Packard with all the newest accessories."

I half expected to find a small clip reading, "A stranger visited the homestead of Mr. and Mrs. Joe Steward. The very large stranger traveled by foot and appears to have come from a heavenly origin to deliver a message..."

No, that story wouldn't play well, but the thought made me smile anyway. It got me to thinking about Amos and how he said not everything was as it seemed. Apparently, something about Mary's cross had not set well with at least some of the local churches. Amos's words kept coming back to me. "There was less mercy in them churches than you would think". I knew there might be a few judgmental, well-intended, God fearing people in the world. Still, I learned a good bit of compassion from my own church back home.

I did some research into the history of churches in Broken Bow: the Methodist, with our itinerant preachers who rode the circuit of churches to spread the word; Missouri Synod Lutherans established early churches in the town; and then Catholic, Presbyterian and Baptist. The Latter-Day Saints, Assembly of God and Episcopalian all had chapels in Broken Bow.

After a few hours in the library I decided to stretch my legs with a walk around the square. On impulse I wanted to see which churches were open on a Saturday afternoon. I strolled by the Apothecary, Hardware Store and Insurance Agency. At one corner was a beautiful old limestone church. The bell tower reached toward the heavens, the stained-glass windows depicted the assent of Jesus with remarkable detail. The heavy oak doors were intimidating, so I passed it by. I kept walking until I found the Presbyterian Church with a beautiful welcoming red door; I found it locked. I checked the Lutheran, but it was locked up tight as well. I headed back to my car when I noticed a man in a dark suit coming out of the Assembly of God Church. I walked toward him. He stopped to greet me. He was a slim fit man of about thirty with a finely trimmed mustache. He wore his hair a little long for a preacher, but he was smiling.

"Good afternoon," I said. "Could I ask you a question?"

"Sure," he said. "I was just headed out but if you need some help I'll do what I can."

"Well, sir," I was unsure what I wanted to know but I heard myself blurt out, "Do you think angels still visit people today?"

He stepped back, took a good long look at me. "I'm not sure what you're asking me, son?"

I realized how strange this was and decided to just walk away. "Never mind," I said turning to leave.

"Son, now don't run off," he said and moved in front of me. "You caught me off guard. Why don't you come inside where we can talk."

I was embarrassed. "No, it's alright," I said with a wave of my hand.

He moved closer. "I insist, please come with me." He was standing in front of me, pointing toward the church door with an open palm and outstretched arm.

I couldn't think of a way to get out of there without being rude so I walked with him to the church. He unlocked the door and led me to his office located just off the assembly hall. He offered me a chair across from his desk and we both sat.

"What is this all about?" he asked.

My mind was racing trying to come up with a way to fashion a question. I decided to take the reporter's role. "Well, I'm talking with some of the church leaders in the community to see what they think about angels. See, I'm a reporter, I'm working on a story, sort of a take on the idea of God's presence and how he speaks to us today."

"I see," he said leaning forward to place his elbows on the desk. "You asked about angels outside."

"Yes," I said. "Do you think angels speak to people today or are they just in the Bible?"

"The Holy Spirit moves and speaks to us," he said. "The Spirit of the Lord is ever present, always in tune and working for those who will hear the call to do God's will. Son, are you saved?"

"I am," I said. "So, the Spirit is not an Angel?"

He smiled a smile intended for fools and children. "The Spirit is God. The Holy Trinity, Father, Son, and Spirit are one. See when Jesus ascended into Heaven, the Book of Acts tells us he sent the Spirit to empower his followers here on earth until he returns. We are baptized for the forgiveness of sins. Then a second baptism of the spirit is given to a select few. Were you baptized at birth or of your own accord?"

"I was baptized at birth and confirmed at fifteen," I said fully prepared to defend my salvation.

The preacher smiled, "You know Peter asked the Philippians if they had received the spiritual baptism. A baptism which gives us the powers to heal the sick, cast away evil, prophecy and receive the will of God. Let me ask you son, have you been born again, have you received the Spirit?" He lifted an eyebrow to punctuate his question.

I got up to leave not ready for a laying on of hands or anything "Thank you, that's all I needed to know." I had almost reached the door when the young preacher said, "If you think you've seen an angel then you've met the Devil."

I turned with my hand on the door to see him standing behind his desk. "Excuse me?"

"The Devil is a lion seeking to devour the weak. He will present himself in many ways to fool us. Have you been visited by the devil; are you battling his demons?"

"No," I said with a scoff.

"Son, don't try to battle the Devil alone." He pointed toward the Sanctuary. "We can go into the church and pray. Jesus is the only one who can help you. He wants to help you. He wants to save you from the Devil. We can do all things through our Lord Christ Jesus. But you must be born of the Spirit by confessing Him as Lord. Let Jesus into your heart and be reborn a new creature in Christ."

"I'm not, the devil is not, I'm not battling any one. It was just a rhetorical question," I said turning the doorknob and heading for the exit. The Preacher came after me, calling to me from the door of his office.

"Angels are not of this time. We will see them during the rapture, battling the forces of evil, on the great and terrible day of the Lord."

I didn't stop to hear the rest. I rushed out the door and hurried toward my car. I was anxious and angry. The whole encounter upset me. I slammed my hands on the steering wheel as I started the engine and drove off in a greater hurry than I intended. I looked toward the church as I drove by to see the preacher standing on the sidewalk. His face a expression of concern and judgment.

I headed out of town, driving along the North Loup River. I calmed down by looking at the trees as Amos said to do. Sure enough there were plenty of cottonwood trees splitting off at the trunk to form a V. White oaks with outstretched arms, but none with branches growing in such a way as to resemble a cross. There were cedar and pine trees planted as wind breaks. There were dogwood and maple trees, but none could've been carved into a cross.

I drove to the cross, got out and climbed through the fence to stand beneath it. It towered over me, its arms stretched out to the horizon. I looked out over the valley down toward the road. I could imagine the cross from the vantage point of a western traveler; it must call out to them, a guide to safe harbor, a refuge from the long journey.

I walked over to where the old chapel stood. The limestone-block corners stood firm. There was the steeple from the reservation, its pointed peak as sharp as the spear of destiny. The roof's cedar shake shingles were warped and brittle. The old whitewash on the Dutch lap walls was blistered and curling to reveal the weathered boards. A small door, hinged to open out, may have once been painted a welcoming red. The elements had long since softened it to a rosy pink. The stained glass was all still there, a few delicate triangles cracked, but none broken out. Spring weeds were going up, taking their stand next to the dull brown prairie grass. The place looked a long time forgotten. It's fading stance a stark contrast to the churches in town. Maybe the journals would tell me about this place and what it stood for. Why a messenger of the Lord would require it to be built out here. The footpath I stood on passed by the chapel leading toward the homestead; the other way led back to the road. The path in either direction was sadly overgrown; time and neglect encroaching steadily to hide the pathway to the small sanctuary. I followed it back to my car by the side of the road with a heavy heart and plenty of questions rattling around in my head.

Chapter 17

It was almost dark by the time I got back to town. I dragged Main street, circling the square twice looking for Amanda, before finally parking so I could see cars pass. I sat listening to the radio. The local jock was playing a string of hits, Pat Benatar's new one "Hit Me with Your Best Shot", Rick Springfield's "Jessi's Girl" and Phil Collins "In the Air Tonight"

Somehow, I felt as if I'd been waiting for this all my life. When you're young everything is possible, you hope for something meaningful and dramatic to happen. You don't wish for tragedy only for significance. I prayed for destiny to call, and when it did, I hoped I would be brave enough to answer. That's how I choose to remember that night.

Amanda drove by in a beat up, red and white, nineteen seventy-two Chevy pickup. I honked when she went by. She waved to me from the cab, like a schoolgirl. She pulled into the spot next to me, driver side to driver side, so we could talk from the comfort of our vehicles.

"Howdy stranger," she said.

I nodded, "How did it go with Uncle Jimmy?"

"Fine," she said without looking away. "Hey, do you mind getting some beer for us?"

"Who's us?" I asked.

"Well you, me and Jimmy silly," she laughed.

It had been an odd day, the night was mild, the moon was full and anything could happen. "Sure, I could go for a beer. What kind?"

"Any kind, just not Shaffer's. That stuff tastes like piss. Coors would be best," she said with a dimpled grin.

"Sixer or twelve pack?" I asked.

"Make it a case. We'll get a party started," she said.

"What about seeing Uncle Jimmy?" I asked with a little alarm. I hadn't waited around all day to get drunk with some high school kids.

"Jimmy will drink his share," she giggled. "More than his share. Besides it's polite to bring something."

"Okay," I said. "You want to wait here or ride with me?"

"You park yours over there," she pointed toward the hardware store, "and hop in with me. Uncle Jimmy won't allow that thing on his property."

I did as Amanda instructed. She drove us over to the Kwick Mart where I picked up a case of beer. The old woman with reading glasses on a chain and too much blush on her cheeks kept looking to see who was in the truck. She looked me and my ID over several times before taking my money. I chuckled to myself, imagining the naughty bit of gossip to follow in our wake. I sat the case on the floorboard between my legs and sank into the warn bench seat of the truck.

"Miss Percy give you the stink-eye?" Amanda asked.

"The lady inside? Yeah, she looked me over pretty good."

"Nosy old bitty," she said with a frown. "The old bat's been standing behind that counter as long as I can remember. Probably hasn't been laid since I was born."

I had to chuckle as Amanda backed up and headed out. With a screech of the tires she squealed, "Whooo-we!"

We drove north, away from the river. She looked at me with eyes to dream of and a smile to break a young man's heart. The windows were down, her hair blew around her head like a living thing. She shook her head every now and then to keep it out of her face. She reached over to crank up the radio. "Shake It Up" by the Cars was on and she sang along. She had a terrible voice, but she bounced along to the beat.

I tried to casually ignore her little act. I couldn't tell how much she really liked the song and what was just teenage foolishness. In a small town you have to make your own fun. Sometimes flirting with trouble is the most fun.

"How far to your uncle's place?" I asked.

"Oh, we're not going to Jimmy's right now," she smiled. "I'm taking you parking."

"Whatever," I said. "You are very sweet and well pretty, but I.."

"Not that kind of boy?"

"What, no, that's not it..."

"Relax paper boy," she said with a little mockery in her voice. "I'm just joshing with you. Uncle Jimmy's place is just up here."

Chapter 18

James McCray, aka Uncle Jimmy, lived in an eight room, two
story farmhouse. The house, barn and yard were framed by cedar
trees. A long gravel drive led to a wide covered porch. The front
room was lit up, the upper floor dark. She parked along the side of
the house and shut off the engine.

"Now listen," she said brushing the hair from her eyes. She
made a point to look directly at me. "Like I said, Uncle Jimmy can
be a little squirrelly, so just sit down and have a beer. Let me bring
up the journals and we'll just see how it goes, OK?"

I nodded, opened my door and grabbed the beer. Amanda
waited at the side door. I stood with her for a moment under the light
of a naked bulb above the step. She smiled a cunning little smile
before opening the door and calling out. "Uncle Jimmy, it's Amanda,
I brought a friend. Don't shoot."

Jimmy was a little guy not more than five foot seven, with dark
hair and mustache, squinting blue eyes with a suspicious glint. He
called from the front room, "What the hell are you up to Sissy? You
bring some beer?"

"Uncle Jimmy, you know I wouldn't just drop in without beer,"
she said as we entered the room. I followed behind with a case of
beer held out in front of me to present as a gift and a shield, just in
case he had gun at the ready. The large front room was cramped with
too much furniture and a clutter of knickknacks and inherited
antiques. The floor was covered with a fading rug. A formal couch
with matching love seat sectioned off the room into a smaller square.
Jimmy sat in an overstuffed leather recliner next to a gun case
holding a half dozen rifles; to his right stood an end table with a beer
and a revolver close at hand. I counted two shotguns on the rack over
the console entertainment center next to a well formed six-point
buck.

"Uncle, this is my friend Willy Beam. The one I was telling you
about from the paper," she said.

I sat the beer down and offered Jimmy my hand. He took it and
gave me a firm handshake. Amanda picked up a beer and handed it
to Jimmy. He finished the one from the table and took the fresh one
offered.

"What are you kids up to?" he asked.

"Nothin' much," Amanda said as we sat down in the love-seat
next to Jimmy. I sat on the couch across from our host. He turned his

attention to the television set. "I was watching this movie, mostly because it's the only damn thing I can get. I can play some music if you want."

Amanda offered a shrug with a casual nod of her head. I did the same.

Jimmy hopped up and went to the console entertainment center. The hinged solid wood top concealed a turntable, AM/FM radio and eight track player. "Man, I got some great albums here. Let me see," he said thumbing through a selection of records in a wooden box with a faded seed corn logo on the side.

"Here it is, this is the one," he said. He took the record from the sleeve, held it very close to his face, squinting to read the titles on one side then he flipped it over, placed the record on the turntable. He turned the switch to start it spinning, then took an LP brush and dusted the record. When he was satisfied it was dust free, he very carefully reached over to position the needle.

"What are we going to hear?" Amanda asked.

He flipped the switch and the arm lowered onto the spinning record. The speakers, not only in the console, but also mounted on the wall behind, began to pop and crackle. "You'll see," Jimmy said, grabbing his beer and rushing to sit in the recliner. Suddenly the bass notes from Aqualung by Jethro Tull, "da dunt dunt dunt dunt da, da dunt dunt dunt da" Jimmy playing air guitar as the speakers rattled my back teeth and threatened to knock my heart out of rhythm. Jimmy sang along with every word, nodding his head to the beat in his leather recliner. I took a beer and leaned back in my seat. Amanda shrugged and did the same.

I love Jethro Tull, the album; the song "Aqualung" is one of my all-time favorites, but tonight the six minute and thirty-eight second song took forever to finish. When it did, Amanda stood up and went to turn the volume down. "Jimmy," she said. "I, we, need to ask you about something, okay?"

Jimmy stopped rocking and took a big swig of his beer to finish it. "Okay, get me another beer first."

Amanda handed her uncle a beer and sat down in the love seat across from him. "Jimmy, Willy here," gesturing in my direction with her beer hand, "has been talking to Grandpa Joe."

Jimmy looked toward me with an odd expression. I suddenly felt like an unwelcome guest.

"Joe told him Aunt Mary Ann kept journals and you might have them?"

Jimmy took a long pull on his beer but didn't say anything.

After a long still moment Amanda asked, "Jimmy do you have Aunt Mary's journals?"

He stood up and walked out of the room without saying a word. He went to the kitchen. We could hear him open and close the refrigerator. It sounded like he opened a cabinet and then the sound of a chair being moved.

"What the hell?" I mouthed to Amanda.

She held up a hand, "Shush."

We could hear Jimmy talking to himself but couldn't discern the gist of the conversation. I looked to Amanda, her expression was caution. I felt as if we were stalking a wild beast and must remain very still so as not to spook it. After a few minutes Jimmy came back into the room. He looked at me carefully, not turning his back to me as he went to sit back down. He rocked back and forth, took a swig of his beer before asking, "Joe told you to ask about the journals. I've been waiting for this. Never thought it would happen tonight, never."

Amanda interjected with excitement, "So, there are journals?"

"Yep," Jimmy said. "I got them after Joe went to the home. Mary asked me to save them long before the cancer took her."

"What do they say?" Amanda asked.

"I don't know," Jimmy said. "I've never read them."

I started to ask why, when Amanda asked, "Where are they?"

Jimmy turned to ask me, "So you've come to read Mary's memories?"

"I guess," I said. "Yes, I'd like to know what's in them."

"What did Joe tell you?" he asked. "What is the name of the stranger?"

"Gabe," I answered.

"A man," Jimmy asked?

"No, not a man," I answered

"Not a man, like you said" Amanda echoed.

"No sir, not a man. Mary told me Gabe was not a man, not of this world anyway" Jimmy said. He was fidgety and resumed rocking. His penetrating stare studied me. "What else did Joe tell you?"

I wasn't sure what he wanted to hear. I understood my answer was critical. "Gabe told them to put up the cross and build the chapel."

He nodded at my answer, so I kept going, "Joe said I would need to get the journals from you, if I wanted to find out more."

He looked up at the celling, still rocking, his deliberation pronounced in every creak of the rocker. He didn't look at me but asked, "Do you know what you're after?"

I had to think for a moment then decided to go with the truth. "I'm after a story. The story of Mary and whatever she knew, about the cross and chapel, and the traveler. I want to know her story."

"You think it's just a story?" he asked now looking at me. "This has all been foretold."

Amanda broke in with frustration in her question, "What does that mean?"

Jimmy stood, challenging me, "It ain't just some damn story, not made up like some kind of fairy tale. Not any bedtime story neither. It's true, every word of it."

I stood and looked him square in the eyes. "I thought you said you've never read them."

"I don't need to read them to know what they say," he turned toward the gun rack. He rubbed his chin while slowly shaking his head. He whispered to himself, "It's been foretold." Suddenly, without another word, he walked past me and out of the room, up the stairs to the floor above. We listened to his footsteps overhead, following his movements with our eyes.

I mouthed, "What's he doing?"

She shrugged, not the happy carefree manner as before, but an awkward movement of anticipation and maybe a little fear. He moved some things around. A heavy object dropped on the floor causing both of us to flinch. We heard him move slowly over our heads until he reached the landing and then came down the stairs. He re-entered the room with an armload of notebooks. He walked over and sat them on the couch beside me.

"Those are the first of 'em. You read those, and we'll see about the rest."

I carefully picked up the one on top. The cover had faded, there were water marks on one corner. The heavy cardboard cover was in good condition and on the front was a month and year.

"How many are there?" Amanda asked suddenly standing next to me.

"Boxes, maybe fifty," Jimmy said.

"Fifty?" I asked.

"Hard to say, I've never counted them all," he said.

I opened the one in my hand. The penmanship was clean, well formed, flowing with grace in each letter. The tails of the cursive g's and f's fell below the line and the small c's were delicate in their connections. My penmanship was terrible, a jerky mix of cursive and printing. This was a strong elegant hand. I leaned the notebook toward the light to read the first few sentences.

August 25, 1965

It's so hot, temperatures near one hundred all week long. We need the rains to come but today, not a cloud in the sky. Joe's worried we'll lose some of the herd if it doesn't rain before the week's out. I can hardly stand to cook. We may have fresh vegetables and fruit preserves for supper.

"Are these in order?" I asked.

"Order of what?" Jimmy replied.

"Of date, time, importance." I said.

"Don't know," he said. "The ladies boxed'em up. I just took the boxes and stored them away upstairs."

"And you've never read them?" Amanda asked.

"None of my business, just my responsibility."

I thought that was odd but then again everything about Jimmy was odd. But he seemed more relaxed now that he'd handed over the journals. He took his beer and returned to the console to cue up another record.

I mouthed to Amanda, "Can we go?"

She nodded, "Jim, we've got to go, but I'll be back, OK?"

"Sure, whatever," he said. "You're leaving the rest of the beer, right?"

"Right," we both agreed as we headed out the back door.

We drove in silence back toward town. I held the stack of journals on my lap. They felt like a secret treasure. I couldn't wait to open them, to pore over them, to see what they might reveal. I was anxious with anticipation. I replayed in my head the strange chain of events leading me to this night. I normally wasn't so introspective or thoughtful about stories or the people in them. I connected with fictional characters but this was different. Mary had me hooked.

When Jimmy went to get the journals I could hardly keep from following him upstairs. My heart was racing when he put the stack of journals in front of me. This was more than a story; it was a mystery. The spiritual mystery of Mary Ann Steward, her cross and the chapel, her journals, and whatever they held was mine to discover. I was compelled to know it all.

"That was trippy; right?" Amanda said, pulling me back into the truck from wherever my thoughts had wondered. "I mean, Jimmy has always been strange, but he freaked for a minute. When he gave us the journals he just chilled out. Like it was nothing, like we borrowed the toaster or something."

"I thought you went to see how he was before we went out?"

"I did," she said turning her head to look at me for the first time, or the first time I noticed. "He was fine. I told him I was going to bring a friend out who had been to see Joe. He was cool until we got out there. Then he was..."

"He was what?" I asked, "What's the deal with your Uncle Jimmy?"

"He was in Vietnam. My dad says he came back with head wounds, not so much that he was shot in the head, just not quite right in the head. He gets a little freaky sometimes when the family gets together, and it gets loud. With everyone talking at once. He just has a hard time but I think he used to be worse"

"He lives alone out there, on the farm?" I asked.

"Yeah, he gets along fine by himself." She slowed down and turned off the road and into a pasture. We hit a bump; I flew up and hit my head on the cab, almost losing control of the journals.

"What the hell!" I yelled.

"Hold on." She turned sharply down a rutted lane into a grove of trees. We came to an abrupt stop by a stock tank.

"I told ya' I was taking you parking," she said with a laugh.

"You're crazy," I laughed too.

"I'm just kidding. I just needed to stop. I want to think and talk for a minute. This is one of my favorite places."

"Where is this?"

"This is Miller's pond." She killed the engine and turned off the headlights.

"We used to go swimming here when we were kids." Amanda looked out toward the pond. "I just delivered my Aunt Mary's personal journals to basically a stranger, and my Uncle Jimmy, who

I admit is a little messed up, was freaked out and said some really strange things. I know you told me the stories from Mr. Tensley, Uncle Joe and all but until I saw how Jimmy acted, I didn't really realize, I mean, I thought......" she leaned her head on the steering wheel... "I don't know what I thought exactly. It's all so crazy."

She took in a big shoulder-raising breath and exhaled. We sat still for a moment, replaying the strangeness of the evening. My mind drifted back over the course of the day. The darkness hovered, the silence stretched out until suddenly she said, "So, what do you plan to do with those," pointing at the journals in my lap.

"I was just thinking about this day. I mean, how I got here, with you and the journals," I fumbled over my thoughts. "In all honesty, I'm a little freaked out myself. I don't know exactly what I'm going to do with these, if anything. I just want to read them because I've got to know what's in them. Don't you?"

"I want to know what's in them, too. Hell yes," she looked very intense, "but after that what?"

I didn't answer. She shook her head back, adjusting both her hair and her attitude. "I just realized I don't know you. We've talked a couple of times and I went along with this just to see if you were full of shit. Well, it seems you're not."

"Look," I said putting the journals on the seat between us. "I'm as surprised by all this as you are. When I got up this morning I had no idea the day would turn out like this. It's amazing and yes a bit freaky but exciting too, right?"

"I don't know," she said, pulling her hair all over to one side of her head. "It's crazy alright and spooky. I mean freaky. Come on, Jimmy acted like, he said 'foretold'. What the heck is 'foretold'? I mean, really?"

"You're right," I sat upright in the seat, taking a more formal posture, "we don't really know each other. First, I can tell you, nothing like this has ever happened to me. I didn't think for a minute when I first came across the story in the paper, that it would lead to something as strange as this. All I know is I've also got a burning need to find out what happened."

"For your story, for the paper?"

"Maybe," I said. "I just know I've got to know what's in these journals. But I promise, I will not hurt you or your family."

She looked at me with daggers in her eye. "If you do, I will frickin kill you." This was not an idle threat.

I held up three fingers, "Scouts honor," I said. "Cross my heart and hope to die, stick a thousand needles in my eye."

She smiled and we laughed a little. "Tell me about yourself, Willy Beam."

We talked for good long time. I told her about Des Moines and Valley High School, Ames and Iowa State, how I got to St. Paul and the paper. I told her about Sarge and Melvin. She told me about her family and school. Her friends and what she hoped for college. "I want to go and see places, ya know? I want to go to Omaha and Kansas City, Saint Louis, maybe Dallas."

She talked as if these were exotic ports of call and I guess for a girl from the Sandhills they were.

"Everyone's so sad here, ya know? It feels like everything is changing and not for the better. All my friends' parents are splitting up. Things are coming apart. It just sucks."

"I'm pretty lucky I guess. My parents are still in love," I said. "They've got their problems, but they are, from what I can tell, happy."

"Well," she said, "the rest of the country's on the brink of a mental breakdown. Not that anyone would ever talk about it. God forbid the facts interfere, much less interrupt the soap opera that's being so carefully portrayed by everyone."

"I guess I'm not sure what you mean," I said.

"For Christ sake, are you kidding me?"

When I shrugged she looked exasperated in the most amazing way. "Everyone, and I do mean everyone, is so full of crap, it's a joke, no one gets it." She moved forward on her seat and turned to face me. "Seriously, do you not see it?"

I shrugged again, to which she looked at me slack jawed. "Come on Willy. Okay here's what's going on. The assistant football coach is sleeping with the girls' basketball coach, and his wife is pregnant. Everyone is playing some kind of part, from the salesmen to the checkout girl. My friend's mom takes Valium like its candy and drinks a pint of vodka a day. Her dad is trying to keep up appearances, but he's going to lose the farm and there's nothing anyone can do about it. Even the president of the United States is a plastic haired actor." She was wound up now but she had my attention. I was listening, for the first time really listening to more than the words but the ideas pouring from her mouth.

"Everything's so fake, plastic and disposable. My friends and I all know, beyond a shadow of a doubt, that our parents are a bunch of hypocritical assholes. They say one thing and do another. Oh, we know about the screwing around and the drinking. Their addictions and if it's not alcohol or sex, it's some other sin nobody wants to talk about. We are the bastards of the revolution, Willy, the least supervised generation with the easiest access to almost anything, except the truth."

I had to admit, she was right. No one ever really talked about any of it. I knew five guys in school who spent time in rehab for drugs and stuff. Their parents spent lots of money for treatment but none of them came back any less messed up from what I could tell.

Then she said something that scared me a little. "You know, sometimes I get this image in my head, a flash of light, sort of a perception of a stark windowless room with a harsh naked bulb swinging back and forth; around and around casting scary shadows on the floor. It's covered by broken glass, all jagged and dangerous."

I didn't say anything. She looked away, down at her hands. I wanted to reach over and take her hand in mine, but I didn't.

"I'm sorry you're having a bad time," I said.

She laughed, flashed a smile complete with dimples to let me know she could put up a facade as quickly as anyone. "It's not all bad. My friends, we spent a week in the summer by the lake. Amy's parents have a cabin there. It was great. The air is fresh, no smell of cow shit. We laughed and sang, drank beer, and swam. The girls laid out to tan, no lines," she smiled a wicked little smile. She was playing a part now, performing to satisfy my concerns that cropped up when she dropped her mask. She had been too truthful a minute ago and now she was not lying as much as hiding the pain for my benefit.

"I'm adopted," I blurted out. "My parents couldn't have children, so they adopted me. I was just a baby, so they didn't tell me until just last year."

She looked at me with intrigue. My heart was pounding and my breathing heavy. I wasn't sure if I could tell her this. I hadn't even verbalized it to myself. "See, it was toward the end of my final year at college. I was filling out an application for my first reporters' job. I really thought I was going to get it too, but they asked for my place of birth. I don't know why, maybe for a reference check or something. Anyway, I had put down Des Moines, IA. That's where I thought I had been born. That's where we had always lived, but when I didn't get the job I called to ask why. The editor said I had provided inaccurate information on my application. I told him I didn't know what he was talking about. Then he told me. There were no William Frances Beam's born in any of the Des Moines, IA hospitals in January of 1960."

She turned to face me now, sitting sideways on the seat with her legs crossed and Indian style. She nodded for me to go on. "I went and checked the records down at the courthouse and I wasn't born in Iowa. I checked all the microfiche for all the area hospitals and found nothing."

"What did your parents say?"

"They have always been very honest with me, or so I believed; so when I asked my mom about it she cried and then she told me a unbelievable story."

I cleared my throat. I hadn't planned to tell her anything like this, but I went on. "She hadn't been able to get pregnant. They had tried for years and nothing. I guess my parents had been on the waiting list to adopt but every time a newborn was available something happened to prevent them from adopting. They prayed and prayed about it and one day their pastor called. A lady was at the church and she had a baby boy who needed a home and they needed to come right away down to the church."

I took a deep breath; this was the part I didn't understand. "Mom said they met with the minister and he told them this was 'a very unusual situation' and he wanted them to be open minded. There was a baby who had been brought to the church. The woman who brought the baby was older, and it was not her child. She had assured the minister that the baby had been given freely. The woman said she had been given a sign that a couple in the church was waiting on a child, a newborn to adopt. The woman didn't say how she knew this or who gave her the sign. My mother was nervous and excited but when they put me in her arms, she knew it was the miracle she had been praying for. They only met the lady that one time and never heard from her again. They knew nothing about where I came from. The minister instructed them to go away for a couple of days, maybe a long weekend and come back with news they had adopted. They should say 'they didn't want anyone to know, just in case it fell through again', and that's what they did."

"That's amazing," she said. "I mean really unbelievable."

"I sometimes think it's unbelievable, too," I said.

"You think she made a story like that up?"

"No, my mom is a terrible liar," I said. "I just feel like there's got to be more. There are so many questions and she had no real answers."

She said, "What's wrong? That's a great story, a fantastic story; a Goddamn miracle!"

"Yeah, I know it's a good story and my parents are great, really great. I don't know. I mean, someone didn't want me, ya know."

"You don't know that. Besides someone did. A sign, man," she said with great care. She put her hand on my shoulder. We sat in silence. I wanted to tell her more but couldn't share the doubt and emptiness I felt. The idea of being a bastard was not something I thought I'd ever get used to. We derive a lot of who we are from our families, our parents and the heritage and traditions of the family. I thought I knew my family and I did; they will always be my family, the ones who cared for me, raised me. But somehow, still, it felt like a lie, a lie of omission; if not a lie, certainly less than the whole truth.

"You should be happy. Your parents prayed for a miracle and got one," she said. "My parents got hammered one night after a barn dance and surprise, surprise. Here I am. My brother is fifteen years older and my oldest sister is forty-three years old. I have a niece who was a grade ahead of me in school. Do you know how fucked up that is?"

"I don't know if it's messed up or not. There are plenty of surprise or "oops" kids. The couple gets out of rhythm or I guess hammered and the next thing you know. Why's that so messed up?" I asked.

"Why is it fucked up?" she said with warm sarcasm in her voice. "You want to know why? Well, first off, I'm a mistake. Call it whatever you want. I was not planned, not hoped for or anticipated. My mom and pop have ten grandkids and will more than likely have great-grandkids before I get married." She looked at me expecting a strong reaction.

I shrugged. "Still they're your parents; you're their kid. They didn't give you away to a stranger, a woman from God knows where. You have an odd situation, but you have a family."

"My family is so messed up. I sometime think I was left on their doorstep by some stranger." She intended to be funny, but she wasn't. Although, I couldn't say it myself, she had voiced what I believed to be the truth. I was left on the church doorstep by some stranger and given to my parents, not by some miracle, but simply by chance. Thank God they had been good decent people with a room and love enough for me.

"I'm sorry," she said. "That was stupid. I didn't mean it the way it came out."

"I know," I said. "It's alright."

"No, it's not," her eyes pleaded with me to forgive her.

"It's okay. I promise. It's no big deal," I said.

The disappointment in her face made me want to take it all back, to somehow turn back the world, just a few moments so she would look at me with compassion or desire. Almost anything except the sad look, she wore now.

"Look what happens when people are honest," I said.

She bit her lower lip and turned to look out the window. We sat there, lost in the awkwardness. I was searching for something important, or clever, or silly to say but nothing worth saying came to mind.

"I'm glad you were honest with me," she said then turned to look at me, her eyes were soft, full as the moon. "I want to know what's in Aunt Mary's journals too."

"We'll find out together."

Chapter 19

I woke up late on Sunday, the church bells ringing, calling the congregation to worship and me from my bed. I made coffee, wrapped a blanket around me and cleaned a place at the table to read the journals.

June 4 1948

These are my memories, my best remembrances of the life changing events that happened after Gabe visited me almost three years ago. I realize now I should have started writing from the beginning; recording everything that's happened but I didn't, so now I'll try to remember. I vow to keep better account of what happens around here in the future. He came to the back door, but I truly don't recall him knocking. He was there, and I knew it. I remember looking at him through the screen door. He was tall, not a giant but certainly the biggest being I've ever seen. I sensed he was powerful yet gentle in nature. His eyes were soft, his features pleasing and his smile comforting. I invited him in instantly, without hesitation. He didn't speak to me, not in words but somehow, I understood everything he conveyed. As crazy as it sounds I could truly understand his intention, his questions; not like I was reading his mind, more like he was directing mine.

Anyway, he came in and sat at the kitchen table. His presence filled the space. He told me his name was Gabe and he'd come from afar to ask me a question. If I was called to build a place for the lost and hungry, for the injured or hurt, the sad and afraid would I be willing to build such a place? Would I allow our ranch to become a safe haven for the wanderers and the lost?

It was such a bizarre thing to be asked and yet I said, 'yes', without hesitation. How could I say no? I would never turn someone away and Gabe knew that. Just then Joe came in and he sat with us. Time stood still, or it rushed by, I'm not sure which. Over the next few hours Gabe instructed us how, where, and when we were to build a chapel and commission a cross, where to put it; how it was to be made and who was to make it. I remember Joe drawing up plans with Gabe adjusting and correcting them as Joe drew. Joe has always been very handy, a rancher has to be, but the plans he constructed were simple and artful; like a draftsman's plans.

Gabe told me where to find a tree for the cross and to have Amos Tensley make it. He said to have it up by the spring of this year, 1948. It was to be a beacon for those who were seeking shelter. Joe went out with the plans and it was just Gabe and me. He looked at me and he pulled me in to his thoughts. I know this sounds unbelievable. It was so easy to do and so hard for me to explain. It was like a dream, not really a dream. He said I was chosen to be God's hands, here in this place. I asked, "why me?" I had a soul full of compassion and mercy and there was far too little of both in the world. I would need to be strong and courageous, for those coming would be weak and afraid. I must trust in the Wisdom of the Lord; it would guide me.

I'm not sure God chose the right person. I'm not very big or strong, I've never been very brave or outspoken. Gabe said God chooses whom he chooses. I remember asking why not someone from the church, why not a minister or priest. Gabe smiled and said, "There are those who find comfort in the church and it's good they do but not all do. Those who need comfort and cannot find it in this generation's religion, will find it here." Gabe was right, so far. There are lots of folks who need comfort and find very little anywhere. Why they find it in my little chapel in the middle of these Sandhills is a mystery to me. I read once there is not enough religion in the world to save it but there is more than enough to destroy it. I guess that's right.

I spent all day Sunday reading the journals. Mary kept regular entries on an almost daily basis. She kept a record of the activities on the ranch alongside the events, visitors and happenings at the cross and chapel. I read and read until I fell asleep. I woke up in my dream and was standing at the foot of the cross. I looked up to a brilliant blue sky. The color was so powerful, refreshing and clean. The door to the chapel was open and I took refuge there. Inside it was cool and filled with colored sunlight filtered through the stained glass. I smelled fresh fruit, old paper and candle wax. I was drawn to the platform, just as before; this time the huge Bible was open to Proverbs chapter nine. A light illuminated the verses.

"Wisdom hath built her house; she hath hewn out her seven pillars: she hath killed her beasts; she hath mingled her wine; she hath also furnished her table.

She hath sent forth her maidens: she crieth upon the highest places of the city. Who so is simple. Let him turn in hither: as for him that wanteth understanding, she saith to him, Come, eat of my bread, and drink of the wine which I have mingled. Forsake the foolish, and live; and go in the way of understanding."

I looked out over the pews. A congregation of people, the same as before looked back at me; some sitting, others standing around the small chapel. Their faces looked peaceful, comforted and safe. They smiled shyly or grinned foolishly, none looked unhappy. I thought to ask them why they were here and then wondered why I was here?

A pulsing bright light filled the doorway again. I heard the ringing, high pitched and startling. I opened my eyes and turned off the alarm clock.

Chapter 20

Trees along the river are suddenly marvelous with color. Their red, orange and yellow leaves beg for illustration against a purple indigo sunset overlooking ripe tan cornfields on crisp autumn evenings. The season of harvest calls for sweaters and letter jackets. That time of year brings smells of freshly cut fields of corn and beans, of football fields marked with chalk and concession stands tempting with buttered popcorn and grilled bratwurst. Fall is my favorite season; a fantastic experience for the senses. My mind recalls jack-o'-lanterns and Halloween costumes, bonfires and roasted marshmallows sandwiched between chocolate bars and graham crackers, melting with romance. Morning frost stinging my nose and ears, with an anticipation of snowfall and hot chocolate by a Franklin stove. I recall the youthful anticipation of harvest festivals with marching bands on parades, and harvest queens riding on vintage cars with frozen smiles and practiced waves. That is how I chose to filter my memories. I frame them with crepe paper and stream flickers of championship football games played on the Friday after Thanksgiving. I long to see the University of Nebraska Cornhuskers battle The University of Oklahoma Sooners for the Big Eight crown in Memorial Stadium. Those are the memories I cling to.

But the harvest of 1982 was full of anxiety. The price of corn hovered right at two dollars a bushel, a dollar less per bushel than two years ago. Cattle prices were stubbornly low and beans not much better. Harvest should bring the settlement of debts and balancing of ledgers. Instead it delivered anxiety and loss. The anticipation planted in the spring and nurtured all summer grew into a tall harvest of angst and sadness. The fallout from the bitter harvest would have a powerful influence on the children of the era; a long tale of shattered legacies and new dreams. I heard Harold Perkins, the old farmer who wouldn't let them take his land, put a shotgun in his mouth. He was not the first nor would he be the last to reap death from that bitter harvest.

The one saving grace, the one great distraction from the bleak truth was and still is Cornhusker football. Everyone, from Omaha to Sidney, Ogallala to Sioux City young and old, man and woman is a Husker fan. Nothing united the state like the Big Red. There was one game more anticipated than all the rest: the game adorned with every expectation; the game for which all the rest had been previews; the game which showcased legendary players at their best; the game filled with stories and moments to mark a life. The annual contest was always on television, one of the few times Nebraska games were televised in those days. This year the Sooners from Norman Oklahoma were coming to Lincoln to battle for pride and championship. The Big 8 crown was on the table and a trip to the Orange Bowl and perhaps a shot at the National Championship.

The paper somehow secured media credentials for the game. Sarge held a raffle and I won a coveted media pass. Mike Lowden from the sports department and I were going to the game. I had been to other games with my father as a kid, but I was going to the NU vs. OU game, the unofficial state holiday, with 76,000 Big Red fans in attendance at Memorial Stadium for a two O'clock kick off. I cannot tell you how excited I was, except to say that a flock of foolish butterflies in my stomach threatened to fly me to the game.

I decided to drive so I could go home to see my parents for the holiday weekend. Mike rode along but, was going to see a buddy in Lincoln and he would get a ride back to St. Paul on Sunday. It was great to have someone to talk to and replay memories of past championships; to recall the great games of the rivalry. Mike had been at the '71 game of the century when Johnny Rogers "put'em in the aisles" with his historic punt return, securing him the Heisman trophy and the team a National Championship game.

We arrived at noon and parked in the Bottoms north of the stadium. It was cold and clear, not a bad day for this late in November. We hurried across the railroad tracks and the practice fields on our way to the stadium. I tried to maintain an even pace but the closer we got to the gate, it was all I could do not to run. We entered Memorial Stadium proudly showing our media passes and walked out to the sidelines. There is no place like it on all the earth. The turf as green as summer, the oval stadium framing our view, looking up at a brilliant blue sky, the teams in shades of red warming up as the growing crowd watches in simmering anticipation.

First, it was just kickers and punters on the field, the rest of the team in the locker room. We stood behind the goalposts and snapped pictures. The backs and receivers came out and Mike and I tried not to gawk or point. Instead we nudged and nodded toward players like Turner Gill, Mike Rozier, Roger Craig, Irving Fryar; the big boys, Dean Steinkuler, Dave Remington and the Williams boys; Jamie and Toby. I realize now they were just a few years younger than I was, but there in Memorial Stadium, they were the stars of the show.

The players all returned to the locker room. We found a place in press row behind the south end zone. The fans filled the seats to capacity, every game a sellout since the Kennedy administration. The energy and expectation rumbled in the air until the band played Hail Varsity and the team rushed back onto the field with the cheerleaders racing ahead of them as if chased by wild beasts. Everyone rose in one voice to cheer.

The Huskers took the opening kick and proceeded to go three and out. A muffed punt return gave Nebraska the ball at the Oklahoma forty-one-yard line. I'd never heard such a roar when the ball was recovered. It's one thing to be up in the stands, among the crowd and adding your voice to the cheers, but down on the field with camera in hand, the explosion of sound sent chills up my spine and made me wish for ear plugs. I had a small place in the corner with the other photographers. I did my best to seem unfazed by the experience, like the veterans around me, but I couldn't control the smile on my face. These were some of the great, future legends of the game and Oklahoma had its own star players: Tony Casillas, Steve Sewell, Jackie Shipp, Stanley Wilson, Kelly Phelps and a freshman named Marcus Dupree.

The fumble led to a Nebraska touchdown by Turner Gill, who rolled out and then cut up field, avoiding a tackler as he sprinted to the end zone for a 7-0 lead. Red balloons, held by the 76,000 fans in anticipation of the first score by the home team, were released into the air. They floated up to be carried northeast by the wind, filling the Lincoln sky with the signal to all; the Cornhuskers were on the board. I snapped a picture of it not for the paper but for my own collection. I still have the picture today. The vantage point surreal, the tradition and pageantry captured in a still frame to recall the game; the emotion and the elation.

The Sooners ran a power I formation for the first time in the Switzer era, shelving their traditional wishbone for Dupree's combination of power, speed and vision. The young man was a force who deserved to be featured behind a gifted fullback like Wilson. The fullbacks for Nebraska were eligible linemen with numbers allowing them to occasionally carry the ball but only on trap plays or the belly option. Wilson was a true runner with speed and power of his own. He proved his value during the next drive, taking a hand-off up the middle; he was initially stuffed by the interior of the Nebraska front, but he bounced back from the pressure, stepped to the side and rushed off to the left for a twenty-yard gain inside the Nebraska five. The Sooners capped the drive in their famous wishbone formation; a quick option pitch from Kelly Phelps to Dupree allowed the back to high-step to the end zone untouched for the tying score. Memorial Stadium was filled with the Sooner fight song.

Oklahoma followed up their first scoring drive with a field goal. Then Coach Osborne opened up the play book and allowed Turner Gill to throw the ball. Gill completed a quick out to Irving Fryer, first to one side and then to the other. Moving quickly across mid-field, Nebraska set up one of the most magical and imaginative plays of the day; the Bounce Rooskie.

The Huskers lined up in a classic pro left formation, the tight end and flanker to his left with Rozier in the I formation. Gill took the snap and turned to his right as the backs charged toward the right side of the line as if the play was off tackle. Gill stepped back from the line, turned to his left to throw a skip pass to Fryer who has taken a step back from his position at the line of scrimmage.

Gill threw not just a pass but a lateral that skipped up off the turf like a rock on a pond. It bounced up into the hands of Fryer who then threw a pass to tight end Mitch Krenk. The ball was slightly overthrown, so the receiver had to stretch out, fully extended to catch the ball. He tipped it up and back to himself, juggling it for just an instant. Collectively the crowd sucked in a breath which seemed to bring the ball back into the arms of Krenk, who was tackled inside the fifteen-yard line.

The crowd went crazy. What a call; what execution; what trust in the players to create such a play, to call it in the biggest game of the year and then have it work. The momentum swung back to the home team with a rushing touchdown. After that the Big Red drove down the field like a well-oiled machine, marching seventy yards with a mix of toss plays and the obligatory fullback traps with a reverse to the flanker mixed in to keep the Sooner defense off balance. The Huskers scored again from fifteen yards out and once again the crowd roared in approval.

The next Sooner possession brought the best of Kelly Phelps, the OU quarterback, who mixed option run and roll out passes in a fluid exhibition of skill and spirit. He guided the Oklahoma offense down the field with efficiency until a false start penalty put them behind the chains. On a third and five, the Nebraska's line stood up to the young tailback from Mississippi, now wearing crimson and cream, to force a fourth down pass, which went high over the receivers' head.

On the next drive the Huskers featured the future Heisman Trophy winner, Mike Rozier, until he took a nasty hit at midfield and was lost for the game. Gill was unable to connect on three straight pass attempts and OU got the ball back.

Phelps tried to hit a long pass down the sidelines. The Nebraska safety intercepted it and returned it to the Oklahoma thirty-yard line. Nebraska couldn't convert, and the field goal attempt went wide right to end the half.

"What a game," Mike said in my ear. "Nothing better than getting paid to watch football on a Friday afternoon."

We moved up into the press box during halftime to be among the writers from the Omaha World Herald, Lincoln Journal, Daily Oklahoman plus AP and UP writers. This was why I went to journalism school; to be here and now in the middle of this.

Mike warned me, "Listen kid there's no cheering up here. Don't comment out loud. If there's a questionable call keep it to yourself. We can talk but keep it low and no yelling." I nodded my understanding. Decorum and partisan reporting was the rule of the press-box.

"They'll kick us out of here," Mike said. "I for one don't want to have to answer to J.P on Monday, understand?"

I took a seat and looked down onto the field. From this height the green and white field looked like a pool table. The angle made it hard to judge the trajectory of the ball in flight. It was exhilarating and overwhelming. I wanted to say something but kept my thoughts to myself.

Oklahoma received the second half kick-off. Steve Sewell returned the ball out of the end zone, but was dropped at the fifteen yard line. On first down, Dupree was thrown for a loss of two back to the twelve. Phelps' pass sailed high on second down bringing up a third and long. The Big Red had them backed up in their own end, answering the bell for the second half with fire in their belly.

Then it happened. Phelps turned to his right, pivoted back to the left to hand the ball deep in the backfield to the talented tailback. Wilson delivered a kick out block on the defensive end, allowing Dupree space to run. He made a cut at the twenty-five and in a flash was gone. A man so big should not be able to cut and run away from a defense like that. Dupree was no ordinary freshmen running back. His eighty-seven-yard run was electric. He strolled in to the end zone with the ball held high and once again the Oklahoma fight song filled Memorial Stadium. The visiting fans sang, "Boomer Sooner, Boomer Sooner, Boomer Sooner, OU!"

Rozier tried to make a go of it the second half but was clearly not the same runner he had been to start the game. Charley McBride's boys got the message to key on Dupree. The Big Red defense swarmed to the ball forcing a three and out on the next OU possession as well.

In the middle of this great rivalry, in a game which for both teams represented the success of the season, a championship at stake, the play clearly reflected passion and intensity and yet sportsmanship wasn't overlooked. After every hit the player offered his opponent a hand up, a pat on the behind. There was a mutual respect among combatants even during the fierce competition.

Roger Craig took over at I back. He ran with power and grace, at once lowering a shoulder to punish a tackler, next spinning to avoid another would-be tackler. A pass or two from Gill, aided by a penalty on Oklahoma put the Big Red on the threshold of another score. Craig took the ball to the right, bounced to the outside and the band struck up the fight song, "There is no place like Nebraska, good old Nebraska U. Where the girls are the fairest the boys are squarest" as the Huskers took a 28 to 17 lead.

The Sooners responded with a drive keyed by Sims. Not the legendary Billy Sims, the Heisman trophy winner who plagued Husker Nation only a few years ago. No, this was Fred Sims. That was the beauty of this great rivalry game; an unexpected player comes to the game and offers his best to his team and fans. Freddy Sims was not the power and grace of Dupree. Fred didn't possess the size of his namesake, but he came with momentum and spirit on his side.

After a completion by Phelps to convert a third down and eight, Sims got the call. He took the ball to burst through the line, then to the outside on his way to a first down at the Nebraska twenty-seven-yard line. Phelps ran the fullback belly to Wilson for a few yards. Then back to Sims on the power toss. He broke a tackle and fought his way down to the twelve. Phelps next went to the speed option, pitching the ball to Sims, who turned up field only to be met by the defiance of the Nebraska safety. Sim's helmet exploded from his head. The ball bounced toward the sidelines. I could feel the hit at the top of Memorial Stadium. The crowd exploded with approval for the play and the players. Sims got up, casually picked up his helmet and put it back on his head as he jogged back to the huddle, nodding to let his teammates know that he was okay.

Phelps took control now, with the ball in the red zone, running back to back option plays, first right then to the left, putting the ball inside the five. Stanley Wilson went over the top for the score, making the game Nebraska 28 and Oklahoma 24 as the third quarter came to a close.

It was all going so fast, the players, the clock, the afternoon shadows stretching across the field. To me it felt as though the hours were minutes. Mike and I smiled, nodded to each other but neither said a word above a whisper.

To open the fourth Nebraska took the ball and began to drive. The defense now felt the desperation of the game. Each hit more defiant, each play important. The Huskers drove the ball to mid-field with a standard mix of runs and passes, Gill throwing on time, Craig running fearlessly behind the great offensive line. On a second down and six the NU offense popped the fullback trap which had worked so well all day, but this time they fumbled. A Sooner scampered from the pile with the ball. Phelps and the offense raced back onto the field with opportunity at hand.

Dupree returned to the game, running with new determination. Phelps completed a pass to mid-field, which was followed with an inside hand-off to Wilson for a couple of yards, then right back to Dupree off tackle. The freshman dragged Nebraska defenders with him as he picked up a first down.

You never know who will respond at a critical moment in a game. On Oklahoma's side, Freddy Sims had come in to provide the spark the Sooners needed and was now riding like a wave toward the goal. I wondered who would answer on the Nebraska side of the ball?

Enter Dave Burke, a corner back from Utah, wearing number 33. The defender came up on a first down and launched himself into the big power back, knocking Dupree backward for the first time all day. When Phelps rolled to his left on the next play, determined to deliver a pass to future NFL great Steve Sewell, Burke came hell bent for leather. It appeared Sewell would catch the ball inside the five for a first and goal and possibly the game winning score. Burke lowered his shoulder and lowered the boom, jarring the ball loose. The incomplete pass brought up fourth and six. Once again, Phelps rolled to his left looking for a receiver to complete a first down pass. The open receiver appeared at the twenty-yard line until number 33 came into the play to knock the ball to the ground. The Sooners were turned back by the kid from Utah in scarlet and cream.

Nebraska took over, but the determined defense forced a punt. With five minutes to go, the game remained in doubt. The Sooners moved the ball across the forty when a questionable pass interference call gave them hope. I had to bite my tongue not to yell. The Big Red bowed its neck to force four incomplete passes, the last pass knocked away by none other than the hero of the day, number 33, Dave Burke.

Still the proud Oklahoma defense forced one last punt. The Cornhusker punter pinned them deep in their own end of the field. Oklahoma tried a throwback pass that was intercepted with only seconds on the clock. The crowd left their seats, filling the sidelines around the end zone, unable to contain their emotions as they stormed the field with only seconds left on the clock. The fans had to be removed from the field so Turner Gill in triumph could kneel on the ball to seal victory. The Big Red machine rolled, all of Nebraska cheered, we couldn't stop grinning. Once out of the press room we both let out a cheer and slapped hands. It was the best day ever, but there was more excitement in store.

Chapter 21

We joined the throng of fans spilling from the stadium and into downtown Lincoln. All along O Street from Tenth to Twenty-Seventh Street and from R to K Street the restaurants, bars and clubs were full of people: drinking, laughing, dancing and celebrating the victory.

We stopped into Barry's where some of the other journalists gathered. We were finally able to cheer for the Cornhuskers as fans and not reporters. They recalled each play and turning point; the injury to Rozier and Craig's ability to step up and run with power and grace, the Bounce Rooskie from Gill to Fryer to Krenk, and the defense that, all except for the one big play coming out after the halftime, shut down Dupree. I drank and laughed along with all of Nebraska on this Friday evening. The game having ended just after five, allowed us time for drinks, food and other opportunities to support the local economy in the dance clubs, rocking with live music.

We had booked hotel rooms and planned to stay for the night on the newspapers' dime. We ate steaks at Misty's around eight and dropped into the Zoo Bar on 14th Street to hear the Blues. After a half hour we agreed this was not a night for the blues. We walked on down O Street to a little dive with music and people spilling out the door. We squeezed in and mingled.

Mike believed himself an expert on both sports and women. He said, "After a game like today, the girls will be out for a party. I tell ya, they'll be dripping wet after a win like that." He gave me a jab with his elbow to punctuate the point. "I'm telling you kid," he said after a swig of beer. "We are going to get lucky tonight. You stick with me, I'll get you laid."

Truth be told, I was hoping he was right. I could use some companionship. There had not been much opportunity to date since I took the job at the paper. I'd met a couple of nice girls around town; nice girls were not what I needed tonight.

"Now listen to me Willy," Mike yelled over the music, "keep your eyes open and your head on a swivel for a couple of young ladies looking to party."

The music was loud, but the band was just okay. They had an amazing drummer. The lead singer seemed more interested in how his hair looked than staying on key. Mike cruised the place a couple of times trying his best pick-up lines. After several rejections he returned to report all the girls were stuck up sorority bitches. When the band finished its set we moved on to another club.

There were plenty of places to go and a variety of venues. Hard rock blasted out of one doorway and disco balls spun over the dance floor of the next. We peeked into some and stopped into others. Mike truly knew his way around; he seemed to know someone in every place we stopped.

The bar at 16th and O was the place we stayed after paying the ten-dollar cover to get in. The band was hot. They played everything from Dire Straits to Pink Floyd. The singer was good. He did a respectable job covering AC/DC and the lead guitar was out of this world. The place was packed. I spotted a group of girls on the edge of the dance floor, moving to the beat so I asked one of them to dance.

We elbowed our way on to the parquet floor and danced to "Mony Mony". We yelled, "Get Laid, Get Fucked" with the rest of the bar when the lead singer paused during the chanting chorus.

She had a nice smile; she danced great; her feet moving to a simple step-ball-chain rhythm, inviting her hips to move along with her arms. I wasn't a bad dancer, plus I played mean air guitar at the right times. When the band took a break, she thanked me and walked away. I found Mike leaning on a stand-up table on the edge of the dance floor. He handed me a beer and said, "She was hot. Did you get her name?"

"No," I admitted. "Too loud to hear; may have been Kerry or Kathy."

"You should go for that," Mike said with a wink. Just then I felt someone bump into me from behind. I turned to see who or what it was. A fight had started a few feet from us. The bystanders, moving to get out of the way of punches, fell back into each other. A ring formed, people moving back, surging outward away from two red faced farm boys who had squared off after the initial punches. The bouncers made their way into the crowd to break it up. Their pushing and shoving caused the crowd to reluctantly part with people falling over each other. I started moving to get out of the way. Suddenly a girl fell into my arms. She had been pushed by the crowd. Her foot got stepped on and she fell as I was moving. Out of reflex I put out my hands to catch her. She put her hands out to break her fall and so I caught her under one arm and across her chest. My palm caught the swell of her breast as I lifted her up and away from the fall. I adjusted my hand placement as I pulled her to me. We both stumbled back into Mike who put his hand in the middle of my back to steady me and protect his beer. "Whoa there big boy," Mike said. "Easy now."

"You alright?" I asked.

"Yeah, thanks," she said breathless. She looked down at her feet. I followed her gaze to see she was missing a shoe. "You've lost a shoe," I yelled.

I spotted a pointy-toed yellow slipper being kicked around by the milling mob. I stepped around her to retrieve it. I had to excuse myself a half dozen times as I made my way toward the prize. It got kicked just as I was about to pick it up; by sheer force of will and good luck I was able to grab it before it moved again. When I stood up to show my prize, I was directly in the path of a pair of pissed off bouncers, escorting one of the fighters from the bar. I took a glancing blow to the shoulder from one of the guys. The hit spun me around. I stumbled and ducked, then made my way back to the table.

"My hero," she exclaimed. "I guess that makes getting felt up worth it."

"Sorry about that," I said with a grin.

"I didn't mind," she laughed. "I'm just glad you didn't let me fall on my face."

"I'm Kim," she said. "And this is my friend Amy." She pulled a tall redhead over to the table. Amy nodded first at me and then at Mike.

"I'm Willy and this is Mike," I said.

"Nice to meet you," she said. "So Willy, huh. Does that mean you have a little willy or that you're a big dick?" she smiled with a devilish twinkle in her eye.

"I don't know," I stammered. "I guess you'll just have to find out."

Mike stepped in, "Would you ladies like another drink?"

"I would," Kim said, "I lost mine in the fall."

"I'd take one," Amy said as she moved to lean on the table between Mike and Kim.

"I'll be right back," Mike said. "Stay right here kid." he ordered and added "Nice catch," patting me on the back.

The band returned to the stage, I imagine at the request of management to get the music started again after the fight. The guitar struck a chord, the bass did the same just to check the sound, then the drummer counted off "One, two, one, two, three, four."

The lead singer leaned into the mike and broke into the opening of "Too Much Time on My Hands" by Stix.

"I love this song," Kim exclaimed. "Come on, let's dance!"

She grabbed my arm and off we went. She was small, maybe five-three, with short hair, cut so it hugged the back of her neck; the top was all teased and back combed to stand at attention. She bounced onto the floor with her arms in the air. I willingly followed her bouncing style until we found our space and sang the chorus along with the crowd of dancers.

She spun and moved away from me and then came back shaking her shoulders, coming right up close inviting me to do the same. When I did, she spun away and danced back to where she started. It was a playful, inviting little boogie. She was blond ambition surging with contagious energy. We danced two more songs in the same bouncing flirting style as the first.

I was sweating; her face glistened with perspiration when the band eased into "We've Got Tonight" by Bob Seger. I half expected her to head for the table. Instead she moved in close, put her arms around my waist and her head on my chest. The crowd thinned, and we had room to sway and turn as the band sang the desperate question.

She looked up at me, "Thanks for catching me."

"You're welcome," I said as we slowly swayed under a sparkling disco ball.

She felt good in my arms. The curve of her body pressed to mine had me thinking all kinds of possibilities. She looked into my eyes as the soaring lyrics begged for comfort, asking her to stay the night. There was an opening for a kiss, but we let it pass and stepped away. We returned to the table to find Mike and Amy leaning in close to each other.

"Mike's a sports writer for the Kansas City Star. He's here covering the game," Amy said with excitement. Mike gave me a wink. I didn't spoil the tale he was spinning. "Yeah, me and Willy here worked the game from up in the press box. The view up there is great."

"So, you're a sports writer too?" Kim asked.

"Yeah, I'm with the Des Moines Register," I lied most convincingly. "What do you girls do?"

"I'm an accounting major," said Kim. "I've got two semesters to go, then law school."

"Really," said Mike with a smile. "You're gonna be a blood-sucking lawyer?"

"Bankers are the real bloodsuckers," Kim interjected.

Amy laughed, "Well, I'm going to be a fashion designer, with my own line of clothing. Kim's going to help me hide my corporate profits from the government and together we're going to take over the world."

"Well, that sounds like it's a done deal," said Mike with a chuckle, then quickly asked, "Hey, you girls want to get out of here?"

The girls smiled at each other and shrugged in agreement. Outside the night was cold; the wind had picked up and we walked back up O street. I put my arm around Kim and Mike did the same for Amy. "Hey, let's head over to the Cornhusker, they got a bar there, that's where Willy and I are staying."

The girls agreed, so we turned down 13th street to the Cornhusker Hotel. We found a warm booth in the bar and ordered drinks. The crowd here was older, full of businessmen and big boosters. The band played fifties standards in a jazzy, mellow background way.

"So, a reporter?" she asked.

"Yeah, first job out of J school," I said. "Iowa State, but I've always been a Nebraska fan. My dad was too." I trailed off. "So, where are you from?" I asked.

"Oh, just a small town out west," she looked down at her beer and peeled at the label. She worked the edge loose with her nail, slowly pulled it off. "I got it, see. No rips, no runs, no errors."

"That's good. What does it mean?" I asked.

"Means I'm going to get lucky, tonight," she said with a laugh. Fifteen minutes later we were in my room. It was wild and hot, I felt like maybe I was just along for the ride. She took the lead. I tried to keep up. There was nothing romantic about it. It was breathless, wet, sweaty and fun. She knew exactly what she wanted, and I was happy to give it to her.

"Wow," I said lying in the tangled sheets breathless. She dug a cigarette out of her bag and lit it. She giggled, "I needed that."

"Happy to help," I said.

"Well, I had to repay the man who rescued my shoe."

"Paid in full," I said.

She rolled over, put out the cigarette, shook her hair and said, "Not yet."

I could try to explain the next half hour; I won't except to say. "Wow!"

I lay like a heap of used towels on the floor thinking, this is the best weekend of my life. She'd come out of the bathroom wearing my shirt. There is nothing sexier in the world than a girl in a man's white button-down shirt, the tail of it just covering her behind, the sleeves hanging down past her hand with only one button done, leaving a little cleavage begging for attention.

She flopped onto the bed and looked down at me. "How you feeling cowboy?"

"Fantastic." We shared a cigarette. I didn't smoke much, never have, but I enjoyed that smoke as much as any I've ever had. We laid there in the darkness, blowing white clouds of smoke toward the ceiling, her naked shape uncovered and unapologetic, next to me.

"When we were at the bar and Mike called lawyers blood suckers, you said bankers were the bloodsuckers. What's the deal with that?" I asked.

"I don't know," she said rolling over to look at me. The street light peeking in through the shades made her eyes blue and sad. She pretended to be interested in the lighter. The sound of the heater fan filled the silence between us. "Come on," I said. "What is it?"

"My family are farmers, or they were, until last year. My great-grandpa claimed a homestead south of Kearney, near Holdrege way back, just after the civil war. My grandpa inherited it from his father and he passed it on to my dad, who was going to pass it on to my brother."

"Anyway, everything was going good. Then one day dad comes home from the bank and he looks like someone has taken his soul. I mean he had this look on his face. It was like he was in shock or was having a heart attack or something. He said the banker was going to foreclose if we didn't make good on the loan."

She rolled over to look at the ceiling. "The harvest came but the markets are bad and the prices too low, there was no way to get the money together."

"What happened?" I asked, knowing the answer.

"They're taking it." She said. "The land, the trucks and the equipment. There's going to be a goddamn auction right there in the front yard."

Her voice wavered. "Now dad is working as a mechanic at the John Deere dealership and Billy, my brother, is working as a hired hand at a neighbor's place. Grandpa," she broke off. She got up from the bed and started looking for her bra. I got up and went to her. She pushed me away. I grabbed her waist, pulling her down onto my lap. She turned her face away from me, her head leaned forward, and she began to sob.

"I'm sorry," I pulled her around, so she was facing me. I put her head on my shoulder. She cried. Her whole body shook with each gasp of air. I stroked her hair and said nothing. After a while she pulled away, wiping her eyes with the back of her hands. Her mascara smeared across her cheeks. She tried to smile but it came out a sob. I grabbed my undershirt from the floor to wipe her face a little. She took it and wiped all the makeup off her face. She looked like a little girl.

"I'm sorry, I didn't mean to make you cry," I said.

"I didn't intend to cry," she said.

I wished I hadn't been such a reporter, asking questions at exactly the wrong time.

"It's so sad, I've seen my grandpa go from being a loving, happy man, to a sad, lost old man," she said. "I'm afraid he'll never recover, never be the same."

I pulled her close. She leaned in and kissed me on the cheek. I kissed her neck. She wrapped her arm around me. This time our embrace was softer, more vulnerable. She held on to me, let me comfort her there in the darkness, with the radio playing low.

Later she snuggled next to me thinking I was sleeping but I couldn't sleep. I lay wide awake thinking about the families like Kim's. I thought, "little girls shouldn't see their grandpas brokenhearted and hopeless." This wasn't economics. This was personal and tragic. Melvin had tried to tell me as much. I guess I needed to feel the weight of it, in my own arms, on my own heart.

Chapter 22

When I awoke she was coming out of the bathroom. Her hair wet and a towel wrapped around her. "Hey you," she said with a wicked little smile.

"Hey, yourself," I rolled over and grabbed at her towel. She scurried away laughing at my halfhearted effort.

"You're a bad boy," she said.

"Come here and I'll show you how bad I am," I teased.

She sashayed back to the bathroom, throwing a flirtatious glance over her shoulder. I heard her turn on the hair dryer. I got up tiptoeing after her. She quickly worked the dryer back and forth first in front and then around the back of her head. She'd washed off her smeared makeup. In the warm bathroom she was cute as hell. I leaned against the door frame and watched her work the dryer and smiled.

"What?" she asked.

I just shook my head. "I lied to you."

"What?" she yelled over the noise of the hair dryer.

"I don't work for the Des Moines newspaper," I said.

"I know," she said, as she turned off the dryer.

"What, how?" I asked.

"Your media credential on the dresser says St. Paul Phonograph."

I lowered my eyes. "I'm from Des Moines; I did an internship at the Democrat. I just thought it would sound better than the St. Paul paper."

She turned off the dryer. "Why?"

"Why, what?" I asked.

"Why did you tell me? Why does it matter?"

"Because I had a good time last night. I feel terrible about lying. So, I needed to tell you the truth."

"Good, I'm glad you felt bad and you told me the truth. You're still not getting this towel," she said with flirtatious challenge in her voice.

"Oh, yeah." Accepting the challenge, we did it on the vanity, in the bright lights of the bathroom, with no makeup or lies to mask our true selves. It was a hot, steamy bit of mischief.

I took a shower while she dressed and put on her makeup. "How about you buy me breakfast, liar," she called from the main area.

We knocked at Mike's room, but they were already gone. So, we went down and had breakfast, just the two of us. I asked if I could see her again. She smiled and said, "Maybe?" She gave me her number on a napkin. Funny I never called her. I thought about it a hundred times, never did. We were what each other needed on that night; a good time, a good lay and a soft shoulder to cry on. I hope she remembers it the same way. After breakfast I drove her to campus. She said goodbye with a kiss on the cheek. She turned and waved as she walked off.

I drove three hours to Des Moines to see my parents. Mom made a belated Thanksgiving meal with turkey and stuffing, creamed potatoes and cranberry sauce. I never understood cranberry sauce, but dad wouldn't allow a holiday meal without it. There were cookies, pie, fudge and peanut brittle.

Mom wanted to hear all about the town and the job, what stories I was working on. She worried I wasn't eating right and all the other things mothers worry about. Dad wanted to hear about the game, as seen from press row. My firsthand account seemed to thrill him more than Lyle Brimser's call on the radio. He had watched the game, but he peppered me with questions anyway.

It occurred to me, while I was talking to dad, that the heroes of the game were not who I went to see. Sure, the teams played great and the star players didn't disappoint but the game was decided by a kid from Utah. David Burke answered the call when the game was on the line. He made the game saving plays when the Huskers needed him most. The same for Freddy Sims, who came off the bench to swing the tide for the Sooners and get them back in the game. Neither David Burke nor Freddy Sims will be revered or even remembered by the fans; still the game chooses who it will. Life doesn't always choose who we expect. God doesn't often choose who's expected. I think it says in Second Kings, "Man looks at the outside but God looks at what's inside..."

We talked about the farming situation. Dad offered good perspective from the accounting side. The city of Des Moines was not untouched by the economics of farming, but it was not crippled by it either. There were still lots of families who were starting to feel the strain. The farm crisis would change Iowa as much as any other state. I stayed until Sunday evening. We went to church in the morning, eating at the club for lunch. Mom beamed and glowed as the ladies at church commented on how good it was to see me, how handsome and grown up I looked. She bragged about the stories I was working on. She overstated my status with the paper, much to my embarrassment. I let her sing my praise as much for my ego as hers. We watched the Vikings in the afternoon and napped on the couch. It was good to be home, but underneath I had a nagging, itching bother. The fact was these were my parents, not my biological mother or father, but my family, the only ones I had ever known. As much as I didn't want it, there was the nagging question. Why hadn't they told me before? Living all those years with a false belief in something made the truth seem more valuable. There was no denying they loved me dearly, desperately and that should have been enough. God knows there are plenty of parents who don't love and care for the children they have given birth to with half the devotion as these two beautiful people. Still the questions persisted, nagged me and left me feeling out of sorts.

We said goodbye as the early sunset called me back to the west. Mom packed leftovers, pie and money. She couldn't hold back the tears when we hugged. Dad had a hard time keeping his emotions in check. I waved goodbye with the two of them standing in the driveway. They looked proud and sad at the same time. I had to look away before they finished waving.

Bob Seger is right about that long and lonesome highway east of Omaha. All I could do was listen to the engine hum and think about the girl I knew the night before. My thoughts drifted to the journals of Mary Ann Steward. I was drawn to a belief they held something important for me. There was a mystery there, a truth there, a spiritual mystery to be uncovered and it called me back to those crossroads in the Sandhills.

Chapter 23

The journals read like a day in the life of a farmer's wife. She recorded the daily events in common everyday language, often as not, starting in mid-thought.

"The clouds kept the sun away today. Joe always worries at this time of year about too much rain, too much wind, too much of a good thing. I feel a bit low on days like this, when it's cloudy and gray. The old folks say whenever there is a heavy fog that rain or snow will follow in the next month. Joe believes it; he reads the farmer's almanac, that's where he gets these things. He swears his grandma kept records and it's true."

There would be entry after entry just as common and folksy, but then I'd find something else.

April 8th, 1959

Last night something called me to the chapel. I stopped at the door because there was a strange feeling in the place. I knew there was someone inside, that wasn't unusual by now. This was different, whatever was there felt dark. I took a deep breath and opened the door. It took a moment for my eyes to adjust. I saw him hunched down in the corner up by the lectern. He looked older, worn out, his clothes were almost rags; he had a dark beard and long hair. I thought he might be a hobo from off the train who sometimes stopped for the night. Then I saw his eyes; they were afraid, not of me, for me. I walked toward him. Neither of us spoke as I took a seat in the front pew across from him. I had a thought, no an image, of Gabe. I could see him clearly in my mind and it made me feel safe. Somehow, I knew the man's name. I can't say how or why, but I knew him as Nathan. I said, "You're safe here, Nathan."

When I spoke his name, there was a rush of sounds, like a great number of birds flushed from a tree and the darkness moved about the chapel. It flew about the ceiling and bounced off the walls like a trapped barn owl. There was a rush of wind and Nathan screeched, then it settled in the corner opposite us.

I stared at it and it stared back at me. It had an inky coldness about it. The only thing keeping me from running was the image of Gabe in my head. It was like he was right there with me and I could almost feel his hand on my shoulder.

Then Nathan spoke, "Make it go away!"

I said, and I swear I don't know where this came from, "I will help you, but you have to make it go away."

His eyes flashed a deadly fear. He scrunched back into the corner and looked away. "Listen to me," I said. "You can make it go. You and only you have the power to make it go and it will go. I know it's made you believe that's not true, but it is. I promise if you say, 'be gone', it will go away.

He looked at me with a dark haunted expression. I could feel the darkness becoming restless, shifting and preparing to pounce. I wanted to run. Only the presence of Gabe kept me in place.

Then in a voice, rough and soft as a whisper, "Go away,"

The darkness shifted but didn't move. I nodded with assurance to Nathan. He barked, "Be gone." The presence rose up filling the corner all the way to the ceiling. It stood with hovering intimidation over poor Nathan. I stood to face it and said. "Tell it again."

Nathan stood with confidence and said, "Go away and leave me alone."

Then for the life of me, I don't know why I yelled. "Get out of my place, go away and don't come back." The darkness flushed like a covey of pheasants, suddenly flying all around the place and with a terrifying screech it raced toward the doors. A white light filled the space. I swear I thought Joe had pulled up with the pickup and turned the floodlights on. The light sucked the dark specter from the chapel like a vacuum cleaner. There was a gust of wind, the doors banged shut and it was silent.

I turned to see Nathan smiling back at me. His eyes were as bright as a newborn baby. Years had fallen from his face, "Did you see that!" he exclaimed,"

Later in the same journal, June 30th, 1959.

Nathan has stayed with us for a good long time. He was good help around the place and it's been good for him to heal. I've never asked how he came to be in the chapel, but the other day he asked me, "Mary, when you found me, in the chapel, do you remember?"

I told him I did. He said. "I had been lost and hurt for a long time. I was so scared all the time and then you came in to save me. I just wanted to thank you."

I told him it wasn't me who saved him. He had saved himself. He shook his head and said, "No, I'd tried before, but the Shadows were too strong. If it hadn't been for you and the big guy next to you that night, I would still be..."

That's when I knew, it wasn't just a feeling that Gabe was next to me, somehow, he was there, not just in my head but truly with me. He had told me that he would be, but until that night I didn't know for sure. I had almost convinced myself that it was just a dream. Now I know for sure the cross and chapel have become what he told me they would be. I'm not afraid, it just is and so be it.

The entry really shook me up. I didn't know what to make of it. What was the Shadow in the chapel? Was it some kind of demon or a ghost or what? What had happened to Nathan to cause this thing to abuse him? I was really spooked. I couldn't stop reading.

The journals resumed to chronicle the everyday life of Mary and Joe until, as casual as the weather, she would tell a story full of tragedy or miracle and sometimes both.

September 16th, 1955
"I didn't expect anyone in the chapel on Sunday. That sounds strange, but folks who come to our little sanctuary on the hill come during the week, most often on Tuesdays and Fridays for some odd reason. I was changing the supplies by the door. I try to do that every other day, even though the bread and fruit never seems to go bad. I put a fresh pitcher of water and clean towel next to the washbowl. I make the bread myself, wheat and rye mostly because that's what I have baked most often. It's usually gone along with the fruit, but I do find the stems of apples and peach pits left in the pews. I don't always see who comes to visit. There are times I'm called to the chapel because someone needs a little mercy. People carve their names and dates in the cross. I used to get upset about it. Joe reminded me that people need to mark where they've been. I figure maybe it's a comfort to place their names on the cross. I find notes and sometimes small bundles of things left in the pews. I've gone and discovered more than one poor lost person curled up at the base of the cross or sitting quietly in the chapel.

Like I said, not very often on Sunday, so I was surprised to find the Patterson girl, Kelly, sitting on the front pew. She's such a sweet girl, only about twelve or thirteen. She was sitting with her head down, her hair falling over her face. I thought she was praying, so I went about my business. I had fresh pears, peaches, and wheat bread.

I heard her choke back a cry and sniffle. I turned to see if she was all right. The Pattersons live just a section over. I knew the mother had been sick with cancer for a good long time and had passed away over the winter. I went to comfort her. I sat down next to her, but she looked away. I pulled her back against me. I hummed a hymn as we rocked gently back and forth. When she brushed her hair back to wipe her eyes, I noticed her face. She had a real shiner under her eye and her lip was swollen.

I turned her to me and could see she had taken quite a beating. Her lower lip was cracked, her eye swollen and bloodshot. I suddenly had a vision of her father, Bill Patterson, standing over me, his face red with rage. He smelled of whiskey and worse. He was yelling and growling at me. I couldn't understand the words but when he lashed out with a slap of his hand I understood the intent.

I broke away with a gasp when the blow came at me. I asked her why? She said her Daddy was mad a lot; drank a lot, Momma dying made him sad. She had tried to make a Sunday lunch, but burned the biscuits and spilled the flour trying to make fried chicken like Momma had showed her. Daddy got mad over the mess and started yelling. She ran off and was scared to go back.

I took her up to the house, cleaned her face and put a cold washcloth on her eye. Joe came in and I thought he was going to kill Bill Patterson when I told him what had happened. I convinced him to stay with her while I went over to the Patterson's.

I found the drunken fool asleep in the chair. The kitchen was a mess. The house smelled of death and whiskey. I went to work cleaning up the mess and opened a few windows. I had the place put back into order when Bill started to wake up. He looked more than a little surprised to see me. Before he could ask any questions, I started in. I told him he needed to get his house in order. I understood he'd had a bad loss, but it was his responsibility to take care of his kids. He asked what business it was of mine. I told him it was my business when his girl showed up at my place with a black eye. He started to deny it. I stopped him with a wave of my hand. This was going to stop, I said. He was going to put this behind him. He came toward me with fire in his eyes. I slapped him hard across the face. He stared at me like a dying calf in a hailstorm. I slapped him again. This time tears welled up and he started to cry. The tears shook his whole body; he fell to his knees and let out a wail. I thought it would shatter the windows. I put my hand on his shoulder and felt the energy pass between us. He stopped crying and I knelt down to look him in the eyes. He looked away. I took his chin in my hand and made him look at me. I told him he needed to start living and to put the drinking and anger away. His children needed him, his ranch needed him, and it was his responsibility to take care of both. His lip quivered like a child, but he nodded in agreement. I took him in my arms and he cried it out. After a while I stood him up and sent him to the bathroom to clean up. I finished straightening the kitchen. When he came out he looked better. I told him to clean the rest of the house for God sake, then come get his girl up at my place.

I'd fix supper for them. He came up to the house about seven. I told the girl her daddy was sorry, and he would never hurt her again. When he came in the door he looked like a different soul than the one that had been passed out in a drunken stupor just a few hours before. He was clean shaven and dressed for dinner. She ran to him; they hugged for a long time. I hope he's done with the drinking and the violence. I think he just needed a good cry. Men have a hard time crying. They keep it all bottled up and it comes out in angry fits.

I sat there and wondered if Kelly Patterson was still around someplace close. I would like to hear her version of the story, to know if her father had changed after that Sunday. I made a note to look for her and to see if Amanda could help me find her.

I read the journal entries all week. Some I read over a few times. I found them simple, honest and true. Some of the events Mary described in such a casual everyday manner were unbelievable. At times she had such insight, it almost read like prophesy.

June 20th, 1971

Lately I've been thinking about church and my little chapel out here. I wonder why people are drawn to its doorway. Joe and I attend the services in town, always have and guess we always will. We have dear friends and support from our home congregation. I know there are those who talk and judge. Gossip will always serve some people's imagination and I decided long ago there's nothing to be done about small-minded people.

To my point, we see the number of young people, young families in attendance, and it's wonderful. The youth groups here in town are well attended. There is always something going on. I see the huge crowds of people attending revivals held by one national preacher or another. They are preaching to crowded stadiums of people on fire for God and Jesus. The altar calls attract hundreds of hungry souls and take hours to baptize the converted, and still I wonder why people find their way here?

I think it might be some kind of a response to all the hippie stuff everywhere just a few years ago. There's always a pendulum swing to change. The pendulum swings back, an equal and opposite reaction. The thing is, I wonder if the preachers are asking for enough. Is it all a question of saved or unsaved, in or out, heaven or hell, born again, or whatever you are if not reborn. Shouldn't it be about others, about more than self-preservation?

I've discovered walking with God and doing his will is hard. Some days it's the hardest thing to do, to stay on this journey of discovery. It's not a flash of light and a Spirit descends. Maybe it is for some. That's just not been my experience. The way these preachers describe Jesus makes me think of a traveling insurance salesman with protection from Satan with lakes of fire and breath of brimstone. I'd like to tell them God doesn't offer insurance policies and the boogeyman we've created is far less powerful than we imagine. God is not short of resources and all the money in the world can't buy your way into paradise.

I believe in a God full of mercy, long suffering, and unchanging. The Jesus described for our youth today looks nothing like the savior who says, "The kingdom of God is all around you. He who has eyes to see let him see." I fear the pendulum swing when it goes back, and these energetic young people are left wanting. Asking themselves, what, if anything, did I learn in Sunday school or summer missionary retreat? How can I make my world better for the less fortunate? I believe people spend too much time on self-preservation and forget the mercy and compassion so badly needed in the world. That's why I think I find so many strangers drawn to the cross and huddled in our clapboard chapel. They come seeking mercy and comfort, compassion and shelter. We all know our own sins, some perhaps more than others. God knows, every TV evangelist has a prayer and a price tag for forgiveness. I think we're seeking a pathway for life not an insurance policy. We are our best selves when we give of ourselves. Not of our possessions, but of our time. When we show compassion and love for one another; when we stop to answer the question, who is my brother?

Then again, people don't have time to seek answers, particularly to the hard questions; so many will seek the insurance sellers with a Bible in one hand and the collection plate in the other.

I've heard people talk about thin places, those places where you feel close to God. Most of the time those places are on a mountain top or near an epic historic site. I think Mary's cross and chapel were one of those thin places where people experienced the existence of the Divine, but if so, why the Sandhills of Nebraska, for god-sake? The farmers and ranchers out here would tell you living with the weather, battling the insects and just plain hard luck, feels more like penitence at times. Still, there was little doubt in my mind; lost souls, injured in body and spirit found some kind of refuge there. I remembered old Tensley's warning. "...them churches have less mercy than you would think." Did it have anything to do with what I was reading? Were any of the people who came to see Mary and Joe still around? Would any of them tell me how they remember their story?

I called Amanda's house to see if she could help me. The phone rang several times and I was about to hang up when she answered. "Hello."

"Amanda, it's Willy," I said.

"Hey, Willy Beam, the newspaperman. Long time no see," she said.

"I need your help," I said.

"Oh, okay," she said. "That's how it's going be, Huh?"

"What?"

"Don't call a girl for three weeks. No communication for almost a damn month and boom, it's I need your help," she said with loads of sarcasm in her voice.

"Amanda," I started. "Okay, sorry. I've just been reading the journals and my brain is full of questions. I need your help. I need to see Jimmy and get more journals from him."

There was no reply. I thought she had hung up for a moment when I said. "Amanda?"

"Yeah, I'm still here," she said.

"What's wrong?" I asked. "What's going on?"

"Nothing," she said. "Nothing you want to hear about."

I felt like I was back in high school and why not? Amanda was in high school. "Hey, listen," I said. "I'll come up and meet you at the Pizzeria and we'll talk."

She didn't reply, so I said. "I need to see you."

"Okay," she said with a bit of frustration.

"I can be there in an hour," I said. "Will you be there?"

"Sure," she said and hung up.

I was confused, which was nothing new when it came to girls. It reminded me of the joke my dad use to tell. A man found a lamp with a Genie in it. The Genie offered him a wish. The man said, "I'd like to go to Hawaii, but I'd like to drive. Can you build me a highway from California to Hawaii?" The Genie said, "Do you know how far that is? There are mountains and valleys in the floor of the ocean. The current is too strong, it will sweep the piers away. No way. Think of something else."

The man said, "Well, I've always struggled to understand women. Can you help me to understand women?" The Genie said, "Do you think you'll need a two lane or a four-lane highway?"

Chapter 24

I waited at the Pizzeria for an hour. The owner was starting to consider calling the authorities on me for loitering when she came through the door. I stood up when she came over to the booth where I was waiting. She sat down without a word. I lowered myself into the booth and said, "I thought you weren't coming."

"Well, I almost didn't. My parents think there's something going on with you, us, so I had a fight with them about coming."

"Amanda, I'm sorry," I said. "I was afraid this would happen."

She cut me off. "You haven't thought about anything or anyone except Mary and those damn journals. You don't give a crap about me or how any of this has made me look or feel."

"No, I hadn't," I admitted, embarrassed by my selfishness. "I'm sorry. Tell me what happened." Before she could answer I said, "Are you hungry? Let me get you a pop and we'll talk." I hurried up to the counter and ordered her a Mellow Yellow. I sat the drink down and slid into the booth.

"What's this?" she asked.

"Mellow Yellow." I said attempting to be funny. She didn't smile. "Okay, tell me what's going on."

"My mom and dad don't think I should be helping you, seeing you, talking to you," she said.

"Why?" I asked.

"That's what I asked them," she said. "Mom doesn't like anything that has to do with Aunt Mary. Then they started asking who you were and what was going on with us."

"With us?" This could get real bad, real quick, I thought. "What did you tell them, about us?"

"Nothing!" She looked me square in the eyes to assert she hadn't revealed anything about us. "I told them you were working on a story, and I was helping you. I told them we were reading Aunt Mary's journals."

"What did they say to that?" I asked.

"They freaked out! I mean Mom flipped her shit. Dad started pacing back and forth, huffing like a coal train, steam practically coming out his ears."

"Wow," I said. "Look Amanda, I'm sorry. I mean, I can see how all this must look."

I looked away. "I get so myopic. I get fixated on my own stuff." I looked back to her, "If you want to stop, I'll understand."

"You're a real ass Willy Beam." She smiled a beautiful dimpled smile. "You couldn't pay me to quit now."

"Huh?" I asked.

"If my parents are this upset about Aunt Mary's journals, then you can bet your sweet ass I'm going to find out what that's all about. Hell, this is the most exciting thing that's happened around here in my life."

She had perfectly summed up what had me so wrapped up in this mess. The same questions inspired the same motivation for me. Childish curiosity mixed with a hint of rebellion is enough to move the world. If they don't want me to know then there must be a reason. "Good," I said. "Now, we need to see Jimmy and get more of Aunt Mary's journals."

"Not yet," she said. "Not until you tell me what's in the ones you took with you or give them to me so I can read them myself."

"I'll do a little of both," I said and took out a journal to read to her.

March 10, 1964

The cranes have returned. They come like a giant rush of wings from out of the north. They descend on the river and dance in the fields. For thousands of years the Sandhill cranes along with their cousins the Whooping cranes return to the waterways along the Platte River and its tributaries. This migration of the tall awkward birds opens my eyes to spring as surely as Easter bunnies and tulips. It lifts my spirit to see them dance in courtship for the favor of their mate. I could sit by the water and watch until the sun goes down. They are gray and white with a patch of scarlet round their large yellow eyes. They strut on legs two feet long and thin as pencils. They squawk and hop, prance and flap calling the females to join the dance. It is pure joy to see them coming, to awake to see them in the fields, foraging and resting before they head south.

It reminds me of the journey we make from season to season, how everything comes to pass and the joy with each migration. I believe we pass from lifetime to lifetime with a rest in between. I hope for a respite in the fields of Paradise. I don't know if I believe in heaven or hell. I know there is life beyond this plane of awareness. There is a soul, our spirit given by God, not weighted by the restless tides of this body. The spirit returns again and again to bask in the glory of its Creator. I don't begin to understand why we must pass through this earth, at this time, on this planet in the endless reaches of eternity but I know we do. I've come to see the migration of the Sandhill crane as a symbol for our short season of life. We dance for love, and we rest by the river for a while before returning to our journey north to south, birth to death, season to season. We fail to understand the cycle and maybe that's why we repeat it over and over.

"Mary believed in reincarnation?" Amanda said. "No wonder Mom freaked."

"I don't know if she means reincarnation, like coming back as a cow or butterfly or something but she sure believed in more than one life."

"Wow," Amanda said. "I've been reading some of the journals; most of mine are just as common as cow shit. There was this one story. I guess there was a lightning storm. Mary said lightning was striking the ground all around the house. One hit the weather vane on top of the barn, another struck their TV antenna and blew the tube out of the television. She said the wind was howling and several tornadoes touched down across the county. Anyway, the thing was the lightning struck the cross but it didn't catch on fire. In the journal she said Joe saw lightning strike the cross two or three times and it lit up, like it was glowing, but it didn't burn. The next day they couldn't see a mark on it. The storm tore up all kinds of things; it blew over barns and flipped trucks along the road but nothing on their property was damaged. She went to the chapel, there was a family sleeping on the pews. They got caught in the storm and took shelter in the chapel. The father of the family said he was sure lightning struck the cross and the steeple, nothing was damaged, not even one shake shingle on the roof was missing. Mary was amazed"

I then told her the Patterson story and asked. "Do you think any of the people Mary helped would still be living around here?"

"That would be awesome," she said. "I'd love to know what they thought and what they saw or if they even remember any of it."

"It might be awesome," I said. "And it might be something else. We need to keep this between us for now. If we find someone who Mary touched, then we should be careful how we approach them."

Amanda agreed. Her eyes were sparkling, and I could see the wheels turning in that little head of hers. "Let's go see Jimmy," she said.

Chapter 25

We knocked at the side door, no one answered. We walked
down to the barn but Jimmy wasn't there either. His pickup was in
there so we waited on the back porch for a while. I had about
decided to go back to town when we heard the sound of an engine
coming across the yard. Jimmy came bouncing along on the tractor.
He pulled down by the barn and shut off the engine. I noticed there
was no equipment attached to the tractor as we walked down to meet
him.

"What's going on little sis," Jimmy asked as we walked up.

"Not much," Amanda said. "We wanted to bring back some
journals and see about getting some others."

Jimmy went into the barn and we followed along. He took a seat
on an overturned plastic bucket and began cleaning mud or
something off his boots.

"You find anything in them books of Aunt Mary's?" he asked.
"You two find what you were looking for?"

"I found some interesting things," I said. "But I'm not sure what
I was looking for."

"Aren't you?" he asked.

Amanda and I looked at each other, confused by Jimmy's
questions. "Jimmy," Amanda started, "You said you'd never read any
of the journals."

He looked at her sideways and gave me an amused grin; the
type of grin an adult gives to a foolish child. He switched boots to
clean but didn't answer.

"Jim," I said. "Mary recorded some pretty amazing events in her
journals; truly miraculous stuff."

He stood, shook out his pant legs, in a funny little jig until they
covered the tops of his boots. Then he looked me directly in the
eyes, "It don't matter if I read them or not. I know every word is
true."

"How?" Amanda asked.

He nodded and walked between us up toward house. Amanda
and I looked at each other, shrugged and followed. Jimmy walked
with surprisingly long strides for a smaller guy. He covered the forty
yards or so up to the house fast enough, so we had to jog a little to
catch up. He turned as we came up behind, a little shit eating grin on
his face. We fell in on either side of him. "You kids don't have any
idea what you're into. Shit, I must've been out of my mind to give

you those journals. Nothing but trouble's going to come of it."

"Jimmy, you said Willy was the one," Amanda said. "Remember, he knew stuff and you said he was the one you'd been expecting. You remember that?"

His grin turned to a grimace, "I remember fine, little sis. I'm not stupid. I don't forget nothing. I can't forget."

"Look" I said. "I believe the stories in the journals, I do. Have you ever seen anything or know anything about the people who came to see Mary? I'd like to hear their version of the events."

He turned his attention from Amanda to me. "I saw things. I've seen plenty. Things I cannot explain. I don't know if I want to tell anyone about it."

His eyes were piercing, challenging. I'd say he was searching for the motives in my soul, hard to say what he saw. "You get high?" he asked.

"What?" I asked.

He didn't repeat the question.

I grinned "Yea, I get high."

Amanda said, "That's where you were."

Jimmy smiled at her and climbed up on the porch. He reached in his back pocket to pull out a sandwich bag. I looked at Amanda. She shrugged, raised her eyebrows and followed Jimmy up on the porch. I took a seat on one of the mismatched green or yellow lawn chairs on the porch. The sun was falling; the air was cool, not yet cold for early December. Jimmy picked up a ceramic statue in the shape of an elf or possibly a gnome. I've never quite understood the difference. Maybe elves help Santa Clause and gnomes are more mischievous. This one was for sure.

Jimmy opened the bag and offered me a sniff. I inhaled the rich skunky, earthy smell. He broke off a couple of buds and dropped them onto a small tin tray under the gnome. He picked off the stems and tossed a few seeds into a small glass jar by the chair.

I looked at Amanda, "You smoke weed?"

"Sometimes," she said a little unsure. "But only with Jimmy. You won't tell anyone?"

"I won't if you won't," I said.

I hadn't gotten high since graduation; in college there were plenty of J school majors who debated Nixon's prohibition of weed, along with other controversial topics like Carter's Olympic boycott and the Supreme Court ruling on Roe vs. Wade. Iowa had been one of the leading hemp producers during World War II when Roosevelt called on the farmers to grow it for the war effort. Hemp is the male sex of the cannabis plant; it's great for making paper, rope and textiles. Hemp literally has hundreds of uses and it grows wild along the ditches of Iowa. If you smoke enough Ditch Weed you might get high, but mostly likely all you'll get is a headache. It's the lovely and multi colored female which provides the sweet euphoric high. I've pondered the significance of the high coming from the budding female cannabis plant. Maybe the dull workman, serviceable nature of hemp says something about the life of man without woman.

Jimmy took the gnome with its folded hands; rosy cheeks and a pointed hat removed the top of the hat to reveal an opening. He removed the hands, which cleverly concealed a steel pipe bowl. He loaded the bowl, pulled a lighter from his pocket and handed it to me. I took it clumsily at first until I found a neat little thumb hook, on the back of the gnome. I sparked the lighter, put my mouth over the opening at the top of the now bald gnome and inhaled, pulling the flame into the bowl. The yellow fire bent into the green buds in the bowl until it glowed orange. Soon a sweet, warm smoke filled my lungs. I held it for a moment; a little escaped through my nose but I choked back the cough and held it as long as I could. When I let it all go, I felt the day soften. I sparked the lighter again to make sure the weed was still burning. I took another hit and passed it back to Jimmy.

He had been watching me closely. I had passed the stoner's test. Now I was curious about Amanda. I had not pegged her as a dope smoker. She took the gnome, pulled hard on the bong, held it and then puckered lips and gently blew a stream of pure white smoke into the air. I could tell this was not her first time on Uncle Jimmy's back porch, hitting the gnome.

The pipe went around again. I took another hit, but to tell the truth, I was toast after round one. We sat and watched the sunset. The cool evening started to turn cold. We didn't move until the sun had dropped into the west and all that remained were the embers of the day.

"That was pretty," Amanda said. Jimmy and I nodded in agreement; nobody wanted to speak and break the spell. I felt calmer, for the first time in a month. My perception shifted, moved back a little as I became more aware of the beauty and colors of the land and sky. I know pot is supposed to be bad; I've never found it to be anything other than good.

"Man I need some tunes," Jimmy said. He got up and went into the house. I looked at Amanda. She was staring intently at something on the floor of the porch. I started to ask her what, then decided to leave her be. The evening cold made me shiver but I couldn't have moved to find a warmer spot if my life depended on it. Jimmy came back with a boom box. He sat on the floor between us, flipped the switch and adjusted the tuning knob until he got a station out of Kearney. A familiar song, a soft rock ballad, I don't remember its name, but like the thousands of songs I never deliberately learned, I knew the words immediately. Jimmy dragged a propane heater over from the corner of the porch. It was really just an open blue flame propelled through a metal grate by a high-speed fan. The orange glow of the metal was alluring and the heat delightful in the growing darkness.

When the coins started falling at the beginning of "Money" by Pink Floyd, Jimmy sat up to play air bass guitar. He sang along with David Gilmour, in a nice strong voice, imitating the raspy vocals. I bobbed my head and played lead air guitar as Amanda tapped her foot to the deep bass beat. I always loved Pink Floyd. In college we drank magic mushroom tea, dropped the needle on the "Dark Side of the Moon" just as the MGM lion roared for the opening of "The Wizard of Oz". It is surprising how well the soundtrack matches up for a good portion of the movie. Like I said, it's all good fun until the flying monkeys showed up. I've heard the story is a long parable about the political battles between the gold standard and the control of currency by the Federal Bank. In some ways the current farm crisis might be a fulfilled prophecy from Williams Jennings Bryan's "Cross of Gold" speeches from the late 1800's.

The cross of gold and the cross on the hill connected in my mind. I could see the huge Christian symbol glowing like a beacon on the horizon along the road, calling people to come and rest, to be healed at Mary's hands in the chapel at its feet. I pushed the images aside to ask, "Man what do you know about Mary's journals? Did you ever see any of the people she helped?"

Jimmy was drinking a beer, rocking his head back and forth in time to the next song on the radio. "Holy shit dude," he said with a chuckle. "Where the hell did that come from?"

Amanda laughed, "He's obsessed with Aunt Mary and the stories he's been reading."

Jimmy took a long swig of his beer, leaning forward to rest his elbows on his knees. "I asked you down at the barn if you believed what you read. I've often asked myself if I believe."

"Well, do you?" Amanda asked.

"You've got to know something," I said.

Jimmy stood, walked to the edge of the porch and stretched. He put his arms out wide, flexed his hands and fingers, reaching up over his head. He raised up on to his toes; at the peak of his stretch he let out a groan of release and joy.

Amanda said, "Jimmy, I've been coming out here for years and you never said a word about Aunt Mary, her journals or nothing."

"So," Jimmy said, still facing toward the backyard with his hands in his pockets.

"So," she said exasperated. "So, what the hell?"

That made me snort with laughter. That's exactly what I wanted to know. "What the hell?"

Jimmy said over his shoulder. "It wasn't my place to say anything. Truth be told I'd put it away, in my mind. Hadn't thought about what might be in those journals for years."

"How'd you get them?" I asked.

"Mary asked me to keep them before she died. The ladies brought them out when Joe broke his hip. I put them upstairs; just put them out of my mind."

"Jimmy goddammit, "Amanda said. "You're starting to piss me off. There's more you're not telling"

"Little sis, this is an old memory, a long-forgotten thing. I've only half believed they're true sometimes, until this son of bitch here showed up." He pointed his beer in my direction.

"I'm sorry," I said. "But something happened here. Something I want to understand and cannot get out of my head. For some reason I need to know what happened out here. Why here, why this place? It's just such a mystery. I cannot let it go."

Jimmy nodded his head, scratched his chin and said, "I've never told anyone what I'm going to tell you two. I don't know if it will help but here goes. I did two tours in Southeast Asia. I crossed into Laos and then Cambodia. I was 'in country' when all hell broke loose during the Tet Offensive." He grinned darkly. "Charlie rained hell down on us that night. I remember calling out to the lieutenant. I need a damn elephant. He said what? So, I spelled phonetically: echo, lima, echo, papa." He trailed off with the swig of his beer.

"I did and saw things that will never leave me. When I came home I spent about a year out on the ranch with Joe and Mary. Joe let me help raise cattle and take care of the horses again. It was a bad time. Sometimes the only thing that helped was working with the animals; funny how brushing a horse or mucking stalls out can clear your head. Anyway, I noticed how Mary always took time out to go to the chapel. She took fruit, bread and water there almost every day. I asked her about it and she told me how this Gabe character had come to visit and told them to put up the cross and build the chapel. About how some people came to visit the chapel and leave stuff at the cross."

"Did you ever see any of the people?" I asked.

He nodded, "Yeah, I saw plenty of people and not all of them from off the road either. Plenty came from towns around here." He waved his beer in a wide arc. "Some just to pray and talk to Aunt Mary. At the time I had my own problems, didn't pay much attention. Funny, it never occurred to me to ask Mary for help or go to the chapel myself. One day I came up from the barn and saw Mary running back from the chapel. She called for me to come help. I ran up to the building. There was an old guy there, he was hurt, a broken leg. I swear to God his shin bone was sticking through the skin. Well, I grabbed off my belt and made a tourniquet, tried to stop the bleeding. I'd seen plenty of wounds in the war. Seeing the blood and bone sticking out, well hell, I lost it. I started seeing things, flashback. Suddenly, I was there, in the jungle with Charlie, calling to us from just outside the wire."

Jimmy stopped talking. He looked stuck, lost, until Amanda asked, "What happened next?"

Jimmy took a swig of beer and said, "She stopped it. Mary stopped the visions, the flashbacks. She reached out her hand and stopped them."

"How?" asked Amanda.

"That's the part I still don't believe. See, Mary put out her hand and when she touched me the vision just stopped. I was there with Mary and the guy with the broken leg and he was in a lot of pain. We helped him inside the chapel. I practically carried him to one of the pews. Mary took hold of his foot and he yelled like the world was ending. I was holding him down. Mary said she was going to set his leg. I thought she was crazy. She took hold of his leg and pulled down hard. He screamed bloody murder. I looked down and I swear to God, the bone was back in place. The guy's leg was still broke though. Then she put her hands over the wound and pressed real hard with her hands. At first the guy let out another cry, shaking his head back and forth. I was sure he was going into shock. Slowly his face changed, he started nodding his head a little and his face relaxed. Mary took her hands away and I'll be damned if the wound wasn't healed."

"What the hell, how on earth?" Amanda asked.

"I don't know. To this day I don't know. All I know for sure is that son of bitch walked out of the chapel and up to the house within ten minutes."

"You're telling me, Aunt Mary could heal people?" asked Amanda. "An honest to God miracle healer?"

"That's what I'm telling you," Jimmy said.

"What about you?" I asked.

"What about me?"

"You said Mary just touched you and the flashbacks stopped. Had she never touched you before?"

"I've thought about it, and the thing is, I'd never been in the middle of a flashback when she was near. Before it was just a general sadness and anger, nothing she could act on. Mary was never around when the war came back in my head. So, it was like she needed me to be in that state or rather I needed to be in a state of mind for her to act." He took a long pull of his beer, "Plus, she was in the chapel."

"What do you mean?" I asked.

"She needed to be close to the cross or inside the chapel for some reason. She never told me so, but that's what I think. I never saw her do anything really miraculous when she wasn't close to either the cross or in the chapel."

"But you did see other things?" I asked.

"I saw some things, some amazing things, and people left better off after Mary helped them."

"Holy shit," Amanda said.

"It was some shit," Jimmy said with a smile. "I never had another flashback. I still get angry and sad sometimes, nothing like when I was first back. I wanted to die. I had thought about ending it a few times. Not after that day. I never had that thought again."

We sat in silence for a little while then Jimmy said, "I'm hungry, let's eat."

Chapter 26

The kitchen smelled of homemade soup and cornbread. Jimmy went to the stove to stir the stew in a ceramic Dutch oven. The simmering rich brown aroma filled the room, wafted to my nose and filled me with memories of home.

"When did you put this on?" Amanda asked.

"It's been cooking since lunch. I put the cornbread in when I came in to get a beer," Jimmy said with pride.

"Man, that smells so good," I said.

"Well grab a bowl and sit down," Jimmy said, pointing to a stack of soup bowls on the counter. Amanda and I took a bowl and stood like kids at a mother's apron, waiting to share the beef stew. He dished out helpings and brought the cornbread over on a plate along with real butter and cold beer. I've had fancier meals but never better. The warmth from the kitchen stove filled my heart. The tender free-range fed beef melted in my mouth, corn, carrots, tomatoes and celery in a light broth with a hint of salt and pepper. I ate one bowl and without manners or permission took another along with two squares of cornbread. We ate without conversation, expressing our appreciation for the meal with head nods and raised eyebrows. Amanda laughed when I slurped the broth from the bottom of the dish, it didn't stop me.

"Wow, that was amazing," I said.

"The weed or the soup?" Jimmy asked.

"Both," Amanda said, we all laughed in agreement.

We sat in the yellow light of the kitchen, full and content, mellow and friendly. "So," Amanda began, "Jimmy, did you ever talk with Mary about what happened at her place? I mean did you ever discuss stuff?"

Jimmy stood up, started collecting the dishes and moved to the sink. He stacked the bowls and turned on the water. He put in some dish washing soap and dropped in the silverware.

We waited for a reply. I'd learned to let Jimmy answer in his own good time. I could've sat there all night looking at the expression on Amanda's face. She was just a teenage girl but would be a beautiful woman. We stared at each other across the table. I wanted to know what she was thinking.

"Mary had some strange ideas about God and heaven," Jimmy said standing at the sink cleaning the dishes. "She believed churches had it wrong somehow. She talked about the Fullness of God and the

Eons. She believed our souls were eternal and we all returned to the light of fullness. To tell the truth I didn't understand much of it. I bet if you keep reading those journals you'll find some of that stuff." He stacked the bowls in a drying rack. "She knew things, she understood things more complicated then I could ever explain. I think Gabe told her some things we aren't supposed to know."

"Why do you think that?" I asked. "Did he come back again after the first time?"

"I don't know," said Jimmy. "I just got the feeling that Mary and Gabe communicated."

"Did you ask her about how she healed the man's leg?" I asked.

"I did," Jimmy said. Once again, we waited while he hunted for a tea-towel for drying.

Amanda asked, "Well?"

Jimmy put the silverware in a small holder at the corner of the tray and slowly began to dry his hands. "She told me, with the faith of a mustard seed."

Amanda asked, "What in the world does that even mean?"

"You know like Jesus said in the New Testament, 'if ye had the faith of a mustard seed, you could command the mountains to stand up and walk into the sea.' I think Aunt Mary had that kind of faith."

"Do you think there are other people around here we could talk to?" I asked. "Who would remember things?"

"I don't know," Jimmy said coming back to sit at the table. "I would imagine there are, why?"

"We'd like to talk to them," I said. "I would like to hear their side of the story. See if it matches up with whatever I read in the journals."

"That might not be a good idea," Jimmy said.

"Why is that?" Amanda asked.

"Come on sis, you know how people are. They keep things to themselves, besides things that happened out at Joe and Mary's place, well they get people upset."

"How?" I asked.

"Man, you ask a lot of damn questions," Jimmy said, smiling. "Look, what Mary talked about, and what she did didn't sit well with some folks. They, some of them, thought she was some kind of a witch or something."

"A witch," Amanda exclaimed. "Mary wasn't a witch!"

"Well, I can tell you this," Jimmy said. "Folks are quicker to believe it's the Devil before they believe its God. Funny how people pray for a miracle and then when they see it, they call it a curse."

Jimmy agreed to let us go up and look through the journals. Amanda and I went up the narrow staircase to the second-floor landing. The hallway was dark, even with the bare light bulb beaming from above the staircase. We guided ourselves along by touching the wall. I was still pretty stoned, so the shadows we projected in the hall danced like phantoms. I located the door, turned on the lights and found boxes of journals on the floor, stacked on the bed and atop a bookcase. Amanda noticed the spirals and then the brighter colors of some of the notebooks. We decided those might be newer editions with more recent entries. She started leafing through those and I took up a box of the older ones.

"Let's look for the date and skim a few pages to see if anything catches your eye," I suggested.

We went to work. I found a lamp and surprisingly it had a working bulb in it, which helped. Jimmy came up with a portable mechanic's light and hung it on the door. The harsh glare gave the room the feeling of a field laboratory. I was into a box from nineteen sixty-three and four. Mary's elegant handwriting was familiar to me, I could almost hear the voice of the author.

March 11th, 1963

It's been a hard winter and it feels like snow is coming again. Joe's been working so hard to keep the cows alive in this mess. I keep hoping spring will come but winter stretches for as far as I can see out my window.

The snow had piled up in front of the chapel door and I couldn't get the door open. I spent half an hour with a shovel clearing the way to get in. I know only a fool would be out in weather like this and there are plenty of fools who are called here even in snow two feet deep.

I took that journal and the next three notebooks. There were roughly two months per notebook. Mary wrote only on one side of the pages and often her entries were two pages or more. She sometimes wrote poems or just doodled on pages. She could've been a sketch artist with a little training. I moved to another box and grabbed a random notebook halfway through the stack.

October 23, 1963

It's been so warm this fall. Long days without a cloud in the sky, but plenty of storm clouds around us. Visitors have been coming and going a lot this year. Plenty of them passing through, moving to the west before the winter comes. There was a young family stopped with car trouble the other day. Joe offered to let them sleep in the house, but the man insisted on sleeping out in the chapel. I thought it odd and was called to investigate a feeling around one o'clock in the morning.

I took that book as well. I kept going adding journals to my stack. I looked over and Amanda was doing the same. Jimmy had picked up a few notebooks and was reading.

"Jimmy," I said. "You really haven't ever come up here and read some of these?"

He shook his head no. "Really?" asked Amanda. "You're crazy, I'd have to know. I can't believe some of the things I've read so far."

"Like what?" I asked.

Amanda began to read from the journal in her hand.

"May 2, 1973; kids from town have been coming out here drinking and smoking on the weekends. I sent Joe out to check on them. He took the truck with the spotlights on it and headed up to the cross. He was gone for a good while when I heard him call me on the base radio in the house. He said someone up there needed my help and so I got my coat on and went. There was a whole group of kids gathered around Joe's truck when I got there. One of the girls was hysterical, crying and screaming, kicking and thrashing around. I asked the kids what she was on, but no one wanted to admit to anything. Then the Phillips boy said she had eaten mushrooms. I swear I don't understand kids these days. Anyway, Joe and I got hold of her and took her up to the chapel. I held her real close and whispered in her ear. She struggled something awful. Slowly I was able to calm her down. I told her the colors were good and the light was love. I repeated this over and over until her crying became sobbing, until I thought my heart would break. I asked her what was wrong to make her cry so hard. She said he took it. He took it and she couldn't get it back. No one would ever love her because he took it at night when no one was around to stop him. I got an image of an older man sneaking into her room and I could feel her fear. Poor soul was broken inside like a glass doll. I held her and rocked her like she was my own child. I couldn't put the pieces back together."

"It goes on," Amanda said, "Aunt Mary was amazing.

I collected a dozen or so notebooks and put them into an empty box. Amanda did the same. We took our collections down stairs and back into the kitchen. "Now, you've got to bring those back. I'm responsible for them and I want them back."

"We understand," I said, and Amanda agreed. We took our journals and left.

The night was cold and clear. I could feel the stars shimmer and move against the jet-black dome of the atmosphere. I noticed the big dipper and then Orion's belt, I picked out Venus and Aries the ram. I admit I was pretty high, and very aware of everything. I smelled the cold in the air, felt it settle on my face and water my eyes. The hum of the engine, the roll of the tires on the road added a rhythm to the ride. It occurred to me to ask, "Hey, how long have you been getting high?"

She curled up next to the door with her hands inside her coat sleeves. "What?" she replied in a sleepy little girl's voice.

"You heard me," I said. "How often do you go visit Uncle Jimmy and suck the gnome's head?"

She giggled, and then moved over to lay her head on my shoulder, "I don't know, maybe once a week this summer. Jimmy was real paranoid about it for a while. I think he liked the company."

"I didn't get high until college," I said.

"Well," Amanda said pulling her feet up in the seat and snuggling into my shoulder. "You didn't have the shit I have to deal with."

"What shit is that?" I asked.

"I don't want to talk about it," she said.

I liked her snuggled against my arm, curled up on the seat beside me, so I let it go. That day, the gnome on Jimmy's porch, the warm meal and the drive back to town, the memory of it all stirs an emotion I can't quite explain. It's a good thought whenever it passes by. It was late, much later than I had thought. It would be close to midnight before I got home. I was worried about Amanda.

"Are you OK to drive?" I asked.

"I'm fine," she assured me. Before she got out of my car she asked, "Hey, what do you want me to do when I find something important in the journals?"

I told her to write down the information in a separate notebook. Try to look for names she recognized or family names from the area. "If it's real important call me at the paper."

Chapter 27

I was at my desk working on a story for the Wednesday edition, the social happenings from Dannebrog. Mr. and Mrs. Arnold Allen had hosted family and friends in celebration of their fiftieth anniversary. Their oldest, James Allen from Minnesota attended with his wife Kelly Patterson-Allen and their three children. The gathering was held at the First Christian Church of Dannebrog. It was big doings in a small town. When I graduated from J school I knew I would have to earn my stripes as it were. I expected to write obits and classified ads. Covering the social happenings of small towns within the circulation of the Phonograph was the most painful and humiliating writing I could think of. Every small gathering recorded in bland newspaper style. Who, what, when, where and why using the vocabulary of an eighth grader and the imagination of a drill Sergeant. Sarge yelled for me from the door of his office. "Beam, in my office, now!"

Without hesitation I grabbed up my notebook and headed for the editor's office. Sarge's office had frosted glass windows halfway down the walls on three sides; the interior wall had woodgrain paneling. This effect meant you could see shadowy movement, but no clear impression of what was going on. I cautiously entered, prepared to bolt for the door if he began to throw things. "You wanted to see me," I said.

"Sit down," he said with a cigarette jutting out from between his lips as he shuffled papers. He stacked the papers into the IN box on the right corner of the desk, took a puff on the cigarette and let out a billowing cloud of smoke to mix with the haze of smoke clouds hovering overhead.

I took the chair, but wasn't comfortable. The furrow of his brow let me know he was upset, but for the life of me I couldn't figure out why. I was ahead of schedule on my stories. I hadn't been late to work or missed a deadline. His question made me realize I was thinking too narrowly in my evaluation of his frustration.

"Beam, what in the hell have you been up to?" he asked rhetorically. "I got a call this morning from the sheriff up in Broken Bow. He says you're up there messing around with some schoolgirl. Tells me the father is considering statutory rape charges. Folks are upset and I need to know what in the hell is going on!"

All I heard was rape charges and sheriff. "Sarge, I don't know what to say. I, I'm."

"You're what Beam? Son you better start talking, or the shit is going to hit the fan," he said.

"I've never so much as kissed Amanda Steward," I began.

"So, you've been up there sparking with some little girl," he said with enough disappointment to shatter my esteem.

"No!" I said, "I've been working on a story and she's been helping me with some background work."

"A story for the paper?"

"Not exactly," I said. "It personal. Just an idea really."

"You better explain," he said crossing his arms.

"Okay," I took a deep breath. "I came across a story about..." here I hesitated, which caused Sarge's eyebrow to raise in a suspicious way. "Son, you better not bullshit me," he warned.

I took a deep breath. "There is a cross and chapel outside of Broken Bow, the story about the light burning out?" I hoped he remembered the article. "Anyway, there is a huge cross just outside of Broken Bow. I found the man who made it, Amos Tensley; he told me an amazing story about a lady named Mary Steward. Mary and Joe Steward owned the land the cross is on; Joe's still alive and living in Ravenna. The thing is, this story is unbelievable, crazy really but from what I can find out it may be true."

"Son, you better start making sense real soon," the big man said leaning forward.

"See, this story has me and the more I dig, the deeper it pulls me. I can't let it go and I feel like I'm at the edge of something important."

"Let me see it," he said.

"The thing is, I haven't written anything, yet."

He scowled at me. "What does this have to do with the girl?"

"She is the niece of Mary Steward. She's just helping me with research some", I hesitated to put a word to it, "historical elements of the story." I couldn't decide just how much to tell him. I wasn't sure if I could put it into words, or at least ones that wouldn't get me institutionalized or jailed.

"Joe Steward claims his wife was visited by a stranger, an angel, for the lack of a better word. The angel, Gabe, told them to commission the cross, the one Tensley made, and build a small chapel for people who needed a place to rest. Amos told me a remarkable story before he died."

"Died?" Sarge barked.

"Yes sir, he told me this incredible story just a week before he died. I have journals, written by Mary Steward, telling about events and people, locals and travelers, who had spiritual, even supernatural experiences while staying there. I'm talking real honest to God miracles." I took a breath and went on. "Now, I know this sounds crazy but this woman has recorded hundreds of events, in the most straightforward, common everyday language. It's hard for me not to accept them as something significant." I couldn't believe I had said this out loud.

Sarge was leaning back. "Tell me one of these significant events."

I thought hard about which story to tell. They were all running together in my head. "I have her journals, one is in my desk. Let me go get it."

He motioned with his head to go. I ran to my desk, pulled out the journal on the top and returned to his office. I hadn't read much of it, but I hoped it would provide some proof that I wasn't crazy. I wasn't sure how it could prove I wasn't a rapist. I rushed back into the office, dropped in the chair and begin rifling through the pages.

"Willy," Sarge said. "Give me the journal."

I didn't move to hand it over. I had worked so hard to get these. I'd been to Uncle Jimmy's and dug around in the attic for them. Could I trust Sarge with them? What would he do with it?

"I will give it back," he said. "I promise." His tone was softer now; his face less red.

I begrudgingly handed it over. "Sir, I know this must sound silly, but these stories are real. The whole thing is unearthly, but somehow I know it's for real."

That was the first time I'd said to myself or anyone else that the stories were real. I told Jimmy I believed them, that didn't make them real. I knew Mary was able to heal people, mend broken bones and maybe even souls. She was touched by something greater and she used it for good. Something else I knew at that moment; there was a reason I had hold of this story, or it had hold of me, in particular. I had to follow it for a reason. I didn't know why or what it would lead me to, but I was going to find out.

"Okay," Sarge said. "Let's pretend for a moment that I believe you. What have you done to get the sheriff and everyone all worked up?"

"I don't know," I said. "I honestly don't know..."

It started snowing around lunch time. I could see the hard cold pellets dancing and swirling in the wind. It was just a dusting at two o'clock, but by four, the flakes were falling sideways like white rain. The snow piled up on cars and along the sidewalks. The first snow of the season always felt magical carrying the promise of the holidays, of Christmas and New Year's, of candy canes and hot chocolate, the smell of pine trees and turkey with stuffing. I don't pretend to be anything but nostalgic, a fool for traditions. The sight of snow falling outside the window filled me with a holiday spirit. I was such a child. Working in a newsroom full of men who knew this white stuff falling on the roads and bridges could mean accidents, stranding people with possibly tragic outcomes made my images of jolly old elves, twinkling stars atop a fur tree with presents beneath seem extremely naive.

"Oh, shit this could be bad," Mike said, standing by the teletype, pulling a weather report from off the wire.

"Check with the sheriff and keep a scan of the monitor tonight," said Sarge. "Someone's going to end up in the ditch before this is done."

"Or worse," another replied.

Sarge called the troops to attention. "Alright people, this storm is expected to dump ten to twelve inches overnight with wind gusts thirty to forty miles an hour. The temperature will drop quickly. The weatherman says the wind chill factor is going to feel like fifteen below. If you need to get home to take care of pipes or family, better go do it now."

A couple of the guys went for their coats. Sarge went on. "I'll need someone to stay and keep tabs on accident reports and possible news stories. Willy, I think you'll be fine for the job."

I was a little surprised; then again it made perfect sense. I was the one to stay and hold down the fort. I had no family or pets that needed me. I could do this. "Sure boss," I said.

The rest of the staff began to finish up projects and gather up material to take home. I knew many of them would work at home and still be in early the next morning. It would give me a chance to review my story before submitting it for Sarge's editorial cutting. I felt like I was getting better at cutting out the bull-crap, as Sarge called it. Sarge liked the news to be crisp and true, not big on speculation or conjecture so his style was my style, sharp and clean. Still I liked to wax a little when I could.

"Willy, can I see you in my office," I heard Sarge say. His tone bothered me. It was not like him to use a mild address.

"Hey boss," I said standing in the doorway.

"Come in," he said and nodded toward the chair. I cautiously again took a seat.

"I've been reading this journal," he said. "You're correct; there is some truly unbelievable stuff in here." He tapped the cover of the journal on his desk. "Tell me again how you got this?"

I wasn't prepared to tell everything about how I got them, what to leave in, what to leave out?

"Well," I began. "I got them from James McCoy, the nephew of Mary and Joe Steward. I believe he got them from Joe before he went to the home." Sarge's face was fixed in that "go on" look he would give me when I'd only half answered a question. "James is Amanda's uncle, or at least that's what she calls him, I'm not exactly sure of the actual family tree."

"How many of these notebooks does Uncle James have?" Sarge asked.

"I don't know, a hundred, maybe more," I said. "Why?"

"And you've seen them?" Sarge asked.

"Yes," I said. I wasn't sure where this line of questions was going.

"How many of these books do you have?" he asked.

"I had six at first and then we went back the other night and we took a sampling from several boxes, so about fifteen or so."

Sarge looked at the journal on his desk. His gaze was odd, sort of lost in thought. I was curious and cautions. What had he read, was he upset, or mad? Was he worried about the phone call earlier, and was I about to get fired?

"'Night boss," Bill from sales said, sticking his head in the door and breaking the spell.

"Goodnight, drive safe," Sarge said. He got up from his chair, walked over to close the door. I was close to panicking. I was about to get fired. Would I still have to stay all night? He must have gotten another call from the sheriff. I was thinking "Oh, shit, Oh, shit here it comes."

"Will, I want you to consider dropping this whole thing up in Broken Bow. Whatever work you've done on it has been a distraction. It would be better if you let this be." He was standing, towering over me. His expression was now of a commanding officer, a drill instructor.

"What," I began.

"Listen to me son," Sarge said. "This stuff is no good. This business with the girl looks bad. These journals are distracting you from your job. You have the potential to be a good newspaper man, but if you go tracking this stuff it could ruin that."

I was intimidated by his stance and demeanor; it left me with little room to argue.

"Okay," I said. "But..."

"No 'but' son," Sarge said. "You need to return these things, stop going up to Broken Bow and stay away from this girl. Is that clear?"

There was nothing to say, "Yes sir."

Later, I sat in the dim light of the newsroom and watched the snow come down; big white blowing flakes were piling up against the doors and windows. The wind howling out of the north caused the snow to swirl, obscuring my view out. The blizzard piling up around the building made me feel lonely. I was sad for me and mad at Sarge for his power over me, confused by the sheriff calling and a little angry at Mary for dragging me into this mess. Mostly I was disappointed in myself for being such a coward.

But I was just too caught up in the whole thing now. Even though I told Sarge I was done with it, I wasn't. My gut told me there was more, more to the story, more than just Mary's side of the story and it bugged me not to know. Wasn't that the nature of a good reporter? Didn't the instinct to dig when people told you to stop make for a good reporter?

I was still perplexed by Sarge. True, I didn't know him very well, but in my time here he never looked unsure or pensive. Sarge was black and white, good and bad, clear lines of delineation. Today he was clearly upset, not just about the call from the sheriff. There was something in Mary's journals that bothered him, made him uneasy. The uneasiness was important, maybe the key to something and everything.

A crackled voice from the police monitor pulled me from my thoughts. "Single vehicle accident, Hwy 281, ten miles north of St. Paul, south of Hwy 22 near Wolbach. Officers on scene to investigate."

I logged the information as Sarge had instructed. He said to record anything and we would follow up in the coming days. I thought we could just pull the accident report from the sheriff's office later. The boss was adamant; we needed our own record to refer to so I kept an ear open for updates, but I was only half listening; my mind drifted to the journals. Sarge had given me back the one he read. I took the journal from the drawer in my desk. Its cover was dark blue with a manufacturer's logo on it along with the months and year; July and August 1961. I let it fall open and began to read.

July 12, 1951

Joe and I walked the fences today and it was hot. It must've been 98 degrees or better and the ground is so dry. If we don't get rain soon we'll have to start selling off some of the calves. Can't keep em alive and it's better to get something for them, even at a loss. We keep praying the good Lord will send rain, and if he don't, we'll make do.

July 15, 1951

The radio weatherman says a storm is coming. I hope it brings rain and not a bad storm. The clouds are angry this morning and I can smell rain in the air. That smell makes me happy, but something in the wind makes me uneasy. Joe went to put feed out; I hope he makes it back before this storm hits.

July 16, 1951

We got an inch and a half of rain in the gauge. The whole world smells clean and fresh as Eden. I love the smell, it refreshes my soul to breathe it in and feel the dampness on my skin. Joe was happy to see it rain, maybe we can keep the calves as well as the cows. I know the humidity is going to rise and it will be sweltering this afternoon. But we give thanks for the small miracles and take the good with the bad then make the best of it. What does the Bible say, the rain falls on both the righteous and unrighteous.

July 20, 1951

We went to town shopping this morning. The heat was rising up off the sidewalk something terrible. It made my head hurt by the time we got done. Saw Betty and Nadine, had a good visit while Joe was in the hardware store. Nadine looked tired. I know those kids are a handful still she just didn't look like she was well. I told Joe I was worried about her and so we planned to stop by and visit her on Sunday.

July 22, 1951

The chapel called me today. I hadn't felt a pull like this in a while. Oh, there have been plenty of travelers and visitors. Most just need a place to rest and a drink of water, a cool spot out of the heat. It's always strange to me this little chapel stays so cool in the summer when everyplace else is so hot. Anyway, I went up to check on the place and there was a soldier there, a teenager. He was all dressed up in his uniform sitting on a pew with his head down. He must've been praying and came to full attention when I came in. He had the most intense brown eyes. He looked like he was going to salute. I almost chuckled. I could tell he was so pained in his heart, I couldn't stand to hurt him.

He said he was back from basic training and was about to be deployed. He was worried about his family and being so far from home. I let him talk for a while. His father, Galen Parks, had a farm over close to Palmer and his brothers were helping with that. His mother was real worried about him. He supposed it was normal for her to worry. It took him a while, but he finally got around to the fact that he was scared of going to war. He knew it was possible, likely in fact that he was going to have to kill. He remembered the Ten Commandments posted at his grade school and his momma telling him, 'Thou Shall Not Kill' and as much as he wanted to defend his country he didn't want to spend eternity in hell for it. I offered to pray with him and we did. He was still so worried that I decided to tell him the secret.

The monitor crackled again. "Dispatch, this is unit 210. I have a truck off the road near Saint Libory, south of 59 off 281 and Saint Paul road. Send tow truck, trailer is blocking the south bound lane."

"Roger; any injuries?" asked dispatch.

"Negative. Driver is uninjured. Just need to get the road cleared ASAP," the voice said. I recorded the incident and went back to reading:

I decided to tell him a secret that Gabe had shared with me. "We're the creation of a loving and merciful God, a God of light and forgiveness. We are made up of three elements, matter, spirit and soul. The matter, which all this earth is made of is our body and it's a temporary thing. The spirit is the energy that makes us alive, able to walk, talk, think, eat, sleep, breathe and all the other good and bad things we do in our bodies. That is a fleeting energy that will leave this earthly body someday. Our soul, the breath of God, made in the image of God, from the light at the center of the universe, is eternal and will return to God. Hell is a creation from the imagination of man. Yes, there is real evil in this world and we should never invite it in, but our souls belong to the Infinite and will return there. He asked how that could be. If there was no hell then why be good? I told him because there is accountability, you will meet the God of the Universe and there will be an answer to give. I believe the loving God will offer mercy at another time for all of us."

I stopped reading. I sat looking at the snowfall and listened to the wind howl. A dawn of understanding rose in my thoughts. Maybe a problem Mary presented to the churches, to the community as a whole was the fear of hell as a powerful motivator in the Christian faith; the need for salvation from hell, the reason for the cross, the crucifixion, and resurrection all centered on a fear of damnation. What was Mary talking about? This was blasphemy to some and foolish to others, but no Hell, what was the alternative?

The alternative was love. God is Love, right? But then again, the punishment for sin is death and damnation. The wages of sin are death, wailing, and gnashing of teeth, a casting into outer darkness. I've occasionally thought of God as an angry old man demanding to be loved or else, but I knew that image was sinful. I heard a teacher at camp say the simple and complicated commandment of Jesus is to love thy neighbor, without limitation or restrictions, without question and without boundaries. If God commands us to love and forgive our neighbors as he has forgiven us, then how can Hell be the place where so many of us will end up?

I paced the room, talking this through to myself. Was this what bothered Sarge? Because it bothered me. I know Jesus is the example of faith. His death, burial, and resurrection the bridge to God and salvation. But what about all the people who never heard of Jesus or those Jews who came before? What about all those who came before Jesus? Did God condemn all the souls for thousands of years before the crucifixion to an eternity in hell?

It seemed harsh and unfair, to have been born in Egypt or North America or China, a thousand years before Alexander or Cesar, to be punished for time and fate. I thought about the Indians and their everywhere god; was that a different voice of God? Mary said we all return to the Infinite. Did we return to be judged, to have sentence passed, and then cast to the lake of fire? That's not how I read her secret. She said, Hell was a figment of our imagination, but accountability was required. She was talking about the infinite nature of a soul; the soul we cannot see or touch or measure, but everyone is sure we have. Science couldn't identify the essence of the soul, but it must exist. This was unknowable, well beyond my level of reasoning. I spent the rest of the night pondering the passage of Mary's journal while keeping track of the accidents and incidents.

I trudged home around five o'clock in the morning. There was a foot of snow on the ground, drifts twice that high and mounds of white plowed from the streets by the city road crew. I thought as I made my way along. "The practical, logical, safe thing to do is to mail the journals back to Jimmy and forget the whole thing. The job, my career, my health would be better off if I took Sarge's order to heart. My father would tell me to be smart, do your job and leave this crazy business with all its questions in Jimmy's attic. It wasn't worth it."

I had all but decided to be practical. Then, just as I reached the foot of the steps up to apartment, I decided all that logic and practicality was really just another name for cowardly. It stunk with the sick sour skunky odor of self-preservation. There are a handful of moments in a person's life when you have to truly confront yourself. Rarely, in a modern lifetime, does the average citizen really have to decide on a course of action; knowing the consequences will reverberate throughout a lifetime. Okay, that's a little melodramatic, but I knew in my heart of hearts, my next move was going to somehow define what I thought of myself for years to come. I could choose inaction to avoid making a decision. I've done that before and would do it again. But to lie fallow, to just let it be, would feel as timid as lying down and taking a beating. So I walked to my apartment in the muffled cold, along streets blanketed in snow my decision in hand. I decided I would have to be more careful about who I talked to and careful about Amanda. I'd need to be more focused at work, but my time out of Sarge's newspaper offices was my own and I wouldn't let it go. I couldn't, not yet. There was a reason I had come here, a purpose to all this; an explanation would only be revealed by following the story wherever it might lead.

Chapter 28

Winter came with an angry blast, with ice in its breath and snow following in its wake. I stepped out on the landing of my apartment, tasted the swirling flakes and watched a full moon beam its cold blue light on the rooftops to create jagged shadows in the street below. I shoveled snow from my doorstep and scraped ice from the windows of my car. I was afraid the weather might keep me here for Christmas, but the day before the holiday the sun broke through, snowplows moved, and my pathway home was clear. My arrival late on Christmas Eve brought tears to my mother's eyes. She cooked for an army. Dad and I were obligated to do our best to consume the feast. It took a supreme effort and several settings to make a dent.

I got a sports coat, three pairs of slacks, button down shirts, practical items like underwear and socks, along with a new pair of dress shoes. Long gone were the days of toys and games. The things I needed were things I could use for my new grownup life. I appreciated them, smiling and thanking my parents for each gift. Secretly, I had wished for something selfish, impractical, and childish.

Christmas day, 1983, across the Great Plains, was one of the coldest on record with dangerously cold temperatures from Wichita, Kansas to Fargo North, Dakota. A hundred and twenty-five cities east of the Rocky Mountains set record lows for the day. My father commented on a story in the news in which long range forecasters predicted as to the coming of a next ice age. It warned that these types of winters would become the norm in the coming decade. We stayed close to the fire. I slept out in the den to be warm. We watched "M.A.S.H.", "Dukes of Hazzard" and "White Christmas". Later, Mom put Dean Martin's Christmas album on and we drank hot chocolate.

The weather was still bad when I packed up to head back. Mom was holding back tears as I waved goodbye. Dad had already gone off to work. He put a hundred dollars in my billfold, which I found when I pulled over for lunch outside of Lincoln. The heater in my car was having a hard time keeping the car warm and the ice off my windshield. I stopped at a station at the York exit. The attendant didn't find anything wrong, "It's just cold," he said with a shrug.

It was starting to sleet by the time I reached Aurora. I thought about stopping in Grand Island, but it was only thirty miles to St Paul. The sleet turned to ice; the ice began to form on my windshield. When I got to Helgoth's corner, my view of the road was the size of a softball. I pulled over to scrape the ice off. The wind chill was dangerously low, and I was sure frostbite was forming on my nose. The side windows were completely iced over. I rolled the driver's side window down a little to see before pulling back onto the road. It's a narrow road with a shallow shoulder; my wheels spun in the ice. I pressed hard on the accelerator to get off the shoulder. The tires screeching as they spun, then one caught at the edge of the pavement. Suddenly the car lurched forward and sideways onto the road, into the oncoming lane. I looked up to see a truck coming, its headlights bearing down on me through the frosted haze of the windshield. The driver blew his horn. I was sliding and all at once the car righted itself, jerking hard right, back into the north bound lane and out of the way of the oncoming semi. I felt the blast of air fill the cab of the car through the open driver side window.

My heart was pounding. I let go an exhale I must've been holding in expectation of my impending doom. I pulled off at the next county road to gather myself. I couldn't explain how I had gotten out of the way of the truck or why I was sitting here in one piece and not a bloody mess strung halfway to Grand Island. I know some would simply thank their lucky stars and drive on. I didn't. I couldn't.

I recognized the significance. I felt it was a sign, perhaps an angelic intervening. I know this is where the skeptic brushes such moments aside as chance or luck. I'm not a skeptic. Besides, it was my life and I hadn't had time for it to pass before my eyes. I took a deep breath and prayed. I thanked God for saving me and hoped he would see me the rest of the way through.

A team of scientists at the Arctic Circle recorded temperatures of minus 128 degrees. The temperatures stayed so low for so many days, the scientists believed their equipment had stopped working. In fact, that winter was one of the coldest ever recorded on the planet Earth. In Nebraska, the total snowfall for that year was twenty-one inches, the most snow to accumulate since the twenties. The wind never stopped blowing. The cold stole my breath away in a second. All one could do was lower one's head and lean into it. I felt like I was leaning into an oncoming storm. I worked at the paper, covered the basketball games for the area teams, and read Mary's journals. She was my Valentine during the coldest, bleakest winter of my life. I read each journal cover to cover, over and over. She was amazing and humble in her ways. I could imagine some people in her situation would become self-absorbed or think very highly of themselves. Mary went about her day as a humble rancher's wife until someone needed her.

June 4, 1957

I went to the chapel yesterday to clean and lay out more bread and fruit. There was a young family there with a very sick child. The poor thing was running a very high fever. The mother, Debra, was so worried. The father, Sam, said they left out of Wyoming that morning and the little girl was fine. After lunch she had thrown up. They thought it was something she ate, but as the day went on she started running a fever. They were headed for Fremont where he had family. They pulled over when the child got sick again. He saw the cross and had a notion to bring her to the chapel. The poor thing was burning up, even though she was bundled up in a blanket. There was a terrible flu going around. I read somewhere where thousands died from it in Hong Kong. The news was warning of an influenza outbreak like they had back in the World War I years.

I had the father move the girl, so she was lying on the platform. I asked the mother if she would pray with me. We prayed together in silence and then something came over me. I knelt over the child three times. They must've thought I was crazy. I knew it was what I was supposed to do. I asked for the fever to pass. I went back to the mother and asked the father to join us in prayer. The father looked as spooked as a heifer in a hailstorm. He took my hand and prayed with us. I again went and knelt over the girl and asked for the sickness to pass. Then a third time I prayed with the family. I remembered the old healing prayer from my youth.

O merciful God, our heavenly father; we beseech thee in the name of this child, Melanie, and the family who loves her so. Lord we ask for thy healing power that she may be restored to health, body and mind. We pray in the name of Jesus Christ our Savior, Amen.

I then went a third time and knelt over her. Previously she had slept, her breathing shallow, her face pale and damp. This time, I felt her move beneath me. She opened her eyes and smiled. I felt her brow and it was cool. I took her by the hand and she got up. She was such a lovely little girl. She ran to her mother and hugged her. They made a perfect picture huddled there together hugging. I almost cried. I invited them up to the house for supper.

I wished a hundred times over I had picked up a box so I could keep reading. I would find myself at loose ends, wanting to know what had happened at the cross and chapel in the late summers and falls of 1957, 58 and 59. I read and reread the journals I had, looking for clues, searching for meaning. I found myself daydreaming about what the rest of the story was? What happened after they were touched by Mary? But there was no way to know.

I took solace in the small gyms reporting on the area basketball games on Tuesday and Saturday nights. I love high school basketball, all basketball for that matter; with the smell of a clean swept hardwood floor and the leather of the basketball, the bright lights and warm popcorn. I grew up watching Iowa Hawkeyes basketball. I chose Iowa State for journalism but, Big Ten basketball was the best, with the volatile Bobby Knight and the undefeated Indiana Hoosiers; Magic Johnson and Greg Kessler from Michigan State. My all-time favorites were Lute Olson and the seventy-nine Iowa team led by Ronnie Lester, with a great supporting cast of Kenny Arnold, Steve Waite, Steve Krafcison, Vince Brookins, Kevin Boyle, Bobby Hanson and Mark Gannon. They won the outright Big Ten title that year and went all the way to the final four.

During the semifinals game against Louisville and their high-flying point guard, Darrel Griffith, aka Dr. Dunkinstien, Ronnie Lester scored the first ten points of the game. Then he twisted a knee. Iowa hung tough until the end, finally losing by eight to the great Denny Crum team. The Cardinals would go on to win the NCAA tournament. I think about what might have been if Ron hadn't gotten hurt; I loved that team.

I played a lot of basketball and was pretty good, good enough to come off the bench at Valley High School when I was a sophomore and start most of my junior and senior year. I played intramural games at Iowa State and cheered like a banshee at Cyclones games, but in my basketball heart I was a Hawkeye.

Covering local basketball games was a respite for my troubled spirit. The St. Paul team was alright. They lacked any real height. The tallest kid was six foot one at best. They listed him at six three; all coaches lie about the height of their players. The Greely and Centura teams were good. They played tough defense and a motion offense based on screens and back-door cuts. Everyone played the same old boring two-three zone defense. The kids had no patience for breaking the zone. You have to make it move from side to side to open up the lane and then when you get inside the zone, don't rush. Be quick but don't hurry, fast but don't rush. Look for the shot first, then to the corners. When the zone collapses, its holes are exposed. The problem is, it takes discipline and coaching. The zone makes players impatient and so they jack up a shot from the outside. The percentages are low for most high school players to hit consistently from eighteen to twenty feet out. Instead of working for an easier shot, they take the first open shot and miss. Therefore, the zone defense wins.

It was odd for me to watch girls play full court basketball. In Iowa the girls play three on three with the center line as the divide between the two halves. I'm sure it was intended to protect the "delicate nature of girls" back when the game was invented but because of tradition and coaching it had stayed that way in Iowa. Since the 1970's, Nebraska girls played full court like the boys and it was strange for me to watch. The problem with girls playing five on five is the scores are so low. Sometime the winning team only scores twenty-five points or less. Still, getting paid to report on basketball was not a bad gig.

I prayed for warmer weather and my prayers went unanswered. The snow kept falling and blowing, with mounds of it pushed to the side of the road on the four lanes or piled up at the edge of parking lots. My images of soft holiday snowflakes had become crusty, black, ugly piles of mush. Through the cold, I slogged back to my apartment. With the leftovers and supplies sent back at Christmas long gone now, I dined on variations of ramen noodles, mac and cheese or hamburger helper. The nice thing about helper is it can last for two meals. The menu this evening would be tuna helper tetrazzini, on account of lent. Whenever Ash Wednesday came around, the price of tuna dropped to accommodate the Catholic's commitment to not eat meat during lent. I made no such commitment; but, when tuna is twenty-five cents a can, I could be persuaded to eat fish.

I had achieved the proper boiling point and reduced the heat when there was a knock at the door. I jumped at the noise. I approached the door with excitement and suspicion. I peeked through the blinds covering the plate glass in the top half of the door. It was dark; a pale moonlight gave an eerily silver shadow to the person on my doorstep. The figure had turned away but from the shape and size, it was a girl. She turned back toward the door and to my shock, it was Amanda hopping up and down and blowing in her hands.

I jerked the door open and said, "What are you doing here?"

She brushed past me and into my small living room. She looked around at the modest furnishings, hurriedly tiptoeing over to stand by the heating vent. "It's freezing out there," she said.

I repeated my question, "Amanda, what are you doing here?"

She replied in a mocking voice, "Could you be a little happy to see me? It's not like I had to sneak out and drive on icy roads all the way from Broken Bow to see you or anything."

She pulled off her scarf and blue stocking cap and shook out her hair. Dancing in front of the heater she said. "Something smells good, what's for dinner?"

I was standing by the door with my hand on the knob. Her comment about the smell made me rush for the stove to check the tuna and noodles. I fumbled with a spoon as I stirred the simmering concoction. With some effort I saved it from sticking to the pan and becoming a mess. The distraction gave me a moment to think. "Why did you drive on icy roads from Broken Bow?" I asked.

"To see you!" She called. "Why the hell else would I come to Ain't Paul," she smiled at her joke.

I put the lid back on the pan and returned to the front room. "Amanda, you shouldn't be here."

She stopped prancing by the heater. "Why not? You said you needed my help and then you just disappeared. I was worried and then I got mad; you wouldn't take my calls, when you told me to call, so I decided I would come see you."

I walked over to stand in front of her. "Look, I'm sorry I got you mixed up in this. I should've left you alone and..." I looked down at my feet and tried to find some explanation.

"And what," she said with real sadness in her voice.

"Amanda, honey," I said. "They called my boss, He said I should stay away from Broken Bow and you. It could cost me my job."

"Who is they?" she asked. "My father, that fat ass Sheriff Barkley?"

I nodded and looked down at my feet, again.

"Well, I say, screw'em if they can't take a joke." She smiled and let out a little laugh.

"This is no joke," I said. "I wanted to talk to you, but was afraid I'd get you in trouble, more trouble than I had already caused."

"Willy," she said with a cock of her head, "I was born in trouble and have been looking for every opportunity to cause more ever since."

"Well, I wasn't and don't need trouble now," I said.

"What," she said with a touch of anger. "You're going to start some crap and then just walk away? You're a coward if you make me go."

I could say nothing. I tried to look upset. I wanted to send her away. I truly wanted to do the responsible thing, but now that she was here, I was really glad to see her. I had been so alone.

I shook my head and asked, "Do you want some tuna helper?"

She nodded and took off her coat while I went to get two plates and then cleared a place to eat. We sat on the couch, our plates on the garage sale coffee table and ate tuna tetrazzini. We watched Happy Days on my thirteen-inch black and white TV, as the wind howled and rattled the windows.

"So, was there something in particular you risked life and limb to come see me about?" I asked.

"Oh crap, I completely forgot," she jumped up, hurried across the room to where she dropped her things and shuffled through the bag she had dropped there with her coat. "I've been reading the journals and I found something interesting." She brought the notebooks over to the couch and sat with them on her knees. "There's an entry from August of nineteen sixty-one that got me thinking."

She opened the journal on top, hurriedly flipping through pages. Her excitement was hardly contained; her face lit up as her eyes danced across the pages. "Here we go," she said, holding the book sideways, inviting me to move closer to read.

"I'm very happy, we've sold the cows and calves at a good price and Joe won a ribbon at the State Fair prize for Belted Galloways. It's been a good season. Elizabeth has settled out west. She sent me a postcard from California last week and it was hopeful. Somedays my thoughts wonder about that precious child. My hopes are great for him and the young couple. I know they will be good parents. I miss him and hope the best for him. Maybe someday I'll see him again. God only knows how or when that will happen."

I looked up, "What? I don't understand."

"This is the only entry I can find from that winter. This is the only reference I've found about a baby." She bugged her eyes a little to prod me to follow her thinking. After a pause she said, "I've been organizing the boxes, trying to put them into order, and some are missing."

"Missing?" I asked. "What's missing?"

"I can't find some of the journals from nineteen sixty."

"What do you mean, some?"

She exhaled in frustration. "Okay, here's the deal. I go along with the dates, most of the journals are in order. The boxes are in some semblance of order, going back to nineteen forty-seven. When I get to nineteen sixty the months from January to about mid-April are there, then it gets spotty."

"Spotty," I say, more interested now.

"There are a few weeks towards the end of April that are gone. She started a journal in May, then nothing until Thanksgiving and only one journal the week of Christmas."

"Then what?"

"Then nothing," she says with a mixture of excitement and anticipation. "There's nothing until later February of 1961."

"Are you sure?"

"Hell yes, I'm sure. I've got most of the boxes arranged. Well there's one more group of boxes to work on, but they all seem to be from later. Nothing before seventy-one. Then I was looking through a stack of journals, not in a box and that's where I found this entry."

I re-read the entry. I didn't really get what Amanda was poking at.

"Don't you see?" she asked. "There's a reference to a baby, a baby boy that Mary gave to a couple who didn't have a child."

Slowly a realization blossomed in my mind. I didn't really want to touch it. I looked at Amanda. She was smiling, almost bouncing up and down with excitement. "It's you," she said. "It's got to be you!"

"No, it doesn't." I said with plenty of uncertainty in my voice.

"Yes, yes, hell yes it does," she said. "Look, it makes perfect sense."

"It doesn't make any sense," I protested.

"It could be you," she responded. "It's you. I know it's you."

"Where are the rest of the journals?" I asked.

"Exactly!" She was almost hopping up and down. "That's the question. What happened to the journals? Why are all the rest of Mary's notebooks there and in order except a six or seven-month time in 1960?"

"Wait! A pregnancy takes nine months," I said.

"Well no shit Sherlock," she replied. "The mother may not have known she was pregnant for a couple of months or she may not have gone to Mary until she was sure. Come on reporter, ask the questions."

I started to roll it around in my head. Amanda was right, there were some real interesting questions.

"I'm really happy you brought me this, but I'm not sure, not ready to..."

Amanda dropped her shoulders. "Are you kidding me? Come on, I bring you this unbelievable gift. A true mystery with all kinds of possibilities and you're all, mister doubting Thomas?"

Her eyes flashed a fire of anger. "Well screw you!" She slammed the journal closed and got up. She went to her things and started picking them up.

Amanda's outburst caught me off guard. "I'm sorry," I said. "I just need a minute to get my brain around it. I mean it's a little much, don't you agree?"

She didn't reply, she just threw on her coat and pulled her stocking cap from the pocket.

"Wait," I said. "What are you doing?"

"I'm going home," she said. "I came all this way to show you this and, well, I expected you to be a little more, more excited, inquisitive maybe."

"I'm sorry," I stepped between Amanda and the door. "Stop, okay, let me think about this a moment."

Amanda stood her ground but didn't move to leave. I put my hands on my hips, ran one hand through my hair and exhaled. My mind was racing with questions; some I didn't really want to ask. The wind blew. The windows rattled. Amanda stood impatiently silent. "Okay, so Mary helped a girl, named Elizabeth, who had a baby and she gave the baby boy to a couple somewhere, that's all we really know," I said.

Amanda stuck out her chin, "We know there are volumes of Mary's journals missing that would cover the time that Elizabeth would've been pregnant."

"Which means what, exactly?"

"Are you deliberately being an ass?" she asked. "It means someone didn't want them talking about the pregnancy or the baby left for anyone to find."

"Why?"

"I don't know," she said. "That's what makes it interesting! Maybe she's the daughter of someone who didn't want people to know she had a baby out of wedlock. Maybe the mother was raped and someone is covering up a scandal or maybe her family wanted the evidence gone. There are all kinds of possibilities and one of those possibilities is that you are the baby."

"All right, let's just slow down a minute" I said, "the 'who' may be the motive for removing the journals." My mind was starting to work and the mystery started to pull. "Who put the journals in the boxes, or better yet when?"

"I asked Jimmy again if he put the journals in the boxes. He said they were given to him by some ladies from the church, but he didn't know which church. I think Joe broke his hip in 79. That's why the family sold the land. He couldn't manage the place any more. I remember daddy talking about buying the property, but for some reason the family let it go."

"Maybe Joe needed the money for the nursing home?" I asked. I turned and picked up a notebook from the coffee table and looked around for a pen. I saw one on the stand by the phone and crossed the room to get it. Amanda had to step aside to let me pass. The way to the door was open. She could leave if she still wanted to. To my relief, she put down her things and went over to pick up Mary's journal.

I sat on the sofa and began to scribble in the notebook. I always think better with a pen in my hand.

"Who is the first question but why may lead us to who," I said. "The how isn't important right now. We already know the what. When could be important and might bring us back to who."

"The question we need to ask is what," she said. I looked up as she sat next to me on the couch.

"What?"

"Yes, what," she said with a smile.

"No, we know what," I said

"We don't know what. We don't know crap about what."

"I know crap. What crap don't you know?"

She smiled, "What do you think you know?"

I smirked, "The 'what' is the pregnancy, the unwanted pregnancy of a girl in the early 1960's. Maybe she was a teenage girl with few options, probably scorned by her family, friends and church. That's enough of a what."

"Why scorned?"

"What?" I said, "It's just a word. I could use another, rejected."

"How about 'judged'?"

Okay, 'judged'," I said. "What difference does it make?

"The words we use are important, you should know that. How we use them says something about what we feel about people and things," she said.

I stopped to consider her. She was not just a girl to be protected or sheltered, instead, she was a person to be respected with whom one could debate, discuss and disagree. "You think 'judged' is better than 'scorned'?"

She shrugged, "I think maybe they should be joined."

"So, she was scorned and judged, which left her with no other option than to turn to Mary."

"Maybe she didn't turn to Mary?"

"What do you mean?"

"You've read enough of Mary's journals. People didn't turn to Mary, they were led to her, to the cross and chapel."

"You think?"

"I know!" She was only a foot away. Her hair had fallen onto her face. She brushed it aside with a flip of her head and a brush of her hand. I caught myself staring. Then it happened. I don't know who moved first. Suddenly her lips were on mine and my arms were around her. She pushed me backwards and down. She was so warm, her lips hot, our breathing urgent. I don't know when I've ever been so desperate. She pulled her shirt over her head, I unhooked her bra and she was pulling on my belt. We moved to the bedroom and she took charge. I thought maybe I was taking advantage but ultimately it was her passion that was satisfied. I was just happy to ride along.

I lay there in the stillness. Amanda's head was resting on my shoulder, snuggled up under the blankets. The room was cold, but she was warm and soft. I stared at the ceiling trying to work it out in my mind. Who took the journals? Who even knew Mary kept journals or what was in them? When did they get access to the boxes and what did they do with them? I thought, "Please let them not be destroyed." The 'what' may be important. My gut told me the 'who' was what we were looking for. The other what, where, why and how were clues to who.

Amanda stirred; I looked at the beautiful girl lying next to me. I remembered my college roommate saying, "Things get complicated after people take their clothes off." This situation had already been career damaging; now it could get life threatening if her daddy found out. I was sure Amanda could keep her secrets, just like I was sure tonight was not her first time. Those facts didn't make it any less dangerous. I've never been good at keeping secrets or telling lies. Amanda might be able to keep things quiet, but could I?

I woke up before dawn when I felt Amanda move. She was sitting on the side of the bed pulling on her jeans. She looked over her shoulder at me and raised an eyebrow. "I've got to go."

I nodded and said nothing. She bounced up off the bed, danced into her jeans and looked around for her bra before realizing it was out in the living room. Her hair was a mess and her mascara smeared. "You're beautiful," I said.

"Bullshit," she laughed as she adjusted her bra before pulling her shirt over her head.

"No, you're beautiful, to me." I got up and took her in my arms. She was looking around for her boots. I touched her face with my fingers to draw her attention to me. "You were what I needed."

She bit her lower lip. I pulled her to me and kissed her, soft at first, then with mouth open and desire. She pulled away a little, "I've got to go."

"In a minute," I said as I picked her up and playfully tossed her back on the bed. She giggled as I leaned over her. "I need to get back, before I get in trouble," she said with a smile.

"I thought you were trouble," I said. She resisted a little, just a little before she giggled and threw her arms up in surrender. This time she allowed me to feel I was in control. Truly, nothing was in my control. I hadn't been joking about her being trouble. We might be headed for trouble; at that moment I didn't care. I was emboldened, rebellious and fearless. She made me want to be that way. I wanted it to last, knowing full well nothing lasts, except memories and our regrets.

She left for good, before the eastern skyline turned to gold. I kept the notebook she left, along with the fragrance of her perfume, in my bed. I made coffee and got ready for work. I should have realized nothing would be the same after that morning; nothing would be as good as it had been in those frozen moments before sunrise.

Chapter 29

I made it to mid-afternoon before the big man called me into his office. "Willy, sit." I took the hard-wooden chair across from him and waited. "I thought I told you to stay away from that girl."

I was stunned, and my face betrayed my guilt.

"We agreed you would stay away from Broken Bow and leave the girl alone, correct?"

"Sir, I've not been to Broken Bow to see the girl." It was technically the truth, at least I could stand behind it.

"You're full of shit," Sarge snorted. "I got it on good authority a truck with four county plates was parked by your apartment until after midnight."

"So," I said with a shrug.

"So, boy, I suspect a girl was in your apartment last night."

"Yes, there was a girl at my apartment. I'm a grown man, and who comes to see me is my business," I said in defiance. Before Sarge could say another word, I attacked his position. "I'm twenty-two years old, out of college and of age in the legal sense. If I had company stay past midnight, that's none of anybody's business, sir. This little town knows everything going on and nothing about what's happening. I may have a girlfriend. She may be from North Loup or Ansley and she may drive a truck with four county plates, but that's between us."

Sarge leaned forward, drumming his fingers on the desk. "Are you telling me, whoever came to see you last night was not the girl from Broken Bow?"

I weighed my answer. "I'm telling you, and anyone else who wants to know; it's none of your business."

His eyes probed mine for weakness or hesitation, any hint of fear. Sarge curled his upper lip, snorted and sat back, and crossed his arms over his chest. "Willy, my boy, you're playing with fire and it's going to get you burned."

I held my gaze until he said, "Get back to work. I want to see the second draft of the Allen story before the end of the day."

"Yes, sir," I said, as I stood to leave.

Sarge wasn't finished, "You're leaving those journals alone I hope."

I stopped at the door, "Sir, I will read what I want in the privacy of my own apartment. I believe Orwell's Big Brother is at least a year away."

I hurried from his office, hoping he didn't come after me. Sarge had fought the communist in the bitter cold and he was not above letting me know just how proudly he had served his country.

That afternoon I strolled down Main Street on my way home. The sun broke through in the west, descended from the clouds like a character in a children's book. The glowing yellow light completely filled the space between the rows of buildings along the brick paved lane. As it touched down on the cobblestone street it paused, its fullness framed in my view with a ceiling of clouds with orange and purple highlights; it's borders the dark brick buildings on either side of the street and the base, an antique herringbone pattern of bricks at its feet. Its stunning yellow warmth, announcing beauty and wonder, were still in plain view, for those who have eyes to see and ears to listen. The majesty of God is all around us. The harshness and cold cannot stay. The season of darkness sometimes stretches out the long nights of winter, but must give way to renewal, revival and spring.

I needed to see the sunset as much as I needed Amanda to come crashing into my apartment. I may not have known it or wanted it, but I knew the bright untamed light was what I needed as much as anything. I felt a burning desire to explore the past and embrace the future, no matter the cost.

Here's my advice. When you're young, take chances. Risk big, dream bigger, and travel to new places. Make a bold regrettable move. The days of adventure are different for each of us. The size of one's comfort zone is malleable, but whatever it is, takes the chance. There will be plenty of time for safe bets and easy ways out. There are lots of avoidable conflicts, time to slip by, protect your losses and save face. There are only a few days in your whole life when you can risk it all on a game of pitch and toss; fill the unforgiving minute with sixty seconds of passion and running without fear of consequences. I don't promote reckless endangerments or criminal activity, but risk is a reward in your youth. Regret is a nagging bitch attended by a legion of haunting sadness.

That day, in the light of a magical sunset, was one of my days. I ran to my apartment, jumped in my car to chase that setting sun, toward Amanda, Uncle Jimmy and his stash of journals. Tomorrow I might be out of a job. So be it. I had enough money saved to make it a few months here. My parents would lend me a little more if I promised to come home by June. Sometimes you just have to say, "What the fuck!"

I headed west, but then at Hwy 11, detoured south following it down to Hwy 58, then up through Rockville. I cut off to 68 rolling down through Ravenna. I found myself walking up to the nursing home to visit Joe Steward. I hadn't thought about going to see him; I just stumbled upon the need to see Joe. I approached the nurse's counter with a cautious smile asking if I could see Joe Steward. She pointed toward a large dining area in the opposite direction from Joe's room. "He's having dinner. If you want, you can join him."

I walked toward the low hum of conversation. The dining room had a dozen round tables with six or eight chairs around each table. The food was served family style with bowls or platters of food at each table. A nurse sat with each group to help serve and clean up if something got spilled. It was almost like a church social.

I looked around for Joe, scanning the room for someone who looked familiar. Then I saw him looking at me. I tentatively waved and walked toward him, I couldn't be sure, but I got the feeling he had been expecting me.

"Hello there," he said turning in his chair to greet me.

"Do you remember me?" I asked.

"Why yes," he said, "You're Willy Beam, the reporter from Iowa."

"Yes, that's me. Can I join you?"

There was a chair open next to him with a plate and silverware set for a guest. Joe gestured for me to sit. "By all means, have a seat young man," he said with a spry smile. Two women dined at the table with us. One, frail and frayed, was dressed in a housecoat, her hair a mess. Her over-sized glasses fit poorly on her deeply wrinkled face. The other woman looked as if she might be coming from Sunday church in a fine fitting dress with a high collar, with her hair styled and sprayed, and with a bit of makeup and lipstick and her smiling eyes. The church lady nodded a socially correct welcome. The housecoat lady began to gum her meal without any sign of recognition.

"Willy, this is Gladys Thompson and Edna Bower," Joe said. "Ladies, this is Willy Beam. He's with the paper over in St. Paul."

Gladys, the church lady, said, "Very nice to meet you." Edna kept eating.

I nodded to each lady as I sat down at the table. "Very nice to meet you," I said. A nurse come over asking if I was going to eat. "No, thank you. I just stopped to say hi to Joe."

"You should eat," Joe said. "It's meatloaf. The cooks are very good." Something in his eyes convinced me to agree. His whole demeanor was something I hadn't anticipated. I wasn't sure what I was expecting since I hadn't planned to come. I thought maybe I would need to remind him who I was, to jog his memory about when I was last here. He acted so happy to see me and I was pleased to see him, like seeing a great uncle or grandfather. The nurse brought me a plate of meatloaf with mashed potatoes and green beans. Joe was right; it was good, like a home cooked meal, a damn site better than tuna helper.

"How's the story coming?" Joe asked.

"Which story is that," I replied.

"The one about Mary's cross and our old chapel."

I didn't recall we had spoken about me writing a story. I remember asking about Mary and the journals. Maybe I had led him to believe I was working on a story. I didn't remember telling him I was. "It's coming along," I said, realizing there was something I wanted to ask Joe. "Sir, could you tell me about Mary? What she looked like, how she was, anything about her would be helpful."

He grinned as he carefully chewed a bit of meatloaf. I thought he had missed my question with all the sound around us. I started to ask again when he said.

"Mary was my angel. She was as pretty as a picture from the day I met her till she passed. Never another woman caught my eye like she did."

"Where did you meet?" I asked.

He grinned, and his eyes twinkled "At a barn dance in the spring of forty-four. I was home from the service. She was standing against the wall with some of her friends. She was taller than the other girls, but that's not what made me ask her to dance. It was her eyes. They were as green as a field of spring grass and as inviting as heaven."

"I bet she was a doll," said Gladys leaning into our conversation from across the table.

"Oh, she was," said Joe. "To me anyway. Those eyes and her dark hair, I was smitten from the get go. We danced the Liddy, and then the band struck up a polka and she never missed a beat. She was sweet as pie and tough as boot leather," he said with an air of respect. "She was strong willed and stubborn as a Dane. She could be determined, and nothing was going to change her mind."

"How tall was she?" I asked.

"About five-six, as I recall. You know when we first got married and took over the ranch she would help with calving. I once saw her turn a breach calf around and pull it out without help or harm to the cow or calf." He laughed, "She was covered from head to foot in birthing fluid, but she held that calf like a baby and laughed with delight. I've never seen such joy."

"What else," I asked to keep the memories flowing. I realized in the course of Joe's story that I didn't know Mary the person at all. I knew her from her writing. I had some idea of how she saw herself and the world, but I didn't know her, not as Joe did.

"When I first brought her up here," he remembered, "the old place didn't have indoor plumbing. Had to go out to the well for water and we had an outhouse. Oh boy, she was not happy with that arrangement, believe you me. First thing I had to do come spring was get a pump house built and pipes run for indoor plumbing. She threatened to leave me if I didn't get her an indoor water closet."

"We didn't have indoor plumbing at our place until the kids came," said Gladys injecting herself into the conversation. "In fact we didn't have indoor plumbing until nineteen fifty two."

We all listened and smiled, and then I returned to my questions. "So, you and Mary didn't have any children?"

Joe shook his head slowly the smile fading. "No, she was unable to bear children. It broke her heart and mine too. All her sisters and brothers had a tribe of kids, not Mary. Sometimes on Sunday afternoons, when we had been over to my folk's place with all the kids around, running and playing, getting into trouble and causing a mess, we'd get back home and she would sit and cry. We tried and tried, each time something went wrong. It was terrible."

I hadn't intended to broach such a tender subject. I was embarrassed to have asked in such a casual way. Gladys went back to eating, not wanting to comment on the subject.

Edna said, "God's will."

I looked at her and asked, "Excuse me, what?"

"It's God's will. When something like that happens, my momma always said it was God's will. Either to teach a lesson or make you stronger. God only gives us what we can handle." She went back to chewing her food. The nurse at the table, who hadn't said a word to this point said, "Edna, that's enough" and began removing the plate and silverware from the table.

Joe was looking toward the windows across the room; his

expression morose. I was angry with Edna and myself. I had asked a painful question on a painful subject without thinking and Edna had opened up an old wound.

"Joe, are you alright?" I asked.

He slowly turned to me and nodded. "Can you walk me to my room?"

I helped him out of his chair. He walked bowlegged and gimpy. I remembered his hip had been broken; the injury forced him off the ranch. We walked slowly with Joe using a stout wooden cane as I held onto his other arm. His grip was strong as a vice. The old cowboy was strong but fading. I helped him into the recliner and took a seat in the hard-wooden chair by the bed.

"I've heard people say that all my life. God's will. Bullshit." He spit the words and wiped his mouth. "If it's God's will then it was his blessing that gave her the soul to endure it. If God willed it then God sent Gabe to have us build the chapel and the cross. To help people. I sometimes think it would've been too much for Mary to care for a child and for all the folks as well."

I sat with my head down and my hands clasped in front of me. The light from the hallway peeked into the room. A floor lamp gave the place a warm yellow glow; on a nightstand was a picture of Mary, standing next to a younger Joe. She was pretty or had been when she was younger. In the picture her arms were covered to her elbow, her face a little weathered. Her eyes were green, and her dark hair cut short. She had broad shoulders and a sturdy frame. They were smiling in front of a crowd of people beside a stout looking bull with a wide white stripe around its middle.

"That was taken at the State Fair in 1960. We won blue ribbon for that bull. He was a belted Galloway with good bloodline, he sired great beef cattle."

"Is that the breed you raised?

"Mostly the Galloway, yes." He leaned forward to tell me about his passion, cattle. "The Belties were great for the Sandhills because they have a heavy coat. We could leave them out in the pasture most of the year because they'll eat damn near anything, not just hay. Hell, they loved the rough prairie grasses and still produced a nice marbled beef." He paused and grinned, "Do you know where they come from?"

I shook my head no. "They are from the Scottish moorlands around a place called Galloway. Mary called them Oreo's because they looked like the cookie to her."

"Did you breed them for market?" I asked.

"Mostly for the stockyards in Omaha and Kansas City. They gave good milk too. We kept a few for the milking. Mary would churn sweet milk into homemade butter and cream." He closed his eyes, enjoying the remembered tastes of homemade butter on warm bread. We talked for an hour about the ranch and the life there. I could tell he loved the land and the life. He remembered stories of cold winters and hot summers, floods in the spring and sudden changes in the weather from September to October. I got the feeling they were happy memories of a life shared together. There was a pause in the stories, so I asked, "Joe do you remember a girl with a baby coming to the chapel?"

His face got serious and he rubbed his chin, "There was a girl who came to stay with us for a time. She was with child when she showed up at the chapel. Mary brought her in and we took care of her till the baby was born."

"Do you remember the year?"

"It would've been in the spring of sixty. The same year we won the blue ribbon for the Oreo bull," he said.

"Do you know her name or what happened to the baby?"

He looked me square in the eyes for a drawn-out moment, as if he were considering the answer. When I didn't look away, he said, "Her name was Elizabeth, but she didn't name the baby. We took care of it for a month or so. We took it to a couple in Iowa she knew needed him. She kept her journals; you should be able to find all this in the books over at Jimmy's place."

I didn't tell Joe some of the journals were missing. Somehow, I knew it would upset him and there was nothing to be gained by telling him. "Do you know who packed the journals in the boxes?" I asked. "Jimmy thought it was some church ladies but he didn't know who."

"No, no I don't know exactly who boxed them up for me. I had broken my hip and was laid up for a bit. When I moved over here the folks from the church came out to help."

"Do you know if anyone besides Mary ever read the journals?"

"Not that I'm aware of," he said.

"Did anyone else know what she wrote about? Anyone know she kept a daily record of the ranch and things?"

"I'm not sure." Joe said with a scratch of his chin. "Why are you asking? Is something wrong?"

"No," I lied without looking at my shoes. "I'm just curious. I had hoped to interview some people Mary may have written about. I thought if people knew about her journals it might be easier to ask about them."

Joe looked at me with a glint of suspicion but let it go. We talked a while longer. It was getting late. I had stayed well past sundown. I wouldn't make it to Jimmy's tonight. I had more information and a lot to think about. I had to admit, maybe Amanda had a case. I was certainly more curious about the baby boy Mary referred to in the journal. I had a name, Elizabeth. Maybe her family, my family still lived there. I wasn't convinced but was leaning that way. I felt better for knowing but worse as well. It was one thing to read something, to suspect something had happened a long time ago to someone else. You can feel empathy or sympathy, but when the bastard might be you, it's something altogether different.

As I drove back to St Paul I got a sick feeling in my stomach like when I was a little boy watching the Wizard of Oz. Right then I could hear the green faced bitch cackle as she sent out her hordes of monkeys to dismantle the Tin Man and strew the Scarecrow all over the forest floor. The same fear settled into my bowels and made me wants to hide from the truth. I still remember how mad I was at my parents for not telling me I was adopted. Now, I was willing to consider a new idea. Maybe they knew how afraid I would be. Maybe they wanted to protect me until I was old enough to face my flying monkeys.

Chapter 30

It was a week before I could make it to Jimmy's place. It was early evening, yet he wasn't home. I tried the side door and like most farmhouses the doors were never locked. I felt odd about just going in but I had to look at the journals. I went straight up stairs and into the room with most of the boxes. I pulled the chain on the light hanging from the ceiling and looked around. I could see the boxes had been arranged. Amanda had done plenty of work to make some sense from the disorder. It only took me a few minutes to understand her order. I checked a couple of dates and it became clear she had started with the oldest in forty-eight to the left, working to the right for the later years. I scanned the entries from the early years, quickly moving through the late fifties and early sixties. Just as Amanda had said, there were eight and part of nine months missing in 1960 and early '61. The dates resumed in order until I reached the books from seventy-nine. There I ran out of boxes. I pulled a few random notebooks from the seventies.

September 24, 1972

I found a note tacked to the cross this morning. I've found letters and pieces of sheet music from hymn books, a few original songs and poems, like the one pinned to the cross. I thought it was so appropriate for our little place. It read.

If I can pass from here to there
And pass without regret.
For no man cometh without stumble and fall
But all will pass.
For some it's hope, for others fate, for all of us a
Prayer.
If I can pass from here to there
And pass without regret.

I just love that little poem. I wonder about the author, who it was and what they found here. I hope it was rest and mercy. I just know the world is in such desperate need of mercy and forgiveness. I know God is the only one who can forgive sin, but we can all offer a little forgiveness to our neighbors, our family, and our enemies. It's hard to forgive some people but we pray it so often on Sundays, "forgive us our debts, as we forgive others." I think I'll keep this little poem, maybe frame it for the wall in the chapel.

"Who's here?" I heard Jimmy call from down stairs.

"It's me, Willy," I called back.

I could hear him climbing the stairs. I kept looking through the box. He stood in the doorway and leaned against the frame. He asked, "You always break into a man's home to look through his stuff?"

"It's not breaking in if the doors unlocked." I leaned back and looked around at the boxes. "Amanda's been busy."

He nodded. "She's been out here couple times a week and weekends. She told me she thought you'd be back."

"Do you mind?" I asked.

"No," Jimmy said with a slow turn of his head. "Fact is I'm glad for the company. I still think it's going to lead to trouble."

I nodded and started to look through more books when we heard someone else coming.

"Amanda?" Jimmy called.

"It's me," she called as she ran up the stairs, sounding like a herd of buffalo stampeding up the staircase. I wasn't prepared for the feeling of delight when I saw her come into view. Her hair was retained beneath a stocking cap. Her coat hung off her shoulders. A blue sweater with a v neck clung to her curves. She had on faded Levis, cuffed at the ankles to show bunched socks and laced up boots. I took in the sight of her with a smile. She smiled back with a sparkle in her eye.

"What the hell?" Jimmy asked.

We both looked at him. Again, he asked, "What the hell is going on? Are you two?" He looked first at Amanda and then to me. "Oh, hell no! You sorry son of a bitch." He moved with surprising quickness toward me. I jumped to my feet and took a step back.

"Now wait," I said. "Hold on now."

He had me by my arm and collar and spun me around, shoving me against the door. He drew back his fist to strike

"Jimmy," Amanda called. "It's not his fault." She moved to get between us. Jimmy held firm. "I'm going to mess you up," he said in voice far calmer than his intent.

"No," Amanda pushed herself into his field of vision. "Listen to me, Jimmy, I went to his apartment. He didn't do anything wrong."

Jimmy kept his eyes locked on me, "He didn't do anything right."

"Look man," I said with real fear in my voice. "It wasn't like that."

"I went to him. I knew what I was doing."

Jimmy's coal black pupils harbored my destruction.

"I went to his apartment in St. Paul." Amanda was yelling to draw his attention. "He didn't invite me; it was all me. Jimmy, I jumped his bones!"

Jimmy shifted his attention from me to her. He processed the situation while considering the next move. With a snap of his hand he let go and walked away. I leaned slack against the wall. Amanda put her head on my shoulder and we both drew deep breaths.

"So, you're going around sleeping with college boys, are you?"

"Jimmy," Amanda pleaded. "Please don't, okay."

He stormed from the room. We heard him downstairs and the sound of the refrigerator door open and slam shut. Amanda tiptoed over to the door and out into the hallway. I followed at a distance. She looked over the rail down into the hallway and came back with a sheepish smile on her face.

"He'll be alright," she said.

"Yeah, but will I?"

"He's a teddy bear. I promise he won't say anything."

"It's not what he was going to say that worries me," I replied.

We stood in the awkward silence of the room.

"What are you looking for?" She asked.

I looked at the boxes of books at my feet. "I was looking for the rest of the story."

She laughed, "You and Paul Harvey."

"Yeah," I replied. "No, I wanted to see what other entries Mary made about my, my..."

"Your mother?"

"Her name is Elizabeth," I said. "I went to see Joe, he confirmed her name for me."

"I told you so," she said.

"Joe didn't say who the baby was or what happened to it," I said. "Except that Mary took it to a couple in Iowa."

"Ha!" she exclaimed. "I told you so."

"People hate being told so," I said. "Did you find anything else when you were organizing?

"I haven't read much in here. Just tried to get it all in order."

"It's great," I said. "You really did a great job."

She nodded for the compliment. "Let me help."

We worked for an hour digging in boxes, noting the dates, and skimming pages for any clue or reference to Elizabeth or a baby. "She was so dedicated," Amanda said.

"I know, it's incredible," I said. "I tried journaling for a month in college for an assignment. I forgot after a week. What I did write was crap. When I wrote I was usually pissed off or drunk, so it made no sense."

"I bet it wasn't crap," she said. "You write very well."

"It was crap, trust me. I don't string thoughts together very well when I'm upset or six pints gone on nickel draws." I paused, "Wait, what did you say?"

"What?"

"You said I write very well. How do you know?"

"I read; you write for a newspaper." she said with a shy smile.

"You've been reading the Phonograph?"

"I have been known to read the paper." She joked. "Sometimes, the Ain't Paul paper and if Willy Beam, like the whiskey, happens to have a story in there, I might, on occasion, read a little." She went back to looking in a journal but said, "Everyone in the county is just dying to know what cousin Betty from Abilene brought to the anniversary celebration."

"Screw you," I said with a smile of embarrassment, but a little pleased to know she had read what I had written and had an opinion; maybe not a very high opinion. What I wrote about the social events of locals from Burwell, Cedar Rapids and Rockville was a drudgery. Most small-town newspapers fill their pages with social events, church celebrations, baptisms, fundraisers and silver anniversaries or business openings. I wrote my fair share of them. Amanda and I worked in silence for a while. The room was a hodgepodge of boxes, odd sized grocery boxes, some of which had held fruit and other dish soap. They didn't always stack right; the number of notebooks in each box was different so sometimes it took many boxes to complete a year and sometimes only a few.

"Who collected them all and put them in boxes?" Amanda asked.

"Joe said some ladies from the church packed it up," I replied.

"Did he say which church?"

Just then we heard Jimmy coming back up the stairs. He clomped down the hall to the doorway and leaned once more against the jamb. "You guys about done up here?"

"Not yet," Amanda said. "Tell us again who packed these boxes. When did you get them?"

"The ladies from the Auxiliary packed them up."

"When was that?" I asked.

"I don't know, two or three years ago," he said.

"Was it two or three and what month?" I asked.

He shrugged," I don't remember."

"Jimmy, it might be important, try to remember," Amanda pleaded.

He walked over, picked up a journal, and laid it open in his hand. He held a beer in the other hand and raised it to take a swig. "It was two years ago, spring of eighty. I remember Joe fell over the winter of seventy-nine and was in the hospital for a while. He got out, but the family moved him to the home and decided to sell the place in eighty-one." He laid the journal back on top of the box. "It broke my heart to sell the ranch. I wish I could've managed it somehow."

"What month would the ladies have packed these up?" I asked again.

"I think it was May, maybe late April." He nodded his head. "Definitely before June; I would've been out with the Wheaties by June."

Wheaties were the roving band of hired workers who harvested wheat. They would start down in West Texas and work all the way up to North Dakota. Generally, they were high school and college kids working for an outfit with combines on flatbeds. They had contracts all across the upper Midwest and they came back season after season with the harvest.

"I know where to find the 'who'," I said.

"Where?"

"The social column of the Broken Bow Chieftain"

Even though it was early March, it was a cold drive back to St. Paul. When the sun went down the temperature still dropped close to freezing. Once it got below zero, whatever minus it was, it really didn't matter. The degree was damn cold. No, that's incorrect. A friend and biology major told me scientifically speaking, there is no such thing as cold, only an absence of warmth. He thought the idea was somehow profound. I thought it was just semantics. The scientific designation of a state is of no value whatsoever, when the lack of heat inside your car makes your dick shrivel. Definitions are as useless as theology when you're seeking the meaning of things. When contemplating the shades of fate against a clear cold emotion of knowing something for the first time; maybe the only time. The question I kept returning to was, "am I really the baby?" and if I was, am, are; what does that mean? What does it say about God and Angels or miracles in the modern world?

My only perception of God was of a forever disappointed old man. A God who was disappointed at mankind for not having the ability to truly appreciate the gifts he had given us. First, the Garden of Eden, and then the redemption offered by his Son's sacrifice. I never understood, and no one really ever explained this part to my satisfaction. Why would a God, who for generations upon generations condemned the sacrifice of children, first born sons sacrificed by the pagans, the Hittites, Canaanites and Amorites, suddenly change his mind and decide the only thing he could accept as atonement for all time, was the crucifixion of his begotten son? Did he decide the pagans were right? Did he change his position on human sacrifice? I never understood how it worked. I also learned not to ask such troubling questions. It made one appear ungrateful, and if asked too pointedly, sinful.

On this clear cold night with my head full of questions I began to consider a different God; a God who touches small lives in big ways through odd characters. I know there are lots of preachers who have moved people to tears and salvation. I've seen the huge crowds come to Billy Graham and Jimmy Swaggart, Jim Baker, and Oral Roberts, with their message of born again lives. Those warnings of fire and brimstone scared the shit out of me. This God, Mary's God, sent a messenger from a great distance, long before I was conceived, to make space for me in a world which didn't need me and to a girl who couldn't keep me. The nagging question was, why?

That's the rub, the part that really chafed my soul. Why me? Was I supposed to do something? Was I preordained for something? Could it be He just wanted me? If so, for what? To do what and when? I could see the cluster of light on my right, to the south of the highway and asked again, why here? What good could possibly come for me in this place? I wished I had the faith of Mary. Her mustard seed of unquestioning response to a calling was far greater than mine. I wished I were less questioning and more devout. I never could follow anything that way, unquestioned devotion. Asking questions is what made me love journalism. Maybe I needed to stop looking for the answers and start asking better questions.

I parked in the back and hurried toward the steps to my apartment. My head was down, braced against the lack of heat exaggerated by a brisk wind. The first blow caught me on the temple slamming me into the wall. I stumbled back a step and would've fallen but caught the rail and held on. The next blow landed on my chin and I fell, head over heels down to the bottom of the steps. My head was ringing, my eyes unfocused. I got to my feet and ran, weaving, stumbling toward my car. I fell across the hood, staggering along the side to the door. I wanted a place to hide. I pulled on the door, it was locked. I couldn't think where my keys were, so I turned to run. I only took two or three wobbly steps when he stepped in front of me. The man before me was big with a dark beard. He had on a plaid work shirt and jeans.

"You should mind your own business," he said in a deep rumbling voice.

"What, I mean, why?"

"There are things best left alone," he said. Before I could react he landed a fist to the side of my head. I went down. I've never been in a fight before; not one that involved actual punches landed. I'd never been knocked out before, except maybe when I took a baseball to the head in midgets. I don't know how long I was out or how I got to the foot of the steps. I came to in the dark, bleeding and shivering from the absence of heat. It took a great effort of strength and concentration to get my feet to cooperate. The steps were overwhelming. I pulled myself up one step at a time. I had a pain in my side. I suspected he had kicked me while I was down. I reached the landing, fumbled for a key which turned out to be in my jacket pocket. I made it as far as the couch before passing out. I awoke sometime in the middle of the night. I felt like a bruised melon. My tongue was raw and swollen. In the bathroom I spit blood into the sink. My reflection was distorted and a little frightening. I swished my mouth out and spit out a mixture of blood and water. A tooth felt loose, which I knew would upset my mother after all the money spent with the orthodontist. The odd thought made me smile which started my head to pounding like a bass drum. I found a bottle of aspirin and took three. I staggered back to the bedroom and slept until a pounding at the door roused me to a minimum level of consciousness. I don't remember much, only catching flashes of light or images, voices and sounds. I woke in a hospital bed. A nurse was opening the shades. The sunlight exploded in my head. I started to raise a hand to my eyes and found I was restrained by an IV in my arm. I yelled to tell her to close the shades; the pain in my jaw and a sausage for a tongue allowed only a muffled cry. The nurse stopped and came to check on me. Her shadow blocked the light. I closed my eyes. I woke up again hungry and in the dark.

A nurse came in to check on me shortly after I woke up. She was white haired and grandmotherly, smiling and promising me water and ice cubes. She checked my pulse, my heart rate and looked closely into my eyes. "You've got quite a knot on your head young man. We're glad to see you awake and hungry."

After a drink of cold blissful water, I lay in the darkened room staring up at the ceiling. My head still hurt. The pain was a dull throb. My tongue was so swollen, but I didn't taste blood in my mouth. For the first time I considered how I got here. Who found me? How badly was I hurt? I remembered only shadowy images of the ambush. Who had been waiting and why? Had it been because of Amanda or was it something else? I recalled him warning me to mind my own business but had no idea what he meant? Beyond my questions was a storm of fear. I had been beaten and left in the cold, for dead maybe. I wanted my Momma.

Chapter 31

I sat up sipping chicken broth and water, too quickly at first, choking, then sipping more slowly. My throat was raw; the ice water cooled all the way down, soothing, cooling my spirit. Odd, how small things like ice water and chicken broth served with a worried smile by a grandmotherly nurse can revive your being. I slept, this time because I needed to, not because I'd been cold-cocked. The nurse injected pain medication into the IV and I welcomed the cloud of relief filling my veins.

I've heard dreams come after REM sleep, as we come out of a deeper state of rest and rise in consciousness to an alpha level of consciousness. That night I dreamed at the deepest level of my soul. She was there, dressed in a red and black checkered western shirt and work jeans. She was at the chapel refilling the water basin and putting apples into a wooden fruit box, the kind in a 1950's general store. The door stood open, sunlight filled the room with warmth and shadows. I entered through the open door standing between the pews. She smiled at me, not in some vague manner, but directly at me. Her eyes were clear and sharp, and her smile lifted to the corners of her eyes. I felt myself smiling back at her with my whole self. I don't know exactly how else to say it. My smile gave me completeness, the joy in the room radiated from her face and into my heart. Her face beamed a full measure of welcome and mercy to each weary soul who had ever come into this space. It was the essence of Mary, welcoming and merciful.

I looked around, noticing the people sitting in the pews for the first time. They just appeared a cross section of humanity, men and women, young and old, dressed in an array of fashions from different times and seasons. There were families and individuals, some with their heads down in prayer, others smiling at me. I looked for a place to sit, finding an open seat next to a soldier. He was young, maybe seventeen or eighteen, in dress uniform with no chevrons on the sleeves; hat in hand, he smiled shyly. He looked vaguely familiar. I knew him, but as an older man. He greeted me, "Hey, Willy." I was surprised he knew my name. Oddly, he repeated the greeting "Hey, Willy." His greeting became a question, "Hey, Willy, you hear me?"

I started to answer in my dream while begrudgingly awakening. My sight hazy, I saw the soldier standing over me dressed in a brown suit coat. "Willy, can you hear me? There you are," Sarge said with a fatherly smile, "good to see you young man. I was worried about you."

I reluctantly left the community of worshipers in the chapel and came fully awake in my dim hospital room. The suggestions of sunlight peaking around the window shades and fluorescent light from the hallway both seemed paler compared to the light from my dream. A doctor with tired brown eyes and a bald head examined me. "How do you feel young man?"

I nodded my head, not sure my tongue would work; then with some effort I said, "Better."

"Good," he said. "I need to do a few tests to see how much better you are, okay? I'm going to check your eyes for sensitivity to light."

He took a small pen light from his pocket. He pointed it at the pillow by my head then said. "I'm going to shine this in your eyes. Just relax." He moved the light quickly across my vision, blinding me. I blinked from the pain, which throbbed for a time after he moved the light away. He repeated the procedure for the other eye; the sharp pain was more of a pin prick than a knife in this eye. He checked the reflexes in my hands and feet. He helped me sit up, which made me want to throw up. The nurse helped me lay back down. I was out of breath by the time the tests were over. The doctor scribbled in a chart, "Son, you have a concussion. The sensitivity to light should lessen in the next few days; the light-headedness and nausea as well. Right now you need to rest. I'll be back to check on you later."

He and the nurse exited the room. Sarge was in the hall. He had a brief conversation with the doctor and came in and stood by my bed. His posture was ramrod straight but his eyes held some kindness.

"Glad to see you with your eyes open," Sarge said. "When I found you, I wasn't sure."

"You found me?"

"Yes, when you didn't come to work I got worried. You didn't answer your phone. To tell the truth, I was on my way to fire your sorry ass when I found you looking like death warmed over. I called the ambulance."

"Thanks," I said.

"What happened?"

"I was coming home from," I paused not because I didn't

remember, but to avoid the fact. "I was going up to my apartment. I had my head down not looking where I was going and suddenly someone hit me."

"With a bat?"

"I don't know." It hurt to recall. "He was big. I ran, but he caught me."

"I'd say he caught you," Sarge said. He'd loosened his stance to almost a parade rest. "Did he say anything?"

"Not that I remember," I lied. I don't know why. I felt the need to keep the warning to myself, along with where I was coming back from. "Do my parents know?"

"I called your father last night." His voice reminded me of a corporal reporting to a superior officer. "They should be here soon."

"What day is it?"

"It's Saturday. You were out for a little over twenty-four hours."

"Thanks for calling my parents," I said. "Do I still have a job?"

He looked down at me and drew a deep breath. "Do you want it?"

I didn't reply.

"Maybe you should think about going home for a while, back to Iowa with your folks."

"No," I said with too much emotion.

Sarge looked at his boots, then at the wall. I recognized the soldier from my dream. Sarge had been in Mary's chapel. He had been one of the wandering souls seeking clarity or comfort in Mary's chapel. I got a strange feeling; maybe he didn't find what he was seeking there.

"Sarge," I said. "I need to finish what I started. There are things I need to know about Mary Steward and the cross, that chapel and all the people who came to her."

"Why?" he asked, "Why do you need to know anything about it?"

I didn't ask the question I wanted to. "I just do."

Sarge sighed and moved away from the bed. "Your parents will be here soon. You rest for now. We'll talk later."

I closed my eyes and sleep came like a drug into my room. I slept until my parents came. Mom entered with a flurry, rushing around like mothers will do. It was beautiful and exhausting, just what I needed. Dad was quieter and patient; like he can be; it was also beautiful. I've always loved my parents; in that moment when they came to my bedside in the hospital I didn't want anyone else. I was very lucky to be placed in the arms of these amazing people. In that moment I could have been persuaded to go home, back to Iowa. How odd for me to tell Sarge one thing with such defiance only a short time ago, and yet feel so differently now. I could claim it was the bump on my head giving me a wide swing of emotions. Some might suggest it was immaturity or selfishness, and they wouldn't be entirely wrong, but not wholly right either. The doctor came back in to speak with my parents. He repeated the light test. This time the light didn't bother me as much. I sat up and the wooziness was much less. He said I needed to stay the night and could most likely go home tomorrow. Where home was wasn't clarified for anyone but that wasn't his problem.

My parents wanted to stay with me. I insisted they get some rest, so dad took mother to my apartment, so she could clean up. He came back to sit by my bed and have dinner with me. We talked about what happened. I couldn't tell him anymore than I told the others. He looked worried but nodded his head in acceptance of my story.

"Son," he said. "You should come back home with us for a little while, until you are healed."

I didn't answer, couldn't tell him no. "Dad, I would love to come home." His request still hung in the space between us. "But there's something I've got to do here."

"What?" he asked, "What is it you need here?"

"It's hard to explain." I begged off, "I'm really tired, can we talk about it later?"

He let it go.

In the morning mother came back, filling the room and my head with her worried smile and heartening fussiness. I am my mother's boy and one thing a Mommy's boy knows but never admits, is there is nothing better, more healing, warmer and loving than her full attention. When she brushes the hair away from your eyes, there is nothing more special in all the world then a mother's love.

I got out of the hospital that afternoon. My parents stayed three days and two nights. They tried to persuade me to come back with them. I brushed it aside at first with shrugs and vague answers; finally, I had to tell them I needed to stay, at least for a little while longer. They didn't understand, and I couldn't fully tell them why. I didn't tell them about Mary's story. I could never expose them to my need for answers. I feared it would hurt us all too much. I couldn't explain the mystical, spiritual experience I was having or the pull I felt for a higher power. I knew then and know now that I will never fully understand or explain what was going on.

Mom cried. Dad hugged me. I assured them both I would be fine. I would call soon. They drove away with tentative waves and pensive expressions. I watched until they were out of sight and hurried back to my room and locked the door.

That night I tossed and turned until I finally took Demerol. The drug let me sleep and dream, of the chapel filled with travelers seeking sanctuary, of broken souls longing for a healing touch. I met sad hearts in search of drops of joy and prisoners restrained in darkness desperately seeking a light of hope. Their faces were strange and familiar, their names less important than their stories. I felt them, they touched me. I knew them. I awoke in the coolness of my bedroom. My head was groggy and my body ached, but my spirit was clean and renewed. I almost turned over and wrapped myself in the warmth of the covers, to recover a few moments of sleep, but something called me out of my sickbed.

Chapter 32

I was at my desk by eight organizing the stack of papers, notes and messages. I found a message from Melvin to call. There were a few from the people of the small towns I regularly covered for social and business events. There were a few other notes and messages. The one I expected, hoped for was not there. No message from Amanda. My imagination and my heart conspired to choke me. I staved off the sensation to panic. Sarge came into the room with a swish of the door and stomp of his feet. "Beam, what the hell are you doing here?

"Working," I said.

"In my office, now!"

I followed with my notebook in hand, head up and my chin out. Sarge walked to the coffee machine in his office. He poured water from the urn that he habitually filled the night before. He flipped the switch for the machine to brew and walked to the edge of his desk. I continued standing just inside the door.

"I hoped you'd go home with your folks," he said.

"I have a job to do, sir."

"You've got nothing to prove. I'll write you a solid letter for a reference. You've done some good work and for the most part I've been pleased with your progress as a writer. I know editors in Kansas City, Denver, and Des Moines."

"Are you firing me?"

He walked away from the coffee pot and sat at his desk. "I'm," he began then said, "Would you sit down."

"Do I still have a job?"

He nodded, "Now please sit."

I took a chair as Sarge took another sip of the dark black liquid. "I want to know what you're up to. Who rattled your brains and why?"

"I don't know, exactly," I said truthfully.

"You must have some idea."

I nodded, the silence hung between us. "Look son, I will fire your ass if you don't start talking."

"It could be," I hesitated, knowing the truth can be a fragile thing. I was holding back, from my parents, from Sarge and most notably from myself; possibly my assumption was too much for me to say out loud. I didn't trust myself to speak what I suspected. "I think it could have something to do with a story I've been working on, but more than likely it has everything to do with Amanda."

"The girl from Broken Bow," he said with a snort. "Boy, I've told you, girls are nothing but trouble. I told you from the word go."

"I know but it's not what you think."

"What, are you going to tell me some crap about love?"

"No," I said and it wasn't love. It wasn't anything close, but it was something. "She and I are friends. She has been helping me with a story."

"Bullshit," Sarge said and picked up his coffee. "What's this story she's helping with? Don't tell me it's those damn journals again."

"I know," I said. "It's unbelievable, these journals are significant, somehow."

"To whom?"

"To me," I said. I should have told him everything. I might have laid it all out on the table. Then again, there was no good way to explain any of it without sounding completely insane. I hardly understood what was going on.

"I'd like to say I admire your stubbornness," Sarge said. "But I think you're just being plain stupid."

I didn't disagree. Still I kept the dreams to myself. I held to my suspicion that I was the bastard child of a girl from the Sandhills. Sarge finished his coffee in one big gulp and stood to refill it. I got up to leave the room, then I had a thought. "Sarge, have you ever," I paused, "Were you ever one to visit that chapel?"

He looked at me over his shoulder with an expression I couldn't quite read. It might have been irritation or amusement. "You're trying my tolerance today. If you hadn't just gotten out of the hospital from getting your skull cracked, I'd crack it for you."

I turned to leave, but something made me say, "It's just that in one of Mary's journals she wrote about a young officer who came to the chapel. He would've been about your age and her description struck me as familiar."

"Familiar?" Sarge asked as he walked back to his desk. I was thinking of the soldier I saw in my dream. I thought better of telling him. He already thought I was off my rocker.

"He was a private from one of the towns around here, going to war, the Korean War."

"It was a police action," Sarge said with a bit of sarcasm. "And there are plenty of boys from around here who fought in Korea. The

VFW club is full of them on any Saturday night."

"Well sure, I know," I said, not exactly sure how far to push or where it would lead. I once heard a good journalist never asks a question for which he doesn't have a follow up question. I had asked without thinking, now I had only one option. "She described his uniform as having a long coat with a belt and Marine symbols."

Sarge began leafing through his notes and messages. "Willy, if you have a question other than the ones you've already asked, then ask it or get the hell out of my office."

I nodded and left his office, glad to still have a job but carrying a nagging feeling of something missed, an opportunity passed.

Chapter 33

I shuffled through the messages again and stopped at the ones from Melvin. We hadn't talked in weeks and now here were two messages in a few days. He might have heard I was hurt or maybe not. I picked up the phone, called, and got no answer. I hung up and sat there wondering about Melvin. We worked together on the farm projects. He was my reference for all things agricultural, but I didn't really know him.

On a whim, I decided to drive out to see Melvin, to see what he called about and if it was my health, then to let him know I was fine. The sky was a moving shade of blue with only threads of clouds, suggestions or tokens of white cotton candy left over from a distant recollection. It was still cold, traces of snow filled the ditches. The first few cranes of the Sandhills pranced in fields. Soon those fields would be full of the great gray birds, as angular as herons.

I recalled the entry from Mary's journal. The migration of these amazing birds was as predictable as the season, a metaphor for our lives. I had missed last season's migration but had heard plenty of stories from local bird watchers and seen pictures. A gallery of pictures cannot do justice to their awkward courting dance nor the sound generated by thousands of wide graceful wings as they cross the fallow fields along the rivers. Their gliding descent; wings outstretched and arched like parachutes, their gentle, casual hop of a landing, followed by happy honking call to each other. Thousands of them standing at attention; their long necks and sharp narrow beaks a striking silhouette against a western sunset.

The amusement of their dance; great gray wings splayed out, prancing and hopping about on thin legs, as they work to attract mates. They stay for only a few weeks in March, resting in harvested corn fields along the wide shallow Platte and Loup rivers. Naturalists estimate they've been migrating to these plains for thousands of years, and yet each time they come, it's a spectacle. They come to these crossroads of land, water and spirit; a promise of spring as reliable as the calendar, to dance, to love, to be revived before moving on.

I left my observations of the itinerant birds and turned on the radio. I'd always been a rock music guy, maybe a little too much pop but never a country and western fan. We made fun of the hicks who listened to that twangy stuff in college. Now living out here with windmills and cattle, cornfields and Cornhuskers, I had gotten a taste for the twang. That spring a singer named Razzy Bailey had a ditty, and KZ100, Nebraska's biggest FM was playing 'She Left Her Love All Over Me' in heavy rotation.

I thought about our night together. My romantic nature had me daydreaming images of her love all over me. The problem, I suspected was someone else had caught wind of our affair, and I had the medical bills to prove it. Someone, a big someone, wanted me to know they weren't 'razzy' about it. My thoughts of Amanda were complicated, not just because of my images of her as a lover, but also because of all the mixed up, twisted and converging story-lines leading me somewhere or nowhere at all.

I turned down the long gravel drive to Melvin's place between two white railed fences. A Massey Ferguson tractor with a snowplow on the front was parked by one of the out buildings. A group of strategically placed maple trees surrounded a late nineteenth century farmhouse. Melvin's place made me think of a Terry Redlin painting. I parked in the round in front of the house and walked up to the door. Judy, his wife, opened the door before I could knock, "Willy, are you alright? We heard you were in the hospital."

"I was, better now," I said lowering my head, so my bruises were not so noticeable.

She was gentle and smiling as she waved me inside. "I've got some fresh brewed coffee or would you like tea?"

I chose the tea, following her to the kitchen and sat at a small kitchenette table by the window. The walls were white; the linoleum floor was a bold print of interlocking green and yellow squares with diamonds inlaid with folk art flower shapes. The explosion of color made my head ache. The kitchen smelled wonderful of bread or maybe a pie.

Judy handed me the tea. "What brings you all the way out here?"

"Melvin called the office and left a few messages so I thought I'd take a drive and see what he wanted." I took a drink of the rich amber tea and thought how agreeable tea made with well water tasted. "I called earlier, and no one answered," I said.

"Oh, well its calving season and we've been out to the barn quite a bit," she said with a frown. "Calves are like kids, they come whenever they want and usually in the middle of the night. I keep telling Mel we need to put a line down to the barn."

"How are the calves looking?" I asked, not knowing the proper language to ask about such things.

"Good," she said, "good," with a smile strained at the corners. She looked down at the tabletop instead of in my eyes. The odd pause in the niceties hung there until she said, "Mel will be coming up for lunch soon or you can walk down to the barn if you like."

The back-screen door clanged and rattled with my departure. I walked on a well-traveled path toward a three story, red Dutch style barn. Its high peak stood thirty feet above its base which spread out in a wide stance, a hundred feet across. I could smell the sour sweet nature of the animal dung mixed with ancient wood and fresh hay at the entrance to the barn. A pair of propane heaters blew heat from a blue flame at either side of the entrance. The dark coolness of the barn felt earthy and inviting.

"You look like hell," I heard Melvin say with a laugh. Like some homespun apparition he materialized from a stall at the far end of the barn. He leaned a pitchfork against one of the support posts; a great wooden timber, standing true and sturdy, reaching up to the roof trusses twenty feet above us, and walked towards me.

I laughed too, "Well I feel worse."

"What brings you all the way out here on this fine spring day?" His voice was friendly, laced with good humor. He extended his hand and I shook it. Melvin laid his forearms over the gate that stood ajar at the entrance of an empty stall.

"You called the office a few times," I said. "So I decided to come see what you wanted."

He nodded but didn't reply.

"Anyway, your wife said you guys have been busy with calving."

"Yeah, pretty busy." He changed the subject, "So, you feeling better?"

"I think so. My head still hurts some. I get a little lightheaded from time to time, but you know," I said with a shrug.

"I heard someone rattled your brains pretty good. Any idea who or why?"

"No idea, who" I said. "Why, maybe. Did you want something?" I asked, changing the subject.

Melvin stood away from the gate and slapped his gloves against his leg. "You remember the Taylors?" Dust flew from his action, specks of earth and hay exploded into the shadows, floated into the light, dissipated and disappeared.

"The old man borrowed money to get his boy started with his own place. You know how tough it's been, for everyone. Anyway, the kid is behind with the bank. The old man is the co-signer; it looks like they could lose both places."

I put my hands on my hips and kicked the dust at my feet. The news hurt me somehow. I closed my eyes, trying to keep my emotions from welling up at the corners of my eyes. I recalled sitting on the porch with the Taylors back in the fall when Sarge first started down this road of investigation into the farming crisis. I could see the old man, red faced and defiant, shouting at Bill Oldfather in the bank, and Mrs. Taylor, Eunice, hospitable as a grandmother serving me lemonade. Of all the farmers I'd met, my hope for each one of them was captured in these fragile images.

"Is it for sure?" I asked.

"Not a hundred percent for the dad," Melvin said. "But the boy's place, definitely."

A cow moaned a few stalls over. Her bawling started low, then rose in octaves and vibrato until it choked off at the end of a sharp squeal. The wind rattled the stark branches of the trees like dry old bones.

"I know you've been tied up with other things. I don't know if you're going to stick around, but the folks around here, some of them are in trouble."

"Are you in trouble?"

He turned, walked a couple of steps away, and stood facing the exit with his fists on his hips. "I'd be lying if I told you everything was fine. I can say we're in better shape than most and I hope we'll be alright." He looked up, "but I don't see how this thing gets better anytime soon."

"I keep reading in the Ag News where it says in six months prices will begin to rise," I said.

"Wishful thinking," Melvin said. "What else are they going to say? Truth is, I don't know if anyone knows how bad it is or how bad it's going to get."

"How bad do you think it'll get?" I asked.

"Desperate," Melvin said. "With land prices what they are; hundreds of farms and ranches are over extended. The banks and farmers both could be desperate to the point of panic. The guys over at the State Ag Department don't have anything else to say. Like the rest of us, all they can do is hope for the best, prepare for the worst."

I looked down at my shoes, a light brown powder settled on my white Nike high-tops like shit on paper. "I still don't get it," I said. "I've asked everyone and there's plenty of finger pointing and blame laid, lots of options, still no real answers."

Melvin pushed back the ball cap and scratched his head. "That's because there's no simple explanation. Everyone wants there to be some easy answer; a straw man to blame. If there's a reason, then it's definable and it's fixable. If it's not fixable, then folks want someone to blame, someone to direct their frustrations towards. Truth is, the nature of things is anything but simple."

"I know," I began.

"You don't know," Melvin interrupted me. "Everyone knows something and still wants it to be something else. We want simple in a complex world. My grandpa, when he was getting up in years, liked to talk about how much simpler life was when he was a boy. The truth be known, when his father, my great-grandfather, worked this land, it was hard to scratch out a living. I've studied history, and lots of farmers quit farming, just gave up or had to go someplace else when my father was a boy. The same thing is happening now. A lot of people are going to have to find a new way to make a living. Farming has never been an easy life. Nobody ever did it to get rich. It's a different way of life, a good way, but like everything else it changes."

"Change is hard," I said.

"Change is constant," he said turning to look back at me. "My dad loved to say, 'shit will happen and things will change'. Well, right now shit has happened and things, they are a changin' and there's no one to blame but the seasons and circumstance, forty years of bad farm policy, and partisan bureaucracy. "

"So, what can I do about it? Why call me?"

"I thought you'd want to know about the Taylors." He shrugged, "I wanted to see if you were alright."

"Well," I said. "I'm sad to hear about Taylors but I guess I'll be alright"

Melvin stirred the dirt with his boot. "There's something else."

"What?"

"I think you getting beat up has something to do with the article you wrote. I believe someone didn't like your depiction of Harold or the Posse. You know Harold committed suicide?"

"No, when?" I asked in astonishment.

"Yep, last week. The son-in-law found him. Put a twelve gauge in his mouth, horrible mess."

"You think my story..."

"No, hell no!" Melvin said with a wave of his hand. "Harold lost his farm and with it his hope. He took his life because he couldn't face the idea of losing it all. But it's possible his son-in-law needed to blame someone. I been thinking maybe he needed to vent his anger and some college boy news reporter would be a prime target."

I had been thinking it had something to do with Amanda but now... "He said, I should mind my own business."

"What?" Melvin asked.

"The guy who jumped me, he said I had been warned to mind my own business," I said. "You really think he would blame me over a newspaper article?"

"I don't know, but it's possible. I told you those conspiracy groups can be dangerous. The son-in-law could be a member of the Posse. You're part of the system working against them and maybe an easy target. Someone to blame."

"Someone to lash out at," I said. "But I'm not part of the system."

"It don't matter how you see yourself," Melvin said. "Listen, I want you to be careful. These groups might see the newspapers and its reporters as just another pawn of the Jewish bankers, who are taking away their way of life."

"I didn't write anything inaccurate. I was just reporting. Someone's got to write it, don't they?" I asked.

"Yes, they do." Melvin agreed. "I think your account of the auction and the farm crisis was well written and important. We need to keep a record of the people, the families who are affected by this tragic set of circumstances, even if not everyone will be happy with the news."

"Come on," I said, trying to find some reassurance to let me sleep at night. "You really think some grief inspired nut job would ambush me for a newspaper story? Hell, I write mostly about silver wedding anniversaries and church bingo winners."

"Well, it might take a nut job to think beating up the social columnist for the paper would make a difference," Melvin said. "Meanwhile, I'm hungry," he said. "and I'm sure Judy has lunch ready." He put an arm around my shoulder and turned me toward the house.

After a good home cooked meal and a glass or two of Judy's sun brewed ice tea, I headed back to town. The sun felt good streaming in my driver side window; it was nice to have a day with sunshine. The bank clock at the corner of Main and Hwy 281 showed the afternoon temperature at forty-two degrees. Ten degrees above freezing felt like a heat wave. The sun on my face, nature's warmth filling the little Honda made me optimistic. Melvin's assertion that the ambush was retaliation didn't make me feel safe, but it allayed my concerns about my relationship with Amanda. The notion that a relative of Amanda's wasn't out to kill me somehow made me feel better. Not safer, but better. Melvin's theory made more sense, still I was missing something.

When I got into the office I went to my desk and started making calls. I called the Taylors to see if they would talk to me and got no answer. I called Mr. Oldfather at the bank; he was busy. I returned a couple of calls I'd missed from when I was out. I checked the calendar to see what events usually came up in the spring. I needed to make my rounds to villages and towns. I decided to call tomorrow to see who was around. I was making notes when the phone rang. I answered it, "Phonograph, this is Willy."

"Willy, it's me, are you alright?"

"Amanda?"

"Yes, who else?"

It was a fair question. "I'm fine."

"What happened?"

"I can't talk right know," I said. "Call me at my place, around ten, alright?"

"Okay," She said. I hung up.

I needed to think and couldn't find the power to do it right then. I've since heard of treatment for people who have traumatic brain injuries. A woman used mild electronic pulsation and sound waves to reboot a person's brain after a head injury. I could've used a reboot right then. Turn it off for twenty seconds and turn it back on, the solution for every IT call center since the modern age of computers. I needed to reboot my brain and rethink my situation.

I told Sarge I was going home to lie down and left for the day. Back at my apartment, I swallowed two of the prescribed pain pills, pulled the shades and put a pillow over my head to block out any trace of light and dreamed.

The chapel was filled with shadows with colored shards of light stabbing through the windows. I could hear the wind whistling around the structure, gusting with enough force to uproot the whole thing. I was cold. My hands felt numb and my teeth hurt when I inhaled the icy interior of the night. How I got there, why I was there, were not questions I had in my head. I was only aware I was there and had no questions beyond the harsh reality of my situation and how I would survive.

Suddenly, the door of the chapel burst open. The wind blew the icy night in upon me. I turned from the cold, pulling my coat collar up to cover my ears. I heard footsteps and a gentle voice speaking to me, but the wind carried the voice away from me. Someone touched my arm and I went with her. She led me across the windswept expanse toward the soft yellow lights of home, warmth, and safety. I didn't look at the woman who was guiding me along. My attention fixed on the home and the light where the promise filled my every thought.

Inside, she sat me beside a small cast-iron Franklin stove, radiant with heat. She placed a homemade quilt across my legs and wrapped another around my shoulders. Speaking gently, she scurried around me in a comforting tone. The wind and cold, no longer a threat to my soul, I began to thaw. The quilt's healing powers engulfed me. My mother had quilts like this, made of scraps and love; a pattern of blue and goldenrod flowers fading into the cream-colored background. There is no better cure for what ails you than to be wrapped up in a homemade quilt with prayers sown into its very fabric. The woman brought me warm soup to sip. The broth and the quilt renewed me.

The shrill ring of a phone startled me. She brought the receiver to me on a long springy cord and said the call was for me. The phone was still ringing as I put the receiver to my ear. With the sound of a ringing phone still piercing the air, I looked at her and in that instant, I recognized her. Mary Steward said, "Answer the call, Willy."

"Hello," I said. My voice sounded deep and scratchy, so I spoke louder, "Hello, I'm here, hello."

"Willy, are you okay?" It was Amanda. I hadn't missed her call. "You sound like you're asleep."

"I am, I mean, I was." I pulled myself up into a sitting position. The phone slid across the nightstand and crashed to the floor with a high-pitched ring of the bells inside.

"Willy, are you there?"

"Yeah, sorry, it's fine, I'm fine." The phone landed up right, so I didn't bother to pick it up. "I was having this crazy dream."

"About what?"

"It's not important," I said. "How are you, is everything alright?"

"I'm fine," Amanda said with an ironic laugh. "You're the one who got beat up. That's why I called, to see what happened."

"I don't remember much. When I came home, someone was waiting for me. He ambushed me and..."

"And what?"

"He said I needed to mind my own business," I said waiting to see how Amanda would respond.

"What does that mean?"

"I was hoping you might know."

"Me, why would I know?"

"I thought maybe, well that, someone had found out about..."

"About?"

"About us."

There was a long pause and I thought maybe she had hung up. Then she said, "What about us?"

"You know," I said.

"Know what?" She paused.

"That you and I..."

"Did the deed? Got it on? Had Sex" She said with a laugh. "Really, you think someone rattled your skull because of me?"

"I don't know."

"Who do you think would come to St. Paul and ambush you for sleeping with me?"

"I don't know," I said a little exasperated. "Some ex-boyfriend or an older brother maybe."

"Willy," she said, "There is no ex-boyfriend, but my brothers maybe," She giggled. "Hey, if Jimmy didn't crack your skull when he had you in his sites, you're safe."

I was relieved but needed to heed Melvin's warning.

"Willy, are you still there?"

"Yes, I'm here. Sorry, I couldn't talk before. Why did you call again?"

"To check on you, again. I heard you were in the hospital. I was worried."

"You called before?"

"I called last week and spoke to your mom. Didn't she tell you?"

"No, no she didn't."

"That's weird," she said.

"What did you tell her, what did she say?"

"I just told her I was a friend of yours and I wanted to know if you were alright. She said you were resting and she would tell you I called."

This, more than anything upset me. Even now it's strange to know, to realize, that my mother failing to deliver a simple message from Amanda, disturbed me greatly. My mother's sin of omission made my stomach ache.

"She didn't tell me you called," I said. "And you're sure this had nothing to do with me and you?"

"I'm pretty sure. If my parents or someone else knew and wanted to send a message, they would start with me, not you."

"Well, I'm glad you're not in trouble."

"Do you think it could have anything to do with Aunt Mary's journals?"

"I don't see how," I said. "Only a few people know about them and we've not said or done anything with them. We still don't know the 'who'."

"I thought you knew where to find the 'who'," Amanda said.

"What?"

"When you left Jimmy's, you said you knew how. We were talking about who and how to figure it out and you said you knew where to find the 'who'."

I was drawing a blank. "I did?"

"Yes, don't you remember? We were talking about the ladies who boxed up the journals and you said 'I know how to find the 'Who.'"

There was nothing, no recollection of the conversation or the direction I was going. "I don't know."

"Oh, I know," she said. "The social pages, in the paper, the archives. You thought there would be a story about the churches helping Uncle Joe move off the ranch."

I vaguely recalled the idea or maybe I just thought it sounded like a good idea. "Okay."

"You really don't remember. Willy, I'm worried about you."

"Don't worry; the doctor said there might be some gaps in my memory." I was worried about me for a lot of reasons. Amanda and I talked for a while about nothing much at all. Funny how two people can stay on the phone for an hour and say nothing at all, to just listen to her smile.

Chapter 34

I didn't know exactly what to do next except work. So, I wrote stories for the Ladies Auxiliary and their Memorial Day plans in St. Paul. I wrote a story about the migration of the Sandhill cranes from an interview with a local conservationist and enthusiastic bird photographer. I recorded the comings and goings of local dignitaries and church gatherings. I traveled around the small towns keeping up with the agricultural news, along with the local theater group's production of "South Pacific", and took photos of the high school basketball games. I read and reread the journals I had.

I was working on a wedding anniversary for Mr. And Mrs. Alfred Lutz, their fiftieth, when I realized it, or rather remembered it. I had written a story about another wedding anniversary, some months ago, and had overlooked a vital clue. I rushed over to the stack of papers from late last year; right after the big snowstorm, before Christmas. I dug through the stack with barely contained excitement. How had I missed it? I uncovered the Sunday edition for December twelfth. There in the social section: Kelly Patterson-Allen. I had a very strong sense that this was the Kelly Patterson from Mary's journal. It was highly possible. She had married a boy from Dannebrog, James Allen, and now lived in Minnesota.

I almost ran back to my desk. The guys in the newsroom looked up at my frantic movements but chalked it up to youthful foolishness or insanity; either way, it didn't distract them from their work. I looked in the phone book for Arnold Allen. My hands were shaking as I dialed the number. Before I could think of what I was going to say, Mrs. Allen answered. "Hello," she said in high pitched musical voice.

"Mrs. Allen?" I asked.

"Yes, who is this?"

"Mrs. Allen, this is Willy Beam with the Phonograph. I wrote a story last winter about your anniversary."

"Yes, I remember," she said with the hint of a question in her tone.

"Well, the reason for my call is about you daughter-in-law, Kelly. I was wondering if she is from Broken Bow by any chance?" I asked hoping beyond hope I was right.

"Well, yes." Mrs. Allen said. "As a matter of fact, she is. She and James met at college. She's such a sweet girl."

I cut her off, "I'm sure she is. I was wondering if I could get

James and Kelly's phone number?"

"Well, I suppose but what is this all about?"

Now I was stuck. This was as far as I had gotten in my head but now I needed a good excuse, one that didn't sound crazy. "Well, see." I began, then it hit me. "I'm working on a story about homesteaders in the Sandhills, and I believe the Patterson's were one of the Kinkaiders who were able to apply for 640 acres of land. I wanted to ask Kelly if she had any records or information about her family's place."

"Well, I don't know. I've never heard her talk about that, but I suppose it's possible. Let me get you the kids' number. They live in Fridley, just on the northern edge of Minneapolis. It's lovely in the summer, but just too darn cold up there in the winter for me."

"Yes ma'am," I agreed. She gave me the number. I repeated it back to her to be sure I had it right. I had a lead and hoped Kelly Patterson was willing to tell me about her trip to the chapel when she was twelve.

In the meantime, I was late for a basketball game in Broken Bow. The basketball season was winding down; conference tournaments and district winners would advance to Lincoln to play for state championships in each of the state's divisions. As I said, watching high school basketball games was a joy for me. I was covering the games for work, but also because I was curious to see Amanda play basketball. She was a forward, not much of a scoring threat, a strong rebounder, and good defender. I chuckled the first time I saw her on the court, those short shorts and high tops. Her curly hair pulled back in a ponytail, a fierce expression on her face, and of no surprise to me, a willingness to play a little rough. Nothing flagrant, but she had sharp elbows and knew how to give a hard foul. Amanda played most of the game but scored only four points for the Lady Indians who lost 32 to 24. Not a lot of scoring, but plenty of effort. I credited the defense of both teams in my story, being generous in my coverage.

The boys took the court as soon as the girl's game was done. I took the opportunity to get a pop from the concession. The crowd from both towns spilled into the lobby for a smoke break. Parents congregated along the hall near the trophy cases or took a trip to the restroom.

I took a turn at the urinal, washed my hands and proceeded to the concession. I bought a pop and a candy bar and was walking back to the gym when Amanda came out into the hall. Her face was still flush from the game, but she had changed into a cheerleader outfit. She rushed up to me, "I want you to meet my mom."

"What?" I said.

"Come on, she's right here." She turned and waved to a dark-haired woman standing by the doors. Before I could voice my concern at meeting her parents I was standing in front of Katie Steward.

"Willy, this is my mom," Amanda said with a pull on the woman's arm.

"Nice to meet you," I said and extended my hand.

Amanda's mother shook it evenly. "Very nice to finally meet you," she said.

I wasn't sure what to say next and clearly neither was Katie.

Amanda was excited, "I can't believe you're here, are you covering the game?"

"Yeah," I held up my notebook as a way to show I was there to do a job. "You played great." I said.

"I'm terrible, but thanks anyway" she smiled. "I've got to go," and rushed off leaving me and Katie Steward in the hallway of the Broken Bow gym. We stood in an awkward space between the trophy case and the concession. I nodded and started to move away, when she said, "I wish you would leave my daughter alone."

I wasn't sure what to say, so decided to ignore it and move away. She stepped to block my path. "I don't know what kind of a stunt you're trying to pull, but Amanda is in high school and you have no business messing around with her."

"Mrs. Steward," I said. "I'm not messing around with anyone. I'm here to cover the game for my paper."

"You know that's not what I'm talking about." She put one hand on her hip and pointed her finger like any scolding mother would. "This funny business with you and my daughter has got to stop. For the life of me, I don't know why Jimmy would ever let you two get into those journals, but they are full of a bunch of crap."

"Mrs. Steward, I'm sorry." I said, trying to excuse myself from her accusing gaze." I need to get back to the game."

"She's still in high school for God's sake, you should be ashamed of yourself," Katie Steward said accusingly.

People were starting to look our way. A few men by the trophy case stopped their conversation to see who Katie was talking to. I stepped to one side and walked away. There was no point to win by making a spectacle. I got a couple of steps away when I heard Katie Steward say, "Nothing good ever came from digging around in the past and you need to stay away from my daughter."

I went back to my seat by the announcers. I felt fairly confident that Mrs. Steward would not follow me to the middle of the stands; all the same I kept my eyes on the game. I tried to concentrate on the score and my story, but the confrontation had me rattled. I wanted to run out of the gym at halftime but kept my seat. I saw Amanda coming towards me. I pretended to be in conversation with one of the officials.

Amanda said. "I'm so sorry she yelled at you."

I looked around at her and then to the crowd. I felt like every eye in the gym was on me. I looked away but could feel the pressure all around me. "It's alright, just let it be," I whispered with a forced smile.

"No, it's not. I wouldn't have introduced you if I thought she would act like that, the old bitty," she said a bit too loud.

"Amanda, please, not right now." I begged.

She looked at me with real hurt in her eyes. Thank God the buzzer sounded for the second half to start. Amanda ran off to cheerlead and I turned my attention back to the game. The excitement of the game, which went down to the wire, kept me from focusing on my uncomfortable situation. I had known getting involved with Amanda would be trouble. Sarge warned me and here I was in the middle of it. Like everything else going on around me, I didn't clearly understand. What did she know about me and Amanda? I had a good idea what she suspected. There were too many unknowns. One thing was clear; I was going to get the hell out of Broken Bow as soon as this game was over. No dragging Main Street or hanging around to talk to coaches. I would just have to write the story from my notes and leave the coach's comments out.

The St. Paul Wildcats missed a last second jump shot to lose 58 to 57 to the Broken Bow Indians. When the final horn sounded I gathered up my stuff and made for the exit. I fell in with a crowd of St. Paul people for cover, rushed out into the parking lot and headed east on US 92 within ten minutes.

How had this gotten so complicated? I knew the answer was my own foolishness and dogged stubbornness.

In an act of more foolishness or divine inspiration, I stopped at the crossroads: the Loup Rivers, the railroad and a convergence of highways. The moon was full and bright as a lamp in a blue-black sky. I looked to the north, and there shining like a dream, was the cross, illuminated not just by the light at its foot, but by the moon and all the stars of the universe. I pulled to the side of the road, got out and walked up the slope toward the cross. I was winded and chilled by the time I reached the fence line. The night air hurt my teeth and made my nose run. I climbed through the fence to stand beneath the cross. Its great arms stretched out from the weathered trunk. A hymn, "The Old Rugged Cross" suddenly filled my head. I hummed the tune and then sang out "On a hill far away stood an old rugged cross." I had forgotten part of the verse but the chorus; "So I'll cherish the old rugged cross, till my trophies at last I lay down; I will cling to the old rugged cross and exchange it someday for a crown." The song returned good memories to me.

I walked toward the chapel, the shadows darkening its entrance. The door hung loose at one hinge; faded gray weeds covered the step. I pushed on the door and it came open. It smelled musty, but not unpleasant inside and it was surprisingly warm. The pews were still upright as was the lectern on a small platform, just like in my dreams. It seemed strange for this place to feel so familiar. The floorboard creaked as I walked toward the front of the chapel. The moonlight flooded the space around the lectern from the skylight. The Bible was gone, but I stood there in the moonlight on the low platform and looked out over the room. I would've been surprised if the pews had been full of people like in my dreams.

I bowed my head to pray.

I prayed for understanding. I prayed for help. I prayed for mercy and wisdom. I prayed for all the souls who had passed through this place. I prayed for direction. I prayed for the farmers and ranchers, all the families and lives hanging in the balance. I prayed in my head at first, in silence with moonlight falling over me, and then recited the Lord's Prayer from memory. I raised my eyes to the moon bathing me in its light. I stood there a long while looking up at the moon letting the Spirit of the chapel heal my soul.

I left the chapel and walked back to my car. The situation was still the same, out of my control. I was still a long way from home, but for the first time in forever I felt whole and right. My head never bothered me again after my stop into the chapel.

I got back to my apartment around eleven o'clock, after filing the story at the Phonograph. I drove around the block twice looking in all four directions before crossing the street and going up the stairs. I may have looked paranoid. That didn't mean they weren't after me. The phone was ringing when I got inside. "Hello."

"Willy," it was Amanda. "I'm so sorry. I cannot believe my mother acted like that. Please, don't think I set you up or anything. I had no idea she would say something to you. I just wanted you two to meet and..."

"Amanda, calm down. It's okay. I promise it's going be alright."

"You left in such a hurry." Her voice was hoarse. I could tell she had been crying.

"I'm sorry," I said. "I was a little freaked out. I'm alright now. Your mom has every right to be concerned."

"She's a mean old bitch and I told her so." Amanda's voice cracked. "I'm so mad I could just spit."

I laughed. I couldn't help it, being mad enough to spit struck me as funny. I heard her smile and let out a little laugh. I said, "Amanda, you should apologize to your mother."

"I will." Her voice was childish and small, "but not tonight. Maybe tomorrow."

"Well, don't spit," I said. "Listen, your mother said one thing I thought was strange, 'nothing good ever came from digging up the past'. I know you said she didn't like anything to do with Mary, but do you have any idea what she meant?"

"I told you she thought Aunt Mary was full of shit. She told Daddy that Mary was crazy. Said all the strange stuff around the cross was spooky, and unnatural, like maybe Mary was a witch or something. I told you she's a bitch."

So, it's a fact, a prophet is not respected in his hometown. Maybe that's what Amos was talking about.

"Listen," I said. "I found Kelly Patterson."

"What, no!" She almost screamed, "Where?"

"I remembered a wedding anniversary I wrote about back in December for the Allen's from Dannebrog. The daughter-in-law was Kelly Patterson-Allen. I called Mrs. Allen and she gave me Kelly's number in Minnesota."

"When are you going to call?" She sounded better now, back to normal. "Oh, can I be there when you do?"

"I don't know," I replied. "I haven't decided how I'm going to ask her. I mean, it's going to sound strange any way I ask. I don't want to come off like a crackpot."

"I think she'll be glad to talk. I mean maybe she's been keeping it bottled up all this time and wants to tell someone."

"I don't know." I said. "She might just hang up on me."

"I bet she doesn't." Amanda said with confidence. "Anyway, when are you going to call?"

I stalled, not sure if I wanted anyone around when I called. I knew Amanda wanted to be a part of everything, but her enthusiasm might be distracting. "We'll talk about it later but right now I've got to get some sleep."

"Willy, talk to me a little while longer, please," she begged like a child. It was juvenile and foolish, but I stayed up and we talked about nothing until after midnight.

Chapter 35

A few days later I stayed late at the paper. I waited for everyone to leave, pretending to work late on a story. Finally, I had worked up the nerve to call Kelly Allen. I considered what to say and how to ask her about the experience with Mary Steward at the chapel. I couldn't come up with a reasonable thing to say without sounding crazy. I knew it was a risk using the company phone to make a long-distance call about a story I had explicitly been told to leave alone, but I did it anyway. Somehow, I felt if I called from work, it would make it more professional. Truth be told, I really didn't want the call on my bill. Even with my parents paying it, I didn't want to answer for the toll.

I imagined all sorts of responses, but finally I just picked up the phone and dialed. My hand nervously shook a little as I punched the numbers. It was after six o'clock. I should catch the family at supper, but at least she would be home, I hoped. The phone rang two, three times before a girl answered.

"Hello," said a soft high-pitched voice.

"Hello," I said, clearing my throat. "Is Kelly there?"

"Who's calling?" the girl asked.

"My name is Willy Beam with the St. Paul paper," hoping the failure to specify which St. Paul paper might bring Kelly to the phone.

"Mommy, it's for you." I heard footfalls on a hardwood floor; my heart pounded with every step. A woman whispered, "Who is it?" There was a pause, but I couldn't hear the reply.

"Hello," she said?

"Hello, Mrs. Kelly Allen?" I asked.

"Yes, who's this?"

"My name is Willy Beam. I'm with the St. Paul Phonograph in Nebraska. I'm sorry to bother you this evening, but I'd hoped to ask you a few questions?"

There was a pause before she said, "About what?"

"Well," I began. "I know this may sound a little strange, but I've come across Mary Steward's journals." I paused, "Do you remember Mary and Joe Steward?"

Her voice was tentative with an edge. "I remember, yes. What about them?"

"Mrs. Allen, I'm not sure how to ask you this, but Mary recorded some amazing events in her journals, many of them happening near the old cross and chapel. Well, see one of the entries is about you and your family. There is a story about, well, after your mother died, you came to the chapel on a Sunday afternoon. Your father, well, do you remember?"

The questions hung on the line for a few unsteady breaths. "I remember."

"I don't want to bring up bad memories. I just wanted to ask because I hoped you could tell me if any of it's real? I wanted to know if the entry is true and if it is, do you..."

"Listen, I'm sorry, but I'm trying to put supper on the table and don't have time for this." The line went dead.

I listened for a moment, confused by the sudden disconnect. I pulled the phone away and looked at the receiver as if it could reveal the reason for the abbreviated call. I considered calling her right back, to try again. I wanted to know so desperately, to hear her side of the story. Maybe my desperation came through and alarmed her. It didn't matter now. She'd hung up. If I called back, she might get upset enough to call Sarge and complain. I didn't need to be fired for insubordination. That wouldn't look good on my permanent record. I put the phone back in the cradle and laid my head on my desk.

I rested there thinking. I had to try something. The opportunity was so close. If I couldn't call back, what could I do? The answer was too obvious, I could write. I pulled out a clean sheet of paper and loaded it into the typewriter. I wrote to Mrs. Kelly Patterson-Allen in Fridley, MN. I told her the story of how I came to find the journals and how she was one of the few people Mary Steward named, in all her entries. I typed verbatim the entry from Mary's journal and asked, did she remember the day? What happened to her father? Was Mary a healer of body and soul or was it just her perception? Would she please share with me the rest of the story, because I needed to know, not for publication, but for my own understanding? I asked her to call or write, providing my phone number and mailing address for both the paper and my apartment.

I addressed the envelope, then decided to make a Xerox copy of the journal entry, so she could see it for herself; I wasn't making it up. It was there in Mary's handwriting. I folded it all together, stamped it at the postage machine and ran to mail it before I lost my nerve or changed my mind. For better or for worse it was down the mail slot. It would be on its way by morning. Whether I got a reply or not, I felt better.

Chapter 36

Spring in Nebraska brings storms. The day can be sunny and bright, full of promise. Then suddenly, ominous clouds begin forming in the southwest. You can see the rain falling out of dark towering black and gray thunderheads way off across the plains. You're standing in the sunshine, then the wind picks up and the temperature starts to drop. You know the storm is coming. You can hear the storm approach like a stampede of horses. Suddenly the trees are bending, and water is overflowing the gutters, rushing and rising in depth and velocity. Sometimes hail, the size of golf balls and worse, beats crops, livelihoods and hopes to piece. A few years ago, a cluster of tornadoes ripped through Grand Island, all up and down South Locust Street; the town looked like a war zone. Spring can be like that in tornado alley. The farmer prays for rain; when it comes, he prays it doesn't cost too much. I felt a farmer's anxiety as April blew in, praying to find answers but at the same time hoping the revelation didn't cost me too much.

Before I headed off to Broken Bow again, I went to see the preacher. I visited the First Methodist Church in Saint Paul a few Sundays, not every Sunday but enough to not be a stranger. The music was familiar, comforting, even uplifting. I liked the minister. Pastor Brad Hopkins was a tall man who spoke with a gentle voice, which tended to squeak when he got excited. He was younger, maybe late thirties, with a wife, Kristal, and two little girls, Emma and Ashley.

Pastor Hopkins kept regular office hours at the church Monday through Thursday from nine to noon and one to five. The First Methodist Church in St. Paul was typical of most area churches with its wide stone steps leading up to stout doors. A soaring white cross sat atop a steeple and stained-glass windows depicted scenes from the Bible. The walls were made of dark red brick with each window trimmed in white. The office sat to the side of the main church; a miniature of the larger building, except for the cross atop its peak. The office looked to me like a calf standing beside the mother church, not yet mature enough to have grown its cross or blossomed its stained glass.

Mrs. Meyers, the secretary, smiled when I came in. "Hello Mr. Beam. How may we help you, today?"

"Is Pastor Hopkins available?".

"I'll see," Mrs. Meyers said getting up from her desk to walk over and peek into the open door of the pastor's office. I heard her tell the pastor I was here. I felt my stomach flutter. I'd thought about this meeting before coming and prepared myself with questions and notes. Still I was nervous.

"Tell him to come in," Pastor Hopkins said in his high tenor voice. Mrs. Meyers waved me in as she returned to her station. The office was large, a full fifteen by twenty-foot room, lined with bookshelves reaching up to the ceiling. The shelves and woodwork were old, dark and smelled of mineral oil. The preacher sat behind a large imposing desk beneath an over-sized window looking out over a well-kept lawn. He came out from around the desk to greet me. "Willy Beam, from the newspaper, what a surprise."

"I hope I'm not interrupting," I said as we shook hands.

"Not at all," he replied and pointed to a pair of chairs next to a small round table. I took a seat with a notebook on my knees. The pastor sat casually, crossed one leg over the other, laying his arm on the table. "What brings you in today?"

"Well sir," I began.

"Please don't call me sir, I'm Brad."

"Okay, Brad," I said. "I have a question or two I was hoping you can help me with?"

He nodded and looked toward the notebook still in my lap.

"What is the church's stance on angels?"

He smiled, his eyes searching my face for sincerity or humor in my question. I held his gaze and waited. He sat up in the chair, adjusted his shirt sleeves and said, "I don't know the official stance on celestial beings, but I'm in favor of them. Why do you ask?"

I anticipated his question and planned my reply. "I've been told a story, by someone who I believe is honest and sincere, who encountered an angel many years ago. After some research, I've come to believe it is true. So, I wanted to know if the church still believes that angels appear to people today."

Brad glanced toward the window, then the open door. He got up and walked over to gently close the door. When he returned, he placed both forearms on the table, cleared his throat, and said, "Why don't you start at the beginning?"

"I'm not sure we have the time for me to start from the beginning," I said. Brad raised an eyebrow as I exhaled and let it go. "There was a woman from a town near here. She passed a few years ago. Her husband and many of the people she knew are still alive.

I've spoken to her husband and believe the two were good, loving, honest, Christian people. I've been given journals, recorded in her own hand, which tell a story of an angel. This angel visited the home of the couple back in the forties and gave them a mission with very specific instructions to build a cross and a small chapel. They followed the instructions and for over thirty years or more, she recorded remarkable, even miraculous events, most pertaining to the cross and chapel. I believe the stories and the events to be genuine; that is they are true." I paused and then said "So, I'm wondering if angels still come as messengers of God?"

Pastor Brad pulled his hand up, his thumbs pressed against his lips. He clearly didn't get up this morning prepared to answer theological questions on angels. "Are you asking me if I believe in angels or if the church does?" I nodded. He lowered his hands to rest on the table and went on, "If the question is, do I personally believe in the existence of angels, then the answer is yes. I've never knowingly had one visit me, but I believe because of my faith."

"And faith is belief in things unseen," I said. "My question is, does the church allow that everyday people, as common as dirt, can meet angels and after that, visitation; heal people, body and soul?"

"I have many examples where people have confided in me of their experiences with things, possibly angels, which they believed saved them, helped them, interceded for them in time of danger," he offered.

"I know," I said. "I've heard similar stories. That's not exactly what I'm talking about."

"What are you talking about, then?"

I opened the journal in my lap and turned to a page I had marked. "This is one of the descriptions of the angel from her journals," I said before reading. "He was well over six feet tall. My Joe is about six two and Gabe towered above him. He had broad shoulders and dark eyes. His hair was long, down to his shoulders. He was handsome. I couldn't say how old he was. When he first approached I thought he was about fifty but when he came into the house and we sat for a while I swear he looked to be half that age."

"I cannot say he spoke, but I perceived a strong radiance. I felt as though we communicated more than talked. I look back now and realize I should have been afraid, but I wasn't. He put me at ease. What he asked us to do sounds crazy now, but at the time it was perfectly reasonable for him to ask, and for us to accept. I know he was not of this world, but he knew this world and its troubles all too well. I can write it here with complete certainty, Gabe was an angel, a messenger of God, and I couldn't have refused his request any more than Moses could've refused going to Egypt."

I looked up and into the face of Pastor Brad. I had read the entry from Mary's journal a dozen or more times. I'd had months to mull it over and consider it. I had dropped it on him, on a bright and peaceful spring morning, with no real warning. He was wide eyed for a moment and cleared his throat. "That's very interesting. Who did you say wrote this?"

"It was a woman from the area, I'd rather not say who." The events of the past few months had made me wary of giving out too much specific information.

"I'm not sure what you want me to say," he began. "Clearly this woman, this couple, had a divine experience, an encounter with someone whom they believed was sent from God."

"But do these types of things really happen?" I asked.

"It's obvious it really happened for this couple. In the end that's all that matters," he said.

"Is it?" I asked. "All that matters?"

He cocked his head and said, "Yes." There was a pause before he went on. "We want to know God. We pray for him to reveal himself or his will to us. Why should it be such a surprise when it actually happens?"

"Because it almost never does," I said.

Brad smiled. "I think it happens more often than we allow. In this modern world we ask for proof, scientific evidence, for most of the elements of great power that exist, that science can prove; we don't see them with our eyes. Rather we sense them. We know their effects, we can predict their coming; in some cases, we've harnessed their power but they are beyond our vision. God is like that. Love is indeed a power not scientifically definable. Still, I know its a great power when I look at my children and my wife."

"I understand what you're saying. What I want to know is, why here? Why this place, of all places? Why this woman, this couple?"

Brad said, "My thoughts are not your thoughts, neither are my ways your ways, declares the Lord."

"What?" That was the exact same passage Joe used when I asked him why.

"It's from the Prophet Isaiah," Brad said. "We don't know, nor will we ever fully know the thoughts of God. He chose her because she was the person he called, and here, because, well maybe it's a crossroad, a way station for those who needed help." He shook his head. "Willy, I'm not the kind of preacher who will give you a simple answer or theological argument to worry about. I'll tell you this, God has his reasons. You will have to seek the answers for yourself. If I can help you I will. I'm afraid this is your question to seek. But to answer your original question, I believe this woman believes she had an encounter with an angel and her faith, it seems like, had a powerful and important impact on a great many people. That, my young friend, is God at work. Now, I have my cross to bear," he said with a smile.

"What cross is that?"

He sighed, "A number of the churches are trying to form an association to help the farmers and ranchers in the area."

"Really," I said with surprise.

"Yes, so many of the families are in such distress. We've talked about setting up a hot line, a crisis line of sorts, so anyone who needs help can call. There have been a number of suicides. We feel if there had just been someone they could turn to; someone to understand and listen and to offer them a little hope."

"Who is we?" I asked taking out my notebook.

"There are churches from all across the state, every denomination and every congregation is involved. There is a group of pastors and elders meeting later this week to discuss plans. We're really just in the planning phase right now."

"I would be happy to do a story on it. The paper can help get the word out," I said.

"That would be great. When we have a little more information and some volunteers trained, I will certainly call you."

The meeting with Pastor Brad was helpful and reassuring. The fact was he didn't try to perform an exorcism or force me to repent for my line of questioning, something I was sure might have happened at a few of the denominations I might have asked. The idea of an ecumenical alliance of churches joining forces to help when it seemed nobody else could or would was exciting. It restored my faith in people and the church.

At the same time, he left me holding the same bag I went in with. Not that I expected him to take this cup from me but a little more guidance would've helped. What can one do if all signs and indications are that your God has put a task in your hands?

It had been interesting. The story was intriguing and shadowy but now it was more than a curiosity. The journals from the summer and fall of 1960, which someone wanted to hide, could be damaging to someone, possibly me. I spent the next few days working and considering my options. I was getting tired. This quest was now a burden, my enthusiasm was faltering.

Never-the-less, later that afternoon I found myself at the library spinning microfilm and trying to read poorly photographed copies of local papers. There is a skill to spinning the film at a rate fast enough to skip the ad pages and still slow enough to digest the column titles. I was looking at dates, reading the social history of Broken Bow and thinking 'I loved the smell of books'. The Saint Paul library was a converted store front, with a narrow aisle and a few small reading tables in the back. It did have one small microfiche viewer and a file cabinet with back issues from local newspapers.

After checking with Jimmy and Joe, I narrowed my search to between May and June of nineteen-eighty. The bad news was the Broken Bow Chieftain was a daily; the good news was, the social and church news was published only on Wednesday and Sunday. This helped me considerably. The activity can be tedious, but for a wannabe newspaper writer who can get distracted by good writing, it was fun. The national events of historical, maybe global importance were surrounded by the most random and trivial local news. Scanning these stories, reading a few and summarizing others in my mind, led me to an idea. If I had gone back fifty or one hundred years and scanned a similar collection of newspaper archives, I would find the same historical and trivial stories. The names and the places would've changed the style of writing, but not the mixture of everyday events; business and economics, politics and legal cases, social and obituaries, even editorial and opinion pages. The structure, long ago, was established and replicated. I imagine in the future, fifty or one hundred years, the same random and trivial stories would still trump the historical and important stories. We are distracted by the novel and the tragic, while the truly important and historical bore us, or we just fail to recognize the difference.

The farming crisis felt the same way to me. The tragic and dramatic impact on the people around me, in this place and hundreds of little towns like it, was transformative. The children of this generation would know the ramifications for decades. Many of them would not fully understand the ripple effect these losses would have on them. I sat in that cramped little library and considered how it would all play out. Who would be the winners and which ones the losers? Would we even know the difference in the long run?

I scrolled the pages as I mulled over the questions and consequences in my head. I was distracted by a sound; someone dropped a book on the solid oak floor. The reverberation bounced off the windows. I looked around to see the sheepish smile of a boy peeking around the corner of one of the rows of books. I smiled back, turned my eyes back to the screen and there it was.

In the church section, April 12th, 1980, "Ladies Auxiliary helps pack up Steward Ranch". The story was short, just a few lines. Still it contained a list of some of the ladies who helped: Betty Sue Anderzhon, Tammy Watkins, Pam Ott, Susan Hampton, Margery Lamkin, Helen Hitz and Ann Bailey. These names meant nothing to me. I suspected one of them knew where the missing journals were and more than likely had a good reason for them to be hidden away. What that reason was, I didn't know for sure, but I wanted to, needed to, find out.

Chapter 37

I needed Amanda's help to find the members of the Ladies
Auxiliary. I waited until the weekend to call her home number. Her
mother answered. I hung up. I called Jimmy's; he didn't answer, so I
decided to take a drive. I let the wind blow through the car to air out
the decay of winter, to wipe away the foul spirits of the past few
months, and to enjoy some warm air swirling around my head. The
open expanse of the countryside budding in spring colors lifted my
spirits. I could smell the first promises of wildflowers. The rolling
green dunes bisected by the ribbon of asphalt promised only passage
through and not the conquering of, this wild beautiful landscape. I
thought of winding roads of life through a vast wilderness of time,
until the smell of the feedlots choked my senses. I considered the
profound effects of man's encroachment on the beauty of the earth.

I tuned on the radio just as the FM station out of Ord dropped
the needle on the guitar riff from Def Leppard's "Rock of Ages". I
played steering wheel guitar and sang along. I've always enjoyed the
comfort of a steering wheel in my hands; the possibilities of an open
road framed in a windshield, and the magic of a good song playing
on the radio. While subconsciously aware of the act of driving, my
mind drifted to other roads, my destination, what lie ahead, and
daydreams not yet realized. I passed by small communities, caught
glimpses of life at intersections, flashes of color, the blur of a face
distorted in the blink of an eye. I recognize the lives at these
crossroads, of people with personal stories and private struggles; the
landscape shifting; the persistent advance of technology, rapidly
changing, progressing toward something worse or better. Who could
say? These split seconds of time, perceptions I couldn't hold on to,
passing thoughts that drifted along with me on my journey to the
crossroads. Perhaps the discovery of something important;
something recorded in the stolen journals of a modern-day Saint.

I came up out of the valley to catch site of the cross standing in
the sunlight, resolute and unyielding, against a clear blue sky. I
perceived what it must symbolize to travelers along this lonely road.
What it has always promised for lost souls seeking hope and shelter
from the harshness, the prejudices, the loneliness of this life. A
weathered cross and its small chapel offered safe harbor for a time,
giving hope and love; the greatest gifts of the Spirit to this harsh and
dangerous world.

I cruised the square a couple of times, drove out to Jimmy's place, but didn't find Amanda. I came back into town and stopped at the convenience store where I had first bought her a case of beer after the football game. That memory seemed a long time ago. I went inside to get a pop and some chips. When I came out I saw her truck go by. I hurried after her. When she stopped at the light I pulled up behind her, honked twice and waved. She pulled into a parking spot on the square and I pulled in beside her.

"Hey stranger," her friendly easy greeting made me smile. "Where you been?"

"I've been looking for you."

"Well, I've been right here," she said. "I can't imagine why it took so long for you to find me."

I walked up and leaned my forearms on the truck window and stuck my head in. She didn't back off or divert her eyes. Those eyes are something I still recall with lustful intent.

"How are you?" she asked.

"Better, much better now." I said, "I found the names of some of the ladies who helped clean out Mary and Joe's place." Pulling my notebook from my hip pocket, I handed her the piece of paper. She bit her lower lip as she read the names. While she was reading, I looked around to notice the bustle of business, a mother with two children in tow went into the drugstore. A man in overalls came out of the hardware store with a lawn mower blade in his hand. A couple entered the café just as two high school boys came out, one of the boys holding the door for the couple as they went in. There was wholesome, small town activity all around. I still felt some level of suspicion, my fight or flight disposition very much aware, which was natural but it made me uneasy anyway.

"I know most of these names," Amanda said. "And just who we should go see first."

"Great," I said. "But I don't want to get you in trouble with your parents or anything."

"Willy, don't you know by now? I've been trouble looking for a place to happen since day one." She smiled and handed me back the paper.

We started by looking up Betty Sue Anderzhon. Amanda said she lived on Fifth Street over by the Hinky Dinky grocery store. Amanda left her truck parked where it was and rode with me.

"What do you want me to ask Mrs. Anderzhon?" Amanda inquired as we pulled up to the house.

"I thought I would ask the questions," I said.

"Oh no," she laughed. "That's a bad idea."

"Why?"

"Why? Because you'll come off like a reporter and start asking questions that will get us nowhere."

"Like what?"

"Trust me," she said. "Just let me lead. If you think of something you must ask, do it gently. Don't ask anything until I get her talking." With that, she opened the door and started for the house.

The small bungalow sat back from the road with a winding sidewalk leading up to a covered porch. Amanda knocked on the door and when there was not an instant reply, she knocked again and called out, "Mrs. Anderzhon, are you home?"

We heard footsteps and Mrs. Anderzhon call, "I'm coming, I'm coming. Keep your shirt on."

Mrs. Betty Sue Anderzhon was a plucky woman of about five foot six. Her air was dyed a light brown and styled to set like a bee hive atop her head. It was held in place by a pale-yellow scarf to complement her pants suit. "Amanda dear, what brings you to my door?"

"Hello Mrs. Anderzhon," Amanda said with the sing-song voice of a little girl. "We wanted to ask you about something, do you mind?"

We were welcomed into the small comfortable living room. The light from a large front window, filtered by a sheer yellow drape, warmed the room. We took a seat on a simple modern sofa. The room hadn't been updated since the 1960's I thought.

"Do you kids want anything to drink, tea or water?"

"No thanks." I began

"That would be awesome," Amanda said with a wide dimpled smile. "We'll take tea, thank you."

Amanda gave me a look that said, "Shut up and follow my lead."

"What brings you young people to my door today?" Mrs. Anderzhon asked as she placed a tray with three glasses of tea on the coffee table in front of us. She sat down on the edge of the recliner across from us.

"Thank you for the tea," Amanda said and took a sip. "We have been going through some of Aunt Mary's things we found out at Jimmy's and we had a question we hoped you could help us answer?"

"I'll try," Mrs. Anderzhon said.

"See, there are some journals, notebooks really, of Aunt Mary's."

"I remember," said Mrs. Anderzhon. "There were a lot of them as I recall."

"Yes, and they are fascinating," said Amanda. "We've," she paused to nod in my direction, "we found some very interesting things in them. But some of them are missing."

"Oh?" Mrs. Anderzhon said with a note of interest.

"Yes," Amanda went on, "there are several months from the year nineteen sixty. We wondered if they got damaged or misplaced or something when the Auxiliary helped Joe pack up everything."

Mrs. Anderzhon looked at Amanda oddly, like she didn't understand and said. "Do you think I did something with them?"

"Oh no." Amanda said quickly, "No, that's not what I meant at all. No, we just hoped you might remember the notebooks and if you recall some of them missing or damaged."

Mrs. Anderzhon sat down her glass of tea. "You know, it was some time ago when we helped pack up all of Joe's and Mary's things. I don't remember anything about the notebooks, except there were a lot of them."

Mrs. Anderzhon looked up toward the ceiling and then gazed toward the window. There was a long pause which I filled by taking another drink of tea. It was strong and earthy, full of minerals, a taste I've come to love. A large clock in the corner ticked away the seconds as we waited. I hated this part of any conversation; my professors and Sarge had told me time and time again to wait, to let it be. I hated it still. Amanda didn't seem to mind at all. She sipped her tea and looked around at the room. She turned and smiled with a little shrug. The seconds ticked away. Suddenly Mrs. Anderzhon returned from her wandering mind, "I vaguely recall something about those notebooks but just cannot put my finger on it."

"Like what?" Amanda asked.

"It was something about, well," she looked confused. "I just don't quite remember. It will come to me. It always does. When I stop thinking about it, it will come to me. Do you kids ever have that happen?"

"Yes, I do," said Amanda and I nodded in agreement. "We would be very grateful if, when you think of whatever it is, that you would call me or Willy at the paper."

"Oh, you're with the newspaper?"

"I'm sorry, where are my manners," Amanda said. "This is my friend Willy Beam, from the St. Paul Phonograph."

"Nice to meet you," Mrs. Anderzhon said and extended her hand. I sat forward and shook her hand. "Very nice to meet you too."

"Well, a reporter," she said. "Does this have anything to do with a story you're working on?"

"No," I began.

Amanda interrupted me again. "Yes, yes it does. Willy has been working on some local history and part of it has to do with Aunt Mary's place, the cross and the chapel. Do you remember anything unusual about any of that?"

"Well, dear, there was always something unusual going on up there." She smiled in an apologetic way. "I don't mean anything bad, just strangers coming and going. Lots of rumors about it all. Mary was a dear woman, so brave and spiritual in the end."

"What do you mean spiritual?" I asked. Amanda gave me a look, but the description of Mary piqued my interest.

"Well, I don't know. She was always very in tune with spiritual things. She had a great understanding of things. I remember when she passed." Mrs. Anderzhon paused and said to Amanda. "She was such a strong woman, not afraid at all. I know she was ready to go on."

"Thank you," Amanda nodded. "Was there anything in particular, an event or maybe something she said? To make you think of her as spiritual?

"Well, let me think." She looked toward the ceiling again and then back to us. "There was one time when we were playing bridge together. We couples got together twice a month. It was always a good time; four or six couples would rotate. One time you would host and the next time you were a guest. Rotating kept it fresh and different. We always enjoyed playing cards with Joe and Mary. Joe is such a character and Mary was so bright and smart. Joe and my Al were both in the service and they talked cattle and farming. We weren't in agriculture directly; then again everything depends on cattle and corn." She smiled and took a sip of tea. The pause lasted for a few beats longer than I could stand. Before I could utter something stupid, Amanda said, "What did Aunt Mary say, while you guys were playing cards?"

"Huh, oh yes," The old lady smiled. "Sorry, I was thinking about how much we enjoyed cards." She cleared her throat and put down the tea. "We got to talking about God and the Bible. Al said something about prayer. He was in a twit over the courts taking the Lord's Prayer and the Ten Commandments out of the schools. You know the country has never been the same since that awful woman got prayer taken out of the schools. Anyway, we were talking about the Bible and how it's the Word of God and Mary said something which has always stuck with me. She said she didn't believe in the Bible, that the Bible was a window through which we might glimpse God but it was not God. I remember Al got upset with her. She said there was a big difference between inspired and authored."

"Did you ask her what she meant?" I asked.

"Al did. He was really upset at Mary, so she told him. 'I can be inspired to act, to write, to paint, to preach, to build because of God, but that doesn't mean God wrote or painted or built it; I did. The Bible is the same way. They wrote the prayers and poetry, laws and history to praise God. God didn't write it for them'".

Mrs. Anderzhon picked up her tea and took another drink, "Al was so angry he almost asked them to leave; then Joe made a joke, and everyone laughed a little. Joe was always so good at settling things down when Mary got things stirred up."

"Did Mary stir things up a lot?" I asked.

Mrs. Anderzhon cocked her head to one side and looked away for moment, then said, "She had a way of telling the truth that set people on edge. Mary was a sweet woman, would do anything for anyone. I can tell you she didn't suffer fools. She spoke with such authority. I somehow think her tone, no, that's not the right word; her certainty, made men uncomfortable."

Amanda chimed in, "Is there anyone she made uncomfortable who might have wanted to hide her journals? Anyone who might want to keep a secret?"

"I don't know," Mrs. Anderzhon said. "Maybe, let me think on it. There is still something but..."

"But?" Amanda asked.

"Cannot think what it is. When I do I'll call you, Amanda dear."

We thanked her for letting us stop by and for the tea. She followed us to the door. As we were about to step off the porch I pulled a Colombo; Peter Faulk in a prime-time cop show. The offbeat detective would ask his questions and start to leave, leading the suspect to believe the interview was over, and just as Columbo reached the door he would turn and say, "One more thing. You said, such and such, did you know...?" The question was often random, seemingly out of nowhere. The character in question would always answer and the revelation would somehow expose a hidden fact which led Colombo to solve the crime.

So I pulled a Colombo. "Mrs. Anderzhon, just one more question. Did you ever hear anything about a baby that Mary and Joe cared for? Maybe a local girl who was pregnant and they helped her?"

The old lady looked confused for a moment and then a light went on, "Yes there was the Ott girl. Oh, what was her name? Sweet as could be, Pam, no that's her mother. Jenny, that was her name, Jennifer Ott, she didn't stay around though. It was quite a scandal, her and the preacher's boy. My Al always said preacher's kids could be the wickedest things."

Amanda jumped in, "Was Pam Ott one of the ladies who helped pack up Joe and Mary's things?"

"I believe that's right," she said.

"Do you remember the name of the preacher?" I asked.

"Why yes, it's the Reverend Troutman, Peter Troutman."

"Thank you," I said. "Have a great day and if you think of the other thing please be sure to call."

On the drive back to Amanda's car we talked. "Jenny Ott gets pregnant by a local preacher's boy. Mary and Joe take care of the girl and the baby. Mary writes about it in her journals and twenty years later the mother takes the journals, Why?"

"I thought Joe said the girls' name was Elizabeth?" Amanda said.

"I know, but maybe the Reverend Troutman didn't know about the other girl. Maybe he just had time to read a small reference to a baby and assumed it was the one he was looking for. But why would it matter, why would he take them?"

"Why again." Amanda said. "We are always back to why."

"Well, that's the problem with questions. They have to have a who, what, when, where and why," I said.

"Maybe in your paper, she said. "Sometimes people just do things, without thinking, without motive, just because. It was there, I did it. Haven't you ever just done something because?"

"I did you just because," I said with a smile.

Amanda looked at me with surprise and shock. "What in the hell." Then she smiled, "I think you have that backwards."

"Yeah?"

"I did you just because." she laughed a coy little laugh. We smiled at each other. She was so fresh and full of spunk. "I'd do it again," she said. "Just because."

I thought about turning the car for the country, find a secluded turnout and see about some "just because". I didn't. Instead I brought the subject back to Mary and her journals. "We should see if we can find Pam Ott."

"I know where to find her," Amanda said. "Why don't you come to church with me tomorrow? I'll introduce you."

Chapter 38

In Nebraska, as well as most Midwestern communities, Sunday is for the most part, a separate, holy day of rest. Unless one's job is essential to the well-being of the community or one is some kind of deviant, drunk or heathen; one is expected to attend the service of choice and to ask for forgiveness, tithe and receive the sermon with somber reverence. One isn't required to sing, but if one can carry a tune, or make a joyful noise, one should raise his voice in praise. I didn't mind worship and have no particular disagreement with God. Like Johnny Cash said, "My arms are long enough to fist fight with the All Mighty." I considered myself more spiritual and less religious, a cliché for my generation. I find religion to be discouragingly hypocritical, while full of the best of intentions.

This Sunday morning, I could have benefited from an uplifting, God loves you no matter how messed up you are, kind of lesson. I had a feeling this sermon might go down the path of the vengeful, jealous God, whose wrath was being visited upon the community for its lack of obedience to the will of God.

Standing there looking up at the bell tower above the stone facade arched over the door of the Lutheran church, I could imagine a white haired old man with self-righteousness in his gait and condemnation on his lips rising to the pulpit to address the congregation of farmers and bankers, lawyers and retailers, housewives and nurses, teachers and store clerks, all huddled in their family pews. The preacher would be delivering a call for the trumpet of the Lord, followed by avenging angels, thundering down to judge the quick and the dead. I almost turned and walked away.

Amanda saw me standing outside. She came out to get me with a smile of pure delight. It was that same smile that caused me to agree to come here in the first place. "What are you doing out here?" she asked, putting her arms in the crook of my elbow and pulling me toward the doors. She wore a wool skirt and black high heels. She smelled of Vanderbilt perfume and her hair was curled, styled and teased. She looked so different, sweet and young, too young.

Katie Steward gave me an awkward smile. Bill Steward politely shook my hand, not smiling. Her brothers and their wives and children all milled about; smiling and nodding as Amanda introduced me. We moved as a group to the sanctuary. The family sat in two rows on the middle right-side of the church. As I suspected each family group had their regular pews and sections from which to worship. The organ cued the congregation to rise. The choir sang the first of three hymns followed by a prayer read from the Book of Common Prayer by a lay-minister.

"Almighty God, Father of all mercies, we give thee our most humble and hearty thanks for all thy goodness and loving kindness to us and all mankind. We bless thee for our creation, preservation, and the blessings of this life; above all, for thy unfailing love and redemption for the world by our Lord Jesus Christ, for thy grace and hope and glory. We beseech thee, our Lord God, to give us a strong sense of thy mercies, that our hearts may be thankful in your presence. Amen."

The layman, dressed in a fine black suit, walked to the lectern. "Good morning," he said to the congregation and the congregation returned the greeting. "We have a few announcements this morning..."

I looked around at the families and good folks of Broken Bow, their faces upturned and eyes forward and bright, listening to names of the sick and infirm in the community, along with upcoming events and social gatherings for the week. These were good, devout people of God who were trying to find salvation for themselves and their families.

I realized my invitation to church was not just an opportunity to meet Mrs. Ott. I could've refused or made an excuse not to come, but I wanted to. I wanted to be seen and introduced to people in Amanda's life. I wanted to see how they would act toward me, if they would be hostile or welcoming.

Suddenly, everyone rose around me. I stood with the congregation alongside Amanda. She looked so very pretty with her hair curled and makeup on, and her dress and heels; she was a doll. I hadn't seen her this way and it made me uneasy down deep in the pit of my stomach. She noticed me looking and smiled while giving me an elbow in the ribs at the same time. This wasn't just anything.

When a girl invites a boy to church it means something. It's not as big a deal as meeting the parents, but it's up there. I realized, standing there, next to her in the light of the stained-glass windows, all made up and smiling, that I would disappoint her.

We stood through another prayer and sat for the sermon. The Pastor, William White, clothed in a robe and the collar of a priest with Bible in hand, stepped up into the pulpit, adjusted the microphone and smiled.

"Good morning," he began. "The Gospel reading this morning will be from the book of John, 6:35 to 40.

"And Jesus said unto them, I am the bread of life: he that cometh to me shall never hunger; and he that believeth in me shall never thirst. But I said unto you, that ye also have seen me, and believe not. All that the Father giveth me shall come to me; and him that cometh to me I will in no way cast out. For I came down from heaven, not to do mine own will, but the will of him that sent me. And this is the Father's will, which hath sent me, that of all which he hath given me I should lose nothing but should raise it up again at the last day. And this is the will of him that sent me, that everyone which seeth the Son, and believeth in him, may have everlasting life: and I will raise him up at the last day."

"Blessed be the Word of the Lord," said the congregation in unison.

Rev. White closed the Bible before him and adjusted his notes. "Jesus is the Bread of Life and we are all called to partake of his flesh and blood. This was a difficult thing for the Jews to understand. It can be a difficult thing for us to understand but the promise is real. The promise that we will not be hungry or thirsty is real, of this I'm certain."

He paused and looked around the hall, "Now some of you may be thinking, 'Now Bill, I was hungry this morning and I was thirsty just before I came into the church.' I myself must admit, I get hungry and thirsty all the time; in fact, I could stand to be a little less hungry." He took a step back and patted his belly which was ample. The congregation chuckled appropriately.

"So how do we understand this statement, this promise of Jesus? If we look back a few chapters we see that Jesus has just fed a great multitude, five thousand men plus their families, with five barley loaves and two small fish. This miracle is what prompted this discussion among the disciples. They believed this bread is like Moses and the manna that fed the Israelites in the desert. Jesus is talking about more than manna, more than barley loaves. He is speaking of a spiritual bread and water, living water for the soul, which quenches our spirit. We all need to be fed in the Spirit and I know some of you may be thinking, spirit's fine, it's all well and good, but we've got crops to raise. We feed the world from the corn, wheat, cattle, and beans we grow right here in Nebraska."

He looked down at his notes and then lifted his hands to grip the sides of the pulpit. He raised his head, "And we know all too well the delicate, fleeting nature of our crops. We live and die with the price of corn and cattle. A hailstorm or wind, flood, or drought can destroy all that we have built. If not an act of God, then the malice of men can uproot us from our homes and all we hold dear. Then what?"

I could see the preacher was going to hit close to home. There were plenty of farmers and business men, families like Amanda's, who were asking the same question.

"What then?" Reverend White asked the congregation. "What do you do when it's all gone? How will you respond when faith is all there is? When you are truly hungry and thirsty. We will need that promise of living water, spiritual water, and the promise that comes from the sacrament, the bread of life. We are called to help each other, to do the will of the Father in Heaven, to act with compassion and mercy for each other. When we see a family in need, we must respond as a congregation, as a community. It's not enough to look out for ourselves. Jesus said in verse thirty-six, 'I've come to do the will of the one who sent me.' He was called not to do his will, but the will of the Father. Are we any less called to do the will of the Father?"

He let the question hang over the congregation. "I know in these times of trouble, when our well-being, our livelihood is threatened; it is easy to point fingers and get angry. We must submit to the will of God. God's will can be hard. Later in the seventh chapter we read that many of the people who had been following Jesus in verse sixty say, 'This is a hard teaching. Who can accept it?' You may be tempted to say the same thing; to question the will of God. I too am troubled by the tragedy I see around me. I hear some people say, 'God is judging us for our transgressions, for our trespassing.' He may very well be." Pastor White repeated the phrase almost under his breath, "Indeed he may be. I will not deny God's will does not allow our sin to go unrecognized or unchecked. We've all sinned and come short of the glory of God, but he will not abandon us. We, who are marked as Christ's own, will be guided by the Spirit and lifted up by the mercy of our Savior, Jesus Christ."

The preacher arranged his notes. He looked up to the ceiling and then out over the crowd. "What are we to do? What is to become of us? These are questions you may be asking in your homes and farms and businesses. And I tell you this, drink from the living water, eat of the bread of life, repent and pray for God's mercy and trust in the Holy Spirit to lead you. When you are in need, don't be too proud to ask for help. When you see others in need, be the hands of God and help, where you can. The Lord will not give you more than you can handle, more than you can endure. Trust in the Lord and feed yourself on the Word. Hard times don't last; faithful people, strong in the Spirit, do. Amen"

The choir rose with the first blast from the organ and the congregation stood to sing as one. I lifted my voice as well, sadly off key, I added my voice to the congregation. Later, after the closing prayer and the benediction I followed Amanda up the aisle to the exit. We had almost reached the door when Amanda stopped. "Mrs. Ott, how are you this morning?"

A large woman in a dark blue dress with orange and yellow flowers on it turned to Amanda. She wore big framed glasses and her lips were bright red, a stark contrast to her pale skin. Her eyes were brown and watery behind the glasses. "Well, hello dear," she said.

"Mrs. Ott, I want to introduce you to my friend Willy. Willy Beam this is Pam Ott."

"It's very nice to meet you," I said.

Chapter 39

When you go to church with someone, obligation and good manners dictate you to eat Sunday lunch with the family. The Steward clan gathered at the restaurant on the square. Amanda rode with me the ten blocks from the church.

"I'm so happy you came to church," she said with her bright dimpled grin.

"It was good," I said. "Do you think we can go see Mrs. Ott later today?"

"She said we could stop by, so I guess, if you want to."

Her mood changed with the subject, "Why wouldn't I want to go?"

"I don't know, no reason I guess."

"What?" I said a bit exasperated.

"Nothing, I just thought maybe you and I could spend some time together, alone."

"How will your family feel about, you and me alone, just because?"

"Who said anything about, just because?" She cut her eyes. "My brothers didn't beat the crap out of you outside the church building. Still it could all depend on how you do at lunch."

"How I do at lunch?"

"Yeah, Daddy will want to get a good look at you before he lets his little girl take off with some college boy," she said, teasing.

I pulled up to the curb and watched the family pile out of their trucks and Sunday cars. They were good Nebraska corn fed kids; wide at the shoulder and broad across the chest, with arms thick as my thighs.

"You'll be fine," Amanda said as she climbed out of the door. I wasn't so sure.

Her brothers gave me a little grief about being from Iowa, Idiots Out Wandering Around, and for Hawkeyes football. I proudly told them about going to the Oklahoma vs. Nebraska game. Once I assured them that I bled Husker Red and wowed them by re-telling all I saw from the press box in Memorial Stadium, they let me be.

Amanda smiled and laughed; she was proud I held my own against her brothers. Katie even smiled. Bill just watched and listened. I didn't take his neutral position for acceptance, just observation. He looked as if he had other things on his mind. He knew his little girl could handle most anything she set her mind to.

We had pot-roast with whipped potatoes, bacon and onion seasoned green beans, fresh rolls with real butter and brown gravy over the whole mess. It was comfort food served from a local diner by a woman who could've been your grandmother. News stories and clips from back in the day showed of what was in style. The latest cool stuff like: car phones, Rubik's cube, spiked hair, and mullets; valley girls with songs and a movie to highlight their strange dialect, and odd clothes. The fads and styles of the eighties eventually made it to the Midwest. There were girls who wanted to be Madonna or Cindy Lauper and guys who tapped into the rebellion of the Clash or tried to be preppy in the style of Tom Cruise and Rob Lowe, but not around that table on that Sunday.

These were country boys whose boots were worn for comfort, not style. The girls followed the big hair fashion of the times, but more in line with Barbara Mandrel and Rosanne Cash, the Judd's, or Reba. Those valley girl wannabes lived in Omaha and Kansas City, Des Moines, and maybe Lincoln. They would've looked out of place in Broken Bow or St. Paul. The fashion trend for the girls in the Sandhills was FFA jackets and Four H t-shirts with their daddy's denim work shirt as a jacket. They wore boot cut jeans bought at the feed and surplus store, faded by work, not bleached to look stonewashed. On Sunday, maybe some dress or slacks for mom and a western style sports jacket with a bolo tie and Stetson hat for dad, whose boots would be polished to a high sheen.

This was the collection of good people I dined with on that Sunday afternoon. I felt foolish with my penny loafers and button-down shirt. I'm sure to them I looked the perfect fool. Amanda may have liked that I dressed different and didn't own a pair of boots. I liked her tough country girl dress and wild hair. Still it was her sweet smile and flirty green eyes I recall the most.

After lunch we went to see Mrs. Pamela Ott, who lived on 8th Street, a block west of the fire station. The sad little house sat only a few strides from the sidewalk, surrounded by a chain-link fence with a simple metal latch on the hinged gate. The siding was a pale green with white trim.

Amanda stepped up on the concrete steps and knocked at the wooden screen door. The sun was streaming down overhead, reflecting off the house with harsh effects on my eyes. This was not what I had expected to find. This house looked ill-kept in a neighborhood that was fading: there were cracks in the sidewalks and ill kept yards full of dandelions and clover, trees overgrown and unattended, dead or dying branches dangling in the upper tiers of the canopy.

We heard a rustle of movement from inside, then the door groaned as it opened. Mrs. Ott was dressed in a housecoat, a large billowing light blue thing buttoned up the front; slippers to match, a clear indication she was resting for the afternoon.

"Hello," Amanda said. "Did you remember we were coming by?"

"Yes, yes," Pam said. "Come on in." She moved back out of the door and we followed her inside. The ten by ten living room was over-furnished with a love seat and a recliner, a large console television set, the kind with a flip-up lid to hide a record player, and AM/FM radio with big cloth covered speakers on either side of the TV screen. I had helped my father move a similar sized system and can attest to their incredible weight.

Mrs. Ott took a seat on a cloth covered recliner; Amanda and I scooched behind the coffee table to sit on the loveseat. A small dog, a mutt mix of terrier and something unintended, rushed in and barked at us. His tail was wagging but his attitude wasn't welcoming in the least.

"Hush now," Mrs. Ott said to the dog. "Come here and stop all that noise."

The dog licked his lips and looked from us to his owner. Then with a few hops across the hardwood floor jumped up onto her lap. She placed the dog to her side and gave him a pat on the head. "Virgil here is all bark and no bite," she said with a smile. "Now, what do you young people want with this old woman on a Sunday afternoon?"

"Well," began Amanda, "the thing is we've been going through some of Aunt Mary's things stored out at Jimmy's place and there are a bunch of journals."

Pam Ott nodded and smiled, "Mary wrote all the time, she had such beautiful handwriting."

"Yes, she did," Amanda agreed. "The thing is, there are a few missing." Mrs. Ott kept rocking and petting Virgil. Her mouth was turned down at the corners and her lips disappeared.

"Do you remember helping pack up the journals?" Amanda asked.

"How do you mean?" the old woman asked.

Amanda shrugged, "I don't mean anything, just wanted to know if you remember packing up the journals?"

"Like I said," Pam Ott looked away, "there were plenty of them. We just packed up the lot along with everything else."

"Did you read any of them?" I asked.

"Did I read them?" Pam Ott waved her hand and laughed. "No time for reading. We were working out there for two days, lots of stuff just piled up. Joe being a widower for a few years, then laid up with his hip; the stuff had piled up. No telling what might have happened to some of the journals."

"The thing is," Amanda began, "there appears to be only about a half dozen or so missing, all from the spring and fall of nineteen sixty."

"Oh, well that is odd," said Mrs. Ott.

"Yes, it is," Amanda went on. "We've been racking our brains trying to figure out why just those six or eight months."

Mrs. Ott continued to rock, a blank expression on her face, giving no reply nor offering any thoughts. Amanda had cast the line, but Pam wasn't biting so I joined in.

"There were a few references just before, in May, of a girl who was pregnant staying with Joe and Mary. Do you recall anything about that?"

The old rocker slowed a bit and Mrs. Ott quickly smiled. "I know Mary always had people coming to stay with them. The old chapel attracted all kinds of strangers. I wouldn't be surprised if one of them was a pregnant girl. I don't remember anyone specific."

"Well, that is strange," said Amanda looking at me and then back to the old lady. "When we talked to Mrs. Anderzhon, she was sure that you would know something about the girl."

Mrs. Ott shook her head, not saying anything for a few cautious rocks of the chair. "I don't wish to be rude. I'm really tired. It's been a busy morning with church, I was up early to help with the Sunday school class. It's amazing how much energy five and six year olds have." She smiled with her lips, but her eyes were sad.

Amanda and I took the hint.

"We are sorry to bother you, we'll be going." Amanda stood up. I got up as well. Amanda moved toward Mrs. Ott and took her hand. "Thank you for letting us come to see you."

Mr. Ott rocked forward, forcing poor Virgil from his comfortable seat on her lap, and stood. We turned toward the door when I noticed a number of pictures on a table by the phone.

There was a family portrait, Mrs. Ott was much younger, maybe in her forties. Mr. Ott, looking older by at least a decade, stood by her side with two children in front, seated on a low bench. The boy looked about fifteen with short hair and glasses, a blue checkered western style shirt and blue jeans. The girl was a bit older. She was tall, like her father, with a pale blue dress with puffy sleeves and a high collar. She wasn't unattractive, just awkward with a forced smile to hide her teeth.

"Is this your family?" I asked picking up the picture.

"Yes, yes, it is. That was always one of my favorites. The kids were just into high school."

"What are their names?" I asked.

"Henry, named after his grandfather and Jennifer named after my mother."

"Are they still around?"

"Henry is," she said. "He's in North Platte. Works for the railroad. He has three boys."

"Little ones?" Amanda asked.

"No," the grandmother said, talking the picture from my hand and pointing to another on the ledge. Three boys, all in their teens, stood next to an older version of the boy in the picture. "They're all grown now, college or married with babies of their own." She beamed and pointed to a picture of an infant laying on its belly on a blanket with a small tuft of hair held up by a blue ribbon. He had a wide toothless smile.

"Oh, what a cutie," Amanda said with a gush only girls can offer at the sight of a baby.

There were other pictures of the boy with his kids and a picture of Mr. and Mrs. Ott together in a frame engraved for their silver anniversary but no other pictures of the daughter.

"Does Jennifer have any children?" Amanda asked with a smile.

Mrs. Ott's smile, which had been there just a moment ago when talking about her grand-babies, faded and her eyes looked toward the floor. "No, I'm afraid she's gone."

"I'm so sorry," Amanda said with complete sincerity. "I had no idea."

"What happened?" I asked. Amanda gave me a look. I held my ground trying to look empathetic.

Mrs. Ott reached for the picture in my hand. She took it and looked at it with a deep sadness, then pressed it to her bosom and said, "She went away, to California, after school. We missed her terribly. We didn't hear from her for a long time. Then a few years ago, I got a call from a nurse in Sacramento who said Jenny was dying of cancer." The word cancer caught in her throat. Her eyes watered at the edges. "I'm very sorry. I need for you to go now." she said not looking at us, but rather at the pictures on the wall.

We left, as quietly as we could with a simple wave of our hands, closing the door behind us, leaving Pam Ott to her pictures and her sadness.

We sat in the car studying the little faded house. It leaned a little, the roof line slanted to the south, the galvanized steel gutters gapped from the roof and the downspouts rusted. The paint around the windows was cracked and peeling; weeds held sway in the yard and were encroaching on the sidewalk.

"She's such a brave soul," Amanda said.

"How so?"

"Her son isn't in North Platte with the railroad any more. He lost the farm and moved out there hoping to get a job with Burlington Northern. He hurt his back somehow. Dad said he was not doing very good." Amanda wiped her nose and her face, it smeared her mascara a little at the corners.

"She was a farmer's wife all her life and when the farm was gone she lost everything."

"What happened?" I asked

"Same song, different verse. The bank loaned too much, crops were destroyed by a storm, and insurance didn't cover the loss, no more credit, and no way to save the land." Amanda shrugged. "Nothing to be done, it sucks. She comes to church every Sunday and Wednesday, Momma says, for the food as much as the fellowship. I don't think she eats right, diabetic maybe."

"You think she took the journals?" I asked.

Amanda shrugged, "If she did, it's alright with me."

"Why, would she take them?"

Amanda stared off. "Maybe because it makes her happy. Maybe she reads about a baby being born and thinks of her little girl. Maybe she imagines her grand baby, wrapped in a blanket and held close in her arms. Maybe the why isn't important, maybe this whole damn thing is a waste of time."

I started the car and drove off. We didn't talk for a few blocks. I started to defend the mission. Then I thought of Pam Ott's sorrow and the quiet tears streaking her face, holding the family picture. Maybe the why wasn't as important as it had seemed a few hours ago.

Chapter 40

I took Amanda out to her family home. I had never been to the farm, west of Broken Bow on Callaway Road. We turned between two sturdy iron fence posts onto a winding gravel drive leading back toward Mud Creek. The hard-packed drive ran like a ribbon through the low green hills leading up to a large two story house. Trees encircled the yard, a Quonset hut stood back from the parking area, and next to the parking area, a traditional Nebraska red barn. I parked next to her truck, my Honda Civic looking much out of place in this landscape.

"Thank you, for coming to church," she said.

"Thanks for lunch," I said trying to be cool. For the life of me, I couldn't think of a thing to say. She looked toward the barn. The yard was still, the air was warm and for the first time, neither of us said a thing. Amanda was always more comfortable with the silence but this time she looked as unsure as I felt. What was the next move? What were our options? Was there anything else to say or do?

"You want to see something?" she finally asked.

"Sure," I said.

"Go back to the road," she said. "There's a place a little ways from here."

We rolled the windows down and the air rushed through the car like a whirlwind. She directed me down a minimum maintenance county road. The dirt road was washed out at the edges, so I had to drive down the middle. Thank God on a Sunday afternoon there was little or no traffic. We topped a rise and a green carpeted valley opened up before us. Low rolling hills decorated with growing afternoon shadows and lazy clouds painted the landscape in darker greens and yellows. Along a hillside, standing in groups, and alone, were cows; red and cream heifers beneath a slow turning windmill. The scene was so lovely and authentic; the blue sky, those cows grazing on a green open landscape beneath a rusty old windmill, was unforgettable.

"Turn here," Amanda said without looking at me. I turned toward the creek on a rutted trail. She had me park in a stand of trees clustered along the river. As I breathed in the landscape, I understood why people out here held this land so dearly; something which is so harsh and so beautiful, untamed and bountiful. This land was what their ancestors came for, a promise of land and the hope of building something to pass on. This land once teemed with buffalo and Indians, Pawnee, Sioux, and Cheyenne, who followed the great shaggy herd across this landscape. If I closed my eyes, I could almost imagine the primitive romantic scene of the buffalo hunt, thundering and exhilarating, right here in the valley. I could sense why the Sandhill and Whooping crane migrated across this land to rest along the rivers before heading south. This wild and beautiful land could be harsh and unforgiving, but on that day it looked like paradise.

We followed a footpath leading down to the water. The land dropped off sharply along the bank and a small dock stuck out over the waist deep water, flowing along at a leisurely pace.

"This is good," Amanda said.

"Good for what?" I asked.

"Just because," she said leaning in to kiss me. She tasted like bubble gum and smelled of the spring wind. She was uninhibited, without hesitation or guilt. It was amazing, how "just because" sex helped to toss away the worries and let go of the 'why'. We were young and there was too much tension, too much pain to deal with, and "just because" chased it all from our minds. Later we sat on the edge of the dock dipping our feet in the water. I couldn't stop grinning like a fool. We watched the sunlight fade and the landscape darken until finally she said. "I need to get home. Mom will be waiting supper on me soon."

I dropped her off at her house, watched her run like a little girl across the yard, up the back steps, and with a glance over her shoulder disappear into the house.

On my drive back to St. Paul, I listened to the King Biscuit Flour Hour on KBBN 93.3 FM with host Bill Minkin. "We've got one of my favorite new bands. This live performance was recorded a few years ago at the Orpheum Theater. With the success of their new album, "Unforgettable Fire", I just had to play a session by U2 with Bono, The Edge, Larry Mullin Junior and Adam Clayton" The intro faded, and my speakers came alive with "G-L-O-R-I-A, Gloria"

Ever since, I was a huge fan. I would be one of the few who braved the storm to see them live at Red Rocks in June. Their passion rang like bells in my head. My Ipod holds at least a hundred songs by U2. They made me think deeper and wider about the world around me and beyond; at the same time, I felt as though Bono sang to my heart, marking critical moments in time with lines which opened ravines of memories in my soul. When U2 broke into "I Will

Follow," it carved the memory of the day with Amanda, with such clarity and sadness; I could hardly listen to it without melancholy splinters irritating my eyes. I was well aware one of us would walk away and the other couldn't follow.

Chapter 41

I worked on stories, did my job, the novelty of it gone, and the illusions of grandeur a memory. Sarge seemed to always be in a foul mood. The thought occurred to me that a little "just because" would improve his mood, but I couldn't think of a woman with the fortitude to give it to him. He ranted about my copy; the red editing pen bled over two good stories. I didn't care. I made the changes and verified the facts. The content remained the same. I would like to tell you how Sarge's harsh editing made me a great writer. I won't, and it didn't. It made me want to do something else. Maybe I don't take constructive criticism well, or maybe I don't have a passion for the news. I know the more he circled and marked, the less I wanted to be a newspaper man.

I was working on one of my revisions on Thursday morning when my phone rang. "Phonograph, this is Willy."

"Mr. Beam," said the older woman on the line. "This is Sue Anderzhon."

"Mrs. Anderzhon, how nice to hear from you," I said with a surprised smile on my face.

"I called to tell you I remembered," she said. "I remembered what it was about those notebooks of Mary's that you and Amanda were asking about."

"Yes," I said hopefully.

"Are you two still working on a story about the Steward place?"

"Yes, yes I am," I assured her.

"Well the thing is," she began. "I was cleaning up some old notes from the Auxiliary meetings, and I came across a scrap of paper. It was a bulletin from the Church of the Nazarene and I remembered."

"Remembered what?"

"It was the preacher; Reverend Troutmen of the Nazarene Church. He came by the Steward's when we were cleaning up. He helped pack up a few things; mostly he was looking through the notebooks. He asked if he could take a few of them, for research or something. I told him they weren't ours to give, but he assured me he would return them when he was done. I knew I shouldn't have let him take them. With him being a pastor and all, I thought it would be alright."

"Do you know if he is still around, in Broken Bow?"

"He has moved over to a church in Pleasanton, north of

Kearney. I don't know which one. I suppose it would still be a Nazarene church."

"Mrs. Anderzhon, this is great news. Thank you very much," I said.

"Well, I knew it would come to me. I just had to let it rattle around in my brain till I found it," she said much pleased with herself.

"I'm so glad it did," I said. "Do you know anything about Reverend Troutmen?"

"I didn't know him well. I remember he was a very abrasive man. He was strong minded and stubborn. I know that's not a good thing to say of a preacher, but he could be a bully with people who he could intimidate. He never held much over me and I should have stood my ground when he asked to take those journals. I was busy you see, and no one was around, so I let him take them."

"How would you have known? I'm sure he had a good reason for taking them," I assured her. "Do you remember the reverend's first name?"

"I do," she said. "It's Frank, Franklin B. Troutmen. I don't know what the B stands for, but it's here on the bulletin."

"Thank you very much for the call. We'll see if we can't find him," I assured her.

"Well I hope so. You will let me know when the story is coming out. I'll want to read it," she said.

"I sure will," I said. "I'll have to get the whole thing approved for publication by my editor, but when it comes out I'll be sure to mention that you were instrumental in our research."

"Well now, that would be sweet of you," she said. I could hear her smiling on the other end of the line.

I looked in the phone book; first for the church, and next for a Mr. Franklin Troutmen. There were several churches in Pleasanton, none of them the Nazarene Church and there was no listing for Troutmen, Franklin or otherwise.

I looked in the Kearney listings, still nothing. I began looking in the phone book for the name in the other little towns: Ravenna, Sweetwater, Hazard, and Litchfield. I read the listings as they would appear on the map along Hwy 2 on to Mason City, and finally Ansley where I found a listing for the Rev. Franklin Troutmen.

On my way to Broken Bow, I drove through Ansley, a small hamlet at the crossroads of Highways 2 and 183. The tiny village might have once held great promise, with both Mud Creek and a branch of the Burlington Northern railroad passing to the west of it; in my memory it was a wide spot in the road.

My first thought was to call to make an appointment. I decided to wait to talk to Amanda. Just then Sarge roared, "Beam, get in here." I dropped what I was doing and rushed off to see what he wanted.

When I entered Sarge's office, he was standing by the fax machine. The pages were slowing spilling out of the odd little printer at a rate of one every ninety seconds. He was sweating and smoking, an unbecoming combination if there ever was one.

"I need you to get over to the Taylor farm. There was a report on the scanner of a disturbance of some kind. I think they went to serve papers on the old man."

"The police are there?" I asked.

"Sounds like it." Sarge pulled the paper from the fax machine and walked toward his desk, reading as he crossed the room. He looked up at me when he reached the corner of his desk. "Are you still here?" he growled.

I ran by my desk, grabbed a notebook, pen, and tape recorder. I was out the door in a minute and headed south out of town within five minutes.

I drove like a mad man and got to the Taylor place within ten minutes. The Sheriff and two deputy cars were parked on either side of the drive, back from the house. I parked behind one of the patrol cars and got out. I didn't see anyone outside the house, but as I walked up closer to the house, toward the outbuilding, I heard voices.

"Jim, please don't do this," Mrs. Taylor said. I slowed my approach waiting at the corner of the house.

"Listen to her, Jim," I heard the Sheriff say. "This is no good. If you have a grievance with the bank, then we can work it out."

"To hell with that sucker, Oldfather," I heard Mr. Taylor yell. "He's been after my land for years, he ain't gonna get it. Over my dead body, they'll have this land."

"Now Jim, calm down," It was Mrs. Taylor again. I wanted to peek around the corner, but didn't want to add to the drama, so I stayed where I was at the corner of the big farmhouse, behind an overgrown hydrangea bush. The sun was hot. I checked my watch, a quarter to three. I didn't see the deputies.

"Jim," it was the Sheriff. "You need to respect the situation. I know this land means a lot to you and your family. I understand, believe me, I do. But the bank has the right to issue a foreclosure, and unless you can pay the note, they can foreclose. Now, it's not fair, it might not be right, but it's the law and everyone has to respect the law."

"The law!" Jim Taylor bellowed. "The law! What kind of bullshit are you spreadin', sheriff? This is my land. I've given everything for this land, sweat and bled for this land, and by God I'll die here.

"Jim, don't say that, please," Mrs. Taylor was crying.

"Nobody going to die today," the Sheriff said in a calming voice. "We all need to just calm down."

I was dying to step around the side of the house and see what was going on. I turned on my recorder on the chance it was picking up the conversation and not just the wind.

Suddenly, I heard yelling and the sounds like a scuffle, then the unmistakable sound of a shotgun blast. I leapt out from behind the bush to see the two deputies wrestling the old man to the ground. His shotgun was pointed at the sky. Mrs. Taylor was standing with her hands over her mouth just outside the back door. The Sheriff had drawn his pistol, pointing it in the air. The three men on the ground were struggling for control of the shotgun. There was a collection of hands pulling in all directions, the gun barrel moving back and forth, up and down, in the desperate struggle for control of the weapon.

The old man was strong, angry, and determined. The young deputies had stamina and authority on their side. It was an even match, but slowly the barrel moved backwards, tipping over like the loser in an arm wrestling contest. Then one of the deputies delivered a quick jab to the old man's ribs, then another, and another. The old man let out a yell when the shotgun fired.

Mrs. Taylor screamed "No, oh God no!"

The deputies had control of the gun. One deputy rolled away from the other two with the shotgun in both hands. The other rolled up on top of the old man, flipping him over on his back. He had Jim's left arm pulled up behind his back and pressed the handcuffs into place. The Sheriff rushed forward to help; within a moment there was nothing except the sound of the old woman crying and her husband's heavy breathing.

The Sheriff yelled over his shoulder, "What the hell are you doing here?"

"Sarge told me to come find out what was going on."

"There's nothing going on here," he said as he got up from the ground. He dusted his pants, walking toward me. "Boy, this needs to stay between us."

"Who's us?" I asked.

"You, me," he pointed his hat back toward the Taylors. "And them."

The old man was still mad enough to fight but restrained at the deputy's feet.

"I got to report something," I said.

"The hell you do," replied the Sheriff.

"But," I began.

"But nothing," Sheriff Griffith leaned in close to my face now. "Tell Sarge nothing happened here. Soon as Jim calms down we'll all leave peacefully."

"Why was he being cuffed in the first place?"

"Son, you need to listen up. This doesn't get reported in the paper. Nothing good will come of it, for you, me, or the Taylors."

We locked eyes, for the first time in my life I stood my ground against authority. I could hear the blood rushing into my ears and smell the sheriff's stale breath in my face. A year ago, hell, twenty minutes ago, I would've cowed. There, in that moment, I would not be censored, or intimidated.

"Sheriff," the deputy called. We both turned our attention to the group sitting in the yard.

Jim Taylor looked pale. He was gasping for breath, crumpled over to his left side. I knew instantly, he was having a heart attack.

"Get the cuffs off him," Sheriff yelled. The deputy fumbled for his keys, trying to remove the restraints. I slid on one knee. Taking Jim by his shoulders and rolling him forward onto me so the deputy could get the cuffs off. We laid him back on the ground. I positioned myself to do CPR.

"You breathe, I'll pump," I said to the deputy.

The Sheriff ran for his car to call for an ambulance.

The deputy, Scott, as it said on his badge, began working in rhythm. I counted as I compressed the old man's chest; "one, two, three, four, five, and breath." Scott leaned down and pushed three quick breaths into the dying man's mouth, holding his nose closed and jaw open. I compressed again and Scott breathed. Mrs. Taylor sat by our side, holding her husband's hand, head bowed in prayer. Her soft frail voice pleaded for his life. After a few rounds with the deputy breathing and me pumping, my arms ached; sweat dripped from my forehead. I wanted to quit, God help me, I wanted to roll over and give up. The old woman's desperate and determined prayer kept me working. Finally, we heard the siren from the ambulance and with it we gained a second wind to hold on. The EMT's pulled up next to the house, unloaded the gurney, and rushed to our relief.

"What's the status?" I heard the EMT's ask the deputy.

"He turned gray and fell over. We've been working on him for a while. I don't know if there's a pulse, he's breathing."

The EMT, Bill Jennings, placed a hand on my shoulder and said, "We've got it. Nice work, fellas."

I rolled onto my side onto the grass, breathing heavily. I could feel the ache in my back. I could hear the sobs of Mrs. Taylor and wanted to cry myself. I closed my eyes, lay still for a moment and prayed. "Dear Heavenly Father, please have mercy. Don't take him yet Lord, not like this, not from this place."

The EMT's lifted the gurney and sped away to the open doors of the ambulance. In a flash they were slamming the doors and speeding away with lights flashing and sirens screaming.

I rolled over and got to my feet. I was lightheaded.

"You alright?" I heard Deputy Scott ask.

I nodded, standing with my hands over my head like I did after basketball practice. I was drained from fighting for a life and the desperate, heart pounding fear of losing the energy of life, pressing with all my strength to call it back into the body.

That's where I base my belief in God, the power of life, the energy which fully animates us, not just the body, but also the mind. That energy cannot be reclaimed or replicated. With all our advancements in science and computers we cannot reclaim life or generate it from the ether. The breath of life, as ancients called it, is not of this world. We feel it, but still cannot touch it. We know it, and cannot name it. It is of a higher power, an infinity source beyond us, holy and apart of us. It is why I still believe, despite all the pressure to concede that there is no proof. For me, the proof lies with what we call the soul. It's more than consciousness, more than bodily function; it is the essence of God in each of us. I felt it in the old man's fainting heart and our desperate struggle for his life.

Chapter 42

The story Sarge got from the Taylor foreclosure was not what he expected. It was some of my best work. I wrote my version of the events with a reluctant interview with the Sheriff. Mrs. Taylor gave me a few really great lines. Mr. Taylor was taken to Saint Francis Hospital in Grand Island where he received a triple bypass and a pacemaker. They cut him from navel to neck, cracked his chest and left him with a jagged pink scar, but he lived. He was still tough as a six-penny nail. His bark was now much worse than his bite. Mrs. Taylor was very happy to have him alive. I got the feeling Jim could've passed with no fear of meeting his maker. He thanked me with some prompting from his wife. Despite his unenthusiastic gratitude, I think he was happy to be alive.

I got some high praise from Meg at the diner. There were a few looks of admiration and a few heart-felt handshakes for my heroic act. Still, there are times even now when I wonder if I did the right thing. I acted on instinct and couldn't have stood by and let him die when it was possible to save him; even so, there are questions in my mind, not regret, just introspections.

In all the excitement of the story, I almost forgot about the Reverend Troutmen and the journals.

Then Amanda called. "Willy?"

"Amanda, what's going on?"

"What's going on with you?" She sounded exasperated, "Where've you been?"

"Work," I said a little annoyed by her tone. "Where else would I be?"

"I don't know, it's just, well you haven't called. I talked to Mrs. Anderzhon. I thought you would want to talk with the preacher Troutman?"

"I guess so," I said a little unsure of what I wanted.

"You guess so?" Her voice raised an octave. "We need to go see this guy and find out what happened to the journals."

"What does it matter now?" I asked. After our visit to Pam Ott, I didn't know how to feel about finding the journals. Would there be nothing but sadness, or worse in the outcome?

"It matters to me, you jerk-weed," she said. "And it matters because of Mary. It matters, and I want to know what happened."

"Okay," I said. "Okay, we'll go see Mr. Troutmen," Her name calling made me laugh.

She laughed and said, "You're such a jerk-weed."

I hung up the phone. Suddenly a folded newspaper landed with a spat on my desk. Melvin was standing behind me with a sad look on his face.

"Christ," I said. "You scared the hell out of me."

"That should scare you more than me," he said pointing to the paper on my desk.

"What, why?" I asked as I opened the paper. The headline sent a chill down my spine.

Farmer Dies in Shootout near Elba by Terrance Moore.

Todd Childers, age 34, died Thursday night in a shootout with Nebraska State Patrol SWAT Team. According to County Attorney Ralph Deardorff, Childers was shot as he ran from a farmhouse toward a makeshift bunker near Elba. Childers had fired at the officers who had been engaged in a six-hour standoff which began at around 3:30, when Childers refused to allow authorities to come onto the property to search for a reported stockpile of weapons and ammunition. According to the Sheriff's office, the deputies, who attempted to serve a warrant to search the property, were threatened. The farmer insisted the no trespassing sign at the gate allowed him the right to shoot anyone who came on his property. He then brandished a weapon and fired over the heads of the officers, who fell back and called for assistance.

Deardorff said Mr. Childers was shot about 10:45 pm as he tried to fight his way from the house to a bunker. He died in the farmyard, armed with a AR-15 army type rifle which had been modified for automatic firing. Deardorff confirmed Childers' face was painted in a military camouflage style; he had numerous rounds of ammunition on his person and a gas mask on his belt. He said Childers fired several rounds in the direction of a SWAT team member as he ran for the shelter. SWAT team members called for him to "Stop." When the farmer refused to obey, and instead fired in the direction of the voice, at least two officers fired, killing Childers.

Deardorff said Childers was the only casualty of the shootout. He said, before the SWAT team was called out, sheriff's deputies tried to negotiate with Childers in an attempt to get him to surrender. Around 4:45 an arrest warrant was issued for a felony resisting arrest with a dangerous weapon.

Deardorff said after the SWAT team was in position, a deputy and the State Patrol attempted to get him to surrender. Childers' wife, Marie, also talked with her husband by telephone from the sheriff's office during the standoff, but the County Attorney could not say what they talked about.

After the standoff, a search of the home revealed a collection of rifles, many of which were army style weapons, along with a stockpile of ammunition and explosives. Also found were pamphlets and literature associated with a right-wing extremist group known as the Posse Comitatus. The wife, Marie, refused to answer any questions about the guns or the propaganda found at the farmhouse. Mrs. Childers was still mourning the loss of her father, Harold Perkins, who committed suicide last month when his property was foreclosed on by Norwest Bank of Grand Island.

Deardorff said part of the continuing investigation was to establish the link, if any, to the Posse Comitatus. Before his death Childers claimed his phone was being tapped. The wife is reported to have said of her husband during the negotiations, "He will never be taken alive."

"Holy shit," I whispered to myself. "This happened last night? Why didn't someone call me?

"The Grand Island Independent covered the story. No one from here was called," Melvin said. "JP is in a mood over this."

"This is the son-in-law I met when I went to Harold's place back in the fall," I said, as much to myself as Melvin. I looked back at the paper and stared at the picture of Todd Childers. His face was familiar, not because I had seen him in the daylight, but because I recalled his appearance on the night I was attacked. My blood ran cold and my hands shook. I knew the dead farmer had beaten and left me for dead on a cold winter's night.

Chapter 43

Amanda and I agreed to meet on Saturday in Broken Bow. We'd drive to Ansley to see what we could find out from the Reverend Troutmen. That week, I made a decision to start looking for work back elsewhere, maybe Des Moines or Kansas City. I had learned plenty about life and work here in the Sandhills, but I'd had enough of a small-time newspaper and small town life. I learned a few things as well. No matter how far away you roam, home is not just a place; it's a collection of experiences, of sounds, and smells captured in the unconscious, and filtered by time. Home is an anchor, a lifeline and a past, filled with influences; both big and small. It can harbor your fears and hold you captive. It's the place your morals stem from, as well as your reactions to tragedy and triumph.

On the drive over, I popped in the latest cassette I got from the record store, Dan Fogelberg, "The Innocent Age." I fast forwarded to the title song. I loved the simple timeless phrases and expressions. I wondered if I was the dreamer, the fool or the sage. I had an unsettled feeling in the pit of my stomach; then again it could've been the convenience store burrito from this morning.

I met Amanda downtown on the square. She was excited. "What is the plan, Stan?" she asked. "Where, what, when and why; that's what I want to know."

"Well," I said with a smile on my face, both for her enthusiasm and the inside joke we shared. "Where, is the First Evangelical Church of Ansley. What, is the missing journals. When, is in about twenty minutes or so. And Why, is because you said it matters."

"Oh, it does, it matters," she said with a clap of her hands.

"I remember when I first showed up, you didn't know or care about the journals and now it matters," I teased.

"I didn't care because I didn't know," she shot back. "Besides, I finish what I start. You have to see things all the way through to the end, no matter the outcome. And I found out some things you've got to hear."

"Okay," I nodded in agreement, because that is so much the way it is out here. You don't leave things unfinished. If you start, you finish; every effort, every endeavor, has value in the process. The experience, good or bad, is a lesson to be learned.

"What are you going to ask the Reverend Troutmen?" she asked.

"Oh, wait, you're going to let me ask questions this time?"

She gave me a playful swat on the shoulder with the back of her hand and said, "Yes, of course, you ask questions anyway. Even if I tell you to let me do the talking."

I remember her smile sparkling with laughter.

"I plan on being straightforward and honest, that's the only way I know how to be," I said.

"You're such a jerk-weed," she said using her new favorite expression.

We headed southeast from Broken Bow. When we drove past the cross, Amanda dug around in a backpack she brought with her. "You've got to listen to this." She took out three or four journals. She turned to a page she had earmarked. "Okay, here it is,"

February 16, 1950

The Minister from the Lutheran Church came to see me today. He came with snow on the ground two feet deep. He started off polite, how do you do, and boy, is it cold out. Then he asked about our intentions for the cross and chapel. I told him my intentions were to praise God. He said the cross seemed to be attracting "unusual sorts of people". Nicely as I could, I said as far as I could tell, a cross will always attract unusual, even extraordinary people. He told me the people coming up here were not in any way extraordinary, but in many ways undesirable. He and the other church leaders were concerned about other things. They were hearing stories about the chapel as well. I asked what sort of stories. To which the self-righteous son of a gun implied that I was practicing some kind of witchcraft or sorcery. So I asked him to leave.

Why is it people are so quick to suspect the devil when something extraordinary happens? Preachers spend half their days praying with families for a miracle, and when one actually happens, they send some smug black collar up here to investigate. People say they believe in the power of God, but then don't recognize it in their own back yard.

"Where did you find that?" I asked.

"It was with the others at Jimmy's" she said. "Wait, there's more." She opened another journal and flipped to another entry.

September 8, 1957

It's been some time since one of the ministers has come up here. I go down to church every Sunday, but they don't come up here very often. Pastor Green from our church is very helpful and understanding, but some of the other congregations are not so enlightened. Anyway, the elders from a Missouri Synod Church called on us today. We sat down to coffee; they were polite for a time. Then one of them asked what type of chapel we had up here. I asked what he meant by type. He turned to Joe and asked if the chapel was affiliated with a particular church or presbytery. Joe told him he would need to ask me about the chapel and the cross. God bless my Joe when he said, he was just the hired help. I almost laughed out loud. They would hardly look at me but directed their comments to Joe. They said it was not proper for a chapel to have no specific doctrine affiliated with it. One of them said the chapel was improper because people who came here to worship were not receiving the word from an ordained minister. I told them that no services took place at the chapel, but all were welcome to come for a moment of peace. That really got them upset. The problem they told Joe, as if I wasn't sitting right there, was people might get the wrong impression. People (sinners, unsaved, even criminals) might think they could be forgiven or saved without actually going to a church. I reminded them that Jesus invited the sinner, the leper, the criminal to come. All are welcome. They warned Joe that if he didn't get this matter in hand, his business might not be welcome in town. Joe stood and politely asked them to leave. I was furious. Joe said to let it go. He reminded me that people don't like the idea of grace for all; just grace for some and forgiveness for the members of the right congregation, and on their terms. I will never understand church leaders who want to control who receives mercy. It's days like this that I'm happy Gabriel came to my door.

"Holy crap," I said.
"Now, this is the kicker," she said.

March 13, 1971
The Sandhill cranes returned to the Loup River. We saw them coming in by the thousands over the past few days. They came gliding in with their wide gray wings and danced to a stop on pencil thin legs. I love to watch them dance and perform for their sweethearts. I was standing out by the fence watching them when a car pulled up. It was the right arrogant Reverend Troutmen. He wanted to know if we had heard anything. I told him again that she was gone and it was none of his business where she went. He

insisted that he needed to know, for her sake. I told him it was not his concern and I would thank him to leave. He started to press the subject when Joe showed up. Troutmen gets real nervous around Joe. He hightailed it out of here. I hope to never see him again, but I wouldn't count on it.

"Why didn't you tell me this on the phone?" I asked

"A girl has to keep her surprises," she said, closing the journal. "Besides, I could've read that over the phone and not see the look on your face."

The church was on the west side of town, just a block from the railroad tracks. The main street was made up of a dozen red brick buildings. Ansley was just a wide spot in the road, a stop, an intersection most people passed through.

We tried the front door on the small one story church and found it locked. I thought it odd this small church in a lonely one stop town would need to be locked. It somehow made me think of the chapel, Mary's chapel, always open to all travelers along whatever road they had come from. Maybe that's why so many people stopped at her chapel, because the door was always open.

We walked around the place to the back, and even though the back door was locked, Amanda pounded on it anyway. A tall man with a bad comb-over opened the door. "Hello, may I help you?" he said in a voice laced with impatience.

"We're looking for Mr. Troutmen," I said.

"I'm Reverend Troutmen," he replied, with a slightly raised eyebrow.

"I'm Willy Beam and this is Amanda Steward," I said offering my hand and gesturing with my head toward Amanda standing by my side. The preacher didn't take my hand, but continued to look at us with a questioning expression. I lowered my hand and went on with my introduction. "We wanted to ask you a couple of questions if we could."

"About what?" Troutmen asked.

"Well, it's a little complicated," I said. "could we come in?"

He looked from Amanda to me and back again, "I don't mean to be rude, but, you see, I'm really quite busy. I'm afraid you've interrupted my work. Is there another time?"

"Look mister, we've driven over here from St. Paul to talk with you about my Aunt Mary's journals. We know you have them and we want'em back," Amanda blurted out in an over loud, demanding voice.

Reverend Troutmen withdrew into the doorway, "I'm sorry, I don't have the time..."

He started to close the door. I grabbed the steel door and pulled; it swung open, flying out of my hand and banging against the wall with a deep hollow bong. The act stunned both the preacher and me. Amanda didn't hesitate; she rushed forward shoving the older man aside and into the church. He turned sideways with her advance then looked from Amanda to me in shock, his mouth open and his eyes wide. I brushed past him to follow Amanda into the church.

I found her in a back hallway between the sanctuary and a small office. The office door was open. Amanda was standing in the middle of the room with her hands on her hips looking around at the shelves of books. I was as shocked as Troutmen but followed Amanda anyway.

The preacher stormed into the room, yelling in a voice that was almost a squeal; "You young people are trespassing and I demand you get out of here before I call the police."

"Go ahead and call them," Amanda said. "We'll tell them how you stole my aunt's journals."

"Young lady, I've never stolen anything in my life," he said in an insulted tone. "And I have no idea what journals you're talking about."

"Yes, you do," Amanda said turning to face him. "Yes you do. We talked to Mrs. Anderzhon and she remembers you coming to my Uncle Joe's ranch over in Broken Bow when the ladies were cleaning up. They were packing up all of Mary's journals and you took some of them. We want them back."

This was not how I imagined this going down. I expected some resistance, but hoped we could sit down, under the pretense of a news story, and get around to the journals in the course of the questions; now here we were, busting into the church, standing in a minister's office and accusing him of stealing. There was no good way out at this point.

"Alright," I said. "Let's all calm down a minute. Reverend Troutmen, I apologize for barging in here like this. We really would like to ask if you know anything about the journals. We've been settling some things with the Steward estate and discovered there are some missing journals. Mrs. Anderzhon seemed to remember you visiting the house while they were boxing everything up, and perhaps you borrowed a few of the journals. We would like to keep all the journals together, as an historical record. Do you still have them?"

My question hung there in the musty air of the office; Amanda was defensive, poised to pounce. I felt myself holding my breath. Reverend Troutmen was stoic, his eyes fixed on Amanda. I found myself caught in the middle of a staring contest. Finally, he said in a restrained, even voice, "I don't have any recollection of your aunt's journals. I'm sure Betty Anderzhon is mistaken. Now, I must ask both of you to leave."

"We're not going any place," Amanda started. I grabbed her by the arm and pulled. She stood her ground for a moment until our eyes locked. I tried to express myself with my eyes and the set of my mouth, "it was time to go."

She started to pull away. I held tight and pulled her to me. She gave in and followed me across the room. We pushed past the preacher and he gave way for us to leave. When we reached the door Amanda said, "I know you've got them. What are you hiding?"

I held on to Amanda's arm for the first few yards, when we got outside, until she pulled away and walked beside me to the car.

"What in the hell was that," I yelled. "What in the hell were you thinking? God damn it! That could not have gone any more wrong. Shit! Damn it to hell!"

She crossed her arms walking to the other side of the car and leaned back on the door. "He has them. I know it and you were just going to mealy mouth him. I want to kick his ass."

"What is wrong with you? He's a preacher. You're going to kick his ass in the church?

"I was only in the office. Hell, it's not like I did do something. I could tell by the look in his eyes. He's got things hidden."

"Like that makes any sense at all." I was pacing and flailing my arms. "He may have them, but we will never know now, will we? God Damn it"

Amanda suppressed a giggle, her shoulders shaking a little.

"What the hell is so funny?" I asked.

She covered her mouth and bent over to catch her breath. "I've never heard your curse like that before."

"Well, I've never burst into a church with a raving lunatic who called the preacher a thief and a liar before," I yelled. "Get in the damn car," suddenly nervous that Troutmen would indeed call the police. "Get in the car now!"

She did as I said and we drove away from the little church without a word between us. I drove to the highway and headed east. When I couldn't stand it any longer I yelled, "Did you lose your damn mind? I cannot believe you did that!"

"He was not going to let us in and when I saw his face and thought about Mary's journal, I just lost it. I'm sorry, it just made me crazy."

"No shit crazy," I said. "Now what do we do?"

"I don't know," she said with her arms crossed and her jaw set.

We drove without talking. I pulled up next to her pickup parked on the square back in Broken Bow. We sat there in silence. I was so jumbled in my thoughts and numb to my emotions.

"I'm sorry," Amanda said. "Maybe we can have Jimmy call him. He's the one with the journals and he's an adult."

"Maybe," I said.

Her voice was sorrowful, "I thought. I don't know, we were just so close. I wanted to know so badly."

"I know," I said. "Don't worry about it. I'm done with this whole thing anyway."

"What do you mean?"

"It's not going anywhere and anywhere it goes, I'm not sure I want to follow, you know?"

"No, I don't know," she said. Her attitude and spark were back. "I want to know what happened to that little baby don't you?"

I nodded. "I'm going to go. I need to think."

She glared; I could feel the disappointment in her eyes. "Whatever," she opened the door. She got out, turned and gave me a look of disgust before slamming the door with all the force she could muster. I put the car in reverse and backed away.

Chapter 44

I got back to St. Paul in the afternoon. I stopped by the paper to see what was going on. I found nothing to keep my attention. I grabbed a sandwich at the café and took a long time eating it. I drove out to the ball fields and sat with the window down watching the wind blow the tree tops, thinking. By the time I got to the apartment it was late afternoon.

I don't know what déjà vu means, nobody does for sure, but we all know the feeling. I believe déjà vu is a sign post, a marker really, letting me know I'm on the right path, a path chosen. I don't mean preordained, more chosen by me, but recognized as part of a larger plan, overseen by free will. I could've gone another way, but because I decided, consciously or unconsciously, to follow this way, and not that, the sign posts assured me I was on the right path. That may be all wrong, but it's how I understand déjà vu.

I approached the stairs to my apartment. A well-dressed man in a dark blue suit with a gray striped tie and a kerchief to match was standing on the landing. He looked down at me. "William," he said. "I must have a word with you."

I stood transfixed for a moment. I had done this before, seen him before. He was tall with dark brown eyes, his hair was short, a business man's style. He was older. I couldn't say how old but his face was strikingly familiar. I knew his face and his manner, in this very place, with the sun behind him, his shadow falling down the steps toward the sidewalk at my feet. The moment was so sharply clear in my recollection; the expression on his face repeated from a previous place, but in this present time.

"Yes," I said and walked up the stairs to open the door. I moved the stack of journals from off the chair in the living room so he could sit. I scrambled for a place to set them, finally settling for the shelf next to the kitchenette. I tried to collect the mess of newspapers on the floor and coffee table, my efforts in vain. He took a seat in the chair.

"Can I get you something to drink?" I asked. "Water, cola, coffee; I can make some coffee."

"No, that won't be necessary." he said. "Please sit down."

I sat on the edge of the couch cushion, leaning forward focusing all my energy in his direction.

"William, do you know who I am?" I nodded my head, but knew that wasn't the right response.

"Well then, let me introduce myself. I'm Gabriel Chamberlain, most people call me Gabe. I oversee the trust for the Steward estate, the trust set up to protect their interests, specifically the small property which contains a cross and small chapel up near Broken Bow. Miss Amanda Steward and you have been rushing around making a number of inquiries. You appear to be looking for answers to old questions, correct?"

"Well," I cleared my throat, wishing I had gotten myself a drink of water. "The thing is, I came across a story in the paper, and then I met Amos Tensley who told me Mary was a prophet, a seer of some kind. The story just got hold of me. I met Amanda and Uncle Jimmy, and he had Mary's journals, which are amazing, but some of them are missing and we wanted to find them." I knew I was rambling, yet the look on Gabe's face said go on, it's alright. "There's this reference in one of them, the journals, I mean, about a baby and there's a whole collection of journals missing. Amanda thinks the baby is me, but I wanted to know for sure. So we went to see the preacher, who Mrs. Anderzhon told us had taken the journals, but Amanda went crazy and yelled at him, and he threw us out of the church. Now I'm not sure what to do."

Gabe had a gentle expression of amusement in his smile. I sat back on the couch, suddenly drained. I felt better. I'd been holding things so close. Then to have it out, even in a jumbled mess of explanation, made me feel better.

"I see," Gabe said.

"Do you?" I asked.

"I think so," he said. "The Steward estate is intertwined with lots of complicated events. What do you seek beyond verification?"

"Well, the journals are full of stories, some of them I can hardly believe," I said not following his question.

"Do you believe they are just stories?"

"No, well, not really, still some are very hard to imagine."

"Very difficult to imagine," he agreed.

"Yes," I nodded. "Sir, are they true? Mary's stories. Are they all true?"

He crossed his legs in a fluid elegant motion. "William, I want to assure you the truth cannot be found in a collection of old books, no matter how special, spiritual, or inspired. The truth is a very personal thing, and therefore, subjective. There are universal truths yes, but a truth held as self-evident for some, is treasonous from another's perspective. Do you see what I mean?"

I did, I really did. So I asked, "What about now, what is the truth for these poor farm families?"

He frowned, "At this time, the truth is yet to be written. I suspect there will be many who in reflection will celebrate the leadership and good fortune for a great many of this era. You, however, will most certainly have your own truth to reflect on. As will the families who are facing a stark truth about their way of life." He cocked his head to one side and shrugged. "The same is true of Mary's cross and chapel. Some will say it is this way. While those who've experienced the healing power of faith first hand, will say the truth is that. The truth is personal; the truth as you see it, is your truth. And lots of people are happy with the truth they have been given and never seek anything beyond its borders. So, are Mary's stories true?" He shrugged letting the question linger between us.

"But why here?" I asked, "Of all the places, why here?"

Gabe looked at me with what I perceived as admiration. "The why requires a lifetime of curiosity. Something you have a great deal of. Be sure and never lose your curious nature."

He gazed up and adjusted his tone. "The desire to know who, what, when, where, and why; the tools of your trade. The fortunes and failures of man sway with these questions. The most perplexing and instinctive question is, where do I, where do we come from? It's the one all of mankind asks time and again of themselves or their creator. Humans continue to seek a resolution, both big and small, throughout time immemorial."

I nodded in agreement, but unsure I agreed or understood.

"William," he said, "you are a superb human being full of persistence and courage. Those talents will serve you well. Now, I would like to suggest you go back home. You have a mother who desperately loves you and a father who misses you very much. These questions of truth and why, will not be resolved in the recovery of a few missing journals. What answers they provide may not resolve anything for you. Mary was gifted at keeping records, but as you well know, her style was folksy, entertaining, fascinating, but often incomplete. You may well find the journals, only to discover a great many other questions. Let me ask you this, if you could find one of these journals, knowing their contents would be hurtful to someone you love, would you still want to read them?"

"Yes, I would," I said as sure of that fact as I've ever been.

He considered me with a level gaze. Then, with a nod he stood, adjusting his coat. I rose with him. He focused his eyes on mine. I was transfixed by the power of his gaze. Then he turned, picked up something from the chair and placed a journal in my hands.

"It's a good story, but it will take you some time to work out what it means to you." He abruptly changed his tone, softening his character and in an offhand way said, "It was very nice to meet you William. I hope we meet again sometime."

I smiled and looked down at the journal. On its cover, in Mary's elegant handwriting, just like all the others, was the month and year; November - December 1960. I looked up to see Gabe standing on the landing staring back at me. The sunlight bathed him in a glowing orange shimmer.

"Wait!" I started after him tripping over the coffee table. I went sprawling across the floor. I quickly scrambled to my feet, and raced out onto the landing, only to catch the trail of his silhouette as it disappeared out of sight. I hurried down the steps and around the corner, but he was gone. I scanned up and down the street, nothing. I looked down at the journal in my hands. Had it been there all along? Did Gabe somehow have it? I didn't see anything in his hands when we met. He had picked it up from the chair but I had moved all the journals and set them on the shelf. I opened the cover, then flipped a few pages...

November 24, 1960. Thanksgiving Day

We have so much to be thankful for. Joe and I went to Mamma's to have dinner with the whole family. It was so good to see everyone. It's amazing how few times we all get together anymore, even with all of us living so close. I was over the moon. I could hardly contain my joy and excitement of having an expectant mother in the house. Elizabeth is ripe to pop. I expect the baby to come within the week. Doc. Rose says it won't come until December, but I don't know if we can stand to wait that long. I'm so excited, you would think it was my own grand baby coming.

Doc. Rose from over in Ord has been such a blessing. He says momma and baby are doing great. He doesn't ask too many questions or look with judgment on Elizabeth. I've known him for years and can always turn to him for help. He's recommended a midwife and she's been out to meet us. I like her a lot. An old soul with wisdom and mercy to share.

I hurriedly skipped forward a few pages and then a few more. Then read:

December 9th, 1960

What a night. Elizabeth's water broke around two in the morning. I sent Joe for the midwife, but with the storm it took forever. Elizabeth was so brave. I figured I'd helped with enough calving seasons that I could bring the baby into the world well enough. It went so naturally. That little girl was so beautiful and strong. I couldn't stop smiling and crying, holding her hand with every contraction. When he finally came we were both bathed in sweat and tears. He is so precious. I can hardly take my eyes off him. Joe and I've talked about it but in the end, we know we cannot keep the little guy. As much as I want to there would be too much to explain and too small a town. Elizabeth is beside herself with pride and heartbroken with having to give him up, but she knows it's for the best, for both of them. I had a dream last week; over the years I've come to trust the dreams. There is a loving couple nearby, desperate for a child. I'm convinced it's Gods will that I take the baby boy to them. I plan to take him to Iowa before the end of the year.

I sat down on the steps and read the whole journal over. I felt such sadness and relief. A settled blessed feeling spread over me as the sun set and my shadow faded. There's knowing you should count your blessings, and there is knowing you're blessed by the grace of God.

Chapter 45

I called mom and dad to tell them I would be coming home. I gave Sarge my resignation, which he accepted. He offered solid advice along with a good reference. He made a few calls for me in Omaha, Des Moines, and Kansas City. I had interviews lined up before the end of the week.

I drove out to see Melvin, to tell him I was leaving. He didn't seem surprised. He asked me to stay in touch; which I have done my best to do over the past thirty years. He survived the farm crisis with his land, but not without some hard lessons learned.

Over the next five years thirty thousand small independent farmers would move off the land; more than during the great depression. It would be another six years before Willy Nelson and John Mellencamp would host Farm Aid in Memorial Stadium; by then the crisis was in full bloom. The Reagan administration would finally take action. They wouldn't fully abandon their theory that the crisis was just a few bad managers who needed to get out of the farming business. They did come to realize that the family farm and its way of life was in jeopardy and made adjustments to help some. For lots of folks in Nebraska, Kansas, Iowa, Minnesota, Missouri, Ohio, Illinois and Colorado it was too late.

The kids who came of age in the wake of the Farm Crisis would seek jobs in cities with more opportunities. The brain drain, as they called it. Some of the best and the brightest from these small towns moved off, taking with them innovation and the "can do" spirit of creation that Dr. Talbert talked about. Their migration from western Nebraska to the east, into Lincoln and Omaha, was the largest since the depression.

To their credit, the churches from around the state came together to do what they could to help. There was a hotline set up for families to call for help, to get answers, or just talk. Their efforts saved lives. They helped lots of families adjust to a new way of life. The churches worked with the state agencies to develop 'experience resumes' for farmers, ranchers and their wives so they could apply for jobs in towns. The church leaders worked with communities to support those who needed help. It was the church at its best, doing God's work, not in some far away mission field but right there in its own community to help its neighbors.

The farmers and ranchers, like Melvin, would get lean, and embrace technology. Like every other industry to emerge from the eighties, consolidation was the process; consolidation not just of dealerships and grain elevators, but small farms to big ones. Consolidation of land meant fewer farmers. Everything changes; only seasons stay the same.

Melvin's boys would become lawyers and financial advisers. They are still the stewards of the land, but they do like lots of others do, lease the land to a larger farmer, but don't work it themselves. In some small way holding on to the tradition, but letting it change as it will.

I went to see Joe before I left. He looked frail and fading.

"I had a visitor," I told him, "Gabe came to see me."

He didn't look surprised, "Gabe has always been around when people need direction."

I thought about what he meant and let it go, "He said I should come to see you before I go back home, to Iowa."

Joe nodded his head. He was lying on his bed, propped up on pillows, a breathing tube across his nose. The sound from the oxygen machine reminded me of old Amos Tensley. The room was not as dark, but the frail old man and the machine brought me full circle.

He looked tired in body and spirit. He was reminiscent and reflective. We talked about horses and cattle. He told me a story of a sweet black mare, a lost calf, and a river crossing, that didn't go as planned. He smiled at the memories. He recalled Mary and planned to see her again soon. I left him sleeping; an honest man's pillow is his peace of mind.

I drove on over to Broken Bow to return the journals to Jimmy. I found him sitting on the back-porch rocking and singing an old Led Zeppelin song.

"Hey Jimmy," I called. He jumped up into a defensive stance, quick as a hiccup, he had a pistol pulled and pointed in my direction. I held my hands up and backed away.

He blinked a few times, drew a big breath, and blew it out slowly. "Man, you should not sneak up on a guy like that."

I nodded, "Sorry, you alright?"

"Yeah, I'm cool." He laid the gun down on the table, turned down the radio at his side and sat back down, "What brings you around?"

I held up the journals. "I wanted to return these."

He motioned me on to the porch. I climbed the steps, laying the journals on an antique milk jug standing next to our friend the gnome. I took the same seat I had before, when the three of us sat out here together.

"You find what you was looking for?"

"I think so, yeah," I said. Realizing at just that moment that I had indeed, found what I was looking for. Not what I expected to find, but what I was looking for all the same.

"You leaving?" Jimmy asked.

"It's time for me to go," I half sang. Jimmy smiled and nodded recognizing the Led Zeppelin lyric.

"Want a beer?" He asked, as he got up to go inside. He returned with a Coors bottle. I gladly accepted. We sat for a while, just looking out across the yard. The day was windy and cool. We watched a flock of Sandhill cranes glide in to land on the edge of the corn field. The cranes were doing their odd little dance to entice a mate; amusing and enduring.

"They've been crossing these grass-covered dunes for thousands of years," Jimmy said. "Season after season they return. You know they hunt them damn things down in Texas. Can't imagine why. They're graceful when they fly, but they taste like shit, and can't dance a lick."

He got up, flopped his arms and raised his knees in a bad imitation of the cranes in the field. I couldn't help but laugh.

"What's so funny?" We looked around to see Amanda walking toward the porch.

Jimmy stopped his silly dance. "We were just talking about mating dances and Texas," He said with grin.

Neither of us said a word. Jimmy nodded, took a sip of his beer and said, "Yep, I believe I'll go see a man about a dog." He hopped off the porch and walked down toward the barns.

Amanda didn't turn to watch him go but waited until he was out of ear shot. "So, stranger, where've you been?"

"I've been planning to come see you," I said

"Liar," she said with a dimpled grin.

She looked so beautiful standing there in the sunlight. Her hair was pulled back in the same ponytail she wore the first time I saw her. I could hardly stand to look at her, with the sadness growing in her eyes. "I'm going back home, to Des Moines," I said.

She nodded, looked down at her feet. I stood and walked down from the porch to stand in front of her. "Gabe came to see me."

She looked up with a hundred questions in her eyes. "He told me to go home, to go see my Mother. So that's what I'm going to do."

"Did none of this mean anything, to you?"

"Amanda, you know that's not true. This all means a great deal to me. You mean a great deal to me but..."

"But what," her voice broke and she chocked it back.

"But it's time for me to go. I've got my answers, and you were right. I was, I am, that baby. Maybe the whole reason I came out here was to find out who I am. And you made that possible." I could feel the raw emotion pulling at my throat, welling up behind my eyes.

"But you're going to go and leave me here, alone?"

I reached out to her. She stepped back and turned away.

"You have your whole life ahead of you." I said. "There are so many things for you see and do. I cannot be here standing in your way." I stepped closer and put my arms around her. She started to pull away. I held her close and whispered in her ear. "You made all this possible for me. I don't want to make anything impossible for you."

She put her head against my chest and I hugged her close, felt her body, her resolve melt into me. We stood there holding on, working up the courage to let go. She released herself from my embrace and looked up at me."I have something for you," she said.

I let go. She hurried past me and into the house. She came back in just a moment with one of Mary's journals in her hand. "I've been reading a lot of these. I found one you should read," I took it, started to open it. "But not now," she said. "Read it later, when you're back in Iowa or wherever."

"Won't Jimmy get mad?" I asked

"Jimmy won't know, besides I think it might help you to understand the Why."

I wish I had a picture of her in that moment. In my mind's eyes I hold on to the ever-fading image of her; as a wish and regret. An old nagging remorse flickers at the edge of my conscious whenever I think of the Sandhill cranes' return in the spring. I see her; laughing and sparkling with all the passion of youth. The years have not lifted the weight from my heart. I still recall all the questions unanswered in that instant; frozen there without the context or references, making it impossible to convey the 'everything' going on in that moment.

In my memory she bubbles with both innocence and desire. I

feel the chorus of a familiar song, and I'm compelled to sing along; instinctively, involuntarily. My recollections are as fragile as soap bubbles in the breeze. I curse the passage of time, and my sudden exit from her life. You just don't realize the fleeting nature of things, or the predictability of time.

I know she'll never be that girl again. I wouldn't want her to be. I'm not that young man. I wouldn't trade one second of the life I've lived. Still, there is a flicker, a weight, no matter how many years pass. I wonder sometimes if it's the same for her. Do I flicker? Do I weigh upon her memory? Are there moments, summoned by seasons and scent, which leak out of the past and take their shape in a dimpled smile she could never fully explain? I hope so. I truly hope she occasionally recalls us; just as I do, in the lyrics of a familiar song and the nostalgic smells of an autumn evening.

Prologue

I found my calling as an advertising salesman. I liked the creative, problem solving process; not to mention the money was better. I met a girl on a blind date. She was smart and funny with beautiful brown eyes and an infectious laugh; to this day her laugh is the most beautiful sound on this earth to me. She still finds me funny, after twenty years and two kids. Mrs. Shannon Beam is my best friend and my biggest fan. I don't know what I'd do without her.

I have a lot to be thankful for. I thank God for all the blessings I've known. For Mary and Joe, for the Cross and Chapel and the refuge it provided me and Kelly and so many other lost and wandering souls in their journey from life to death. I'm thankful for my birth mother and for my parents who loved and raised me as their own. I thank God for those crossroads in the Sandhills. Without them I don't know if I would ever have found my way home. I thank God for my wife and children and all the joy and heartbreak which accompany the raising of a family in this modern age. And finally, I thank God for Amanda, and the journal she gave to me.

February 29, 1976

It's been really warm for this time of year. Joe said it got up to seventy-five degrees on Friday. It's leap year, so we have an extra day and with a full moon, no less. These odd days make me a little sad. When I look back over the many years I remember all the faces of the people who came by here. I think about how sad it is that we call ourselves Christians and don't act Christ like. I think about all the reasons why people come here. I believe this is one of those special places where God allows us to find Him. All I've ever provided here was hope. Hope comes in many forms and means different things to each person, but to me hope is and has been the desire for better. A hope that this too shall pass. A hope someone cares. A hope for mercy and kindness in a hard, tragic world. You know, I think of myself as the inn keeper. The one the Good Samaritan charged with taking care of the traveler who had been robbed, beaten and left for dead along the road to Jericho. Many, who have been beaten down, neglected, and robbed, come here. Some of their own free will, but I believe many were brought to my door by Gabe and others. I'm to care for them until they can move on. Sometimes it's for a night, sometimes for a bit longer. I don't believe this place is unique in this world. God always provides places for people to go. Folks often build monuments or churches in those places, but more often I believe they are unlikely places where the weary and hopeful find rest. I like the idea of being the innkeeper. I don't know, nor do I ever expect to ever know, why. Somethings cannot be explained, and don't need to be, they just are. Thank God!

Dedication

The process of completing my first novel has not been an individual act but the collective work of a community of friends and family. I could not have done it without the love and support of my first reader, my best friend, biggest supporter and sharpest editor, my wife Cindy. I cannot imagine ever finishing this novel without your love and encouragement. Thank you to each of my beta readers: Colleen, Amy, Mike, Karma and Neva. I cannot thank you enough for taking the time to wade through the earliest versions of the manuscript; typos, misspellings and all. Each layer of input, insight and encouragement helped to improve the final draft immensely. To Elle and her fine red pen, your sharp corrections and insightful notes made me consider not just the dialogue but the voices and vernacular of the characters. Your suggestions helped me find the final title for the work. To Carol Ann, your tedious line by line editing was the final polish I needed, thank you. And John for working with me to create the cover; your friendship and creativity is much valued and greatly appreciated. To Charlie Brogan, thank you for your sharp eye and strong editing. Your efforts made this revised edition better.

This, my first novel, is a work of fiction. Any resemblance to any persons living or dead is purely coincidence. The towns are real, but I have taken creative license in places with the geography and description. The characterizations of the towns themselves are simple illustrations and are not intended to reflect the true nature or character of the people anywhere in the Sandhills. I have not lived in the Nebraska Sandhills, only nearby. The author only knows what he knows. If my observations or depictions are in error I apologize. The events contributing to the farm crisis are historically accurate, to my understanding. In my research I have taken advantage of hindsight, personal perception, and economic analysis to convey what was happening all across the Midwest in the 1980's. My hope is that this story makes you think, makes you smile and makes you feel.

Thank you for reading it.

T.B. Kitsmiller

Made in the USA
Monee, IL
11 April 2021